Women
on the Edge
of a
Nervous
Breakthrough

By Isabel Sharpe

WOMEN ON THE EDGE OF A NERVOUS BREAKTHROUGH

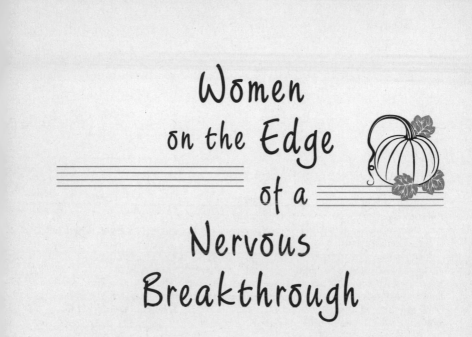

Women on the Edge of a Nervous Breakthrough

ISABEL SHARPE

AVON

An Imprint of HarperCollinsPublishers

WOMEN ON THE EDGE OF A NERVOUS BREAKTHROUGH. Copyright © 2007 by Muna Shehadi Sill. All rights reserved. Printed in the United States of America. No part of this book may be used or reproduced in any manner whatsoever without written permission except in the case of brief quotations embodied in critical articles and reviews. For information address HarperCollins Publishers, 10 East 53rd Street, New York, NY 10022.

HarperCollins books may be purchased for educational, business, or sales promotional use. For information please write: Special Markets Department, HarperCollins Publishers, 10 East 53rd Street, New York, NY 10022.

FIRST EDITION

Interior text designed by Diahann Sturge

Library of Congress Cataloging-in-Publication Data

Sharpe, Isabel.
   Women on the edge of a nervous breakthrough / by Isabel Sharpe.—1st ed.
      p. cm.
   ISBN: 978-0-06-114055-6
   ISBN-10: 0-06-114055-4
   1. Wisconsin—Fiction.   I. Title.

PS3619.H356645W66   2007
813'.6—dc22   2006015946

07 08 09 10 11 JTC/RRD 10 9 8 7 6 5 4 3

One

VERDICT!
JURY REACHES VERDICT
IN ED BRANSON MURDER TODAY—
THE WORLD WAITS FOR TOMORROW

NEW YORK CITY (CNS). It's a cliffhanger in what has been America's most sensational trial since O. J. Simpson's in 1995. After three days of deliberation, the jury reached a verdict in the trial of Lorelei Taylor, which has mesmerized the nation for the last six months. Tomorrow at noon (EST), the fate of Ms. Taylor, accused of murdering her long-time lover, publishing magnate Ed Branson, will be announced.

Comparisons to the Simpson trial have been numerous and inevitable. Now that the nation must wait until tomorrow for the verdict to be read, speculation is rising. Will Lorelei repeat O. J.'s stunning escape from a guilty verdict? Or will the jury this time side with the prosecution?

Ted Branson, son of the deceased, has no doubts.

"She'll get what's coming to her. After what she did to my father, what she's done to me, my mother, to my wife and my children . . . The good ladies and gentlemen of the jury will not let that murdering [expletive deleted] walk free." Lawyers for both sides refused to comment on the possible outcome.

Over the past six months, the nation has been held captive by the testimony, scandal, and lurid details of the trial, but not so captivated as they have been by the woman on trial herself. Though she is dubbed "The Sublime Ms. L" by her admirers, her detractors cite the German legend of Lorelei, a beautiful woman who sat on the banks of the Rhine, combing her hair and singing of her lost love, luring smitten sailors to gruesome deaths on the rocks below.

In less than twenty-four hours, both detractors and admirers will know what the jury of seven men and five women have decided lies in store for Ms. Taylor.

Sarah Gilchrist
Kettle, Wisconsin

Sarah turned on the TV in her and Ben's beautifully redecorated living room. What an improvement over the way her mother had it while Sarah was growing up here. She sat on the cream-colored couch accented with burgundy, teal, and gold pillows, and patted the cushion next to her, allowing her smile to dim only slightly when her husband chose the big leather chair closer to the set. Of course he'd rather be closer, with his vision getting worse. Bifocals soon, Dr. Bradley had said. Honestly, Sarah had told him a million times he needed to take more breaks from his writing or he'd ruin his eyes staring at that little monitor.

They'd both hit forty this year, which made them officially middle-aged, though it didn't seem possible. But of course, Ben went ahead and did what he wanted, which was part of his charm. Far be it from Sarah to interfere. Their teen-age daughter, Amber, had inherited that particular trait from her father, though at age sixteen, *charming* wasn't always the word that sprang to Sarah's mind to describe it.

"Cookie?" She jumped to her feet and offered him the plate—almond crescents, his favorite, made with real butter, and don't get her started on women who baked with that awful vegetable shortening. Those cookies might look good, but they tasted like absolutely nothing, so what was the point? Sarah loved to bake, but she rarely ate what she made, wanting to keep her figure slim.

"Thanks." Ben groped for one, eyes glued to the set. He'd watched nearly every minute of the Lorelei Taylor trial cov-erage when he wasn't working. Of course the trial had been fascinating, not that Sarah had followed the proceedings that closely. And not that Ben shared a lot of the details with her. But all the ins and outs, the infidelity, the abuse, well, she'd almost feel sorry for the Lorelei woman, except murder was never the right way out of a situation. That and the fact that Lorelei was the flashy, tarty, in-your-face kind of person Sar-ah's mother would have called common. In this case, as much as Sarah tried to remain open-minded, Sarah would have to agree.

Plus, the dreadful way Lorelei killed her lover, drugging, then electrocuting the poor man in his own bathtub. They couldn't even say which actually caused his heart attack, the drugs, the electrocution, or the fear. He didn't deserve that, not that Sarah commended him for his alleged treatment of Lorelei, if it was true. But she could see how Lorelei would provoke abuse. The woman was all T&A—trouble and attitude.

The part of Sarah that believed in justice, that believed people were punished for their sins, knew this jury would find the woman guilty. That lent a certain balance and peaceful security to the day, and she looked forward to it. Homemade cookies, a beautiful fall day with a husband she adored, and a guilty verdict. All would be right with the rest of the world, as it was always right in Kettle, Wisconsin.

"Another cookie, honey?"

"Shhh." Her husband pointed to the set with one of his long, beautiful fingers, which she'd fallen in love with the first day she set eyes on him their freshman year at Cornell. Those hands and those deep brown, scholarly eyes.

"Members of the jury, on the charge of murder in the first degree, how do you find the defendant?"

Sarah leaned forward, practically aquiver to see justice done. The camera cut from the juror to Lorelei's face, for once not cocky and brash, but pale and emotionless. Beautiful and lifeless, like a mannequin.

"We find the defendant . . . not guilty, Your Honor."

Sarah blinked. What had they said? *Not* guilty?

Her husband gave a shout of laughter and pounded the arm of his chair. "By God! Not guilty. What a country we live in!"

Sarah set down the plate of hand-formed cookies, each rolled straight out of the oven in a perfectly even coating of powdered sugar. Her husband hated it when she cried, but unfortunately that's what she was going to do.

She bent her head and stifled the sobs as best she could.

Erin Hall
Kettle, Wisconsin

Not guilty. Erin let out a strangled shout, then darted nervous glances around her living room, even though Joe was at work. She couldn't ever be sure no one could hear. Sometimes she felt as if someone was watching her when she knew she was alone, but she hadn't figured out if it felt more like a guardian angel or one of Satan's clan.

The camera fixed on Lorelei's face, so pale before, now flushed and flashing triumph. Lorelei was magnificent. Beautiful. She'd weathered this trial with so much power. Stood so proud when all the shameful stories came out. Teenage prostitution, exotic dancing, *Playboy*. Told all those people what her big-shot boyfriend was doing to her. Erin couldn't even begin to fathom having that kind of courage. To tell someone what was happening. To trust they'd make it right. Or not even to care if they did or not. Just tell the truth, nothing but the truth, and so help her God.

Lorelei killed Ed Branson, Erin was sure. She could picture the scene as if she'd stood next to her while she did it. Could feel everything she felt—initial rage that descended into surreal calm. She'd drugged him first, got him into his bath, thrown in the CD player while it was on. She got lucky when he had a heart attack. The reasonable doubt she needed.

"Not guilty." Erin clutched a couch pillow to her stomach. "Not guilty. Not guilty."

If she said the words over and over, they'd stay real, and no one could take them away from her.

Lorelei had killed her boyfriend who was hurting her, even a powerful, important man like that. Reached a point where she said, *Enough. You can't do this to me anymore. I will fight back.*

So she had. She killed him, naked in his bathtub.

And got away with it.

Lorelei Taylor, née Vivian Harcourt
New York, New York

Emerging from the courthouse should have been a moment of epic proportions. Freedom! God, it had barely begun to sink in. She was free. Not headed for the rest of her life in jail.

Free.

She should have been able to stand in front of the noble columns representing New York City justice, to take a deep breath of glorious carbon-monoxide-laced air and fling her arms wide to embrace this freedom. Then gracefully and with great deliberateness, extend the middle finger of each hand toward everyone who doubted her. Most particularly, Ed's vicious, lying relatives, who'd hated her from the first moment they saw her. Enjoy this moment now and forever, assholes! Lorelei Taylor lives in freedom.

All that and more should have been hers. She'd damn well earned it. But the press, the crowd on the steps, on the sidewalks, overflowing into the street, had other ideas.

Overwhelming noise. Microphones jammed into her face, questions shouted. And behind it, the roaring chant of hundreds. "Guil-ty. Guil-ty."

She held herself tall, waved; Miss America at the pageant, laughing at the sickness of it all, and the futility. They'd see the laugh and the wave and know they'd been right all along. That the Taylor woman had no soul, no emotions, the ordeal hadn't touched her. And if that wasn't the sign of a she-devil . . . oh, they couldn't cross themselves enough times to ward off the evil that was Lorelei.

And if she emerged from the courtroom looking grief-stricken, weary, and humble? See? There you go, they'd been right all along. Proof of a burdened conscience. The beginning of a lifelong hell her subconscious would make sure she lived, and wasn't that justice all its own? She couldn't escape what she'd done completely, no no no.

Any way she played it—further proof of her guilt.

Yeah, she was guilty. Guilty of a lot of things. If you could put someone on trial for a lifetime of fucked-up choices, Lorelei Taylor would do plenty of time. But, ironically, she was not guilty of murdering Ed Branson. And she could shout that from the rooftops every day for the rest of her life, but it wouldn't change one goddamn person's mind about what they were all so sure she'd done.

The crowd surged forward, police sprang into action to hold them back. Lorelei waved again and blew kisses.

In the meantime, she could do a valuable service for her fellow Americans. Provide a convenient focal point for all the hatred and frustration in their small and useless lives.

So happy to help.

Her lawyers read a brief statement, pleased with the verdict, justice done, yada, yada. One pudgy blond in a cheap beige suit, too short and too tight, managed to shove a microphone in Lorelei's face.

"There are a lot of people who seem to think you've gotten away with murder. How do you feel about the not-guilty verdict?"

Lorelei opened her mouth to say, *As good as you'd feel if you took the bug out of your butt*, but her lawyer intervened, squeezing her arm hard to shut down the remark he knew was cooking. Stan was an ass, but he'd saved hers, so she'd do anything for him. Even choke back the impulsive behavior that was always getting her in trouble.

"Oh gosh, how do I feel? I guess extra super-duper happy!"

Even over the crowd noise she heard Stan groan behind her.

The woman narrowed her eyes. Pulled the mike back to her thin mouth that even smudged lipstick and heavy liner wouldn't make look sultry.

"What will you do now?"

Lorelei's sugary, wide smile was sucked off her face and back down into her body so hard, she had to work to paste back some semblance of not caring.

What the hell would she do now?

"Oh, well, the possibilities are limitless, aren't they! I believe I'll begin by running for president. Or maybe Harvard needs a new faculty member, could you check on that for me, sweetie?"

Stan the Man pushed her to move down the rest of the steps toward the car. "Ms. Taylor has no more comments."

Right. No more comments. No more money. No more condo. No more friends. No more life.

And goddamn his cheating, abusive, careless, beloved soul . . . no more Ed.

Two

My Report on Suffragettes in Kettle, Wisconsin
by Sarah Bannon
Mrs. Browley's fifth grade

In 1920, women had the right to vote for the president for the first time. But the men in Kettle didn't want the women to vote November 9. So after the town Halloween party, some women locked themselves in the Harcourt house on Maple Street. They would not come out until the men let them vote. Then the men did let them vote. One woman went home, though, and her husband killed her by beating her.

Comment from Mrs. Browley: *Good work, as usual, Sarah! But the death of the woman was ruled an ac-*

cident. As I'm sure you know, there's never been a crime in Kettle.

Sarah walked along Main Street, taking long, confident strides, enjoying her own grace. She'd been a dancer at Cornell and had danced professionally for a few years when she and Ben lived in New York. In fact, she might very well have gone on to a big career, though she didn't regret her decision to marry Ben and have Amber and give up what she loved.

She smiled and greeted Mrs. Gripentrog, out for a stroll with her miniature schnauzers. Sarah knew she looked nice today, in a new fall outfit from Talbots online—crepe pants in a color called sandstone, and a sage-and-cream striped shell set. Her bobbed hair curved all the right ways this morning, and her face was clear and young-looking, no eye puffiness, no deep lines. People were happy when they encountered someone who looked nice; they always responded more warmly, smiled more openly.

Her heart sped up a little opposite Granley's Stationers; she turned as if by chance and caught a glimpse of Tom Martin, who ran the place. She'd known Tom since grade school; they'd even dated briefly. Very handsome man. He always smiled a little too personally, made eye contact a little too long. Sarah liked that he still found her attractive, though marriage was wonderful, and Lord knew she was devoted to Ben. But little secret crushes were exciting and did no harm to anyone.

She walked on farther, past Stenkel's, the town's general store since 1837, still run by members of the Stenkel family. The early October breeze was brisk, but the sun deliciously warm, and the town looked so quaint and lovely in this light. When Sarah left Kettle for college, she never expected to come back. Funny how love changed that.

Four years ago, Ben had finished graduate school at Columbia. New York City had grated on their nerves and they weren't wild about Amber spending adolescence in the city. Sarah's parents had announced they were selling the house and buying an RV to tour the country. Kettle seemed the perfect place for Ben to launch his writing career. So he and Sarah bought the house from her parents. Sarah gave up her friends and her job and her life and came back to tiny Kettle.

All of which turned out to be a good thing, of course, since they'd been so happy here.

She waved at Mike Curtis, just coming out of Hansen's Hardware. In her opinion, Mike was the town's most eligible bachelor *after* Tom Martin. Most women would probably rank Mike first. Mike had lost his adored wife, Rosemary, a little over two years ago. The two of them had run Mike's business together, and were somehow in physical contact every second as far as Sarah could tell. Made her have a strange feeling in her stomach, but she could never identify it.

After that devastating blow, Mike left town for a year, and had come back harder and with enough grief still in him, poor man, that the women of the town all wanted either to adopt him or to make him forget Rosemary, depending on their age.

"Hey, Sarah." He gave his now-customary short nod; the dazzling-smile part of his greeting had died with Rosemary.

"Hello, Mike." She smiled, carefully keeping pity out of her eyes. Mike got plenty of pity from everyone else in town. But while she was smiling without pity, she also hoped he noticed how nicely her sage blouse caught the green tints in her hazel eyes, and laughed to herself that she should even be thinking such a thing with Ben and her still so much in love. After so much time together. Nearly twenty years. "Been busy?"

"Yes. I'm sorry. I'll be by to fix your porch some—"

"Oh no, that's not what I meant." She waved the unimportant delay away. "I was just making conversation."

"Okay." He nodded, those dynamite blue eyes so serious and intent on her that her heart was unsure whether to melt from pity or silly excitement. Honestly. She had better get a grip.

"I'm off to the Social Club meeting. I'll see you later."

"Next week." He backed up a step or two, raised his hand in farewell, then turned to walk to his pickup.

Sarah turned the opposite way, toward the white wooden Lutheran church on the corner of Main and Spring streets, resisting the urge to watch him get into his truck. Someone might spread it around that she seemed awfully interested in Mike's rear view. Of course she wasn't. Not any more than any other straight woman with functioning sight.

On beautiful days like today, instead of walking straight to church, she walked down to the end of Main Street and back, just to reconnect with the town. Walking the length of Main, seeing the stores of her childhood and many of the same people, was reassuring. Like meat loaf and mashed potatoes. Not exotic, not exciting, but something you could count on for warmth and sustenance.

Two women approached the side door to the church at the same time she did. Erin Hall and her mother-in-law, Joan.

Sarah put on a bright smile at the same time her abdominal muscles—kept strong with exercise—clenched. Erin wasn't so bad. Just sort of strange, and so mousy and dull, you couldn't help feeling sorry for her, even if she made you nervous. But Joan Russell strained every part of Sarah that had been raised by her gentle parents to be forgiving and gracious to all living things. Joan had lived in Kettle all her life, lost her first husband to the bottle, the second in Vietnam, raised Joe by herself, and lived for her own personal grudge list.

Of course poor Erin was on this list by virtue of being married to Joan's son. As far as Joan saw it, there wasn't a woman alive good enough for Joe. Which was amusing since he was a butcher, which wasn't exactly an exalted trade in Sarah's eyes. But since Erin showed up pregnant in high school with his baby, Joe hadn't had the leisure to choose a bride perfect enough for Mom. If such a woman existed. Which Sarah doubted.

"Hello, Joan. Hello, Erin. Isn't it a beautiful day?"

Joan cast a withering glare at the lovely fall afternoon. Her enormous eyes were startling and cowlike, surrounded by cascades of wrinkling tobacco-aged skin. "It'll be winter soon enough, and then my aches and pains will start. You wouldn't say that about a fall day if you had my body."

Sarah put on her sympathetic face and opened the door for the older woman, thanking God she didn't have Joan's body. An inch or two shorter than Sarah, who stood five foot eight, Joan had an enormous bust and a stomach to match. Supporting this abundance, tiny hips, a small rear like a flat forlorn heart, short skinny legs, and size five feet. Top-heavy enough to be tipped over by one good puff of air.

"Winter must be very hard on you, Joan." Sarah spoke in her most soothing, respectful voice, about the only voice that didn't immediately provoke some kind of contradiction from Joan.

Erin stole a brief glance at Sarah. The girl—woman, of course; she was only three years younger than Sarah—always stole glances, as if she honestly didn't think she deserved them. Frustrating, because after one of Joan's comments, Sarah always wondered what would happen if Erin dared a longer look and Sarah winked or rolled her eyes to try to establish a bond.

But as far as Sarah could tell, Erin was afraid to get out of bed in the morning, let alone do more than glance, which Sarah had no patience for. Life should be enjoyed to its fullest, and if you didn't have the guts for that, why bother living?

She followed the two women inside, down the steps to the church basement, to the spartan gray-green room where they met once a week, to chat, drink coffee and eat treats, either homemade—Sarah dreaded Joan's week—or purchased from Sidler's Bakery across the street. The Social Club's job in Kettle was to plan constructive, healthy activities for the residents to keep them out of trouble, not that anything truly bad had ever happened here, or probably ever would.

This week the ladies of the Social Club were going to discuss Kettle's annual Halloween party. Sarah couldn't wait to tell them her idea; she was sure it would capture them. She was impressed herself that she'd even thought of it. Ben had not been enthusiastic, but he had this way of not being excited by her ideas—or at least significantly less than she was.

Betty was already there, enormously pregnant as usual. "Welcome, Sarah, what a beautiful day it is!"

"Lovely. I walked down Main Street and back, just to enjoy it." She wouldn't mention peeking into Tom's store. Betty would feel she had to pray for Sarah's soul and Sarah's marriage, both of which were in fine shape.

"Hi, Sarah." Nancy smiled eagerly at Sarah through glasses so thick, her eyes looked as if they were holograms pasted to the insides of the lenses. Nancy had glommed onto Sarah in Mrs. Johnson's third grade and hadn't let go yet.

"Hello, Nancy. What a sweet dress."

Nancy beamed her pleasure, which made Sarah feel good. Being charitable to everyone was important, so Sarah tried her best to be pleasant. When she herself was perfect, then she could afford to be critical of others.

She helped herself to coffee in the mug she'd brought with her—who could stand the dreadful taste of Styrofoam?—and chided herself for forgetting to bring skim milk. One surreptitious glance at the donuts Betty had brought—raised with chocolate frosting—and Sarah turned away. Betty really should be more careful about her eating habits, gaining steadily as she was. Sarah had seen her at Sidler's buying two dozen donuts for a family of six, two members of which were too young for donuts.

She allowed herself one more glance, but she tried not to pollute her body with too much fat and sugar, so she took her coffee to her usual seat in the circle of chairs, and sat.

"Well, ladies." She lifted her coffee in a gracious salute. Joan hated it that Sarah had unofficially appointed herself chairwoman, but then Joan hadn't volunteered to do all the work

Sarah did. "I wanted to tell you about an idea I had for this fall's Halloween party. As you all know, I am very passionate about growing pumpkins."

She laughed so they'd understand that she was aware she had a fairly strange passion, and that they were welcome to chuckle if they wanted to. "I planted a record number this year—Baby Bear, Harvest Moon, Connecticut Field, Winter Luxury—" She stopped when she realized she sounded obsessed.

"Ben gave me permission to use the next-door lot we bought when the Judds sold it, so I'll have a bumper crop. I thought we could sell pumpkins this year at the party, and use the money to help a child in need. Not here, of course, we have no children in need here in Kettle, but somewhere there are some."

She smiled, trying not to look smug. If people thought you were already overexcited about your idea, they tended to downplay their enthusiasm. Sarah wanted to hear the enthusiasm her idea deserved unencumbered by such a filter.

"Oh, I like that. Very nice. Very nice indeed." Nancy nodded, her dead-straight strawberry-blond hair twitching forward and back over her narrow face. She always spoke slowly, with great importance, as if she were constantly pronouncing couples man and wife.

"Your idea is wonderful, praise God in his mercy, a chance to help a child in need. Sarah, you are so sweet." Betty reached over a plump hand and smacked Sarah's knee, which seemed a strange way to enjoy someone's sweetness.

"Ben is nice to let you indulge that passion," Nancy said. "Fred would laugh if I suggested growing pumpkins."

"Donald would howl! He wants me home taking care

of him. Lord knows he feels neglected enough these days."
Betty laughed that special female laugh that indicates men
are fools, and put a protective hand over her bulging belly,
which bulged so much anyway, you couldn't tell what was
pregnancy and what was Betty belly. Sarah kept smiling and
looked to Erin for her reaction, proud of Ben and how he
didn't mind her growing pumpkins.

Erin stared at Sarah's hairline, as if she was registering
something fascinating. Who knew what went on in that head
of hers? Everything about her was so pale. Skin, lips, eyes,
hair, even her clothes. Yet Sarah thought if Erin made herself
up and got some confidence, she'd probably be lovely. Sarah
even bought her a pretty rose sweater once, but as far as she
knew, Erin had never worn it.

"Good idea."

"Thank you, Erin."

When the silence edged toward awkward, Sarah gave in
and looked at Joan, who was patting her jet-black, poufy
hairdo. Any idea Joan didn't come up with was ignored or
met with resistance.

"What I want to know is who watched the verdict
yesterday?"

A cross between a sigh and a moan broke from between
all the lips in the room except Sarah's, which were pinched
firmly together until she made herself loosen them. The rest
of the women liked her pumpkin idea. It would pass.

"Wasn't that awful?" Betty shook her head of dull blond
curls that looked like a wig no matter what shade she tried.
"That awful woman. O. J. all over again. Is there no justice
except in our Lord's heaven?"

"It was terrible." Nancy nodded again, reminding Sarah of those perpetually nodding animals people put in the backs of their cars. "I cried for him and for the Branson family. Losing a son, a brother, a father in such a violent way. I can't imagine it."

Erin jerked in her chair. Her mouth opened. Color actually rose in her cheeks. "She was protecting herself."

"From what?" Joan blew out a puff of air that very nearly sounded like a rude raspberry. "Him being able to spend any of his own money?"

Erin's glance shot toward her mother-in-law, then down. "He hit her."

"So *she* said." Joan continued staring straight ahead, as if acknowledging Erin had spoken was effort enough. "She had to come up with *some* defense. Someone like her would never come out and admit she killed him. There was never any proof he hit her."

"Lord no." Betty slapped her generous thighs. "A handsome man like Ed Branson would never do anything like that."

"Certainly not," Joan snapped. "He was a gentleman."

"He cheated on her." Erin's face was turning red.

"Men will be men," Joan said. "She wasn't worth staying faithful to for a man like Ed Branson."

Sarah could feel Nancy's hologram eyes on her, waiting to see how Sarah reacted before uttering her own opinion. Sarah felt a prickle of irritation and had to consciously relax.

"Well." She used her gentlest let's-close-the-subject voice. "No doubt she's sitting pretty now. Shall we—"

"She got nothing out of it." Erin sat ramrod straight in her chair, hands clenched together, fingers straining at each other as if they wanted to fly free and attack someone or something. "The family got all his money."

The women in the room shifted uneasily. Sarah couldn't believe this many sentences were coming out of poor Erin's mouth. Who knew if she was working up to one of her infamous screaming fits, the kind she'd had at school sometimes, a horrible tantrum from a child too old to have one.

Sarah would have to smooth this over quickly. "I'm sure Lorelei will find another man to prey on. Now, can we—"

"I heard . . ." Nancy moved her head nervously one side to another, making her hair swing again. She cleared her throat. "You can't tell anyone. Fred would kill me if he knew I blabbed. Promise?"

The women promised solemnly, but of course Sarah knew the town would be buzzing by nightfall. No one would hear it from her lips, though. A promise was a promise.

"You know how it came out during the trial that Lorelei's real name is Vivian Harcourt?" Nancy blinked her hologram eyes. "Well, last night when I was cleaning up from dinner, Fred said Edna Sinclair is being told to leave the Harcourt house."

"What?" Joan bellowed the syllable, her off-kilter body stiffening in her chair. "Edna's been there for years. Estelle let her rent it, furnished, for as long as she needed it. What are you saying?"

Sarah turned her head back to Nancy so abruptly, she got a burning twinge in her neck.

Lorelei Taylor. Née Vivian Harcourt. Broke after the trial. The Harcourt house.

Nancy opened her mouth to continue. Sarah held her breath, feeling as if her morning—no, as if her very life—was starting to teeter slowly out of control.

"It's being kept quiet so the paparazzi don't find out. Estelle Harcourt was Vivian Harcourt's paternal *grandmother*. Mom says she remembers a little girl coming to visit once or maybe twice. Estelle called her Vi." Nancy plunked her hands onto her hips, practically buzzed with power. "That little girl turned into Lorelei Taylor."

Three loud gasps, Sarah's probably the loudest, even though they all must have figured it out thirty seconds ago.

"And Lorelei—Vivian—wants to disappear for a while. And so . . . yes." Nancy took in a long, shuddering breath, no doubt enjoying herself immensely while the rest of the room suffered. "That woman is moving to Kettle."

Tough Choices
by Erin Packer
Mrs. Jantzen's sixth grade

Assignment: Please think of some tough choices someone might face in his or her life, and tell us how you would solve them and why.

Having milk or juice for breakfast can be a tough choice if your life is happy. Choosing to live or die would be tough if you were very sick. Or choosing if you could leave someone you love who is mean to you or not.

Still, having tough choices is better than having no choices at all.

Erin lay in her bed. It was probably her favorite place to be these days. Not like before, when she had more energy. Usually she liked to paint when Joe was at work, or send e-mails. Paint or send e-mails or read *What to Expect When You're Expecting*. She wasn't pregnant anymore, hadn't been for ten years. It made Joe mad when she read it, but she liked to read it and pretend she was still pregnant. Every day she read part of it.

Today was different, though. Today she found out something important that had made electric charges go off in her body, like she was getting shock treatment, or like she was some experiment animal in a science lab. Or maybe like Frankenstein coming to life again. That's how she imagined those things would feel.

The Social Club meeting was usually agony. Especially since Betty had gotten pregnant again, sitting there, plump and full not only of her own life but someone else's. Doubly alive. Which made Erin feel sad and empty, even more than usual.

Nancy mostly sniveled at Sarah's feet, which was tedious. Joan tried to make everyone around her feel bad; that's what she was put on earth to do. She did a bang-up job, too. No regrets for Joan on her deathbed. At sixty, she'd already done more of her life's work than most people did who lived to be ninety.

After Joe married Erin his senior year because she was pregnant, Erin had resisted hating Joan for a long time. It was hard work, but she'd taken pride in it. Then she lost that baby and too many others, and after Joy, whom she carried almost to term, there had been no more babies since, which meant her one potential source of usefulness to Joan had come to an end. That's when Erin figured why bother, and went ahead and hated her. It felt good. An unsatisfying type of power, but it was some.

Sarah was okay. Sarah was smart except for one thing. Sarah didn't realize she was unhappy. Erin thought Sarah fooled pretty much everyone else, except maybe Mike. Unhappy people could recognize unhappy when they saw it. Almost no one else in this town was unhappy, just Erin, Mike, and Sarah. Joan didn't count, she was just a bitch.

Today's meeting might have been horrible, as usual, since they'd had to start planning the Halloween party. Erin stood at that party year after year serving punch, feeling out of place in her hometown, watching other people pretend to be having the time of their lives when it was the same people saying the same things they said the rest of the year, but with costumes on.

Joe always drank too much and leered at other women. The town looked on, wondering what Erin wasn't giving him that made him leer like that, and what did he ever see in her anyway. Then Joe would come home and want to know who she'd talked to and what she'd said to them, and why wouldn't she give him a baby, damn it. And in a mean drunk mood he'd want to do all that other stuff that made sex more exciting for him and hurt her.

She hated parties. So much energy put into forcing people to pretend to be happy on a certain date at a certain time, when real joy came from inside, not from parties or people or pumpkins.

Erin's baby, Joy, was born dead eight months into the only

pregnancy that lasted. Joy was taken away, Erin didn't know where, before Erin could hold her. Nobody mentioned the loss of the baby except Joe. Bad things didn't happen in Kettle. Everybody knew that.

Erin couldn't even visit a grave because she didn't know if the baby had one. She'd made a grave out in the woods, but didn't go often. Her baby wasn't really there.

Now Vivian was moving here. Back to the Harcourt house, which she'd visited a couple of times to see her grandmother. Erin remembered her. "Vi" was three years older and had wandered by and played with Erin one afternoon when Erin was six. When Erin's father had yelled, they'd both run away without stopping to hear what he was saying. They'd hidden in a thicket in the woods behind Erin's house, arms around each other, and laughed so they wouldn't cry. Well, maybe Vi hadn't wanted to cry, but Erin had. Then another day Erin had gone over to the Harcourt house and they'd played with the immense dollhouse in Vivian's grandmother's room, a toy with more furniture than was in Erin's whole house.

Alice came soon after that. She looked exactly like Vi.

Of course the woman Vi grew into—Vivian—might think Erin was a mousy fool. Maybe she would be right. But Erin was pretty sure she and Vivian would lock eyes and understand each other. Maybe not right away. But eventually. And having someone in Kettle who understood her could make life a little more okay. Probably for both of them.

The only person who ever understood Erin was Alice. When her parents found out about Alice, they made Alice leave. Which was stupid of them, and stupid of Erin for sending her, because Alice only existed in Erin's mind.

In Erin's mind, Alice had been beautiful and understanding and kind, and they'd played together every day. They'd gone running, painted, and sat talking in the woods surrounding the town. Alice was the one thing no one should have been able to control.

Sometimes Erin worried that suffering was so familiar, that if the chance for something as strange and ill-fitting as happiness came along, she wouldn't know to make a grab for it.

Three

Vivian Harcourt's Report on The Lorelei
by Heinrich Heine
Mr. Barclay's twelfth grade
Chicago, Illinois

This poem is about a beautiful woman, with one stunning head of hair. She sits on a big cliff in Germany called The Lorelei, at a dangerous narrow place on the Rhine River and combs her alluring tresses, mourning her lost love, which strikes me as a tremendous waste of a woman's time, but then I can't say I miss anyone who's ever left me or died, so I can't relate.

Apparently this woman has a voice Beverly Sills would give her two left teeth for. Men sail by and are so entranced by her beauty, song, and hair-grooming technique, they lose their sense of direction and appar-

ently also their survival instinct. Crash, smash, boats hit rock, body parts everywhere, good-bye sailors. I imagine the bones piled up after a while.

Anyway, no surprise there, all men steer by their rudder, if you know what I mean. But you'd think once word got around that hearing this woman's voice caused death by disorientation, the sailors would start wearing aural prophylactics. Or at least put the gay guys at the wheel.

Vivian—Please plan to meet with me to discuss your grade. Usual place and time. Mr. Barclay.

Lorelei Taylor, used to be Vivian Harcourt and now Vivian Harcourt again, glanced at the white lettering on the green roadway sign: *Kettle 2*.

"Two miiiles to Kettle." She sang the words, first as a nasal country tune, then low and gruff like Louis Armstrong, finally creating a Bee Gees falsetto disco hit, tapping the accelerator so the car jerked down the two-lane road. *Put the pedal to the metal, it's two miiiiiles to Kettle.*

Punchy. Driving too many hours in a row on too much caffeine and crappy food and not enough sleep. To avoid paparazzi, she'd had to creep out of her lawyer's NYC apartment in the middle of the night and into this piece-of-shit car he'd given her, God bless his greasy combover. His son's, he said. Was going to buy him a new one anyway.

She'd been so grateful, she was actually nice to him.

Kettle 1. For God's sake, these people were anxious you

know how long before you hit their town. What was next, *Kettle, 10 yds? Kettle 5'6"?*

Her stomach flipped, then settled as the green forest gave way to farmland and the occasional blue arrow sign pointed out side-road local businesses. Karen's Krafts. Hanson's Venison. Haircuts by Doris. Gravestones. Guns. Worms.

Christ. From midtown Manhattan to Hunt and Fish, USA. She'd probably lose her mind.

A sign flashed by, *Reduce Speed Ahead, 25 MPH*. She glanced at the speedometer, hovering near fifty, and eased up on the gas. No point getting hauled into jail so soon after she got out.

She could still hardly believe it. She'd been so primed to hear "guilty" from the mouth of that prim jury member, that when the "not" came out, she hadn't even really understood for several seconds. Not? As in *not?* As in they actually figured it out?

She was free. Of the specter of lifelong incarceration and, damn it, of Ed. The concepts took their sweet time sinking in. She woke in the middle of the night every night, drenched in sweat, back in jail in her dreams. Or worse, back staring in horror at Ed, dead in the tub, realizing she'd be the first one suspected, knowing she had months of trial hell ahead of her. She still woke every morning nauseated with dread over her fate before it registered she'd come through fine.

A survivor. A goddamn survivor. They could put her on a reality show and launch her into a closet with thirty leopards and a thousand black widow spiders for a week, and at the end she'd skip on out and dance a tango for the cameras.

Free! She laughed, a weird, screechy, manic sound, and nearly choked when her breath caught wrong in her chest. Hot damn. This side of forty, coming to Small-Town America. Who would expect this of Lorelei Taylor?

But since when had she done the expected?

Gas station, lumberyard, diner, and then suddenly Spring Street, on the edge of town. She vaguely remembered the look of Main Street. Quiet, untouched, as if it had stood there since the dawn of time in some isolation bubble protecting it from the decay of progress.

Probably no Starbucks. Shit.

She turned left on Spring, where the white church stood on the corner, steeple soaring up, lofty and self-righteous.

Her elation sank into uncertainty. Was she really going to live here? Trading one prison for another? But what the hell choice did she have? The press and paparazzi were all over her; she couldn't stay in New York. In the days she'd been there since the verdict, she'd been recognized, screamed at, insulted, jostled. Of course, in New York, that was pretty much your average day.

But where else could she go? Stan Combover's legal bills had nearly bankrupted her. She'd depended on Ed to take care of her; he was twenty years older, not in great health, and he'd promised to. But after fourteen years together, the bastard had left her next to nothing. Enough to get by here until the storm blew over, but in New York, gone in a heartbeat. His stinking family must have worked on him not to change his will. Or maybe he was just a rat bastard. God knew she had a talent for finding them.

From Spring Street she turned onto Maple Avenue—did

they not have one original street name in this town?—and squinted at the neat rows of houses, looking for signs of a familiar one. God oh God, it was all so damn precious-looking.

There. White with dark green shutters, looking like home-sweet-home for Donna Reed. The house her paternal great-great-grandmother had built when she moved here from Chicago with her husband, who gave up city life to be a country doctor.

She pulled into the driveway and turned off the engine.

Deathly silence. How did people stand it? She needed a drink after ten seconds.

She opened her door and shoved it way out, stepped onto the cement, pockmarked like bad skin. Her stomach churned, head swirled, the buzzing, bleary-eyed wooziness of too many hours on the road. A glance around, shoving her sunglasses on top of her head. Perfect, orderly houses with perfect, orderly lawns. Nobody around, nothing, zip, nada. She was going to go nuts here.

Wait. A curtain moving across the street. And one next door, to the north.

Jesus.

She narrowed her eyes, then a slow smile spread over her lips. O-kay. If Kettle wanted to see the arrival of Lorelei Taylor, Kettle would.

She took her sunglasses off her head, stuck the end of one temple into her mouth, and took a trip to the end of the driveway in her best do-me saunter. Better if she'd been wearing her Rene Caovilla leopard-print stiletto sandals and a bright yellow miniskirt, but no way would she drive two days in that outfit.

Skintight, low-riding Miss Sixty jeans and an equally tight cropped, scoop-necked top would have to do. She stuck her tits out and made sure her top rode high enough to show off her firm stomach. Pushing forty, maybe, but she damn well didn't look it.

At the end of the driveway, she looked up the street, then down, as if her pimp was due any second and what could be keeping him? Then tossed her hair, made a big show of stretching, arms up, undulating her hips, then bent at the waist to touch her toes, flipping her hair over her head and rolling slowly up.

Across the street, another curtain twitched. She guessed phone calls were being made. *She's here, she's making a spectacle of herself in the street, hurry, before you miss it.*

Grand finale: She drew her hands up her thighs, then straight up over her stomach, cupped her breasts briefly on the way to her shoulders, then raised her hair and let it fall.

There.

If there was anyone on this street who didn't think they knew what she was about, they thought they did now.

She turned back, still sauntering, twirling her sunglasses oh-so-nonchalantly. A movement on the porch of the house south of hers nearly made her fall off her stride. A man, a young man—early thirties, maybe—watching the show unapologetically, one hand on his hip, the other holding a beer, legs apart in a strong stance. Broad shoulders, nicely fitting jeans, T-shirt half covered by an open green flannel work shirt that looked worn and soft. Underneath she could see the bulge and valley of developed pecs, mmmm. That solid masculine landscape under soft cotton was a total turn-on.

Features: strong, handsome. Hair: short, dirty blond. Expression: solemn and unreadable.

"Hi." She stopped at the edge of her driveway and tipped her head, looking him over as if she hadn't already made her assessment. "I'm Vivian."

"I know."

Still no reaction; she wasn't used to that. One way or the other, Lorelei generally made an impact. "I'm your new murderess neighbor."

"I know that, too." He lifted his beer, took a swig.

"Well, you are a veritable encyclopedia, aren't you."

A grin lifted one side of his mouth. That was good. She liked men who could take a joke.

"I'm Mike."

"Hello, Mike."

She let the silence linger, watching him calmly, allowing the hint of a smile on her mouth so he'd know she was interested, amused, in control.

He took another swig of beer and watched her back, apparently comfortable with the silence. If his eyes weren't so intense, she'd say there wasn't much going on in the brain department.

"Aren't you going to offer me a beer?" Okay, she was impressed. She'd had to break the silence first.

"This is my last one."

Brrrrr. All was chilly on the southern front. Apparently Mike belonged in the she's-a-murdering-bitch camp along with most of the country. "All righty then. Nice meeting you."

She turned toward her car, suddenly exhausted and near tears, which freaked her out. She hadn't cried during this entire ordeal except when her cellmate socked her once and the tears had been from surprise and pain. Maybe now that the stress had let up, she'd be able to grieve, deal with the fact that Ed was dead and her life had to go on without him.

Oh, she was so looking forward to it.

"Need help unloading?"

She pivoted on one heel. "What?"

"Do you need help unloading your car?"

Vivian put her hand to her hips and narrowed her eyes. "Was that really your last beer?"

"That's what I said."

She looked over at her grandmother's white one-car garage, and brought the look back to him. "Help would be nice. Thank you."

He set his bottle on the railing and came off the porch with light, easy steps. "Been driving awhile today?"

"From Indiana. Nice traffic."

"You must have started at dawn."

"Before."

He stood next to her while she unlocked her trunk, a solid, silent presence. She was amused to find herself desperately grateful for his offer of help. Lorelei Taylor, who had faced police interrogation, relentless prosecutors, crazed prisoners, angry crowds, Ed's bloodthirsty relatives, and hostile erstwhile friends without flinching, dreaded going into her grandmother's house.

Until the moment she crossed that threshold, the entire nightmare of the last year could have been just that, a horrible fantasy. Once inside, the changes in her life would be undeniable. Kettle, Wisconsin, would be her new home.

Oh. Goody.

She reached into the chaos of suitcases, loose clothes, and bags of shoes and jewelry, and grabbed an armful, waited while he did the same.

"Not enough suitcases?"

"I had to leave in a hurry."

"Right."

His unquestioning acceptance was a relief. She didn't want to share details of the last few days with anyone, not that she would have hesitated to tell him to butt out if he asked. She marched toward the back door with her load of clothes, leaving the sexy saunter for when she wasn't at risk of tripping over whatever her currently invisible feet might encounter.

March, march, march to the end of the driveway, up three steps, pressing the load of clothes against the door with her body so she could reach the keys the tenant had left in the newspaper box. Tight security around here. Didn't they claim there was no crime in Kettle? Hard to imagine. Maybe she should get accused of another few murders and liven things up.

She lifted the lid, half hoping the keys weren't there, though she couldn't stand another minute in the car having to drive off and find them. They were. Two, on a chain with a little dangling plastic Mickey Mouse figure, puffy gloved white hand raised in a cheery wave.

Insipid rodent.

The storm door screeched like a dying monkey, but her key went smoothly into the dead bolt, turned and unlocked; the second key went in hard; she had to jiggle it a few times before she could turn it.

"Come . . . *on*."

The lock gave suddenly, and the weight she'd been leaning against the door propelled her inside, not even giving her the courtesy of a long breath and solemn step over the threshold to experience the deep symbolism of the moment.

Instead, she dropped half the clothes onto what instantly registered as the ugliest linoleum on earth, and gave an undignified grunt, which she followed with some of her choicest curse words.

"Nice mouth."

She glanced back at her erstwhile hero and nearly let him have one of her all-time favorites for his very own.

One dark male eyebrow lifted as if he heard the word she'd chosen for him without her having to say it, and she swallowed and glanced around the kitchen instead, gut sinking in despair.

Oh. God. Either she'd forgotten how bad it was or someone else had come in and wrought Kountry Kitchen hell. Green and blue pastel bunnies hopped around the white walls among sprigs of pink ivy, nibbling flat orange carrots; shiny red apples and mallard ducks cozied up on the cabinets. Cheery curtains with ruffles and smiling yellow and red Gerbera daisies filtered out the daylight.

She thought back to her and Ed's kitchen: granite countertops, hardwood floors, copper, glass, stainless appliances. No bunnies.

She was going to hurl.

"Not what you're used to?"

She turned and looked up at Mike, surprised at his intuition. Men she knew didn't tune in to women's feelings. Or rather, they tuned them out, too busy concentrating on their own, which were always more important and more weighty and, of course, always right.

He was taller than he'd seemed outside, taller than Ed by nearly a foot. Ed had been Napoleon-short and just as complex. Mike was broader and damn handsome, with a farmboy, military edge. His eyes were blue, the shade that always seemed bright and alive, surrounded by dark lashes. Very sexy combination, fresh youth and weary cynicism. She wondered what had happened to start the transition.

"How old are you, Mike?"

"Thirty-three."

She waited to see if he'd ask how old she was. Maybe he already knew; the trial hadn't left much of her private.

He didn't.

"I'll be forty soon." She waited to see if he'd ask when.

He didn't.

"November ninth. All gifts of expensive jewelry accepted. No fur, no cheap champagne, caviar is fine, but only if it's—"

"Are you going to make me stand in your kitchen holding your underwear all day?"

She laughed, a short burst of surprise. "Not today. But maybe we can arrange that another time, hmm?"

He actually smiled, with both sides of his mouth. But not like he thought that was a terrific idea and he accepted. More like his teenage daughter had made her first clever comeback and he was proud while trying not to be.

She suddenly wanted his arrogant silence out of her ugly house so she could be alone and fall apart with no dignity.

"You can take my underwear to my bedroom and I'll follow you. I assume you know the house. I don't remember it."

He nodded and preceded her into the living room, a horror in baby-blue shag carpet with a faded yellow-and-blue floral living room set, then up the baby-blue shag-carpeted stairs to the baby-blue shag-carpeted hallway.

Gran, what were you thinking?

"This is the master bedroom." Silent Mike stood in the hall with his armload of female clothing and jerked his head toward the door on his left.

"Please no more shag."

"Hardwood."

"Thank God." She vaguely remembered this room as something special—some memory associated with it . . . She pushed in and groaned. Old-lady heaven. A canopied bed with an eyelet cover, lace doilies on every flat surface, porcelain cherubs, keepsake boxes, a Jesus wall clock, the ugliest possible blue-and-brown wallpaper on two walls and the remaining two painted, one blue, one brown, gag her.

In the corner, there, the three-story dollhouse—smaller than she remembered, but she'd been smaller then, too—impeccably furnished down to soup ladles hanging over the stove, and tiny crocheted pot holders. She'd played here with someone . . . someone local.

Who knew? Who cared?

"How special is this?" She dumped her armful of clothing on the eyelet bedspread, expecting a cloud of dust. Not a speck. "Clean, anyway."

"Yes." He dumped his load next to hers and tramped off to get another, she imagined. Nice of him.

She lingered, crossed to the dollhouse, and picked up the

tiny figure of a girl, blond thread hair, carefully stitched clothes, tiny padded legs with wire inside so she'd pose. *Emily?*

Jesus, she freaked herself out. Hadn't even thought of this doll in thirty years and the name popped into her head.

Whatever. She put the doll down and left the room, trying to make it down the blue shag staircase without wincing. She had big jobs ahead of her. This house needed shaking up. So did Mike.

And so, she had a feeling, did Kettle.

Four

Excerpt from Sarah Bannon's valedictorian speech
Kettle High graduation

And so I send you off today, exhorting you to turn your energy outward on the world, not only to benefit yourselves, but to make it a better place, with hard work, honesty, kindness, and beauty. The world might see us as young and inconsequential, but it needs and deserves the power of our youth and ideals. I leave you with this quote from Amy Bankson, a Kettle suffragette in the first part of this century. "The power to make a difference is not handed to us, nor is it innate. It is something we must want badly enough to go forth and grab for ourselves."

"Amber, honey?" Sarah sugarcoated her voice, her body tensing the aggravating way it always did when she had to confront her daughter. Sarah was the boss; she shouldn't find this so difficult.

"What, Mom?" Amber managed to inflict an image of weary eye rolling into every sentence. Sometimes it was hard to remember the sweet child who tried to copy everything Sarah did.

"Were you planning to wear that to school?" She tried hard to hold back the over-my-dead-body tone that always set her daughter off. But Amber looked like a slut in her current outfit—tight blue hip-hugger pants and an equally tight knit top that didn't quite meet her jeans, and left nothing to the imagination in the breast department. Somehow Amber had evaded Sarah's genes and managed to grow beautiful breasts, which was wonderful for her, of course, but no daughter of Sarah's would show up in public looking like a slut.

"No, I put it on just to eat breakfast."

"I could do without the sarcasm. And you're not wearing that to school."

"*Mo-om.*"

Sarah's head started to throb. It should be illegal for children to draw out the mom syllable in that particular protesting tone. "Where did you buy that outfit?"

"At the mall last weekend with Tanya. Please Mom, all the other kids dress like this, it's no big deal." Her daughter shrugged and looked down at herself, her beautiful, chin-length, auburn hair falling in wispy, flippy clumps that made it look as if random hairdressers had taken random snips whenever the mood struck them.

Disapproving of today's styles made Sarah feel old. And looking at her daughter's lush, frankly female figure made her feel dried up and even older, and about as sexual as a dead bug.

"It's a big deal to me, Amber. Boys will look at your body instead of at you. No woman wants to be just a body to men." Even as she said the words, she remembered desperately wanting boys to look at her skinny, underdeveloped dancer's body the way they looked at girls who looked like Amber. How different it all was on this side of the parenting chasm.

"Mom, you are so hung up about sex."

Sarah inhaled sharply. "Amber."

"These are *clothes*. The boys will just see clothes."

"No, they won't, honey. Trust me. Go up and change."

"You never let me do *anything*. I am the most restricted girl in the whole *town*. I can't stay out late, I can't wear what I want, I can't eat what I want. You don't like my boyfriend, you don't like my—"

"That's enough, Amber. Go take it off." Sarah's voice came out harsher than she intended. She was generally anxious not to thwart Amber's self-confidence and individuality, but she'd woken up feeling uncharacteristically cranky and disoriented. The day was unusually warm and windy, an abrupt change from the gradual fall chilling she enjoyed so much every year. Her sinuses had responded as usual by making her face feel as if a lead balloon had been inflated behind her eyes. Maybe that was it.

Or maybe it was that Vivian person moving in only a few houses down the block. Mrs. Entwhistle had called yesterday afternoon to tell Sarah to look out her front window. She had, and been treated to a sight that confirmed her worst fears. Brazen, overtly sexual, practically throwing herself at

Mike. She was exactly the kind of woman Sarah dreaded her daughter having any contact with. An especially bad omen that Amber showed up this morning dressed nearly the same way Vivian had been yesterday, though of course Amber had bought the clothes with her trampy friend Tanya before Vivian showed up.

Sarah planned to do the right thing and visit Vivian this morning with one of her carrot cakes made with pineapple and reduced-fat cream cheese frosting. Frankly, she dreaded it.

Amber stomped upstairs, making sure the impact of each foot on each step could be heard throughout the county. Sarah cringed, waiting for the slam of her room door.

Slam.

So damn predictable.

"Coffee ready?" Her husband ambled into the kitchen, freshly shaved and looking so handsome in his usual jeans and cotton shirt. His medium brown hair was thick as ever, though a little more of his forehead showed every year. And his brows had grown wild; she'd suggested he tweeze and trim, but then he wasn't much for her suggestions. A man very much of his own opinions, and how she admired that about him.

"Yes, good morning, dear." She walked up to him, needing the feel of his arms around her. They exchanged their usual quick peck on the lips before he folded her in his embrace.

Funny how she always felt hugging the man you loved should feel like drowning in his arms. She never got the impression Ben was trying to drown her. More like a lifesaving maneuver, careful, efficient, and practical. But then he was a very efficient and practical man, another of his many fine qualities, so it wasn't as if she was complaining.

"I'm ready." Amber clumped back downstairs, wearing her rattiest shirt over the jeans and those dreadful shoes that made her feet look like black boats on top of black bricks.

Sarah chose not to fight. Amber didn't look slutty anymore, and if she wanted to think she was sticking it to Mom by looking ratty instead, she'd get no satisfaction from Sarah acting stuck.

"Juice is on the table, the eggs are ready, I'll dish them up. The toast is in the oven staying warm."

Her family sat and ate in silence, Amber's sullen, Ben's distracted, Sarah's contemplative; silverware clinking against the bistro chinaware she'd gotten from CooksCorner.com, so cheery in bright colors and so sophisticated at the same time. Sarah liked her things to be a reflection of herself, and she liked to think she was cheery and sophisticated.

Breakfast over, she stopped herself from giving her daughter a kiss on her way out the door, and stopped herself from asking Ben for another one as he disappeared into his office. She cleared the table and did the dishes, dried them and put everything away. Vacuumed the floor—should she mop it, too?

No. No reason to keep putting this errand off. Just get to the house, give Vivian the cake, and be gracious and polite so Vivian would know Kettle was a warm and forgiving town, Sarah most especially, being the first to welcome her. Then Sarah could come home and try not to think about having a murderess for a neighbor for who knew how long.

She glanced at the cake on the counter, carefully frosted to a smooth, perfect finish, nestled in a loaf-sized basket lined with a red-and-white checked cloth. She'd decorated the handle of the basket with sprigs of thyme from her garden and a calendula blossom. The basket really looked lovely.

So. She took off the apron Amber bought her at age seven—with Ben's financial help of course—that said *Mom Is Queen of the Kitchen* in green embroidered letters. The M of *Mom* was decorated like a crown. She adored the apron and had actually hesitated to use it in case it got stained, but that disappointed Amber so much that Sarah gave in.

Okay. The apron went back on the hook in her broom closet. She smoothed her olive-colored cotton knit pants from LandsEnd.com, slim fit they called them—and she still had the body to pull off slim fit, unlike some women who seemed to think stretch pants gave them license to stuff—and carefully redistributed the folds of her cream-colored turtleneck under the waistband.

Well. She picked up the cake and walked to her foyer, holding herself tall. Out the door—which she'd had trouble leaving unlocked after all those years in New York, but why bother here in Kettle—south three houses, across the street, and up to the Harcourt house's front door. No one else used front doors in Kettle, but Vivian was new, and using the front door was a measure of respect. Which was always a nice thing to show, even if one didn't necessarily feel much of it.

She fluffed her hair, then tucked it behind her ears and rang the bell, astonished at how nervous she was. Sarah prided herself on maintaining poise and calm in the face of nearly any adversity. She and Ben had had one difficult neighbor in their building in New York, but Sarah had worn her down with kindness. Surely that would be the case here, too. Most people couldn't resist persistent kindness. A shame not many realized it was one of humanity's most powerful weapons.

The dark green door remained firmly shut; Sarah leaned in to listen. Nine-thirty on a Wednesday morning, was Vivian still asleep? Or out? Her car was here. Sarah rang the bell again, tamping down the hope that sprang eternal. If Vivian wasn't home now, Sarah would just have to come back. Much better to get it over with while the cake was fresh and the day young.

There. She heard footsteps up to the door, then a pause as Vivian no doubt peered through the peephole. Sarah put on a pleasant smile so Vivian would know she had a friendly visitor. Most likely Vivian hadn't encountered too many friendly people recently. Sarah would likely be a refreshing change. But then when you murdered an attractive and important man like Ed Branson, you couldn't expect a steady stream of admirers.

The door swished open, Vivian appeared. For a second, Sarah was taken aback by the woman's sheer beauty. She looked like Catherine Zeta-Jones, only more so. She wore the same jeans she'd had on yesterday, and something resembling a laced-up corset, which made her breasts swell carelessly out of the top. Her long hair was perfectly tousled; she smelled expensive and rare and as beautiful as she looked.

"Ye-es?" Vivian drew out the syllable in obvious irritation, which flustered Sarah more.

Honestly. Sarah wasn't exactly an eyesore herself, and she had the distinct advantage of belonging here and letting her loved ones continue living.

"I'm Sarah. Gilchrist. I live up the street." She turned and pointed. "The brick house with the maroon chrysanthemums in the white wagon planter."

"That's the one I would have guessed."

Sarah stayed facing her beautifully landscaped front yard with the antique wooden wagon she'd bought and painted herself, because she had no idea if she'd just been complimented or insulted and she needed a minute to decide.

Better to decide she'd been complimented.

"Welcome to the neighborhood." She held up her cake in the little decorated basket and knew with instant certainty by the amusement on Vivian's face, that she'd decided wrong.

"How nice of you, Sarah. It looks delicious."

Sarah's face burned. She had to work not to hug her beautiful cake back to her chest and go home.

Especially when Vivian drew a long red fingernail across the top of the cake, leaving an ugly groove through which orange-brown crumbs showed. Worse, she opened her lips into a pouty circle and sucked the frosting off her finger as if it were part of a sex act Ben never let Sarah try anymore.

Sarah's goodwill began to dissolve like the sugar and reduced-fat cream cheese on Vivian's tongue.

"Come on in." Vivian took the basket and disappeared into the house, leaving Sarah in an agony of indecision. She didn't want to go into the house of this murderer who insulted her and ruined her perfect frosting. But to refuse would be shockingly rude, and Sarah was never shockingly rude.

"You coming?" Vivian reappeared and fixed Sarah with a look as if she thought her mentally deficient.

"Yes. Thank you. I can't stay long."

"No one asked you to stay long." She disappeared again.

Sarah took a deep breath and stepped over the threshold, reminding herself of the power of persistent kindness. She'd visited Vivian's grandmother Estelle here, and Edna, Estelle's good friend and companion, who had lived here for the past five years after Estelle died. Now Edna had moved to Milwaukee to live with her daughter.

The house was charming. Not Sarah's taste exactly, but she dreaded thinking what this woman would do to it. Sarah and Ben had been at a party in New York once where the photographer husband had hung a full-sized nude picture of his wife in their living room. Sarah and Ben hadn't known where to look. Vivian would probably decorate like that. Except she couldn't be thinking of staying. Once the trial furor died down, she'd be off again to find her next financial protector.

Sarah found Vivian in the kitchen, having cut a piece of carrot cake.

"Breakfast." She lifted the piece and took a huge bite. "Mmm, that is awesome. You want some?"

"No, thank you. I've had breakfast."

"So." She watched Sarah with an appraising look that made it plain she found Sarah lacking. Given the source, Sarah would take that as a compliment, too. "Have a seat and tell me about Sarah."

Sarah sat on one of the kitchen chairs and tried not to stare at the crumb that had shot out of Vivian's mouth during the sentence and landed on the admittedly dingy linoleum.

"I'm . . . I have a husband, Ben, and a daughter, Amber. She's sixteen, and—"

"Did I ask you about them?"

Sarah flinched and felt herself starting to get irritated. "You asked me to tell you—"

"About you. Not your husband or your kid."

A little smile automatically jumped onto Sarah's lips to block any chance of showing her annoyance. "I see."

"What do you do for fun in this town?"

"Well, I'm a member of the Kettle Social Club."

"Yeah? What's that about?" Vivian stuffed the last bite of cake into her mouth and licked her fingers. "You want a beer?"

Sarah stifled a gasp. "It's a bit early for me."

"Right." Vivian opened the refrigerator and pulled out a beer with a red label. "Found this at the supermarket. Decent stuff. Brewed in Wisconsin. It's good."

She unscrewed the top, took a swallow, and dug another hunk of Sarah's cake out of the basket. "Change your mind?"

"No. Thank you." She barely suppressed a shudder.

"What does the Social Club do?"

"We meet Thursday mornings at ten at the Lutheran church on the corner." She pointed in a northerly direction.

"And?"

"We organize events for the town. Right now we're working on the Halloween party, held on the twenty-ninth."

"I love parties! You need any new members?"

Sarah's body grew rigid. She still had the uncomfortable feeling that Vivian was making fun of her. "We are . . . that is . . . I don't think—"

"I'll show up Thursday—that's tomorrow, right?"

". . . yes."

"See what it's about. You don't mind, do you?" Her eyes went innocently wide; she took another swallow of beer.

"Of . . . course not."

Vivian was definitely making fun. She was exactly as Sarah expected her to be. In a word: A bitch. Just what Kettle didn't need. Everyone here was used to Joan. Joan was harmless. But for some reason Sarah felt his woman would not be.

"So tell me, Sarah Social Club . . ."

"Yes?" She couldn't help the slight edge to her voice, even as she kept reminding herself to keep it about kindness.

"What do you know about the very sexy Mike next door?"

A queasy feeling grew in Sarah's stomach, and not just from watching the combination of beer and cake being ingested before ten A.M. Vivian's voice had softened and her eyes had sharpened, and the result reminded Sarah of the big bad wolf just before he sprang from Grandmother's bed. With sudden panic, she imagined Vivian getting similar ideas about Tom Martin. "Mike."

"Yes. Mike."

"He does construction, handyman repairs, that sort of thing, for many of the people in Kettle. He's very good."

"I bet. You sure you don't want a beer?" Vivian poured half of hers down her throat. "It's damn good."

"No. Thank you."

"Is he married?"

". . . No." The word came unwillingly. "He's widowed."

"Oh, too bad."

Clearly it wasn't. "Are you . . . interested in him?"

"If I wasn't, would I be asking questions?"

Fists. Her hands were in fists. The woman was impossible. "I mean in developing a relationship with him."

"No."

"I see." Sarah tried not to show her relief.

"I just want in his pants."

This time Sarah's gasp couldn't be stifled. Her face started to burn red for the second time that morning.

Vivian chuckled. "Does he have a girlfriend?"

"No." She was glad to fling that word at her. "He wouldn't. He loved his wife."

Vivian stopped chewing; her eyes narrowed. "So?"

"He can't bring himself to look at another woman." She made sure her voice stayed free of triumph. Vivian would pounce and swallow her whole, and there probably weren't any woodcutters lurking around to free Sarah from such a fate. But inside she was saying, *Ha, there's one man you won't get in his bathtub*. Mike's devotion to his late wife was something rare and quite wonderful.

"That is totally pathetic."

Sarah drew herself up, leaving her kind smile behind. "Losing a loved one is extremely traumatic."

"Tell me something I don't know."

Sarah's jaw dropped. She *dared* compare her loss to Mike's? "I don't think the circumstances are quite the same."

"Because . . . ?"

"You weren't married."

"Ah, right. That half-hour ceremony explains everything."

"That's not what I meant."

"Then what did you mean?"

Sarah set her lips together and changed positions on the wooden chair. "I meant—"

"That he didn't kill her?"

"Exactly. He loved her."

"And I didn't love Ed."

"How could you love him if you did that?"

Vivian burst out laughing. Sarah couldn't believe it. She laughed and laughed as if Sarah had told a joke or recounted some funny TV episode. Then in the middle of laughing, her features contorted as if she were going to cry instead, but so quickly, Sarah must have imagined it. Because almost as soon as the change registered, Vivian smoothed her features, then stopped laughing quite so loudly, and eventually finished off her amusement with quieter chuckles and a few gasps.

Then she lifted the edge of the corset thing to try and wipe her eyes, but it was too tight and stiff, so she bent down and used the red-checked cloth under the cake, careful not to smudge her overly abundant makeup.

"I'm betting you don't wear much gray, do you, Sarah."

"I'm sorry?"

"Not much gray in your wardrobe? Mostly black? Or white?"

Sarah furrowed her forehead. This woman completely confused her. "I think I better go."

"Awww, you just got here."

"I'm sorry, but I have things to do."

"Like what?"

A forceful puff of air exited Sarah's mouth. Did this woman know nothing of manners? "I have things to do at home."

"For example?"

"I need to leave."

"I'm not stopping you."

Sarah fled for the front door, horrified to feel Vivian's hand on her arm just as she was about to escape. "Sarah."

Sarah forced her last bit of control to stay in place. She wouldn't fall apart here, no matter what. "Yes, Vivian?"

"What do you think of the decor in this house?"

"It's very nice. I like it."

"Come on. Seriously?"

"I—" She closed her eyes. This was the gravest challenge to her composure she'd faced in a long time. Frankly, she'd like to sock this woman in her perfect nose.

"Let me tell you something, Sarah. I want you to listen carefully because this is important." Vivian's hand on Sarah's arm tightened, and Sarah's lids sprang open.

Vivian leaned closer, so close that Sarah could smell the beer on her breath and notice the truly beautiful shape of her mouth. "Around me you can cut the bullshit. Okay?"

Sarah was so startled, she looked into Vivian's eyes, expecting mockery again, and was even more startled to find none.

Her gaze flew frantically around the baby-blue-and-yellow living room. What did this horrible person want from her? "It's a bit . . . dated."

Vivian grinned, then chuckled, then let out a laugh that was more in control, more fun than her explosion in the kitchen.

"I'll see you tomorrow morning at the meeting."

Sarah pulled her arm free and managed to leave without saying what she so desperately wanted to say.

I'll see you in hell first.

Five

<u>Lorelei Taylor's letter to her mother</u>
<u>June 1990</u>

Well I guess I haven't written for a couple of years. I actually called a few times, but Dad always answers and I can't handle talking to him. He should be in jail for what he did to me and it pisses me off that he's not.

I'm moving to New York. I met a guy at a party in Hugh Hefner's mansion, believe it or not—Ed Branson, Mr. Publishing. He's forty-eight, rich as hell, and I know this is going to sound weird, but I fell for him at first sight. And I don't even believe in that stuff.

Anyway, I know I haven't been much of a daugh-

Isabel Sharpe

ter, but you weren't much of a mom, either, especially when I needed you to protect me, so we're even. Still, it didn't feel right leaving Illinois without telling you, so I guess that says something. Maybe when you're an old lady and I'm a saggy, middle-aged ex-stripper we can get together for coffee.

Lorelei, aka Vivian, your little disappointment

Vivian yanked up the last corner of the baby-blue shag carpet in her new living room, a viscerally satisfying popping and ripping sound as the rug came free. Damn hard work. Her hands were raw and covered with scrapes, her attempt at a manicure shot, and now she had about a million staples and blocks of wood nailed to the hardwood floor to pry up.

Some other time.

She'd been working all day, driven by demons anxious to waylay her the second she relaxed. She'd started in as soon as Sarah left—and what was with that woman? My God, Vivian had never met anyone who needed to get laid more thoroughly. That husband of hers must not be getting the job done.

That kind of woman set off evil in Vivian. She'd met too many, mostly at parties with Ed. Inevitably, when the appeal of Vivian's humble origins—and her youth—began to fade, Ed had started sneaking around, with twenty-something Abby, whose *Mayflower* ancestors probably hired Vivian's to shovel their stables.

Women like Abby and Sarah took such pleasure looking down their nose jobs at Lorelei Taylor. She couldn't help wanting to push at that perfect exterior and see if there was anything real inside—guts and organs and pulsing blood. Or whether they were completely hollow, implanted with chips programmed by House and Garden TV and the Home Shopping Network.

With the shit Vivian had just been through, and the bad-assed mood she woke up in, the simple fact of Sarah's existence had provoked her to the sleaze outfit and the drinking-first-thing-in-the-morning show. The rest of that beer had gone down the sink the minute Sarah left. But life was too damn short to waste prissing around pretending a husband and child, a wagon full of chrysanthemums, and perfect carrot cake defined happiness.

So Vivian needled her and had been rewarded with the beginnings of a flareout Sarah couldn't quite block. Vivian would absolutely love to see her lose her shit.

After Sarah left, Vivian had gone to what passed for a su-permarket here. There had to be a strip with bigger stores somewhere—Stenkel's General Store? Jesus. Campbell's soup and SpaghettiOs, raincoats and fishing rods—everything a girl could want.

Then she'd come back here with cans of tomato and cream of chicken soup and boxes of macaroni and cheese, put them away in the duck-decorated cupboards, and arranged the rest of her stuff in the old-lady house. She'd cleared out too-precious knickknacks and girly frilly crap, and opened windows to try to air out the musty smell of aging. Then the carpet; there was no way she could stand that another day. And yes, thank goodness, there was gorgeous hardwood underneath.

Now at barely six-thirty, she was exhausted. She needed a drink. But if she stayed here and drank by herself, she was going to fall apart. Cry over everything that had ever been fucked up about her life, which was practically everything.

She had to do something to block the grief that was rumbling at her like the huge stone ball in the first Indiana Jones movie. Anything to stop the anticlimax release of stress from the trial. Anything to squirm out of facing that the man she loved had been stupid enough to fry his sorry ass in his bathtub, she hadn't been there to prevent it, and now she was stuck without him. In bumfuck, Wisconsin.

A sob tried to come up into her throat—unbearable tightness. She sprang to her feet, breathing hard. Coming here had been a mistake. She should have taken off for Vegas, somewhere she could immerse herself in bright lights, big city, exhaust herself with men and booze and partying and sex, and not feel.

In Kettle, there was nothing stopping her from feeling. Every last goddamn painful neurotic aspect. Not even shredding baby-blue shag carpet could keep her safe. Finding Ed, losing Ed, which had been more screwed up? Fourteen years of her life; she gave all but the last few happily. And even then, when his cruelty worsened, his rejections became more frequent, his supposedly secret visits to Abby multiplied, she hadn't stopped loving him. Which made her a masochistic idiot.

She needed a drink, but not alone. This town must have a bar; it *had* to have a bar. No way could anyone survive Kettle sober, even if he thought he loved it here. She was going out to find the bar, and she wasn't coming back until she was too drunk to stay conscious. What's more, she was in enough of a mean/bitchy/nuts mood that she was going to dress up—*hi I'm Vivian I'll be your town's slutty murderess*—and have herself a ball. These people needed waking up. And she needed to piss people off.

Upstairs to the de-knickknacked bedroom, though she left the dollhouse and Jesus clock alone for now, she yanked off the New York Giants T-shirt that had belonged to Ed. Got out of the seamless ivory bra, too, and put on her laciest black push-'em-together model. Over that, a red ribbed knit top, cut low enough to make the bra worthwhile. People would get what they expected, what they didn't realize they secretly needed her to be, so they could disapprove, feel moral, righteous, superior. They got what they wanted; so did she.

If Ed were here, he'd stop her going out. He knew her moods, knew when she was on a manic high of self-destruction. But he wasn't here. And she wasn't about to deny herself the pleasure-pain of imploding.

She stepped out of her panties, pulled on a thong and a pair of tight black stretch pants. Then her Manolo Blahnik black high-heeled pumps and the full makeup and jewelry treatment and a nice press-on-nails restoration of her manicure.

Okay. Ready.

She stared at herself in the fussy, gilt-framed mirror between the windows facing the street. She looked tired. And old. But the people in Kettle would have plenty to talk about regardless.

Downstairs, outside, not bothering with a coat, she glanced at Mike's house and hesitated, wondering if she should knock on his door instead and see if he wanted to have a drink. Or come out with her.

A car drove past her driveway and into his. A young, attractive blond, with a chin-length blunt bob and a *headband*, for God's sake—had no one a clue here?—carefully outfitted in pleated khaki pants and a perfectly wrinkle-free forest-green shirt, got out, reached into the backseat, and pulled out a covered dish.

Car door closed, she started to Mike's front door as if down the aisle to her beaming groom. Halfway, she glanced over, met Vivian's stare, and nearly dropped the dish.

"Oh . . . hi." She turned bright red and looked back over her shoulder, clearly craving the safety of her car.

Vivian smiled, open and friendly. Even she wasn't messed up enough to pick on Virgin Nelly here. "Big date tonight?"

"Oh." She erupted in nervous laughter. "I just thought Mike might like . . . this."

She lifted the casserole dish like an offering to the gods, and stared at it uncertainly.

"I'm sure he'll love it."

"I hope so." She giggled again and hurried to his door.

Vivian rolled her eyes and got into her car. Mike probably had a regular parade of hot dishes offering themselves. What had his wife been like? Virginal and sweet like little Nelly?

Undoubtedly.

She shot the car in reverse and peeled down the street, just to crank off the neighbors. *Oh that horrible Vivian Harcourt. Whole town went to hell when she moved here.*

News flash, neighbors. It's hell here already.

Up to Spring Street, turn right, up to Main Street, turn

left. That was about as complicated as Kettle got. She cruised down Main and finally spotted a likely looking place on the left, just past the pharmacy. Harris's Tavern.

She parked—there was even parking here—locked her car, and walked up to the brown-shingled exterior with frosted windows and a Budweiser sign glowing red. A few pedestrians passed, glancing curiously. Her nerves buzzed with anticipation; she was spoiling for a scene, a fight, anything but the bleakness of pain.

Hey, Kettle. Here comes your worst nightmare. She pushed open the door.

Her first reaction when she walked into the smoky gloom was intense relief. She half expected the place to be neon bright, squeaky clean, and decorated like a Girl Scout den. Maybe a bake sale in the corner.

But this one place at least, in this fake movie set town, seemed real. Real stink of cigarettes, real battered wood bar with real stools. Real beer-gutted patrons and—she swept the bar one end to the other—no women? Not one?

Oh come on. Every town had at least one blowsy drunk who hung out at the bar. Maybe she was in the bathroom?

Every male eye—she'd guess about sixteen total—was currently on her. Someone murmured something, and a grim chuckle spread across the bar like the wave in Yankee Stadium.

Her adrenaline started pumping. She loved being the center of attention, even attention from hefty rural Wisconsinites suffering from cheese spread.

"Good evening." She smiled at each man in turn, taking her time, noting mostly stares of appraisal or disapproval, but registering leering lust on the face of one particularly creepy-looking guy. And hallelujah, there at the end of the bar, with an unoccupied stool next to him, was sexy neighbor Mike. So he wasn't home to receive his hot little casserole.

She sauntered over and perched next to him, leaning forward as she settled herself on the stool in case he felt the need to ogle her.

Which he didn't seem to, but the icky guy behind him definitely did. She could practically smell his stale, fumey breath.

"Can I buy you a drink, Mike?"

He held up his beer, the same kind she bought for her house and pretended to enjoy this morning, Leinenkugel's Red. Good beer, but not at that ungodly hour.

"I'm fine, thanks."

O-kay. She hadn't figured Mike out. Either he didn't like her, or he just hated her boldness, or he didn't give a rat's ass either way. Or maybe he was 99.9 percent bullshit-free. Rare in her experience. She'd bet on one of the former.

"I'll buy you one anyway. Excuse me." She called to the bartender, shook back her hair, aware most of the men's eyes were still on her, some leaning forward, some back along the length of the bar. The burly bartender, scowling face pink like a ham, kept drying a glass with a white towel.

"Yo, bartender." She spoke louder. What, was the sonofabitch going to ignore her completely?

Apparently. That glass was *really* dry by now.

"What'll you have?" Mike spoke around the mouth of his bottle, then took a sip, not even glancing her way. "I'll order for you."

Vivian let out a low, easy chuckle to hide her anger. "Murderers not popular here in Kettle?"

"That's part of it." Mike put his bottle on the counter, still looking straight ahead. "Women don't generally come to Harris's."

"*What?*" She, who didn't surprise easily, was shocked. "A men-only bar? What the hell century is it here?"

"What'll you have?"

She laughed again. This was surreal. "Irish whiskey, straight up."

Mike raised his finger; ham boy came right over. "Yeah, Mike?"

"I'm switching to Jameson, Frank. No ice."

The bartender gave Vivian a dirty look; she blew him a sultry kiss, which made his look dirtier. He went off to pour the drink. And probably to add rat poison.

"Thank you, Mike."

"It's okay." Mike took another sip, staring at the bottles lined up behind the bar.

"So what do women do for fun in this town? Stay home and bake carry-out casseroles?"

Mike gave her an odd look, beer frozen halfway down to the bar, and for a second she thought he was going to smile. "That's about right."

"How special for them."

The bartender put her drink in front of Mike. She grabbed it and lifted the glass. "Thanks, Frank, darling."

Asswipe. She drained the drink and held it out for a refill. The ham-ster took it this time, though reluctantly.

"I'd like to see what *you'd* heat up for a man at home."

The icky guy spoke to Vivian's breasts; the men behind him chuckled. Vivian sent him a lick-my-boot stare. He was big, dark hair thinning on top, dark brows, dense stubble, big tuft of dark hair poking up from his yellow flannel collar. The kind of guy that was hair all over, but losing it on his head where his ego needed it most. He had pale, almost pasty skin. His nose bent slightly to one side, pink from drink. Jet-black eyes squinted from the afternoon's booze, dark bags puffed under. She couldn't place his age. He could be thirty-five or forty-five. Whatever he was drinking, he was drinking it neat in a big glass, had obviously had plenty, and was planning to stay and have plenty more.

"Who are you?" Vivian tossed off her second whiskey.

"I'm Joe." He introduced himself to her chest and held out a huge hand, which she ignored.

"Well, Joe." She thudded her glass onto the scarred bar. "I'm Vivian, and those tits you're staring at belong to me."

Joe flushed, then tried to recover with a leer while the men of Harris's Tavern laughed raucously.

She pointed to her glass and sent a pleading glance to Mike. He held it up to the bartender, who came grudgingly over with the bottle and poured.

"She's too much woman for you, Joe." One of the men whistled and laughed. "You better go home to Erin."

"They haven't made a woman yet that's too much for me."

"Oh, I think this one is."

Vivian downed her third whiskey, waiting for the familiar glow to allow the pain and mania to leak away. Men were such children.

"You better not take a bath around her."

Laughter, guffaws. Vivian's stomach roiled; her warm glow iced over. Ed in the tub, skin pruned, eyes staring. Sober, she could keep the picture at bay. Stinking drunk worked, too. In between, she was easy pickings.

Big mistake coming out tonight. At her best she could take on the entire bar, have them running for the exit, tails between their legs, and enjoy the hell out of it. But she wasn't remotely at her best. She needed Ed to have told her not to come. Why hadn't he been there to tell her?

This was his fault, the prick. How many times had she told him it was stupid to bathe with his CD player close to the edge? What kind of idiot thought he was immune to that danger? He'd called her a worrywart, and when she'd tried to unplug the player and take it away, he slapped her. So she stopped bringing it up. Fine. Let him fry, it would serve him right.

She just never dreamed he actually would.

"So . . . you ever get lonely in that big house there, Vivian?" Joe posed the question to her cleavage. His words slurred, his glass was empty. He reached behind Mike and poked her in the shoulder.

"Back off, Joe." Mike turned to him. "Just back off."

"Oh, like she's not asking for it. Women like that need only one thing."

"Oh pleez." Vivian rolled her eyes. "What bad movie did you get cut from?"

Mike slid off his stool, threw bills on the bar, and grabbed his jacket. "Come on, Vivian. I'll follow you home."

"No, no. Let her stay." Joe's voice lowered to a deep—and

in any other man, seductive—murmur. On him, it was just creepy multiplied. "Her and her tits are welcome anytime."

"You'd like a glimpse of those, eh, Joe?" This from anonymous jerk number four.

"Let's go." Mike was already at the door.

"Damn right I would."

"We *all* would." The men guffawed, leering adolescents.

That was it. Vivian sauntered after Mike. At the door, she turned, dipped her hands into her bra, and brought out two handfuls of naked breast. "You want to see? Here they are."

Silence dropped over the bar as if someone had pressed a mute button. The men glanced, then looked away, even Joe.

"Jesus." Mike dropped his jacket over her front.

Vivian burst out laughing. Jackasses. Spouting all that macho testosterone, then whimpering at the real thing.

"Come on." Mike grabbed her arm and pulled her after him out of the bar and onto nearly deserted Main Street. She followed, unresisting, still laughing.

"That was priceless. Ha!" She shouted the syllable, tucking her breasts back into her top, absurdly giddy. "Did you see their faces?"

"Yes, I saw."

"You did?" She pouted playfully, finished tucking, and handed him his jacket. "You mean you weren't too busy checking out the merchandise?"

He shook his head, but she could have sworn she saw him hide a grin. Why was he so damn scared of smiling? "You are a piece of work. Get in your car, I'll see you home."

"You don't want to come home with me?" She danced around in front of him, walked backward while he kept coming.

"No, I don't."

"Aw, c'mon, Mike." She stopped his stride with her hands on his nicely muscled forearms and dragged them around her waist, knowing he'd never agree and having too much fun to care. "We could have a most excellent evening."

"Sorry." He pulled his nicely muscled arms away and kept walking, saying a calm good evening to a blond man staring.

"Oh, right." She followed him and winked at the man, who frowned and turned away. "You've got hot tuna waiting."

An incredulous glance. "Come again?"

"A virgin miss came by to drop a covered dish at your house." Vivian unlocked her door and yanked it open. "She's probably still there, waiting hopefully on your front steps. Little sweater thrown over her shoulders to ward off the chill. Shiver, shiver, Mike, warm me up?"

He tightened his lips and looked away. "The ladies of this town seem to think I need regular feeding."

"The ladies of this town are trying to score a big fat Mike wedding."

He rolled his eyes and pushed her into her seat, closed the door. She opened the window, fumbled in her purse, and handed him money for her whiskey. "I didn't mean you to get stuck with my tab."

"No problem." He took the bills and pushed them into his jeans pocket.

"No, come here." She beckoned him closer. "I want to say something."

He leaned forward reluctantly. "I doubt I want to hear this."

"You do." She looked into his eyes, darkened by twilight,

then changed her mind and stared out her windshield. "Thanks for tonight."

"What did I do?"

"You helped me out."

Mike gave a snort of laughter. "I think you did fine on your own."

"Yeah, but I was . . ." She put her hand to her forehead. What? Fucked with grief? Out of her mind? Why would he care?

She put the hand down. Gave him a sultry sideways look and straightened her shoulders so her chest stuck out. "It's like I always say, Mike. Tits are power."

He shook his head and took a step away from the car. "I hate to break it to you, Vivian, but tits are just tits. Even yours. Good night."

She laughed, not sure why that was funny, or if it was funny, and watched him walk to his car, start the engine, and wait for her to pull out ahead. She drove slowly back to her weird old-lady house in the weird, silent, beautiful neighborhood, liking the sight of his lights in her rearview mirror, liking the idea someone was there for her even for a few minutes—someone she didn't have to pay to be on her side.

Six

Excerpt from Erin's journal
Eleventh grade

November 6—Something weird happened today after school. Jennifer was teasing me about what I was wearing. Like my dad would pay for cool clothes? Right. So I was walking home, feeling sick and angry like usual. And then this kid, Joe, pulls up next to me on his bicycle and keeps riding while I'm walking, even though he almost falls off trying to go so slowly. I figure he's going to make fun of me, too. But he just starts talking. He says Jennifer is a bitch (tell me something I don't know), and then he says he noticed me this year.

At first I'm even more angry. I mean I've been at that school since kindergarten and everyone knows I'm the weird one who has fits. All I'll say about that is they don't know what it's like being me. So they should shut up and leave me alone.

But then Joe keeps talking to me and then he says again he noticed me this year. This time he gets off his bike and tries to touch me. I do not like this. I try to get away. Then he says he isn't going to hurt me. He just wants to touch my hair. So he slides his hand down my hair and says he knew it would be that soft. And then he rides away like he's embarrassed.

I don't remember the last time someone touched me nicely. My mom did, but she left so long ago it seems like a dream.

I want him to touch me again.

Joe was late.

Erin glanced out the front window at Maple Avenue. No sign of a car. Most cars that came down this far were either Joe's or turning around. She and Joe didn't have too many visitors. Sometimes his friends would come by to play cards or watch movies. But not often.

She and Joe lived at the dead end of the street; their house was set off some from the others. Another house could fit on either side of theirs. Behind them lay woods and farmland and a stream she used to imagine joined the Mississippi. She loved the idea of being connected to something as vast and powerful as the Mississippi, though she'd never bothered to find out if the stream fed into the mighty river or not. She didn't want to deal with the disappointment if it just went into Lake Chippewa.

Her stomach growled; she put a protective hand to it. Funny

how gas felt like a moving baby. She was hungry, but Joe hated eating dinner alone; he always said eating alone made him feel as if he were a bachelor. The fact that he hadn't ever been a bachelor, just a child and then a teenager and then a husband didn't seem to matter. He felt like a bachelor when he ate alone. So Erin waited, allowing herself a few crackers to tide her over.

She'd made progress on a painting this afternoon. Towering layer cakes frosted brown and pink and white, yellow tulips, and a plate of blue-silver trout. But once she realized Joe wasn't coming home on time, she couldn't paint. The uneasiness got in the way.

If Joe was late, he was out at Harris's Tavern. Slightly late, say six-thirty, meant he'd stopped for a drink; he'd be mellow, cheerful, and affectionate. He'd tell her how the country should be run, how the town should be run, how the butcher shop he worked at should be run. She'd listen and laugh at his jokes, make him feel interesting and funny, and the evening would be pleasant.

Seven o'clock, he'd have two drinks in him. He'd be harder to cajole into a good mood, tired, more withdrawn, early to bed.

Seven-thirty, he'd find some fault with dinner, with the house, with her attitude, with her appearance, and turn it into a chance to make sure she realized he'd been forced to marry her. Sooner or later he'd mention the lost babies. The first baby was the only reason he married her; where was that baby now? Where were the rest of them? Dead, that's where. And why hadn't there been any since Joy; what was wrong with her? If he knew then that she wasn't normal, he would have used protection. Lots of guys were having sex in high school; he could have gotten condoms without the Stottlers, who owned the drugstore, finding out.

Eight o'clock, he'd come home mean and want sex the way she hated it most.

It was nearly eight-thirty.

She wandered into their bedroom, past her studio, which had been set up as a nursery until Joe went nuts one night, brought in an ax, and destroyed everything. He was tired of her keeping the room that way with the baby dead and no more coming. The crib, the wallpaper she'd put in herself, the changing table, the tiny chair, the rocking airplane for when Joy was older, he'd chopped it all up. Erin hadn't been able to stand it. She'd wanted to take the ax and chop Joe up, but she couldn't get it away from him. She'd ended up with bruises and a cut near her mouth that left a small scar. Another one.

When Joe came back to normal, he'd insisted they make the room over into a studio for her. It had seemed horrible to replace Joy's room with a room just for Erin, as if Joy had to die twice. But Joe's self-loathing and his need to make it right had touched Erin, so she'd accepted his offer. And she did enjoy having her own space to paint in. The one room in the house that was hers. Except Joan really owned the whole place, and never let them forget it.

Erin moved to the window in their bedroom, checked again for Joe's car, then sat in front of the computer. She didn't want to face what was ahead, couldn't stand to sit here waiting. Her legs felt like dancing, flailing, or sprinting. Times like these, she wished she still ran, like she did in high school.

She probably could have been a marathoner, Coach Auburn said. Running set her free the way nothing did, except her trances.

Trances she'd discovered when her father was in his mean moods. She could retreat so far inside herself that she stopped existing. When Joy was born, the nurse said she'd never seen anyone stay so quiet and calm through labor. She'd caught her breath, too, when she saw the scars on Erin's body, but of course said nothing. People in Kettle didn't want to know.

Erin opened her e-mail program and waited hopefully for the system to check the server. She'd sent out an e-mail yesterday, to her aunts who lived near Milwaukee; her cousin; her history teacher who moved back to Chicago; Fran, her freshman tutor in Spanish, now at college in Maine. They were on a list called "Joy."

She hoped one of her e-mails would catch on enough, touch enough people, and be forwarded so many times, that someone would forward it back to her, not knowing she actually wrote it.

Yesterday's e-mail was about a woman who didn't make time to have lunch with her sister. Then her sister was killed in an automobile accident. And now the woman would never get to have lunch with her sister ever again. At the bottom, Erin wrote:

Pass this along to your friends; help their lives be richer in the only way that counts. If it comes back to you, you are richer than Bill Gates, in friendship and in love.

She supposed that was pretty gag-worthy, but those types of e-mails seemed popular. At least judging by the number she got sent, mostly from her grandmother, in an assisted-living facility in Hayward. Maybe you got to like sappy stuff when you reached the end of your life.

After receiving so many of these e-mails, Erin had decided to write her own. She liked the idea of sending part of herself out there. She always made it look as if she'd forwarded the note from someone else. Maybe someday her grandmother would forward one Erin had written back to her.

The rumble of their garage door opening preceded the sound of a car engine in the driveway by a few seconds. Erin's hands fumbled to close her program, turn off the computer. If Joe saw her, he'd want to know who she'd been writing to, what she'd said. He could make her feel guilty asking what she'd eaten for lunch, and he could smell guilt a mile away. Once he smelled guilt, things got unpleasant. Her breath came faster; fear cut sharply into her stomach. She should have had more to eat.

A loud noise from the garage, a metallic clank, like something had been knocked over, a shovel or something. Joe could hold nearly half a bottle and walk okay. If he was stumbling and knocking things over, he was beyond drunk.

She peeked in the mirror, made sure she looked pleasantly neutral. Anything to avoid comment, confrontation, though by now it was inevitable.

"*Er'n.*" His slurred shout increased her adrenaline. Not the nice, excited kind of adrenaline, a dark burn that sapped her, made her tremble. Fight or flight—she could do neither. Just stand and watch it coming, take what he wanted to give her, and tomorrow pretend it hadn't happened. Over and over, year after year.

"*Yes, Joe. I'm coming.*"

She ran the length of the house to the garage door, opened it, smiled welcome she didn't feel. He was trashed. Eyes swollen into slits, lip curled the way it did when he was feeling cruel and horny. Oh God.

"Upstairs. Run my bath."

No. *No.*

"What about dinner? You must be hungry." She drew him into the house, speaking gently, wanting to hold her nose at the way he smelled. Alcohol, cigarettes, and the smell of meat that clung to his hair and skin. Wanting to run out of the house, into the woods, far away until she died of exhaustion and freedom.

"Did I say I's hungry?" He grabbed her arm, yanked her up against him, peered down at her. "*Did* I?"

"No." She shook her head. "You didn't."

"What'd I say?"

"You said to—"

"Run my bath. I wan' be clean." His words slid out, oozy, misshapen, as if the syllables were melting together. "That Vivian woman was at th' bar. She's dirty, Erin. She made me feel dirty. I have to be clean b'fore I can touch you."

Her empty stomach filled with acid and the dark, burning fear of this man she'd once thought she loved. Sometimes she still thought she did. Or could.

But the nights he wanted a bath were always the worst.

Letter home from Sarah
Cornell College
October, freshman year

Dear Mom and Daddy,

I barely have time to write, I've got three ten-page papers due Monday, can you believe it? It's Friday now, I won't sleep until Monday night.

Everything is great, my classes are tough but totally fun, esp. Western Dance History—the prof is completely cool. Everyone claps after each lecture, it's like a performance!

And (drumroll) I met a guy in my Art and Ideology class. His name is Ben Gilchrist. I can't say more right now in case I jinx it, but you know how you said you looked into Dad's eyes and knew, Mom? I think this is it for me. Shhh. Not another word!

Debby just got home, we're going to the library to study, gotta go, sorry this is so short! I'll write again soon.

Love you! Miss you!
Sarah

Sarah glanced up from her copy of *Architectural Digest*, and over at the clock next to her and Ben's bed. Ten-thirty, the news was over, Ben would be coming up soon.

What a day. After that dreadful visit with Vivian this morning, Sarah had scarcely known what to do with herself. She'd gone to the Pick 'n Save out on Highway J, and bought way too many groceries. Filling the house with food felt important, as if she would soon be under siege. She'd bought things she didn't usually buy, too, like sausages, though she bought the lower-fat variety made with turkey. Maybe with cold weather coming, some ancient human instinct was telling her to put on extra pounds for the rough winter ahead.

On some strange impulse, she'd even bought Ben that beer Sarah had this morning, with the red label, Leinen . . . something. Ben had been drinking Budweiser forever because that's what he liked and that's what she bought him. But today she thought maybe he'd like to try a new variety. Of course Ben claimed he'd tried it already, that either she bought it for him before, which she was sure she hadn't, or he'd had one at someone's house, or maybe at Harris's Tavern.

Ben had just nodded at the six-pack she took into his study, where he was immersed in writing some scene of his novel about a monstrous killer who tore children up and drank their blood, and who would want to read that? But Ben said it was a deeply symbolic work, about plundering the planet at the expense of future generations. Even Sarah knew it was all the rage to dwell on violence and misery for entertainment, as if there wasn't enough of the real thing cluttering up the newspapers.

She supposed it was silly of her to want Ben to be excited or grateful that she bought beer she thought he'd like. It was just beer, after all. And Sarah knew she got more excited and grateful about things than most people did.

In any case, it didn't matter.

After she'd put the groceries away, she had her lunch—lower-fat braunschweiger on whole wheat bread, with cucumber and onion. Oh, she'd forgotten how good that sandwich was; she generally had turkey or sliced chicken since they were healthier.

She'd spent the afternoon tending her pumpkins. She loved spending time with them. Down close to the soil she could nurture them, urge them to grow and thrive. No accident plant stores were called nurseries; tending plants was very much like tending babies. Sarah even spent sleepless nights the years disease or vermin struck, though that didn't seem to be happening this year. On the contrary, each globe was growing steadily, gaining strength and majesty.

Working among the vines was peaceful, calming. She could be herself out there in the lot next door, didn't have to make herself pleasant to women like Joan, or hold herself tall and make sure she appeared graceful and gracious. Didn't have to worry her time would be interrupted by Ben or Amber, though of course Sarah was glad to provide them whatever they needed.

She had no serious troubles in her life, but if she did, she imagined that digging and fertilizing and turning the pumpkins would be perfect activities to accompany mulling and ruminating and, finally, decision making.

Of course, Vivian could turn into a problem. But Sarah didn't expect her to show up at the Social Club meeting tomorrow. Sarah had decided that Vivian was just provoking her, for whatever reason she felt she had to. Someone like Vivian would have no interest in planning Kettle's annual Halloween party or the pumpkin sale. She wouldn't show up.

The tired, even tread of Ben's feet sounded coming up the stairs, muted from his slippers, the sheepskin ones she bought him for Christmas from LLBean.com. He'd complained they were too warm, but when she'd offered to send them back, he refused, which had seemed ridiculous. Just because she spent a lot of time selecting them didn't mean he had to wear them if they weren't right. But she lost that argument. Or gave in, rather. Why fight over something so unimportant? She'd save her strength for when they fought over big issues. Except they didn't. They weren't really fighters, she and Ben.

"News over, honey?"

He nodded, sat on the bed, and began taking off his clothes. Slippers first, sliding one foot against the opposite ankle—she didn't even need to be able to see to know. Socks next, they went straight into the hamper, thrown in an awkward motion with his left hand. Pants unbuckled and unzipped; he stood to step out of them. Then he draped the pants on the chair next to her dresser, no matter how many times she asked him nicely to put them in the hamper or hang them on a hook in his closet.

Another battle not worth fighting.

"Anything interesting going on in the world?" She sent a warm and caring smile to his back.

"Not really."

Seiko watch off first, clattering onto his nightstand, then sweater, pulled up from the back over his head, then loosened off each arm. That got tossed on her chair, too, while she reminded herself it didn't matter and pretended to read her article. Shirt unbuttoned, undershirt off, those went into the hamper, and when he missed with his underpants, he didn't bother to go pick them up as she knew he wouldn't.

Such a complicated man, Ben was. Fascinating, really, she found him just fascinating, and so different from herself. Very intense and moody, and the last few years he'd been—

Well, no point thinking about that.

"Are you going to read tonight?"

He made full eye contact with her. "No."

Sarah put the magazine aside then, even though she was in the middle of an article about how Armani designed the interior of his yacht. She turned down Ben's side of the covers to welcome him into bed. Wasn't it amazing how after so many years, they knew what each other wanted, without having to say anything? Full eye contact meant Ben wanted sex.

She took off her own nightgown and her panties, folded them, and put them up by the headboard where they wouldn't get in the way. Ben used to love undressing her, but she supposed her body wasn't such a surprise package anymore that he'd delight in unwrapping. That was what being married a long time—nearly eighteen years—was about. Something richer and stronger grew up in place of that initial excitement. And her relationship with her husband was nothing if not rich and strong.

He moved closer, touched her breasts, brushing his fingers lightly over the tips. She'd never told him how insensitive her nipples were. She was fairly ashamed of the fact. Surely it wasn't normal. Most women went out of their minds at that type of contact from what she'd read in novels, and one of her girlfriends at Cornell said she could orgasm from that alone.

Sarah was sure she was lying. Sarah could barely tell whether Ben was touching her nipples or not.

From there, his hand stroked down between her legs. She spread for him and pushed her hips, made a few encouraging sounds. The truth was, she'd never really thought sex was close to what it was cracked up to be. The novels made it sound like orgasms lifted women off the bed, and sometimes made them scream. Sarah liked being turned on as much as the next person, but she never had the urge to scream.

Actually, she wasn't sure if she'd ever had an orgasm, though she always made climax-type noises so Ben could stop worrying about her and let himself go. Ben didn't scream, either, just made a funny muffled sound and went rigid, before he collapsed.

He climbed over her now, pushed his erection inside her, nestled his head next to her cheek, and began to move. She echoed his rhythm and caressed his back; she'd read that a woman's hands should never be still during sex, so hers never were.

Sometimes she wished he'd look at her or talk to her, but sex for Ben had always been a silent affair. She imagined it was better that way, so they could each concentrate on the feelings in their bodies, but it did seem maybe once in a while it would be nice of him to acknowledge that she was in on the process.

She chided herself for the uncharitable thought and whispered that she loved him, then moaned a little and moved faster. It felt wonderful of course, but somehow she always felt as if something was missing. Probably because—she might as well come to grips with it—she had never climaxed.

Vivian had. Sarah was sure Vivian could climax three or four times in one session, like those women in the books. Those women made Sarah feel like there was something wrong with her.

Ben thrust faster, began breathing harder in her ear. He wouldn't let himself go until he thought Sarah was satisfied, so she thought of Vivian having so many orgasms with no effort and moaned again, bucked against Ben's thrusting as if she was taking something out on him that wasn't his fault. Then she cried out and clenched her muscles. He knew the signal, drove into her harder for about fifteen seconds, froze, and there it was, that muffled sigh-groan in her shoulder, and she knew he was done. He'd kiss her cheek, roll over, and go to sleep in their warm bed. While she had to go to the bathroom and try to get all the semen out of her so it wouldn't soak her panties during the night.

She knew she should tell Ben that she hadn't ever climaxed. She should have told him years ago, back at Cornell when they started sleeping together. But how, after eighteen years of faking, could you tell a person something like that?

She kissed him lovingly on the cheek, swung her legs over the edge of the bed, and on her way to the bathroom picked up his underpants and put them in the hamper.

Seven

<u>Letter from Vivian to her grandmother</u>
<u>August 14</u>
<u>Nine years old</u>

Dear Gran. Thanks for the visit. I had fun at your house. I wish I could live there all the time. You have nice things, especially the dollhouse, and you are really nice to me. Please tell Erin she can play with the dollhouse at your house even when I'm not there. She liked it so much. I think her dad isn't really nice to her.

Love, Vi

If there was a sound more irritating than crows cawing their lungs out at dawn, Vivian had yet to hear it. Police sirens, shouting pedestrians, drunks, crimes in progress—the standard New York repertoire was welcome. Anything but this hoarse alarm tearing holes in the morning silence.

She thrashed to her side, dragging Grandma Stellie's eyelet spread over her ears, and paid with a throb in her head, and a catch-up roil in her stomach. Too much whiskey. Jail hadn't done much to deepen her relationship with alcohol.

Caw, caw, caw, caw.

More than one crow now. Dozens. Hundreds. Every damn crow on planet Earth in the tree outside her window. She was living the early scene of a Hitchcock movie.

Caw, caw, caw, caw.

Shit. She pushed the bedspread down and opened one eye to peer at the ghastly clock she'd left on the wall until she could buy another one. A wooden board with a picture of a white-robed Jesus, hair curling down his neck, standing by a little hut in a garden. His eyes were unnaturally wide and feminine, and he had that vapid "good" expression on his face, like his doctor had prescribed too high a dosage of antidepressants.

No way had Jesus been anemic and bland like that. You had to shout to be heard in this world, and while humanity had undoubtedly changed over the past two thousand years, she'd bet that one fact hadn't and never would. If hell froze over and Vivian went into the Jesus-clock-making business, her Jesus would be the charismatic, passionate, alpha male he must have been to inspire so many people. Not pretty boy on Prozac.

Her fuzzy brain registered the time while the crows attempted the Hallelujah Chorus.

Six A.M. Just shoot her.

She pushed off the comforter and emerged into the chilly air, remembering how Gran kept the house hot enough to dry out a swamp. Ed liked their Manhattan condo overheated, too. And the house in Kennebunk. And the one in Aspen. And Vegas. One luxury overheated living space after another.

Now she had *this* house, though at least it was heated to her liking. When the trial publicity blew over, she'd find a way out of here. It would have to blow over soon. Any press who found her in Kettle would be bored to tears within minutes unless they heard about the incident at Harris's last night. That headline she could do without: *Lorelei Taylor, Stuck Among Boobs, Bares Her Own*. Maybe she should try to behave herself from now on.

Nah.

At the closet, she pulled on her favorite robe, then shut the door quickly, trapping the old-lady smell of lavender that miraculously still lingered inside. Grandma Stellie adored lavender—sachets, bath oil, soap, lotion, perfume . . .

A scent-induced memory popped up, of sitting next to Gran's warm, nonthreatening body, eating oatmeal cookies, drinking cocoa, listening to a *Cat in the Hat* story way too young for her. But Stellie could have read her the Kettle phone book and she would have loved it. Cocoa and cookies and a lavender-smelling grandmother, are you kidding me? It pissed her off, all the kids who got to grow up thinking that was their right.

Yeah, well what didn't kill her made her stronger.

She strode out of the room, down the baby-blue stairs, wincing at the thought of pulling up more carpet with her sore hands and ruined nails. In Kountry Kitchen Hell she winced again. All these creepy bunnies, smiley-flower curtains; how was she going to get this fixed on a nonbudget with her total lack of skills?

Maybe she should live out her sentence here and sell the damn house as is. But when would that be? How long could she tolerate ducks on her cabinets before she lost it?

She made herself bad supermarket coffee, blocking the memories of fresh ground beans and Ed's espresso machine. At least this beat the brew in prison. She cut a piece of Sarah's perfect carrot cake to settle the choppy seas in her stomach, and leaned against the counter for breakfast. She was tired. Nearing forty. Her skills were seducing men, living the high life, and being a wise ass. No one in Kettle would hire her for any job because of her reputation alone. And really, what could she do? Be a fashion consultant? Recommend two-thousand-dollar boots to the inhabitants? How was she going to earn money?

How was she going to fill her days?

A wave of misery started in her chest. She could feel it pushing toward her face, itching to make its watery way into her tear ducts. No way was she standing around for that.

She tossed the rest of her bland coffee into the sink, headed upstairs, showered, put on her makeup—about three times more than she needed here in hicksville—dressed in her jeans and a tight neon-yellow top, then covered up with a sweatshirt that had belonged to Ed.

Jesus on her wall sweetly pointed the way to it being only seven A.M. Three hours until she got to go play committee member with Sarah and check out more townspeople. Maybe make even more nonfriends, apparently one of her strengths here.

Three hours. Better get back at the damn carpet. She had to have something to do.

Half an hour later, she'd barely pulled up two steps' worth, and was still swearing at whoever thought putting a staple every eighth of an inch was a good idea. She grabbed at a stubborn corner for a third furious tug; her fingers slipped and her hand connected violently with the sharp corner of a banister support, hard enough to bring tears to her eyes.

Ow ow ow. She ran into the kitchen and dragged open the freezer. No ice maker. No ice. Christ.

Cold water then, running over her bruise, a blue blood blister already visible under the skin. Her tears thought this would be a nice opportunity for more air time, and she had to blink hard to keep them back. Movement teased her peripheral vision, salt water undulating her view. Was someone outside?

Mike. Backing his truck out of his garage. She yanked off the faucet, pulled off Ed's sweatshirt, and ran, flung the door open, then the screechy storm, not sure what she was going to say, just that she needed like hell to talk to someone.

"Mike." She took a few steps outside into the early October chill and wrapped her arms around herself, regretting her decision to abandon the too-big, too-masculine shirt. *Vanity, thy name is Vivian.*

He turned the motor off and got out of his truck, slamming the door behind him. "Good morning."

No smile, just a nod. He went into his garage and emerged

a minute later, arms full of boards, which he loaded on his pickup.

Vivian crossed her driveway toward him. "Going some-where?"

"To work." He headed for the garage again. "Gilchrist back porch needs rebuilding."

Gilchrist. Sarah. Of the perfect carrot cake and darling decorated basket. Who'd spoken of Mike as if he were her personal savior.

For a second Vivian wasted time wondering if that type of woman appealed to Mike. Her hangover churned up more stomach acid, which turned Sarah's cake into something truly vengeful. "Are nails all you're pounding over there?"

He threw a look over his shoulder, which she deserved for sounding like a jealous grade school student.

"Sorry." She made her voice humble. "Uncalled for."

This time his glance was one of surprise. "Okay."

"I really should have known better than to think you were involved with her sexually." She opened her eyes innocently wide. "Because clearly she hasn't gotten any in years."

Laughter broke out of his mouth, a burst he quickly shut down, and went back to stacking lumber.

What was with him? "It won't kill you."

"What?" He arranged the last board, turned back toward her, and put his hands on his hips. God, he was sexy. Tall and young and confident. Mm-mm good, to the last manly drop.

She sauntered toward him, stopped six inches away, and tipped her head back to stare. This close she could see cir-cles of fatigue under his eyes. Had he stayed up and had a party for one last night? Had Virgin Nelly come by to collect her casserole dish and stayed for dessert? "Laughing. It won't kill you."

"I'm aware of that."

"Then why keep it in?"

He kept the eye contact going a beat longer, then started to move to his truck.

Okay, new topic. She grabbed his arm. "You know, Mike, I woke up this morning and I realized something."

He faced her again, looking exasperated, which made her want to giggle. She had a feeling she'd get to like this man.

"What would that be, Vivian?"

"I need you." She pouted sensually, enjoying the hell out of herself, knowing he was amused in spite of the groan he let slip.

"Do I even want to ask what for?"

"Of course you do." She let her eyes go soft and beseeching. "My house needs an old-lady-ectomy."

"Uh-huh." He gazed up at a branch of the elm that shaded both their driveways. "I've got a lot of jobs lined up. I don't think—"

"Please. I'll help. I want to learn to do most of it myself. But I can't do it all. And I can't live in *that*." She gestured toward the house, horrified to hear her voice thickening into desperation.

Silence. His hands went back to his hips; he stared over her head. She put her hand to his chest, felt the smooth cotton shirt, the smooth muscle underneath. Expected him to step back or flinch. He did neither. Instead he looked down, straight into her eyes with his younger blue ones, and she was astonished to find herself wanting to step back.

"I'll find time to help you."

"Thank you." She took her hand away, even though it wanted to go on a nice leisurely tour. "About payment . . ."

One of his eyebrows lifted. "We can talk about that later."

"I need to talk about it now."

"Okay. Talk."

"I'll pay you the going rate. But I might need time to come up with the money. My cash flow is a little weird right now."

"Don't worry about it."

"I do worry about it."

"Then stop. You have other things to worry about."

"Like?"

"How you're going to survive a small, quiet town like Kettle with all the big, loud grief you've got going."

She did step away from him then, squinted at sun that found its way through yellowing elm leaves and scurried over his wheat-colored hair. "What the hell do you know about that?"

"I left Kettle. After my wife died."

"How did she die?"

"Aneurysm." His lips clamped the word off. "Don't worry about paying me. Concentrate on the little things, like keeping your clothes on in public."

"You didn't like that?"

"People around here don't."

"But what did *you* think?"

Only half his mouth drew back in a smile. "It showed a certain spirit."

She laughed, loud and long, and it was a fabulous relief, like a huge orgasm when you hadn't had one in forever. A certain spirit. She was definitely going to like Mike.

"You know . . ." She sent him a sultry smile, back in control, thank God. "There are other forms of payment."

"Uh-huh." He turned and got into his truck. "We can talk about that, too."

She had to keep her jaw from dropping. "You'd consider it?"

"Absolutely."

This time her jaw did drop, and she had to haul it up and keep looking provocative. Her head started pounding. "So . . . what did you have in mind?"

He furrowed his brows, gazing through the windshield, started his engine, then turned to her. "How about sex twice a week, and you blow me three other days. You can have weekends off. That should cover it."

She nodded over immediate panic, partially digested cake rising to threaten her throat. Well, good for her. She asked for it, she got it. Problem solved. Problem just beginning.

"Vivian."

"Yes, Mike." She managed a ghastly grin that probably resembled a skull's.

"I was kidding. Maybe think before you try that crap again. You should see your face." He chuckled, shaking his head, backed the truck down his driveway, out into the street, and drove with his load of lumber up to Sarah's perfect house.

Vivian walked down the stairs of the white Lutheran church, into the basement for her very first Kettle Social Club meeting, oh boy. She was late, deliberately. If you weren't going to make a decent entrance in a situation like this, why bother? She'd sat in her car in a corner of the parking lot and watched women disappear into the underground den, like rodents escaping the light and danger of open spaces.

An enormously round woman first, then a skinny one, a weird-looking older woman with a weird-looking younger one. And of course, Our Fair Lady Sarah, carrying a picnic basket decorated with rust and gold ribbons, fresh as a meadow daisy, every hair in place, cheerful smile in place, long steel rod in a place not spoken of in good company.

Vivian could imagine her fluttering over Mike early this morning, bringing him homemade breakfast rolls and tea, discussing her porch's needs, naughty bits tingling when his muscles got down to business. Oh, but they must stop that naughty tingle! Good girls never felt that special feeling for anyone but their husbands.

How that uptight bitch Abby ever made Ed cheat . . . But then Ed was nearing sixty, slowing down. Maybe wild animal sex didn't enter into his new requirement list. Maybe Abby was a closet kink-freak, who knew. It didn't matter anymore. Abby didn't have Ed and neither did Vivian.

But, thank God, she did have the Kettle Social Club.

She wandered across a corridor that looked like it belonged in a public school building, smelling of cheap cleaning fluid and the faint appealing aroma of coffee. Voices sounded from behind a door, partly ajar. Vivian flipped her hair back, pulled her breasts up so they spilled farther into the vee of her sweater, and strutted inside.

Immediately her vision zeroed in on Sarah, perched on the edge of her chair, drawn a little back from the circle, indicating leadership. She was talking earnestly, and when Vivian came in, she broke off to force a welcoming smile, but not before an expression of sheer horror came over her flawless preppy features.

Vivian lived for moments like that.

"Hi, everyone."

Unwelcoming silence.

"I'm Vivian, your town murderess, and I'd like to be a member of the Kettle Social Club because I love parties." She gave a cheery wave and pulled a chair to Sarah's right, much too close to be comfortable for her. "So what are we doing?"

"Hi . . . Vivian." Sarah edged her chair away with the pretense of moving it to welcome Vivian into the circle. "I wasn't sure you were serious about coming. I'm afraid we already started. We like to start on time, right at ten."

"Fine by me, Sarah. I don't mind missing a few minutes." She looked pointedly at the frumpy older woman with a jet-black dye job to Sarah's right. "And you are?"

"Joan Russell." The woman glared at the gray-green pillar thrusting down into the room, arms crossed over an enormous, sagging bosom. Apparently that was all the conversation Vivian rated.

And what a shame that was.

Next victim subjected to Vivian's demon presence—in a *church*, no less—a mousy-looking, pale woman. She stared as if she expected Vivian to perform a miracle on the spot, only it wasn't clear if the anticipated miracle would be holy or satanic.

"What's your name?" Vivian itched to whip out eyeliner and mascara, blush, and some lipstick to color in that bland, pretty face. But even that wouldn't do much unless she got the dullness out of her eyes. Was she stupid? Or just weird?

"Erin."

The name, barely whispered, triggered the impression of a shared memory. Had Vivian met her before, maybe on a visit to Kettle? She couldn't really place her face, but the name jogged something. "Hey, Erin. What do you do for fun?"

Erin sank back in her seat; her eyes darted side to side. The room grew creepy-silent, as if the other ladies really, really didn't want to hear whatever Erin did for fun.

Erin blushed, which at least made her look alive. "I . . . paint."

O-kay. Erin was weird. "No kidding, that's great."

"Erin is Joan's daughter-in-law." Sarah made the announcement as if she'd explained the origins of the universe.

Mother- and daughter-in-law sat rigidly next to each other, not sharing so much as an acknowledging glance. Zero love lost there. Having a mother-in-law like Joan would probably make Vivian weird, too.

Next in the sacred circle, the skinny one, a disaster-haired woman named Nancy, whose sharp, turned-up nose seemed to be pulling her upper lip permanently clear of prominent front teeth. She kept flicking anxious glances to Sarah, as if she needed approval for each breath. Vivian dismissed her immediately as a Sarah disciple. Probably gay and didn't know it.

Last was big, blond Betty, of Kmart maternity fashion, enormous and round-bellied, glancing at Vivian occasionally as if she was some fatal disease Betty's baby could catch.

Vivian guessed these would not become her bestest-ever girlfriends.

"When are you due, Betty?"

"December twenty-fourth, the day before Jesus was born." Her hostility dissolved into pride.

"Congratulations, is this your first?"

A ripple of amusement around the room. Betty laughed harder than necessary. "Oh no, the Lord has given me four others in the last five years."

"Your husband's not jealous?"

Betty made solid eye contact with Vivian for the first time, dull, curl-covered head tipped to one side in confusion. "Jealous of the babies?"

"No. Of the Lord giving you children." Blank faces all around. "Instead of your husband giving them to you."

Silence. Horrified. Except for a swiftly squashed giggle that might have come from Erin. Betty turned red; her lips tightened.

Vivian was suddenly desperately tired in every possible way a person could be tired. "Betty, I was joking. I didn't mean to offend you, I'm sorry."

Betty managed a tight nod. Women reshuffled their feet, adjusted their bodies on the occasionally squeaky aluminum folding chairs.

"So. Vivian." Sarah managed to imbue her musical voice with the tiniest touch of disdain. "We were discussing the upcoming Halloween party."

Vivian clapped her hands together; the sound reverberated off the gray-green cinder-block walls. "Cool. I love parties. What's the theme?"

Expectant looks at Sarah, who cleared her throat. "This year's theme is Helping Others."

"Really." *Helping Others?* Halloween was supposed to

be scary and exciting and fun. What was wrong with these people?

Her fatigue grew more desperate, as did her need for caffeine. She made her way to the refreshments, set out on a cheap folding table scarred and smudged with paint, probably from years of cutesy crafts or children's art. "Ed and I threw a Come As You're Not Halloween party once. That was a blast."

A folding chair creaked, probably Betty's begging for mercy. Apparently no one else thought that sounded like a blast. Or maybe they couldn't handle her mentioning the man she supposedly bumped off.

She sighed, poured herself a mug of what smelled like excellent java, and took an appreciative sip. "Mmm, *great* coffee."

"Thank you." Sarah smiled, eyes wary. "I buy it online from a gourmet company in California."

"Did you make these, too?" Vivian picked out one of the cinnamon rolls, oozing sugary icing and pecans, and took an enormous bite, sure Mike had been offered the same this morning. And hadn't Vivian predicted that one perfectly?

"Yes. For others to enjoy." Still wary, Sarah couldn't quite keep her natural smugness from shining through.

"They're fabulous." She spoke through a rich, sticky mouthful and walked back to her place, all eyes on her except Joan's, which were fixed on the floor. "Helping people, huh?"

"Yes." Sarah cleared her throat and sat up a little straighter, which Vivian would not have thought possible. "I grow . . . pumpkins in the lot next door to my house. We'll sell them at the party to raise money for a child in need."

"Sounds like a plan." Sounded like self-indulgent crap. *Pumpkins?* How much money could you get from pumpkins? Sell shots of tequila and hold a drinking contest, then you could make some money. "How much do you figure you can raise?"

All heads back turned to Sarah, who sat stiffly as if she were being questioned by a grand jury. "I'll have well over a hundred pumpkins this year. We can sell them for five to ten dollars each, depending on the size and variety. I grow several different kinds."

"Really." Vivian took another sip of coffee. Who the hell would go to a party at Halloween still needing a pumpkin? And who wanted to buy anything but the standard big orange kind at that time of year? "So even if you sell them all, that's probably only going to make around six hundred dollars."

The women shifted nervously. Color started climbing up Sarah's neck. "Yes."

"How much need is this kid going to be in?"

"We haven't selected a child yet."

Okay. Save the eye rolling for when she got home. "Have you thought about other ideas that might be more lucrative?"

Sarah turned her head and fixed Vivian with a please-die-now stare. "Like what?"

"I don't know, but how many people around here really get excited about pumpkins?"

The women looked at Sarah and provided Vivian's answer: one.

"How about something with broader appeal, shoot for a significant amount of money?"

"What do you suggest?" Ice formed around Sarah's words.

"Oh, I don't know . . ." Vivian shrugged. "A hand job booth?"

Erin snorted suddenly, like a horse with something up its nose. The rest of the women achieved instant rigor mortis.

"Hello? Ladies? I'm kidding." Vivian winked at Erin, who actually smiled, though she immediately ducked her head to hide it. Okay, Erin was weird, but at least she had a sense of humor. "In New York I organized a fund-raising party around a fashion show for a bunch of Ed's friends. The designers and models donated their time and everyone came, because that's what those people were into. We made ten thousand dollars for cancer research."

She looked around the room, surprised to find herself feeling mildly excited. Planning parties was something she was good at, something she liked to do. One look at Sarah's face, however, and she realized her little moment of semi-enthusiastic sincerity had hailed poopballs on the Queen's pumpkin patch.

Tough. If they wanted to help a child in need, and undoubtedly they had no idea how staggeringly many kinds of need there were, six hundred dollars would be a drop in the Pacific. They might as well do it up right.

She studied the squirming ladies, colorless Erin, Nancy with her thick glasses and A-line hairdo that made her look like an Afghan hound, Betty with tresses screaming for highlights and clothes that fought her body shape, Joan . . . okay, well, never mind . . . and an extremely obvious idea popped into her head. "Why don't you sell certificates for makeovers? Women love them and men can buy them for—"

"What, would *you* do them?" Joan finally came to life, glaring witheringly at Vivian's outfit. "Who'd buy one?"

Murmurs in the room. Nancy glanced anxiously at Sarah.

Sarah was still indulging tasteful rage in her Chair of Leadership. "I'm happy with how *I* look."

Vivian bit her tongue. Literally. Because the remark on its tip would serve no purpose.

"And let not your adornment be merely external—braiding the hair, and wearing gold jewelry, or putting on dresses; but let it be the hidden person of the heart, with the imperishable quality of a gentle and quiet spirit, which is precious in the sight of God." Betty folded her hands across what was left of her lap and looked at Vivian with a Jesus-clock expression. "Book of Peter, chapter three, verse sixteen."

For the first time since her not-guilty verdict was announced, Vivian found herself speechless.

"I might want one." Erin nodded too many times, gazing at Vivian. "I would want one."

"Be serious. You don't want one." Her mother-in-law snapped the words out and Erin deflated like a Whoopie cushion, though thankfully in silence.

Speech returned, and with it a strange protectiveness for weird little Erin. "I'm sorry, Joan, *you've* decided she doesn't want one?"

"What would be the point?"

"Ah, the point. Let's think about that one." Vivian gazed thoughtfully at the ceiling. "Maybe . . . gee, I don't know, to look better? Feel better?"

Joan blew a short raspberry. "She'd have no use for it."

Vivian smiled sweetly. "And you know this because . . ."

"Joe wouldn't stand for it."

Erin's body jerked. Too much silence filled the room. Bad

silence. Choking silence. Vivian pictured this Joe person, ultra-conservative, smothering, preaching hellfire and brimstone, forbidding his wife to wear makeup or bright colors.

Then another picture supplanted it, like the next in a mental slide show. Joe. At the bar last night. The huge, creepy, lecherous guy. Was he married to this little rag doll? No wonder he was chatting Vivian up last night. Big animal guys always married wimps so they could stay boss, and then were dissatisfied with the lack of challenge.

Duh.

Fine. To hell with it. To hell with all of it. What had she been thinking? That she could take on a town like this and make even the barest dent? She could come up with the mother of all fund-raising ideas, and still no one would give her or her ideas credence.

She had better things to do than worry about Kettle's social life. Someday she might even figure out what they were.

"Well, I guess we're back to the original idea, then. Sarah?" She managed a conciliatory smile and gracious gesture at the now-victorious Queen. "Please tell us more about the pumpkins."

Eight

Excerpt from Sarah's diary
Sixth grade

Dear Diary,

I overheard Mom and Dad talking. This girl at school, Erin, her mother left. Erin came home from school and there was a note and her mom was gone. Can you believe that? Mom said Erin's father was violent. When I'm a mom I'll be good to my kids all the time. I bet Erin is sad. One time she showed up for school with a black eye. She said she fell, but maybe her father hit her. Maybe that's why she's so weird. I should be nicer to her.

Today Mrs. Jantzen asked what we wanted to accomplish in life. A lot of girls just wanted a husband

*and kids. Not me. I'm going to be famous for some-
thing important, like curing cancer or being the first
woman president or a prima ballerina. No way will I
be a housewife like my mom or Erin's mom, and just
fuss with furniture and gossip on the phone, or get hit
so much I'd have to leave. Ugh.*

Sarah

Sarah drove her 2001 Ford Windstar up their long, paved
driveway. She'd chosen red for the car, since red was such a
bright and cheery color, especially in winter when Wisconsin
tended to fade to gray. Usually that didn't bother her, but for
some reason this year the upcoming months of bare branches
and cold loomed rather oppressively. Silly. Not like her to let
things she couldn't control bother her. Generally she was one
to roll with the seasons, and the punches.

And speaking of punches, what a dreadful meeting this
morning. That Vivian person had done her best to ruin not
only the meeting, but also the party they were planning,
which was going to be terrific. This afternoon Sarah would
call area hospitals to find the child her pumpkins could help.

How Vivian thought she could raise so much money offering makeovers . . . Well, Sarah could only guess that Vivian had no idea people in Kettle didn't want to look like
trash. Someone like Vivian thought she was the center of
the universe itself. Like an adolescent. Like Sarah's daughter,
Amber.

Sarah had been feeling recently that Amber needed to see
people less fortunate than herself. Maybe she needed to vol-

unteer in rural Appalachia or inner-city Chicago or the Deep South. Or maybe she needed to go to Europe and experience cultures that had existed so much longer than hers.

Since Amber would need adult company on this voyage of self-discovery, Sarah favored the last option.

She eased the Windstar into their garage, back much later than usual after her meeting. She opened the lift gate and got out the bag of groceries from Pick 'n Save, and the bag from Bed, Bath & Beyond, and the bag from Granley's Stationers, which made her smile. If anyone were watching, he'd want to know what made Sarah's smile that intriguing.

She let herself into the house and heard hammering out back where Mike was working. Too bad she hadn't been here at lunch to offer him some of her homemade goulash soup or a sandwich, the kind men liked with lots of meat. He'd enjoyed her cinnamon rolls this morning from what she could tell.

"Hi, Ben, sweetheart, I'm home." She set the groceries on the counter and started unpacking. Maybe Ben would come in and hug her, ask where she'd been all this time. That would be awfully nice.

When not even an answer came, she got worried and left the groceries half unpacked on her beautiful granite counter.

"Ben?" She walked into his study and stopped short when she saw him at his desk. Not a blessed thing wrong with him. Thank goodness.

"Mm?" He frowned and tapped impatiently at a key.

"I'm home, honey."

"Oh. Yes." He glanced at her over the tops of his reading glasses, gave a little wave, and went back to work.

She put on a sweet smile in case he decided to glance at her again. "I hope you didn't worry that I was late?"

He kept typing, and she had to repeat the question a little louder. Her voice sounded strained when it got louder like that.

"I didn't notice, actually. Is lunch ready?"

Sarah laughed to dispel a sudden tight feeling in her stomach and moved forward, put her hand on his shoulder. "It's way after lunch. Didn't you eat?"

"I must have gotten distracted." He patted the hand on his shoulder. Sarah saw the words *bloody dismembered corpse* on the monitor and shuddered.

"I'll fix you something now." She left the room, the tight feeling still in her stomach. She'd had lunch at Denver's today, all by herself, which she never did, a Cobb salad, which was unusually fatty for her. But today hadn't felt usual. Vivian had turned everything "topsy turvy," as Sarah's mom would say.

She started leftover goulash soup heating and pulled bread down from the cupboard for his sandwich. The bread hit the counter fairly forcefully, and she nearly tore the bag getting the slices out. Ben wouldn't eat the ends of the loaf, nor would Amber. Sarah always ate them, because she couldn't bear the waste. It would be nice if Ben would eat them once in a while so she wouldn't have to.

She poured Ben's soup into a bowl a little too vigorously so it sloshed over the rim and she had to wipe the bowl and the counter. She took him the soup and the sandwich and a large glass of skim milk, and set it on his desk with a thud that nearly made the soup spill again.

"Thank you." He didn't look up from the monitor or pat her hand again, which would have been nice since she went to the trouble of making him a sandwich *and* heating the soup. Though probably the soup would sit and get cold and she'd have to throw it away in case of invading bacteria.

"You know, Ben, I've been thinking that we've never taken Amber to Europe." She pulled a woolen pill off Ben's sweater and rolled it between her fingers. "She's sixteen and barely been outside of Wisconsin since we moved back here. I want her to have broader horizons. Besides, it would do her good to get away from that awful boyfriend of—"

"Sarah." Her name came out as if he were saying, *Shut up*.

She found herself inhaling sharply. "Well. We can talk about it another time. Eat your soup while it's still hot."

He was already back to typing. She kissed his cheek to show she wasn't at all upset at being dismissed like a servant, then she left quietly, which was probably unnecessary because he'd most likely forgotten she was there at all.

After she put the groceries away, she discovered the new bath mat in the downstairs bathroom looked fresh and neat without the thread-trailing edges of the old one, and it made her feel happier. She thought of calling Ben to come see, but what was the point? Ben wouldn't feel happier; he'd just feel annoyed.

All her morning errands were cleaned up now except the box from Granley's. Just looking at it made her feel funny, which was silly, since all she'd done was march into the store and pick out some thank-you notes and pay for them.

Tom had been there, and unless she was imagining it, on this unusual day he'd stared at her more longingly than ever.

She'd put the thank-you notes on the counter next to his cash register and smiled at him, glad her cheeks were flushed from the chilly day so her eyes seemed brighter and she looked younger.

He'd rung up her purchase, and she'd admired the devastating combination of dark hair only barely flecked with gray, and deep blue eyes. It had been nearly lunchtime, and she'd mentioned she was going to Denver's, just outside Kettle, by the Pick 'n Save and other larger stores. That she'd be eating alone. Then he'd said he went there sometimes, too, and looked at her questioningly, as if he wanted permission to join her.

Oh my goodness. Her cheeks had certainly flushed hotter then. Of course she'd simply thanked him for the notes and walked out. She was a married woman; having lunch with a single man—even an old friend—out in public was a very bad idea. Though she tried to let him know with her eyes—the windows into her soul—that if things had been different, she would have enjoyed having lunch with him quite a bit.

On her way upstairs to change into the slippers she usually wore around the house, she peeked in the gilt-framed mirror inherited from Granny and noted that her cheeks were still pink and that her heathery cotton sweater set, bought online from Nordstrom's, flattered her particularly well today.

Maybe she'd go outside now and check on Mike. Mike would be normal on a day nothing else seemed to be. Too much normal could get dull, she supposed, but not enough became trying.

Back in the kitchen, she arranged a plate of her oatmeal, dried cherry, chocolate chip cookies, and added an apple. Men didn't eat enough fruit when left to their own devices. Mike would appreciate her thoughtfulness.

Outside, she found him bent over, measuring boards laid across a workhorse. Mike was so capable. Ben didn't see the point of fixing anything himself if he had the money to pay someone else to do it. Though it was her money these days, from her grandmother's estate. Her money that made it possible for him to sit in his office for the past four years, writing about blood-drinking creatures instead of having a real job.

Of course she agreed with Ben about hiring people, but there was something sexy about men who could do it all. She wondered if Tom could handle a hammer as easily as he did a cash register.

Right now, however, she felt she could happily sit here and watch Mike's broad shoulders taper to his very nice, very male hips for the rest of the day.

She walked around him, making sure the sun would hit behind her and bring out the strawberry-blond highlights in her hair, at the same time preventing her from having to squint unattractively when she faced him. "I brought you some cookies."

He looked up from his board. "Thanks, Sarah. Those will be a treat."

"You've made wonderful progress." She let her eyes hold a touch of awe. Men loved nothing better than to feel admired.

He shrugged. "Pretty simple job."

"Well, I'm grateful. I know how busy you are."

He shrugged again and ate one of her cookies, biting into it with straight white teeth and crunching with relish. Mike was a good person. She felt so sorry that his sweet old-lady neighbor Edna had been replaced by someone as vulgar and trampy as Vivian. It must be very difficult.

"How are you handling the situation with your new neighbor?" She made sure her voice came out gently so he'd know she didn't judge anyone, no matter how horrendous a human being.

"The situation?" He finished the cookie and reached for another, which she'd offered as soon as his last bite disappeared.

"I mean that she is so . . . infamous."

"That has nothing to do with me."

"Nor any of us, of course." Sarah's stomach tightened again. But Mike must be trying to appear as nonjudgmental as she was. "She's certainly different than Edna."

"You could say that." He smiled then, the full Mike smile.

Instead of returning it, Sarah found herself narrowing her eyes. Because she instinctively felt that smile hadn't been meant for her. "Vivian came to the Kettle Social Club meeting this morning."

His hand hesitated on its way to reaching for a third cookie. Sarah stared into his young, handsome face and had the distinct impression that he wanted to laugh.

Sarah didn't think what had happened this morning at her meeting was remotely funny. "She was extremely disruptive."

"I can imagine."

Again, suppressed humor in his voice. Sarah began to feel aggravated, which she'd never felt around Mike before, or indeed anyone in Kettle with the exception of Joan, who brought on aggravation like summer brought on mosquitoes. "She thought Helping Others wasn't as good a theme for the Halloween party as Come As You're Not."

He outright chuckled. "I'd like to see what she'd wear to that one."

This was too much. "I also heard she caused some kind of scene at Harris's last night."

The laughter went out of Mike's eyes. "I was there."

"I'm sorry you had to see something like that. I'm sorry anyone did." She was relieved he'd stopped laughing and waited for him to share her disgust in a moment that would bring them closer. Even Mike couldn't be nonjudgmental enough to approve of public nudity.

Instead he seemed annoyed, and Sarah couldn't shake the bizarre feeling that it wasn't Vivian he was annoyed at.

She rushed to smooth the moment over, flabbergasted that she'd be required to. "You know how rumors are."

"Right." He turned back to measuring his boards, leaving her holding out the plate of cookies in case he wanted a fourth. He didn't. Neither did he touch the apple.

"Well, I hope she keeps that kind of behavior behind closed doors from now on." She brought the plate, which was starting to shake a little, down close to her body, not pleased at how prudey she sounded. She didn't want Mike, of all people except maybe Tom, thinking she was prudey.

What she did want was to knock on Vivian's door and convince her to leave this town before she ruined it for Sarah and everyone else.

Mike drew a line across his board and turned back, and since his eyes seemed kind again, she hoped her intuition had

been false, and that he wasn't at all sympathetic to his new
neighbor.

"After Rosemary died . . ."

Sarah nearly gasped. In all the months since Mike had been
back in Kettle, she'd never once heard him mention Rosemary's
name, nor had she heard from anyone else that he had. He'd
given Sarah quite a gift on this thoroughly unusual day.

"Yes, Mike?" Her voice came out a reverent whisper, as
Rosemary's memory deserved.

"After she died, I lost my mind. I was so fuc—"

Sarah blinked.

"—messed up, that I couldn't stay here without exploding.
So I left. I behaved badly. I got into fights. I drank too much.
I screwed around."

"Oh no, Mike. You didn't do that." The protest poured
from her, and she didn't even realize how ridiculous she
sounded until she saw Mike looking at her as if she sounded
ridiculous.

"I'm sorry." She gestured with the plate; the apple wobbled
and the cookies very nearly slid over the scalloped white porcelain edge. "It's just so . . . unlike you."

"That's my point."

She had to stare at him while her brain rewound their conversation to try and figure out what point that was exactly.
When her brain finally came up with it, she wanted to gag.

"You're comparing what you went through to . . . *her?*" Bad
enough when Vivian made the same comparison the morning Sarah brought her a carrot cake. "Mike, she's nothing like
you. I'm sure you had . . . troubles when your grief was so
overwhelming, but she's . . . she's *always* been like that."

"Oh?" The rest of his thought couldn't have been clearer if he'd said it out loud. *How do you know?*

Sarah gaped at him. Because how could anyone possibly answer a question like that? How did Sarah know? Just by *looking* at her. "The trial. All those stories."

"All I know is she's a mess right now."

"She's a murderer." Her voice came out so high and desperate, she couldn't tell who was more startled, her or Mike. "She killed someone she'd lived with for fourteen years."

"The jury said she didn't."

Sarah's gasp couldn't be stifled this time. He was putting her world into a large-sized Cuisinart and holding down the pulse button. "But you can't possibly believe . . . She's guilty. She has to be. All that evidence . . ."

He shook his head, turned his back, and started up his saw. The blade bit into the wood, steady along his mark, sawdust spewing over her lawn until the board broke cleanly, and Mike examined the edge as if it held more of his interest than she did.

Sarah suddenly had trouble breathing. She put the plate down on the sawdust-sprinkled lawn, not even caring that he might step on it and break her Limoges. She never cried. She never had a single reason to cry. She and Ben were so happy here.

"Excuse me. I need to go water my pumpkins." She stumbled toward the field, ignoring Mike calling her name, doing her best not to break into a run and throw herself face first into the glorious tangle of vines she'd made possible next door.

Panting, she sank down among her very favorites, Baby

Boos, adorable miniature white pumpkins. They looked so sweet and pure and picturesque against the green vines and leaves and the black plastic she laid down to conserve heat and moisture and discourage weeds. It wasn't really necessary to water them, in fact it could be detrimental to create too much humidity in the late afternoon, making the vines vulnerable to mildew. But she had to get away from Mike somehow. And she always found peace among her pumpkins.

She waited, inhaling the familiar earthy vine scent, for the peace and sense of purpose and calm. Instead she heard Vivian's bitchy voice, *I don't know, but how many people around here really get excited about pumpkins?*

Deep breaths, many of them, while she reminded herself that Vivian's need to destroy something important to Sarah reflected more on Vivian than it did on Sarah. Being upset would only hand Vivian the victory she sought. The other women in the meeting had stood behind Sarah. Selling pumpkins at the town's Halloween party was a good idea. And Helping Others was a fine theme for the party.

A gust of wind brought a chill, and she tenderly stroked the smooth skin of a nearby Baby Boo. Frost would come soon. If it threatened before the party on the twenty-ninth, she'd have to harvest the pumpkins to avoid damage. Cut them from their green umbilical cords and pile them in her shed to protect them.

She imagined herself displaying the pumpkins at the party, by size, by color, some for cooking, some for decoration, some for carving. Imagined how people would be impressed—those who didn't know she grew pumpkins would think back to the previous months and all the hard work Sarah must have been doing while they didn't even realize.

A glow of pride lessened the feeling of dread, until she imagined Vivian again and saw the booth and the woman tending it through Vivian's eyes. With a sense of shock and horror, she saw a middle-aged, frigid woman with nothing to show for herself but a chintzy folding table brimming with attractive squash.

Nine

<u>Letter home from Vivian's ninth grade teacher,</u>
<u>Mrs. Castor</u>

I'm concerned about Vivian's attitude this term.
Adolescence can be tough for all kids, but she seems
to be having an unusually difficult time. She's very
bright, but has started turning in subpar work
and skipping classes. Worse, she doesn't appear to
care or give any indication she understands how
sabotaging herself now could be detrimental to her
future. I think she has a particularly bright one.
I recommend we meet and discuss the possibility
of getting her counseling to see why she appears
troubled.

*Note to Mrs. Castor, scrawled on the bottom
of her letter*

*I appreciate your concern, but Vivian is fine. Just the
usual teenage stuff. My wife and I are handling it.*

Mr. Harcourt

Vivian rolled her trash toward the curb. She'd been about
to work out but remembered Friday was garbage day, so she'd
better set the can out while she thought of it, in case they
showed up to collect before her crow alarm went off. In New
York, she and Ed could drop their trash down the building's
chute the second any accumulated. Here she got to hoard it
for an entire week. Must be completely disgusting in the heat
of summer.

Trash can positioned at the end of her driveway like everyone else's—and how much did she hate to be like everyone
else?—she went back inside and attempted to lift the rolled-
up baby-blue shag carpet she'd torn off the living room floor,
so she could drag it out the front door.

Uh, right.

She took another unsatisfying hold of one end, the coarse
backing grating her knuckles, and lifted with all her strength,
having given up any hope of attractive nails ever again. Instead of coming off the floor, the roll bent like a limp dick
and only got heavier.

Pulling, struggling, swearing, she managed to get the leading edge out the front door, where she stopped and glared at

the stoop. Four steps, a curving walk, and yards of sidewalk to reach the trash area. Mike wasn't home from Sarah's yet. Her neighbors to the north, the most pudgy, Wonder Bread, typically Midwestern couple she could even imagine, had greeted her, the one time their schedules intersected, with such horror and disdain that Vivian was pretty sure help would not be given willingly there. At all. Ever.

With a burst of Super Vivian energy, she dragged the carpet down the steps, where it gained momentum and sent her sprawling back on her superheroine ass on the lawn.

"Need help?"

Vivian twisted up onto her elbow and laid eyes on a teenage girl, sixteen, maybe seventeen, probably walking home from school—the first female Vivian had encountered in Kettle who didn't look like a Talbot's model or a Wal-Mart shopper. She wore a funky black-and-white check miniskirt, chunky black mid-calf boots, and heavy socks up over her knees. An off-shoulder, skintight, black long-sleeved shirt, similar to one in Vivian's old-lady dresser upstairs, emphasized her well-developed breasts. In contrast to her chic outfit, she was sucking on a lollipop, staring at Vivian with childlike curiosity. No hostility, thank God. Vivian had used up her hostility quotient for the day. Hell, for her lifetime.

"Help would be great, thanks." She got to her feet and positioned herself at one end, expecting the girl to go to the other.

Instead, Lolita stood about a third of the way into the giant roll-up and beckoned Vivian closer. "If we pick it up at either end, it'll sag on the ground in the center. This way we can lift it."

Vivian rolled her eyes at her own stupidity. "I would have been here all day."

They staggered with their load to the curb and dumped it. Relieved and a little out of breath, Vivian reached out her hand. "I'm Vivian."

"No kidding." The girl shook. "Amber."

"Thanks, Amber. I think if I had that carpet in my house another day I would have thrown up."

"Yeah, I remember it." She shuddered comically.

"You live around here, Amber?"

The girl nodded and pointed back at the familiar white house with the chrysanthemum-filled wagon. "I think you met my mom."

Vivian choked back a giggle. *This* was Sarah's daughter? Oh yes, there was a God in heaven after all. Mother and daughter must have such a cozy time planning outfits. Vivian didn't have to be there to hear; she'd lived it with her own mother. *You'll go to school in that over my dead body, young lady.* "Yes. I've met her a couple of times."

"And you're *so* going to be best girlfriends."

Vivian laughed, already liking this little Gilchrist. "Possible, but unlikely."

"What do you think of Kettle?" Amber's eye-rolling disdain made Vivian wish Amber was about thirty years older. Or that Vivian was thirty years younger and could make a few different choices. Many different choices.

"It's so much like Manhattan. I can hardly tell I left." Vivian gestured toward her old-lady house. "I'm going in to have a beer, you want one?"

"Really?" Amber's eyes lit up.

"No." Vivian tapped her playfully on the shoulder. "But come on in. I have soda, too."

"Soda?" Amber laughed. "Around here we say pop. Soda is like club soda."

"Okay, I have some . . . pop." She overenunciated the word, and Amber giggled and followed her into the house.

"Do you need to call your mom and tell her you're here?"

"Oh, like *that* would make her feel better."

"At least she'd know where you are."

"I'm fine."

Vivian turned and gave her a steady stare to see if Amber would flinch and start looking guilty, but she held up well. "Diet Sierra Mist? Or Diet Coke?"

"Mom says caffeine after four will keep me awake."

"Diet Sierra Mist? Or Diet Coke?"

Amber grinned. "Diet Coke."

Vivian opened her ugly gold refrigerator, handed a Coke to Amber, reached for a Leinenkugel, and decided against it. Easier to keep the demons back if she did without. And she'd been sleeping like shit, so yeah, maybe not Diet Coke.

"How do *you* like Kettle?" She pulled a Sierra Mist out of the refrigerator and popped the top.

"Too small, too boring, too gossipy. I want to move back to Manhattan and study art."

"Excellent." Vivian took a swig, wondering what it felt like to have known all your life your future was secure. "What kind of art?"

"I do a mixture of photo collage and painting."

"Cool." At Amber's age, Vivian's art was doing a mixture of alcohol and males. "Do you have a boyfriend?"

"Yeah." Amber tried too hard to act nonchalant. "A new kid in school. His name's Larry, he's totally hot."

Aha. She'd guess Larry was boyfriend number one and they hadn't been dating long. Mom Sarah probably wasn't the greatest sexual confidante. Maybe it wouldn't have made a difference if someone told Vivian she didn't have to screw every guy that asked, but it would have been nice. "You sleeping with him?"

"Not yet." She blushed and traced the top of her soda can with her index finger.

"You want to?"

"Sure." She lifted the can to her lips in a jerky movement.

She didn't want to. Vivian felt a rush of protectiveness. "Is he pressuring you?"

"Geez, you sound like my mom."

"Okay, okay." Vivian held up I-surrender hands. "But seriously, you don't have to. If he cares about—"

"I know, I know." She rolled her eyes. "If he cares he'll stick around even if I don't want to."

"Right." Vivian's soda—pop—suddenly tasted too sweet, and she wished for the beer. Why did everyone persist in feeding girls such Cinderella romantic-ideal bullshit? Men wanted into women's pants. And if they couldn't get into one pair, too bad, they'd try the next.

Then brokenhearted Amber would be told, *If he moved on because you wouldn't sleep with him, he wasn't worth having.* Pleez. At sixteen that carried all the weight of a freeze-dried gnat. Girls wanted boyfriends, especially cool boyfriends, and if sex helped you keep them, what was the big deal, right?

They had no idea what a big deal it could turn into.

But then Amber wasn't Vivian. After her adolescent rebellion, Amber would marry a man like Daddy, settle in Kettle, become her mother, and live sappily ever after.

"Did you really flash your boobs at Harris's?"

Vivian nearly dropped her can. *Oh shit.* She expected the news would travel, but somehow when she stood in the bar with her shirt up, she hadn't been picturing young ears like Amber's hearing about it. "Yup."

Amber hooted. "I knew it. The kids at school didn't believe it, but I knew you did."

She gazed at Vivian as if she were the not-very-virgin Mary, and Vivian had to turn away, retrieve a bag of chips from her duck-y cabinet, and pull out a handful while she thought over how to handle this one. "It was a bad thing, Amber."

"It was excellent. It's such an old-guy place, and you did that like you were giving them the finger. The girls at school think it's great. Well, the cool ones. The rest, who cares?"

"Right." Vivian crunched a chip. She really, really didn't want hero worship from kids too young to understand. "It's a pretty bad time for me, Amber. I was pretty messed up."

"Drunk?"

"No. Screwed up, and angry." She passed the bag of chips to Amber. "I wouldn't recommend it. Mike was there to pull me out; you might not get so lucky."

"Mike did that for you?" She sighed. "He is soooo hot."

"Ya *think?*"

Amber giggled. "So are you going to try to date him?"

"I don't think so." She dusted chip crumbs off her hands. "I guess he's still not over his dead wife."

"Oh yeah." Amber's voice dropped to hushed misery.

Vivian glanced at her sharply. Could hand-delivered casseroles be more than a few years away? "Did you know her?"

"Sure, everyone knew her."

"Let me guess, she was just like me, right?"

Amber snorted. "*Not.*"

"I figured." Vivian smiled without meaning it.

"They were so in love, it was like they were joined at the hip. They ran his business together; you never saw them apart. They never fought or anything. It was sooo romantic."

Romantic wasn't the word that sprang up in Vivian's mind. Codependent, however, leaped up with no trouble. Too bad. She'd thought Mike had more strength in him than that.

Amber crunched the last chip of her current handful. "Can I ask you something?"

"Sure."

"Can you help me do makeup like yours?"

Hmm. Vivian studied her natural features. She'd look stunning with a little eyeliner, maybe mascara, some blush, muted lipstick. But put the amount of makeup Vivian was wearing on her, and she'd look like a hooker. "Sure. I can help you."

"Cool! When?"

"Right now okay?"

"Sweet!" She looked at Vivian's exercise clothes. "But were you going to work out?"

"I can do it later. Stay right there." She ran upstairs to get a tray of basics, enthusiasm stirring. Female girlfriend stuff— she missed that. She'd had a few do-lunch friends in New York, but most of her socializing had been couple-oriented, and her leisure time had been hers alone or Ed's.

Back downstairs, she put the tray on the counter. "Ready?"

"You bet."

"Hold still. Now look up." She selected a soft brown pencil and drew a thin line under Amber's bottom lashes.

"What kind of workout do you do?"

"I have tapes." She smudged the line gently with her finger, marveling at the tiny pores and firm texture of Amber's skin. Hers had been like that once. "Step aerobics, free weights . . . I'm actually certified to teach."

"Cool. My mom works out. She used to be a dancer."

"No kidding." Vivian wouldn't mention that she used to be a dancer, too, in Chicago before she met Ed. She was pretty sure in the kind of dancing Sarah did, she got to keep her costume on. "She carries herself like one."

"Yeah, she's in good shape." Amber's voice held its first note of pride regarding her mother. "My friends' moms are always moaning about their weight, but they never do anything about it."

"Human nature."

"Hey, I know." Amber's excitement put the makeup application on hold. "You can teach aerobics classes."

"Oh, like they'd want to come to me to be taught."

"I bet they would. Why don't you? I'll come. I bet my friends would, too. And once my friends are into it, their moms will, too, since they're always whining. Mom says it's just a question of getting off your fat ass."

Vivian froze, mascara wand in hand. "Your mom said, 'fat ass'?"

"She said 'duff.'" Amber made a face, then opened her eyes wide for more mascara. "I wish she was more like you."

Vivian nearly smeared black gunk across Amber's nose. "I'd be a disaster mother."

"But you're cool. You understand what I'm talking about. She just wants me to grow up to be her. I'm *not* her. I want to dress the way I like, and wear makeup and hang out with Larry. She wants me to take ballet and tour Europe."

Vivian raised her eyebrows. "Um. Touring Europe is not exactly hardship."

"Have you been?"

"Sure." She brushed blush across high, young cheekbones. "But not with parents who cared enough to take me."

"I don't feel lucky. I feel like I have Martha fucking Stewart for a mom." She swore with the self-conscious bravado of a teenager who expects to be reprimanded. Vivian let it ride, selected a rosy lipstick, and glided it across Amber's unlined lips.

"There. You look gorgeous."

"You're done already?"

"Mirror in the bathroom, first door on the right."

Amber came back, looking disappointed. "It's not like yours."

Vivian stacked the last tube back into her tray. "My makeup's too slutty for you."

"Well if you think it's slutty, why do you wear it?"

"Because *I'm* slutty."

"No you're not."

Vivian gestured to Amber's outfit. "You can judge?"

Amber giggled—thank God someone had a sense of humor in this town. "Now *you* have to try makeup like *mine*."

"Why?"

"You can't wear that much when you're teaching aerobics."

"Who said I was going to teach?"

"What else are you going to do around here?"

Vivian scowled at the sweet young face. "You, Amber Gilchrist, are entirely too smart. Okay, I'll try it your way."

She went to the kitchen sink, washed her face, and, peering into her little hand mirror, applied the simpler makeup Amber was wearing. Only she was nearly forty, so she got to use under-eye concealer, too.

"There." Vivian gave her cheekbones one last brush and put the mirror down. "What do you think?"

Amber considered her, puckering Berry Rich lips. "You look prettier."

Vivian made a skeptical face.

"I'm serious." Amber gestured toward the hallway. "Go look in a bigger mirror."

Vivian went into the bathroom and stared at herself thirty years ago . . . except she looked thirty years older.

And plain. Ordinary. She could be a suburban mother, driving kids to soccer. She itched to run upstairs, grab her full complement of tubes and tubs and pencils, and fix the mess. But she'd done it for Amber, so she could wait until the girl left.

Barely.

A rap sounded on her back door, the squeak of the screen opening followed. Vivan emerged from the bathroom and saw Mike through the window. Crap. She did not want Mike, of all people, to see her looking like Susie Sunshine.

She walked to the door, feeling absurdly naked, which had nothing to do with the brief outfit of skintight cotton and spandex. She didn't mind Mike seeing her body, in fact she'd very much like to show him all of it, if he'd lower his guard. Why did she feel so nervous showing him her face?

She flung open the door and had to force herself to meet his eyes with her usual boldness. "Hi, Mike."

"Vivian." His blue gaze locked onto hers, and if female nipples coming erect made noise, there would have been a little "ping" sound right there in the silence.

He hadn't ever looked at her like that before. Not even close. Like he wanted to drop to his knees and worship. Sexually speaking. "Ye-e-es?"

He blinked and the look was gone. "I came to help out."

"Well come on in."

He looked past her. "Hey, Amber. You look very pretty."

"Thanks." She giggled, and Vivian didn't need to turn around to know she was the color of a stoplight. Wholesome, handsome men like Mike were the pinnacle sexual fantasy of girls practically too young to know what a sexual fantasy was. Of course at sixteen, Vivian had the real thing, sometimes from men Mike's age, which at the time she counted as a real coup.

Now seeing Mike and picturing Amber, her stomach roiled at the thought of those same men coming on to her. Creeps. They couldn't handle women their own age?

"Vivian did my makeup."

"Did she?" He took a step into the kitchen, suddenly taller and broader than he'd been outside. "Who did hers?"

"Me." Vivian moved around him and shut the door against the chill of early evening. "At Amber's request."

He turned to study her again, and she felt cornered between his big body and the rest of the room. "It suits you. You should wear it that way all the time."

"Who asked you?" She pushed past him into open space. Her question as to whether his dead wife was wholesome or glamorous had been answered, first by Amber and now by his reaction. Screw him. He'd take Vivian as she really was or not at all. She wasn't going to impersonate his wife to get him in the sack.

"Oh my God!" Amber stared in horror at the clock over the kitchen table, a revolting specimen depicting a smiling girl riding a smiling pony. "Mom's going to *kill* me. I have to go *now*."

"Better wash off the—"

"Can't, I have to be home before she goes to yoga. *Shit!*" She raced past Vivian and Mike and bolted out into the twilight.

Vivian shut the door after her and peered through the window. "I hope she doesn't get in trouble because of me."

"What?"

"Amber." She turned to Mike. "I hope she doesn't get it from Sarah because of the makeup."

"I'm sorry." He cupped his hand to his ear. "Was our local hard-hearted exhibitionist murderess expressing concern for a fellow human being?"

"Oh my." Vivian slapped one hand to the side of her face. "It won't happen again."

"Whew." He gazed at the ceiling in exaggerated relief.

"So what are we going to renovate today, Mike?"

"You tell me."

"Okay." She put her hands to her hips. "First, I want every smiling animal, plant, and/or small child removed from this kitchen."

"Replaced with?"

"Oh." She looked around wistfully. "A big iron rack with hanging copper pots. Stainless appliances, stone countertops, a professional range, a—"

"Trying to go back?"

She sent him a suspicious frown. "Back?"

"To New York. To Ed."

Okay, ouch, you win. She opened her eyes wide. "Why would I want to do that? I went to all that trouble to get rid of him, remember? Don't you watch TV?"

"Yeah, I watch it."

"So you know. And you better be nice to me or you're next."

"Uh-huh." He stroked his big, capable hand over the warm, faintly orangey wood of the cabinets. "This house isn't right for that kind of kitchen."

"I can't afford it anyway. But we can nuke the bunnies, right?"

"Consider them nuked. What else?"

"I need you to show me how to get the spiky blocks of wood and all the staples off the living room floor where I tore up the carpet. Then I want to—"

"That'll do us for now." He headed into the living room, his work boots making dull thuds, masculine and comforting next to her tap-tapping white and hot pink Nike cross-trainers. "We can pull these blocks up today. The floor is in good shape, you shouldn't have to do anything else to it."

"Excellent." She stood too close to him, attracted by his size and know-how. Money and power had always been her numbers one and two, but the handyman thing could be a real turn-on. That might have to be her number one in Kettle.

"We can de-cute the kitchen another day."

"Anything that keeps you coming over so I get another shot at luring you into bed."

He turned, not stepping back. "Are you going to keep that up the entire time we're neighbors?"

"No . . ." She straightened his collar, and let her hands rest against his chest. "Just until you give in."

"Uh-huh." He removed her hands from his shirt, guided them back down to her sides. "That will depend on things you're not ready to do."

"I'm ready to do them all, Mike."

"I mean emotionally."

She wrinkled her nose. "What are you, my shrink?"

"Just farther along in the process."

One eyebrow up instead of asking, *What process?*

"Grief."

She rolled her eyes. "Do you have to be so serious all the time?"

He gave her a long look as if he were contemplating something he shouldn't be contemplating. Then he stood back, arms outstretched, opened his mouth, and came out with the most incredible impression of Bugs Bunny she'd ever heard.

"Ehhhh, what's up doc? Of course you know that this means war. What a maroon."

She was so surprised that she forgot to be sexy and burst out laughing, loudly, the way that felt as good as coming.

He watched her, slightly reddened, but smiling. "Okay?"

"That was the very last thing I expected."

"Well, Ms. Prime Time Murder Trial." He puffed himself up. "You're not the only one with secrets."

She took a step toward him. "Tell me more of yours."

"Another time."

"Promise?"

"Let's get to work." He glanced at her outfit. "You should probably put on some clothes."

"Why?" She thrust out her chest. "Because I'm so distracting, you won't be able to concentrate?"

"Because your knees will get lacerated if you land on a staple."

Vivian sighed and started for the stairs. "I think you're going to be the toughest dick I ever went after. At the very least, watch my extremely luscious ass as I walk up the stairs?"

He folded his arms across his chest, stern papa about to deliver a lecture on morality. "Okay, walk."

She made the most of it. One of her most enticing-assed ascents in history. At the top she spun around, wanting to catch his tongue hanging all the way down to the bulge in his jeans.

The bastard had turned away and was inspecting the blocks of wood that used to hold the hideous carpet prisoner on her floor.

A snort of laughter escaped her, then another. Of course he knew this meant war . . . with a worthy opponent. She liked Mike, more than anyone she'd met in a long time. She loved Ed, but she sure as hell didn't always like him. And as the years went on and the fights and his temper got worse, she wasn't sure she still liked him at all.

But she stayed because there was no-friggin'-where else to go.

In her hideous blue and brown room, she changed into her

Blue Cult pink-stitched jeans and a hot-pink top that didn't cover a whole lot more than her workout outfit. On her feet, her favorite pair of pink Kate Spade Mary Janes. And, thank God, she got to fix her makeup, replacing the blah housewife with herself.

Downstairs, Mike took one look and rolled his eyes. "Don't you have any T-shirts?"

"T-shirts won't drive you into a frenzy of lust."

"Don't be so sure." He handed her a bizarrely shaped metal bar, a strip of thick cardboard, a screwdriver, and thin pliers. "Watch. You put the cardboard down first to protect your floor, then stick the blade under the tack strip, near the nail."

"There's a million nails."

"The one pounded down. Then you pry it up." There was a creaking sound as the dusty dry wood gave to his pressure. "For the staples, push the screwdriver under and lift. If only one side comes out, you use the pliers to get the rest. Okay?"

"Okay." She watched his effortless demonstration. "I really appreciate you helping me with all this, Mike."

"Please." He grimaced. "I can't take sincerity more than once a day."

"Hmm." She pretended to think that over. "Then how about after we finish we get drunk and naked?"

"That's more like it."

She giggled, took her tools, and started in. Clumsy at first, she got the hang of yanking up the little buggers, and though some of them crumbled and splintered, a few came up with such smoothness, she felt like cheering. The work was tedious and hand-cramping, but gave her a weird and unlikely sense of pride in the house and her part in making the room look so much better.

Now if she could only afford new furniture. New appliances. New neighborhood. New town. New life.

By the second to last tack strip, they were working side by side along the north wall of the room. Creak, crack, the last strips pulled off, the last staples pried up or yanked out.

Done.

Vivian flexed her sore hands. "Do we have to fill in a million nail holes next?"

"No." He got up and stretched his back. "Call those character marks. Do you have a broom?"

She gave him an I-dunno shrug. "I can poke around."

"I'll get one. Be right back." He left; the back storm door shrieked closed behind him and the room seemed suddenly vacuumed of air and life. No sounds. No breeze. No traffic. Even the crows were quiet.

Vivian didn't do "alone" well these days. Maybe never would again.

She got to her feet, went into the kitchen, and pulled out two beers, opened them both, took a healthy swig of one. She drew her hand over the cold surface of the counter, noting the darkened and occasionally missing grout around the tiny tiles.

What was taking Mike so long? She couldn't bear the silence. First thing in the morning she was buying a CD player and some CDs: Joni Mitchell; Crosby, Stills, Nash and Young; Steely Dan; maybe some Gershwin and Sinatra for times ahead when she could stand to be reminded of Ed. So she wouldn't lose the good memories—dancing in his living room, listening to his god-awful voice attempting love songs in her ear. The closest he got to telling her how he felt. Other people's words, other people's tunes. Nothing of himself that could belong only to her.

Where the hell was Mike?

He showed halfway through the beer she'd opened for him, broom and garbage bag in one hand, paper grocery bag in the other.

"What's in there?" She pointed to the grocery bag.

"Dinner."

She blinked to his face in surprise. "For me?"

"For both of us. The casserole needs heating." He put the bag on the counter, and his boots thudded into her living room, the noise replaced by the scratchy swish of a broom and the metallic tinkle of staples.

A weird warmth flooded her. She didn't generally provoke simple, thoughtful gestures. All manner of bribes and ransom, sure—jewelry, clothing, spa visits, nights out in ridiculously expensive restaurants, trips around the world. But nothing like this anticipation of something she might really need instead of something she wanted.

She turned the oven on and shoved the casserole in. After the radio, at the top of her shopping list—a microwave. Who could have managed here without one?

Now to set the table. Forget the spare, chilly dining room; they could eat in here. Placemats, plates, utensils, napkins—and voilà!

Too utilitarian, like a table the Cleavers would eat at. Like Vivian without enough makeup.

With more of that strange feeling of pride in a house that

didn't feel like hers, she arranged red and yellow pears on a shallow glass dish she'd discovered in a nearly unreachable cabinet. She ducked outside and picked brightly colored leaves from the red maple on her front lawn, ditto sprigs from the blue spruce next to the garage, and ditto ditto from a bush with red berries clinging to naked black twigs. Pears never had it that chic.

Next, truly inspired, on an old-lady flowery-rimmed china plate, she stuck two red and two white votive candles retrieved from a drawer full of them—did Gran's friend hold seances?—and around them she poured a dusty bag of dried black beans, probably bought years ago and abandoned.

She heard him in the bathroom, the sink running while he washed his hands, and for a second she regretted her attempt to fuss up the table. In the next second, she shrugged. Who cared what he thought? If she had to eat leftover casserole some sweet thing brought him, she should be able to leave her own mark.

Mike appeared in the doorway and blinked at the table. "Wow. Who knew?"

"Your neighbor is a woman of many talents: stripper, Playboy Bunny, murderess, and happy homemaker. Beer?" She held one out.

"Thanks." He sank into the chair closest to the door with a long sigh. "This will hit the spot."

"Tough day at the office, dear?" She sat opposite and plunked her elbows on the table, rested her chin on clasped fingers.

"You might say that." He twisted off the cap with his strong hands, very clean for someone who worked so hard with them. "Spent most of the day at the Gilchrists'."

"Where Sarah offered you her nice warm buns?"

He had to stop the beer bottle tipping toward his mouth in order to smile. "She did, in fact. I also heard you had fun at the Kettle Social Club meeting."

"Oh, is *that* what fun is? All this time I never knew. Yes, I was there. Strangely, my ideas for the party weren't approved. Even the serious ones." She felt her mood slip back down, and got up for another beer. "How do you stand it here, Mike?"

He shrugged. "It's home."

"Don't you ever want to get the hell out?"

"I did get the hell out. After my wife died."

Ah, the saintly extra-appendage spouse. "When was that?"

"Two years ago. Roughly."

"Why did you come back?"

He rested the bottle on the table, thumbs gliding restlessly over the label. "Too much of my life here to leave."

"Too much of your wife here to leave."

"Maybe."

She turned away. Her gut tightened; pain started pounding her chest and temples. She did not need this beer or the last one or the one before that. "What was her name?"

"Rose—" He cleared his throat. "Rosemary."

She drank from the third bottle, a long glugging swig, staring out the darkening kitchen window at the fading sky and faint outlines of trees. "And you were in love with her like no woman you've ever known."

"Right." His voice was flat, dead.

Her chest thickened; anger grew in her, anger that wasn't his fault, anger she needed to get the better of. "And she was good and gentle and sweet and everyone adored her."

No answer. Her warning signal. She needed to stop right now, but the fury train thundered on, and Vivian was a first-class passenger.

She turned and gestured with her beer. "And she was a member of the Kettle Social Club and worked at the library and volunteered everywhere anyone needed help and brought the kind of joy to this town it had never known before and certainly not since, because—"

"Enough." He stood up.

She couldn't stop. Rage filled her to where she was shaking with it. "Wild animals gentled at her touch, and—"

"Stop it, Vivian."

"—when she died, angels cried, and—"

"Shut up." He lunged at her, grabbed her shoulders, and practically lifted her off the floor. Her beer slipped and exploded, bubbles hissing furiously. "Just shut the fuck up."

The familiar fear adrenaline raced through her; she was gloriously and fiercely and unquestionably alive, free of the dulling, stupid, endless pain.

"What are you going to do to me?" She gasped the words out in challenge, then laughed bitterly. "It's all been done, Mike. He was a goddamn pro, you're the dust beneath his feet."

His grip on her shoulders gentled; he closed his eyes, bowed his head, jaw clenched so his teeth were probably close to cracking.

Get a clue, Vivian. This was Mike, this was Kettle, Wisconsin. Taunting him would only get her what she hated most. Pity.

"Let go." She started to struggle.

He let go of her shoulders, then wrapped both arms around her so tightly she couldn't move, couldn't breathe. Her face was mashed against his chest, then he backed her against a wall so she couldn't even kick him in the balls.

She fought, wiggling, lifting her feet off the ground as far as she could, so her weight would sag on his arms. Nothing. He was a goddamn fortress; she couldn't fight, couldn't move; she was totally helpless, trapped between the sunshine harvest wall and his body.

She stopped fighting, worked instead to get air back into her squeezed lungs, gathering force for her next attack.

Incredibly, a deep humming started low in his chest, then— oh my God, was she suddenly in *The Sound of Music?*—he started to sing.

"*Over in Killarney, many years ago, my mother sang a song to me in tones so sweet and low.*"

"You have *got* to be kidding me." She pushed against his stone wall body. "For chrissake, we're trying to have a fight here."

He took a deep breath. "*Just a simple little ditty, in her good old Irish way, and I'd give the world if she could sing that song to me this day.*"

His voice was smooth, deep, resonant, freaking Bing Crosby. Pure seductive evil that made her want to relax and give in, let him hold her all night. "So help me God, Mike, if you get to the too-ra-loo-ral shit, I'll—"

"*Too-ra-loo-ra-loo-ral, Too-ra-loo-ra-li.*" He sang on, crescendoing, a grin in his voice now, rocking her back and forth as if she were his daughter. "*Too-ra-loo-ra-loo-ral, hush now, don't you cry.*"

"Mike." She pushed him again, starting to laugh in spite of herself. "Stop, I'm begging you."

"Too-ra-loo-ra-loo-ral, Too-ra-loo-ra-li." His head moved down next to hers, he crooned the last words of the chorus, the way Ed used to sing to her, only ten times better. She stopped moving, stopped fighting, just listened to the rumble in his chest, the tickle of his breath in her ear, more laughter bubbling up—only it didn't feel quite like laughter this time.

"Too-ra-loo-ra-loo-ral . . . that's an Irish lullaby."

He stopped, and there was no sound in her kitchen, in her yard, in the whole of Kettle, nothing but Mike's breathing. Instead of giving her what she'd asked for, what she deserved for making fun of poor Rosemary, he'd sung her a fucking lullaby.

Tears came to her eyes, spilled over, and started rolling down her cheeks, two, then four, then a steady stream she couldn't stop and was past caring to try. He held her, rocked her, and hummed the song again, verse after verse, as if he had nothing else to do for the rest of time but be there for her.

Ten

<u>Letter from Erin's fifth grade teacher,</u>
<u>Mrs. Flatley</u>

Dear Principal Hodgkins,

Thank you for your note, but I must ask again that
you make time to speak with me regarding Erin.
She showed up with bruises again this morning.
As you said, she's an odd girl, certainly, but I don't
think that can be the whole story. My impression
is that she has no one to turn to and I'd like to help
her.

Response from Principal Hodgkins

Dear Mrs. Flatley,

While I appreciate your concerns, I play golf weekly with Erin's father, and he takes care of our family's teeth. I can assure you he's had quite a time raising a child like Erin alone, but what you are implying is simply not possible, especially in this town. I have so far been very pleased with your work this year, your first at Kettle Elementary. I would like to see a long and healthy relationship develop between you and the school. It would be a shame if this issue got in the way of that.

Erin adjusted her head on her pillow and turned to Chapter Seventeen of *What to Expect When You're Expecting*, called, "When Something Goes Wrong." There was a paragraph at the beginning, telling the reader not to read further unless something had gone wrong with her pregnancy. Otherwise, the authors pointed out, reading the chapter might lead to unnecessary worry.

Erin liked the reassuring tone of that paragraph. She liked that the authors cared enough to warn their readers. Erin had read it anyway. She'd been too confident that her baby, Joy, was finally going to be her happiness. The fates could not be so cruel as to take away Erin's mother, leaving Erin alone with Dad, and then take away the one baby Erin had carried past the first trimester, leaving her alone again with Joe.

Turned out the fates were self-serving sons of bitches, like most everyone else.

Or maybe they knew better. Maybe Erin was being selfish wanting a baby so much. Maybe the fates knew Joy could not have been happy with a father like Joe. Erin would have done anything to keep her safe, but maybe the fates knew her efforts wouldn't have been enough. Maybe it was better Erin stayed childless.

It just didn't feel like it.

The advice from the chapter didn't make her feel warm the way it usually did. She put the book away in its special spot hidden under her side of the bed. She didn't even feel like reading today. The world felt different and it was hard to concentrate. She was restless, twitchy.

For the first time in years, she wanted to run. Not run away, she'd wanted that plenty. But just to work her body, like on the track team in high school, before she got pregnant. To feel a sense of freedom, however false. Once she lifted her head high enough above mere survival to realize how trapped she was in her marriage and in Kettle, she'd stopped running. What was the point? Going home after only made it worse.

But then Vivian came. And Erin had allowed herself to imagine that the rigidity and sameness of each day, of each week, month, or year, could vary. And that maybe the people who held her down would get some of their own back from someone strong enough to give it. Because that person sure wasn't Erin.

Two days ago in the meeting, she hadn't been able to take her eyes off Vivian. She was twice as beautiful in person because you could feel the energy and confidence radiating from her. Vivian probably wouldn't stay in Kettle forever, but for as long as she did, things would be better. Even something as little as her suggestion they have a hand-job booth at the Halloween party.

Erin had a terrible time not laughing out loud at that. Even that night as she went to bed, she'd had to stuff her pillow in her mouth so Joe wouldn't hear her still laughing.

The best part of the meeting was how Joan felt uneasy and threatened. On the way home she'd barely stopped bad-mouthing Vivian long enough to breathe. All of a sudden she'd met more than her match in this vibrant, sexual woman who had conquered the man keeping her down. Joan had to understand now that victory was possible. That all women weren't going to lie down and take it like Erin. And that even if they did for a while, it was no guarantee they wouldn't rise up sooner or later and find strength in their own hands. Maybe that made Joan think about what Joe was doing, even for a few minutes. That would be progress.

She got out of bed and made it carefully, tucking the bottom corners of the blankets, leaving the tops loose like Joe wanted. Vivian could live her own life now. Tuck her bed, cook her meals, spend her time any way she wanted. She'd freed herself.

Once Erin bought a bird from a pet store, back a few years after she got married, when she realized the blissful bargain to get away from her father was slowly and inevitably turning into the same prison. She thought a bird would be a good companion. One day the painfully obvious metaphor clicked into her barely adult brain and she'd taken the bird into the woods, set it free, and dumped the cage on the ground. A few days later she'd come back and found the bird lying dead next to its cage. It must have died trying to get back in. Apparently this wasn't the type who knew how to get by in the wild.

Stupid bird.

Except if someone set Erin free, would she know where to fly? She'd run away a few times after Joy died, to her grandma's, to her cousin's. Joe always found her. But if he hadn't, maybe she'd have come knocking back on his door after a few days, too. And if he wouldn't let her in, maybe she'd have frozen to death on the sidewalk. Maybe she didn't know how to survive in her natural habitat, either.

Maybe Vivian could teach her.

She took a shower, dried herself off, and reached for the pretty dusting powder in the white porcelain box, part of the set her mom had given her for her seventh birthday, which she refilled when it ran out. She didn't wear it often, but today she thought smelling good would be nice. On Thursday, when Vivian had breezed into the ugly, stale meeting room, she'd brought with her a light floral perfume. Erin loved that Vivian could bring a room alive for every sense. She'd love to be able to do that. Mostly she crept in and people didn't notice.

She pulled on baggy beige pants, then dug in her drawer until she found the deep rose-colored sweater Sarah had given her two years earlier for helping with the Halloween party. Erin knew Sarah well enough to know the sweater was not a gift, but an attempt to make her over into something better. Sarah had meant to be helpful, but Erin had put it away and never worn it.

Now she pulled it on and checked the mirror in their

dingy and out-of-date bathroom. Erin would love to redo the whole house. Joan had horrible taste. Erin had seen enough home improvement shows that she could probably do the entire renovation herself. But God forbid she change the house Joe grew up in. The one Joan let them live in through the tremendous warmth of her heart, while she languished in a smaller house on the outskirts of town and never let them forget it.

The sweater looked good. She needed makeup, but if she started wearing that, Joe would freak. In fact, she'd have to remember to take the sweater off before he got home or he'd start in with the questions and make her feel guilty for nothing.

Her doorbell rang and she ran to the bedroom and peered at the clock on Joe's side of the bed. Nearly noon. Joe was out playing golf, Joan never came by unless she knew he was home; who was this?

She ran to the front hall and peeked through the peephole. Vivian. Erin turned and flattened herself against the door. Oh my God. A breathless laugh, then she took a deep breath and opened the door, unable to stop smiling. It was like having a movie star show up at your house.

"Hi Erin." Vivian looked stunning, sunglasses pushed on top of her head, fancy-stitched jeans that hugged her hips, a fuchsia suede handbag that matched the stitching in her jeans. Erin window-shopped online a lot, imagining herself in outfits she'd never wear. She was pretty sure that purse was a Kate Spade.

"Hi Vivian." Her voice came out shaky. *Come on, Erin.*

"I'm passing out leaflets about my new aerobics classes,

Monday, Wednesday, and Friday at five-thirty. I'm teaching at my house until I have enough people to get a bigger place. Are you interested?"

Erin took a leaflet. They were done on thick cream paper with a design of fall leaves in one corner and in the other, a woman jumping, arms up, as if she didn't ever expect to land. *Shape Up for Fall.* "These are nice. Did you do them yourself?"

"Yes ma'am." The low, sexy drawl made Erin want to smile again. "On Mike's computer."

"They're nice." She just said that. Could she sound more stupid?

Vivian was studying her; Erin could tell without looking up. Probably thinking the same thing everyone else in Kettle thought, only Vivian wouldn't know about Joe. Erin wished she could toss back her hair and say something brilliant that would convince Vivian they could be really good friends.

"Have we met before, Erin?"

She was so surprised, she jerked her head up and met Vivian's dark, beautiful gaze. "Yes. When we were kids."

"I thought so." Vivian narrowed her eyes. "The dollhouse at my grandma's, did we play there together?"

"Yes. Yes." She couldn't stop nodding and smiling. It was like Vivian was validating her existence. "That was me."

"No kidding. How cool."

"We played at my house once, too. And in the woods behind it. At the stream."

"Hmm. I don't remember that."

No. She wouldn't.

A truck drove down the street. Joe's. How could he be

home already? The golf course was always jammed on Saturdays, and today was warm for this time of year.

He turned into their driveway; the garage door creaked up.

Vivian glanced behind her. "Your husband?"

"Yes." She tried not to sound anxious. "He's back from golf early I guess."

"Introduce me?" Vivian was watching her carefully.

Erin met the dark eyes again and held them this time, communicating what she wasn't saying as hard as she could to someone who would understand. "I don't know if that's a good idea."

"Really." She took a step back. The garage door went down behind Joe's truck. "You sure?"

Erin heard his truck door slam, his heavy steps coming up the stairs from the garage. Suddenly she wasn't sure. The familiar adrenaline surged and started her heart pounding, but not entirely from fear. She wanted Joe to meet someone with strength to equal his.

"Erin." His voice, now his steps behind her, coming toward the front door. "Is that the Lorelei girl?"

"Woman." Vivian shifted her weight even on both feet. "I haven't been a girl for decades."

"Joe, this is Vivian." Erin dropped her eyes so she wouldn't have to see him leering.

"I'm passing out flyers for the aerobics class I'm going to teach. Erin would like to join."

Erin flinched. She hadn't said that.

"She would?" His voice was hearty innocence. She could feel his eyes on her. "We'll talk it over. Nice sweater, by the way, Erin. Have I seen that before? I don't think so."

Damn, damn, shit, and damn, she didn't have a chance to take it off. "First time I've worn it."

"What's the occasion?"

She shrugged, willing Vivian to understand, wanting that bond between them.

"Pretty color, it looks great on you." Vivian pushed her sunglasses abruptly down onto her nose. "So. I'm off. Yours is the last house on this street."

Erin's heart sank. What had she thought, that staring at Vivian would magically enable them to communicate? Vivian probably thought she was touched in the head. Most people did, even Erin sometimes.

So Vivian would move on, and Erin would be left with Joe, who would question her. Why was she wearing that sweater? Who was she trying to look nice for? Why did she want to take the classes, wasn't her life good enough with him? Was she trying to meet someone else? He'd die if she left him, she was the best thing that ever happened to him, he loved her so much sometimes he thought it would kill him.

Sometimes Erin almost wished it would.

"Thanks for stopping by." She couldn't look at Vivian again, or Joe. Erin probably knew more of the sidewalks and yards and streets of Kettle than anyone but bugs.

"Bye, Vivian." Joe's arm came around Erin in an embrace that felt like a threat.

"Nice to see you again, Joe." Vivian reached out and touched Erin's arm. "Erin, want to walk with me? I have a bunch more of these to deliver."

A short, shocked silence. Joe would say no. He'd say they had plans. He'd say he needed his lunch.

"Thanks, I'd like that." Erin nearly fainted. She'd been thinking the words so hard they actually came out.

"Great. Let's go."

"Erin, what about lunch." Joe's voice dropped lower; his arm squeezed her tighter. She'd get it either way now, whether she went or whether she didn't.

"Peanut butter and jelly, food of gods." Vivian grabbed Erin's hand and pulled her out of Joe's embrace, propelled her down the steps. "You can handle that, I'm sure."

"I won't be long. I'll make lunch for you when I get back." She tossed the words over her shoulder, half expecting Joe to charge down the steps and drag her back. But if he started in public, it would be harder for Kettle to pretend they didn't know what was happening. She was safe until she got home.

She fell in step beside Vivian, hardly daring to breathe in case she woke up and found this was a dream. But the sun shone, the wind rustled the changing leaves, and she didn't wake up. So she drank in the companionship and admired the way Vivian managed to look down-to-earth and like a sex goddess at the same time. Maybe Erin would start wearing this sweater more often.

"Pretty day."

"Yes." She chewed the inside of her cheek, unsure how to chat, still more unsure what Vivian expected of her, what had prompted her to want to walk together.

Vivian looked back over her shoulder and Erin copied, terrified she'd see Joe staring after them with his thundercloud eyebrows. But thank God, he'd gone back in.

"Men are so pathetic." Vivian gestured in contempt. "They

put on the macho independent act, and fall apart when we're not there."

"Right." Erin smiled nervously. She wasn't comfortable talking about Joe. He'd been such a forbidden topic for so long, she wasn't sure she'd ever be able to mention his name in public.

"You're the only person I remember from my visits to Kettle when I was a kid." She pushed her sunglasses up into her hair. "Tell me what you remember. I'm curious."

Vivian's words made Erin feel special. She started to relax. "My father used to live next door to you. Not Mike's house, the other one."

"Now home to Tweedle-Dum and Tweedle-Dumber?"

Through force of habit, Erin tried to suppress her laughter and ended up sounding as if she couldn't breathe through a cold. Vivian had nailed the Johnsons.

"You can laugh around me." Vivian turned toward her, and Erin felt her power and understood.

"Thank you." She blinked fiercely to avoid tears, since tears made her sniffle like a schoolgirl and she wanted to pretend for this short time that she and Vivian were friends and equals.

"Before you go on, Erin, answer me this. Is *anyone* in this town not completely bunged up over something?"

She had to remind herself, but she managed to let her laughter out. It felt good. Tickly and freeing. "Very doubtful."

"I thought so. Go on."

"I was six, you were nine." She wondered if it would seem odd to have cemented Vivian's visit in her memory, but she was so anxious to let the story out, she didn't care. "I was playing out back when you came over."

"I just showed up in your yard?"

"We didn't have a fence or anything. I remember thinking you had much nicer clothes than I did." She gave a wry smile. "I guess some things don't change."

Vivian laughed, and Erin felt as if she'd been given a gift. "Then what?"

"Then you came right over and asked me what I was doing."

"What were you doing?"

"Building a house out of a shoebox, with rocks and leaves and grass for furniture."

Vivian groaned. "So I lorded Gran's doll palace over your hut?"

"No." Erin shook her head emphatically. "Not at all. You helped me and then you asked me if I wanted to play in your house when we were done."

"Really. Nice to know I had some kindness in me back then." Her sarcasm was tinged with bitterness.

"You had plenty." Erin wanted to hug her and tell her how they'd run together from her father's anger and how that had been the one time she'd felt she had an ally except for imaginary Alice. She wanted to tell Vivian that Vivian would be okay, which was ridiculous because no one needed to tell Vivian that, and who was Erin to be giving out life advice?

They passed Sarah's house, with the maroon chrysanthemums blooming cheerfully in their white painted wagon. Vivian made a scornful noise. "Here dwelleth the Pumpkin Queen. Abandon imperfection all ye who enter here."

Erin frowned. "Sarah's not as bad as she seems."

"Right."

"She tries to be nice."

"When it suits her."

Erin frowned harder. She wasn't surprised Sarah and Vivian hadn't taken to each other. But Erin would have expected Vivian just to laugh at how Sarah clung to perfectionism like a shield. A transparent shield.

They passed Sarah's house and the pumpkin-filled lot next door, which made Vivian snort and say, "Whatever."

Erin didn't know what to say, so she didn't say anything. She'd thought Vivian's Come As You're Not theme and makeover idea were great, except for once she agreed with Joan. No one would let Lorelei Taylor make them over. The town had voicelessly united to block her at every turn. There had never been a crime in Kettle, and she, being a criminal, came far too close.

In Erin's opinion, there had scarcely been a day without crime in Kettle. Sometimes she thought drug deals and murders and robberies were preferable to the small cumulative evils that went on here every day.

"So Erin, is there a place in town people post these kinds of notices?"

"At the church." Erin gestured ahead to the white building where the Social Club met. "And down Main Street at Granley's Stationers."

"Excellent."

At the corner of Spring and Main, Vivian darted into the church to pin her announcement to the community board while Erin waited on the sidewalk. An elderly woman passed, glaring first up the steps where Vivian had disappeared, then at Erin for the sin of associating with her. Erin wanted to laugh. The same woman probably passed Erin dozens of times in the last thirty-plus years and never even noticed her. Being around Vivian made her visible.

Vivian reappeared through the big wooden doors and skipped down the steps, scowling. Even scowling, she burst with life and passion and beauty. "How long before that gets ripped down? Ten, twenty minutes?"

"If you're lucky."

"Well it's worth a shot." She sighed. "You'll come to my classes, won't you, Erin?"

"I'd like to." Her voice came out dull and hopeless. She didn't offer anything more. Vivian had to understand.

"Then do it." Vivian's words were low and urgent, then as if she were changing into someone else, she smiled and stepped back. "There were notices up for the Halloween party, too. Our Sarah must have been busy."

"Sarah usually is." Erin started walking with her down Main Street, and if Vivian noticed the way people stared or did double takes, she didn't let on. "Halloween is a big deal in Kettle."

"Why's that?"

"In 1920 a bunch of women barricaded themselves in your house to protest men not letting them vote, even though it was just made legal." She grimaced, hating the hypocritical pride the town took in the story. "The men gave in, so along with the holiday, Kettle celebrates the power of women."

Vivian burst out laughing, a long, loud guffaw about as opposite from the way Erin laughed as you could get. Then she grabbed Erin's arm and stopped walking. "*Are* there any powerful women in Kettle?"

She tried to hide the hope in her eyes. "There's you now."

Vivian stopped laughing. She slid her hand down Erin's arm until their hands were clasped, the same way they'd been decades ago when they ran away from the angry sound of Erin's dad's voice.

Then in full view of passersby, who would no doubt carry the story home to their loved ones that night, Vivian leaned over and planted a long, sweet kiss on Erin's cheek.

Eleven

Sarah's entry in her diary
May 26
Morning after senior prom

Dear Diary,

I had such a good time with Tom! He's so sweet and so handsome and so romantic. We danced together almost all evening. I'm sure the entire female half of the class wanted to dance with Tom, too, but no way was I letting them near him.

Sally Jordan had a keg party after at her house by the lake, and my parents said because my grades were so good all year that I didn't have to be back until the next morning! Which is now! So here I am writing

this on no sleep! Not a wink. It was so great. I think
I'm still drunk, but not only on beer!

Tom has got to be the world's best dancer. After in
his car, I let him get to second base, but I stopped him
doing more even though he really wanted to. That's for
my future husband.

He's going to Minnesota to be a camp counselor this
summer, then to UW Madison next fall. He's soooo
cute! He says he wants to go to law school someday,
too!

Anyway, it was a great party and now I have to go
to bed because I'm pooped!

Love, Sarah

Sarah walked into Granley's Stationers, carefully smoothing back her windblown hair. She registered Tom's presence behind the counter, but stopped at the front of the store, pretending to consider some note cards so he'd have the chance to admire her before she spoke to him. She wore pleated, wool crepe pants and a matching short jacket in a flattering shade of rust that she'd bought from Talbots online at a very reasonable price. There was no excuse not to look lovely every day when clothes could be bought at reasonable prices. To complement the ensemble, she'd chosen a cream-colored blouse that set off both her suit and her skin to perfection. The neckline ventured a little farther south than her necklines usually ventured, but she felt a little reckless today, so why not?

She smiled at that thought, hoping her smile looked mys-

terious and would make Tom wonder what she was thinking. Then she turned, broadening the smile into a special
hello.

Of course she hadn't been wrong, he *was* staring at her,
and started when she caught him, which sent a delicious tingle through her body. Innocent, all of it, but so much fun.

She was here to pick up a Cross pen she'd had him order
specially for Ben. A sleek, platinum-plated ball point, to replace the one he'd been using so long it was scratched and
worn. Tom had sent her an e-mail that the pen was ready, and
reading a private note from him, even one so businesslike,
had been vaguely thrilling as well.

*Sarah. I wanted to let you know that your pen has
arrived. Stop by any time. Tom.*

"Hello, Tom." She kept contact with his beautiful dark eyes
as she approached the counter.

"Hi Sarah. You look very nice. As always."

"Thank you." She dropped her eyes modestly. When people complimented you, they didn't want you acting as if you
agreed with them. "Very nice of you to say so."

"You're here to pick up the pen?"

"Yes." As if she were reaching out to touch his hand, she
laid hers on the center of the scratched glass covering the ad-
vertisement for Parker Pens that had been there since she was
a girl. "I've been so busy preparing for the party, but I wanted
to pick it up."

"I'm glad you did."

She let herself thrill just a little at his deep voice saying that. "This morning I found a child at a hospital in Ladysmith who will benefit from our Halloween fund-raiser."

"Good for you, Sarah." He beamed in admiration, and Sarah felt as if she could rise up and float around his store.

"Thank you for your e-mail. It's a nice method of keeping in touch, don't you think?"

He nodded, eyes warm in that way that told her so much more than he ever said. "Absolutely."

"You never bother anyone with an e-mail the way you can with a phone call." She traced the outline of the photographed pen under the glass, wondering if he were imagining her fingers doing something else entirely. "And of course e-mail is always private."

"Yes." His voice lowered to an intimate murmur and, oh my goodness, Sarah suddenly realized how that must have sounded. As if she were inviting him to e-mail her any time he wanted.

"Ben will love the pen I ordered for him."

"I'm sure he will." The warmth left his eyes. He straightened, and only then did she realize he'd been leaning toward her. "It's a beauty."

Sarah smiled, but without much enthusiasm. There. She'd set him straight. Good that he got the message. Wasn't it.

"Ben's such a busy man." To her surprise, her voice came harsh instead of warm and proud as she intended. "Always busy."

She tucked her hair behind her ear even though it hadn't come untucked. She shouldn't have told Tom about Ben being so busy. She should ask for the pen and leave. But at her words, life had come back into Tom's face, and she couldn't bear to crush him again.

"He makes time for you, doesn't he? He'd be a fool not to."

"Thank you, Tom, that's sweet." She hadn't answered his question. Hadn't rushed to say that, oh yes, Ben made loads of time for her and their marriage was so happy and strong.

So there they stood, staring at each other, and a phrase from a romance novel she'd made fun of and secretly loved in college jumped into her head. *Naked need.* That's what they were staring at each other with.

She suddenly imagined herself leaning over and kissing him for the first time since high school. She imagined feeling his hands all over her, she imagined experiencing true passion with Tom, the way she hadn't ever quite experienced it with Ben.

What was she thinking?

The bell on the store's front door rang, a gust of outside air entered the shop, and Sarah quickly covered a stab of disappointment with tremendous relief. Another customer. Good. She didn't need to dig herself in any deeper here. Leading Tom on was the last thing she intended, since of course she could offer him nothing more than mild flirtation.

"Well, Miss Sarah, fancy meeting you here."

Oh no. *Her.* Sarah didn't even want to turn around. No matter how loud or trampy Vivian appeared today, she'd make Sarah look and feel dowdy and unfashionable. Bad enough the woman put makeup all over Amber's sweet, lovely face without clearing it with Sarah first. Sarah was going to speak to her about that, first chance she got.

Tom's eyes bugged out; he swallowed convulsively.

Dark panic threatened, and Sarah had to start her three-part yoga breathing to calm down. Tom would look, of course he would look. Even Sarah thought Vivian was beautiful on the outside.

Vivian undulated—or whatever she got her body to do, it certainly wasn't mere walking like the rest of them found perfectly adequate—up to the counter and held out her hand, tipping forward to enhance Tom's view down her tight sweater. Behind Vivian, a small movement in Sarah's peripheral vision proved to be Erin, actually wearing the sweater Sarah bought her and looking much improved, as Sarah had known she would.

Now there was a strange duo. Had they come in together?

"Hello there." Vivian smiled at Tom and pressed her pelvis against the glass covering the display of pens and pencils.

Her "Hello there" might as well have been *You want to sleep with me, don't you*. Honestly, the woman was desperate to be attractive to people. Which probably covered deep insecurity. Sarah might even feel sorry for her except for an overwhelming urge to tear Vivian to shreds and feed her to zoo animals.

"Hi." Tom gave a nervous chuckle that Sarah wanted to slap him for.

"I'm Vivian."

"Tom Martin." He glanced at Sarah, then back at Vivian, only his eyes took a downward detour before arriving at Vivian's face. "Can I help you?"

"Oh yes, Tom." Said in a low, throaty voice designed to make him think about copulation. "I think you can."

Tom chuckled again, another burst that contained little amusement.

Sarah tried to relax her tight lips enough to smile and show that she felt nothing even approaching homicidal jealousy. If Vivian sniffed out Sarah's attraction to Tom, Sarah would be toast.

"You see, Tom, I want to put up flyers for an aerobics class I'm teaching."

Sarah nearly let out a snort of delight. Who did she think was going to come to a class *she* was teaching? That would be a first-class disaster, one Sarah planned to enjoy.

"Okay if I post one in your front window?" She tossed her hair back over her shoulders in the same way she made every movement, as if it were part of an elaborate seduction ploy.

"Sure. Go right ahead." Tom's eyes dipped up another double-scoop helping. "Sarah, I'll get your pen."

He fled to the back room of the store. Sarah was a little disappointed in Tom. But then it took a person of remarkable strength to face Vivian. Sarah wouldn't hold it against him that he'd gotten flustered the first time—in front of Sarah, no less.

As she'd said so often, when she herself was perfect, then she could afford to judge others. In the meantime, she had the perfect opportunity to bring up the problem with Amber.

"Vivian."

"Sarah."

"Amber came home from your house yester—"

"Oh yes." She turned, wearing concern that would seem genuine on any other face. "My fault she was late. I hope you didn't blame her."

"I would like to ask that in the future you respect my decisions regarding raising my daughter."

Vivian's left eyebrow went up, and Sarah heard herself,

sounding like a prissy, uptight horror of a mother. Damn it, why did Vivian do this to her?

"Uh . . . I just *said* I was sorry she was late."

"I *mean* that I don't let her wear makeup."

"Ah. No makeup." Her voice came out pleasant enough, but Sarah knew she was still making fun. That she thought Sarah was not only prissy and uptight, but unnecessarily strict.

"Amber should be able to enjoy her youth while she's young."

Again the dark brow lifted. "And makeup would get in the way of that how?"

Sarah felt her control slipping. This woman was the absolute limit. "Excuse me if I don't want my daughter growing up to look like a whore."

Silence. Oh dear Lord. What had she done? Her voice had come out much louder than she intended. The words belonged to someone else, not the pleasant, caring woman she tried so hard to be at all times. Tom must have found her pen by now; he was probably cowering in the back, not wanting to come near her.

"You know . . ." Vivian rummaged around in her garish pink handbag, came up with an elongated object, and held it out to Sarah. "I think you need this a lot more than I do."

Behind Vivian, Erin's eyes went wide staring at Vivian's outstretched hand. Then she made a tortured face, as if she was trying not to cry. Or laugh.

Sarah glanced down reluctantly and her face flushed crimson, her throat constricted, a buzzing started in her ears. She knew what it was. And she knew what women did with it. "Put that away."

"No, take it. I'm serious. It's a great stress reliever."

"Put it away." She was whispering, furious, close to tears. If Tom came out and saw that thing . . . "Put it away *now*."

"It's yours. Take it. Great little massager."

Tom's tall form emerged from the back. "Sorry, it took me a while, Sarah. John must have shelved your pen under the—"

He registered the standoff, picked up on the tension. Before he could focus on the dreadful thing in Vivian's hand, Sarah snatched it off her palm and shoved it into the pocket of her rust-colored wool crepe trousers, feeling its weight pulling the light material crooked on her waist and hips.

She tried with every ounce of her considerable inner strength to smile gratefully at Tom, but her body wouldn't cooperate. Her brain was too busy figuring out how to kill Kettle's newest resident without making it look like murder. "Thank you, Tom."

His face showed concern for her, which didn't make her feel better at all. "You're set, Sarah. It's paid for."

"Yes. Terrific." She turned and marched out of the store, the vibrator bumping against her thigh all the way down Main Street. She couldn't even bring herself to call out gracious hellos to passersby.

Bump. Bump. Bump. All the way home to her beautiful house, which didn't soothe her with its tasteful, ordered serenity the way it usually did. All the way upstairs, ignoring Ben's call. He wanted his water freshened, his socks aired, his pillow beaten. He could do it himself for once.

Into their bedroom, over to the wall, where she took the thing out of her pocket and flung it with all her strength into the wicker wastebasket.

A loud buzz filled the room. *Oh Lord, no.* She dug through the refuse and picked up a wad of tissues stuck together. What was that? No one had a cold this week. Was it glue? Had Ben been gluing something? She sniffed.

And gasped. Not glue. He'd been . . .

Without her.

The buzzing seemed to grow louder, as if the thing in the basket were echoing the noise in her head. She groped frantically, hit smooth plastic, yanked the horror up, and flicked the button to off.

The silence in the room was blessed. The roaring in her head was not.

Ben was pleasuring himself without her. Why? If she looked under the bed or in his drawer, would she find pornography? Pictures of some movie star? Or with her luck, of Vivian?

She let the vibrator roll off her limp fingers back into the trash and made sure she'd covered it before she stood and turned. The sight that greeted her was Ben's clothes draped over her chair. The one she'd repeatedly asked him to keep clear.

Did she get *no* consideration? She swept up an armful, stalked out into the hallway, and shoved the pile down the laundry chute, hearing it swish through metal and land in the basement with a satisfying whump. Let *him* find his clothes. Let *him* have to work at something. Besides his penis.

All this time she'd never had an orgasm and he'd been having double.

"Sarah?" His feet padding up the stairs in the slippers she bought him that he hated but refused to return and why the hell not? She put her hands to her hot cheeks and fled again into their bedroom, over by the wastebasket with her back to the window, feeling trapped. He'd take one look and know something extraordinary had happened, and she couldn't tell him what. Probably the only thing she'd ever wanted to hide from him except maybe her silly crush on Tom.

"Sarah." He appeared in the doorway. He'd know. He knew her so well. He'd know and he'd ask, and even though her mind was going a million miles an hour trying to think of a plausible reason she'd be standing next to the wastebasket looking flushed and guiltily furious, it was coming up empty.

His mouth opened as it always did a second or two before he spoke, as if it was able to work faster than his brain.

Here it came.

"Have you seen my green sweater?"

Oh God. She wanted to laugh, but if she opened her mouth, the laugh that came out would be hysterical and evil-sounding. "Your sweater."

"Yes." He gave her a strange look. "I can't find it."

"Where did you look?"

"In my drawer where it always is."

Where it always was, fresh and neatly folded because *she* put it there. "I haven't seen it."

He still stared, waiting for her to turn the house up-side down until she found his precious ugly-as-hell green sweater.

"Maybe you left it at the club? Or in your car?"

He rubbed his head in the gesture that meant this much thinking about inconsequential matters was going to make him cranky. The gesture that always made her want to nurture him and care for him and make his world easy and lovely.

"Maybe I did leave it there."

She sighed, wanting to cry, knowing she wouldn't get the chance even for that. "I'll go check your car."

He came forward and kissed her forehead. "Thanks, Sare-bear. You take such good care of me."

She wrapped her arms around him and laid her head on his chest, eyes closed, inhaling his scent for comfort.

His body stiffened. "Where's the pile of stuff I had over the chair? I need the pants."

Sarah took a long breath. Filled her belly, her rib cage, her chest. Cleared her mind, directed her spirit to a more positive, lighter place. She couldn't let Vivian destroy the richly rewarding life Sarah had built for herself and her family here in her parents' home in Kettle.

"I'm sorry, sweetheart. I thought they were all dirty and put them down the chute." She drew back and smiled lovingly at her husband. "I'll get them right away."

Twelve

<u>Note left on kitchen counter by Ed Branson</u>
<u>Three months before his death</u>

Vivian. I've been called away again this weekend on business. I made reservations for you and whoever at Le Bernardin tonight. Here's a thousand cash to buy yourself something. Not sure when I'll be back or if I'll be able to call. For God's sake don't drink all the whiskey. And Rafael knows you aren't allowed to take the Jag, so don't bother trying.

Ed

Vivian cracked two eggs into a porcelain bowl and whipped them to foamy yellow with a fork. She wasn't much of a cook, but Ed had taught her to make a mean omelet. Their favorite Sunday morning breakfast, with croissants from Fauchon and mangoes or papaya or some other exotic fruit from the fabulously overpriced Zabar's clone food shop on the corner.

This morning the omelet, along with orange juice, coffee, and a donut the bakery woman assured her was made that morning—no croissants worth it in Kettle—all added up to breakfast. For Mike.

Unfortunately, Mike was not at this moment lounging upstairs in her bedroom after a night of carnal pleasures. Sunday morning, he was probably . . . well, who knew?

Vivian would like to know. Ed's routines, preferences, and annoyances became as familiar as breathing. She felt weird not being that close to anyone anymore. Like she was disconnected, free-floating through humanity, looking for a place to land.

She turned the heat on under the skillet and dropped in a tablespoon of butter. Not that she'd like to land on Mike except for a few quickies to get out from under this boulder of grief once in a while. Nothing that would bind her either to staying or to someone so unlike her.

Mike was one of The Good Ones. She was a Bad Girl. She liked men who were a little unavailable, with a tantalizing dash of cruelty. Maybe Mike intrigued her because she'd been through such a time of upheaval and instability that his simplicity and goodness and honesty were a refreshing change. Or maybe the challenge of breaking his late-wife-induced celibacy was just too tempting.

The foaming butter subsided, and she poured in the eggs to sputter and sizzle, shaking the pan with her left hand and stirring with her right. Ed hadn't exactly been a challenge. He'd made a beeline across the room at one of Hefner's Playboy parties in Chicago, put his arm around her shoulders, and said, "I'm Ed. You're mine now."

She'd gone along with it, no problem. An unmarried, powerful, attractive, richer-than-God male? Ideal. The only part she hadn't bargained on was the slow, gradual fall into love over their first year together. Once men knew you loved them, they'd caught you, they'd won, and along with your heart, you lost your power.

When she got out of Kettle, she'd find someone equally rich, but so loathsome that she couldn't come to care for him in a million years.

My, didn't *that* sound like fun.

She folded a third of the omelet over, then tipped the pan so the eggs rolled the rest of the way into a neat package on the waiting plate.

There. She picked up the prepared tray—painted with chubby, yes, *smiling* angels floating through pink and orange clouds—and walked to the back door, one eye on the girl-and-pony clock, which said seven-thirty. She figured Mike for an early riser, but not too early on Sunday, since he didn't have to get up to work.

She crossed to his neat brick house and walked up his front stairs, laughing at the thought that if anyone was watching, they'd be able to count her among Mike's meal-toting suitors. At least she was bringing him something more interesting than a casserole of pasta and canned soup. And with any luck, he'd still be in bed and she could take advantage of his sleepy weakness and serve it up in a way he'd never forget.

A girl could always hope.

Tray balanced on her knee, one hand lifted to ring the bell glowing orange in spite of the early sunlight, she paused and decided on a whim to try the door instead.

Unlocked. Her mind was officially blown. She knew about the no-crime-in-Kettle crap, but Vivian took that as the stuff of legend, nothing anyone would buy into. How could this many people exist in la-la fairyland for so long? What if a psycho lunatic happened by? What if high school kids on drugs or booze decided to go home computer shopping? What if a burglar heard about an entire town of people who didn't lock their doors, and came to party?

Some morning she'd have to get up early and walk into people's houses to catch residents in their showers. *Hi, I'm Vivian. Just wanted to check out your place and see you naked.*

She slipped into Mike's house, carefully maneuvering her tray through the front door so it wouldn't bump or rattle and alert him to her presence.

Done. Even better, she managed to shut the door quietly behind her.

So.

She stood quiet, inhaling the scent of Mike punctuated by French omelet. The place didn't look as she imagined, but then she'd imagined a house that would fit him, and this one had clearly been decorated by the fair and beautiful Rosemary. Who had great taste, the bitch. A cream rug over flawless hardwood, no "character" nail holes here. Overstuffed furniture in beige and/or burgundy, with contrasting and complementary pillows. Glass coffee table with intricate iron support. Wooden mantel and fireplace with glass doors over black brick. It all added up to stylish middle-class comfort.

And it was immaculate. Did Mike even live in this house, or just show up to eat and sleep? Did he clean it himself or did he have a little missy who did it for him? Inquiring minds wanted to know.

She started silently up the hardwood staircase, placing her feet by the wall where creaks were least likely to happen, bursting with the fun of surprising him. The look on his face would be priceless.

At the top of the stairs, a hallway. Door number one? Door number two? Still no noise, was he even home? Then she heard it, the slight swishing of limbs on sheets.

Jackpot.

She pushed door number one open silently and tiptoed into another female-decorated room. An ornate iron bed with an elegant green, gray, and gold comforter, shams, and decorative pillows piled on a wooden chest at its foot. A dresser oh-so-charmingly bedecked with the type of Bo Peep porcelain figures that turned her stomach. And framed photographs everywhere. On surfaces, on walls, in a collage over the desk. Photographs she didn't need to glance at to know the subject. Mike and Rosemary, Rosemary and Mike. Their wedding day, the day after their wedding day, the day after that, the anniversary of the day after that . . .

Vivian returned her gaze to Mike, lying on his back on the right side of the queen bed as if he were still saving the other side for Rosemary, left arm curled around his head, breathing gently through his open mouth, and found herself at an unexpected loss.

The plan had been to speak up immediately. Say something sassy and raunchy, like *Hey, sailor, your best-ever wet dream has arrived with plenty to eat—and breakfast, too.*

Instead, she wanted to do either of two things. Strip and climb into Rosemary's side to defile the holy space with her own naked body, or turn around and take her rapidly cooling omelet back to her own house. This was starting to feel too much like another stupid-assed mistake. Like baring her tits at Harris's. Letting Amber go home without washing her face. Handing Sarah the vibrator in public.

Mike's eyes opened slowly, brilliant blue against the off-white sheets. For some reason that startled her, as if she'd expected their color to fade while he slept.

His head snapped up toward her, then sank back on his pillow. "Vivian."

"I brought you breakfast in bed. To thank you for helping me and to say sorry for being a bitch the other evening." She lifted the tray briefly, hating that she sounded like a girl with a crush who felt totally out of place standing in a bedroom another woman still belonged in. "It's probably cold now."

He dragged himself up to sitting, glancing at the clock, and oh, be still her naughty bits, he wasn't wearing a shirt. His chest, shoulders, and arms should be on display at the Louvre. No fair men got to wake up looking as good as when you put them to bed. She looked like a sideshow freak each and every morning.

"Breakfast." He eyed her with that superior amused look she was starting to hate. "Well, thanks. Very nice of you."

"Don't get used to it."

"I wouldn't begin to."

"Orange juice, omelet, donut from Sidler's, coffee. And of course . . . me."

"You're part of breakfast?"

"Sure." She kept her voice light, moved forward, and set the tray over his lap. Sat on the edge of the bed and let her gaze travel over his torso for her own personal enjoyment. "The best part."

"I'll keep that in mind."

She glanced down pointedly, imagining his A.M. hard-on under the poufy cover. "I hope you wake up hungry."

"Yes, ma'am, I do." He drained the glass of juice, the column of his throat shifting. She should have thought to bring him more. "This looks delicious. Smells it, too."

He started to eat, and she got off the bed and prowled the room, peering at the photographs. Most, as expected, of Mike and Rosemary.

She was beautiful. Exactly as Vivian pictured her. Petite, blond, wholesome, slightly fragile, gazing adoringly at a grinning Mike at the beach. Gazing adoringly at a grinning Mike on a ship somewhere. Quite a few gazing adoringly at a grinning Mike on their wedding day.

"Good omelet, thanks."

"You're welcome." She picked up one of the wedding pictures. "Did you marry her in Kettle?"

"Yes." He spoke with his mouth full. "Her family was from here."

"Yours, too?"

"Mine, too."

"Your parents still alive?"

"Sure."

She blinked and turned to face him. Somehow she thought of him as completely alone in the world. "They're still in Kettle?"

"Yes." He took a sip of coffee. "I have dinner there every Sunday night like a good son should."

Her mouth spread into a smile at his mildly sarcastic tone. She loved when he cracked the sweet-boy mold and showed some spice.

"You close to them?"

"They're good people."

She let him get away with the dodge and looked back at the photograph, at Mike's grin of pure bliss, at Rosemary's sappy devotion. "How about her parents?"

"They moved away."

She wandered over to the closet and drew back the sliding wooden door. Her mouth dropped. Keeping it open for effect, she turned back to Mike, who had the sense to look uncomfortable.

Rosemary's clothes were still hanging in the damn closet.

Jesus. She let out a harsh laugh that was not at all about humor. "I'm sorry, were you planning to let this woman die any time soon?"

"Close the door."

"Why, you don't want her smell to escape?"

"Close it." He thudded the mug back down; coffee sloshed over the rim and scalded the cheery floaty angels.

"Right." She closed the door and leaned against it, arms folded, glaring accusingly. "Now tell me again how you are soooo much farther along in the 'process' than I am."

"Oh for—"

"At least I admit Ed's gone."

"Stop."

"Oh no." She waggled her finger. "This isn't the other night. This isn't about me taunting you where I've no right to. I've got you by the balls this time, fair and square."

He picked up the coffee, took several leisurely sips, apparently not intending to continue the conversation.

Vivian wanted to roar. Nothing pissed her off more than being shut out. Ed's favorite trick, he knew her buttons like he knew fine cognacs and cigars and g-spots.

"What is the point of keeping her clothes here, Mike?" She gestured to the door with the neat row of dresses, blouses, and skirts behind it. "She's been dead two years. How long are you going to hide behind that shit?"

"Probably as long as you're going to hide behind the makeup and big-tits attitude."

She stared at him incredulously. "Excuse me?"

"What I said."

"Like I'm wearing this as some costume?"

"Yes."

She burst out laughing. A big nasty blast of enjoyment.

"You know I hate to disappoint you, sweetheart, but hey, news flash. I don't have an inner Rosemary longing to get out." She spread her arms wide. "What you see is what you get."

"Right."

She laughed again, a hoarse shout of it. He was too damn much. "Sorry to burst your Disney bubble, but it's true. Ask anyone who knows me."

"Who does?"

"Ed did." Her laughter this time sounded strangled. Her body had tightened to the verge of shaking. She needed to back away from this conversation and this room and this house, but her tragic flaw was that she never backed away from anything. "Ed knew me inside out, and look how he treated me. Not like an ingenue, I'll tell you that."

"Ed was an abusive asshole."

"Yeah, but he was *my* abusive asshole. And when it got too much I killed him and solved all my problems." She let her arms drop, as if that explained everything, aware her breath was coming too high, her voice sounding manic, and that he'd pick up on all of it and be fooled by none, damn his Boy Scout honor. "Does that sound like Anne of Green Gables?"

"You didn't kill him."

She tried to laugh again with the same ha-ha viciousness, but it came out a flat croak. "Sure I did. I told you."

"You didn't kill him."

Christ. He was shaking her up. Again. The only kind of shaking she wanted from him was from an orgasm big enough to cause an earthquake, and he kept getting to her. And for some sick reason, she kept coming back for more. She should have stayed home and eaten the damn eggs herself.

"What makes you think I didn't?"

"Instinct." He put the tray on the floor, lay back, and crossed his arms over his face. "Thanks for breakfast."

Dis-missed.

She approached the bed, wanting to tear his hands from his face and scream at him to stop being such a damn disappearing coward. "You don't get off that easily. This conversation was actually about you."

"Leave me alone, Vivian."

She dove onto the bed, moved directly over him, supporting herself on her arms. His body stilled. She doubted he was even breathing.

But she was. Practically panting. Being this close, on a nice cozy bed, even not touching him yet, she felt her body warm and change. She became hyper-aware of how her bra cupped her breasts, how the seam of her jeans pulled between her legs. Her muscles felt strong and her body felt clean and lithe and sensual and alive.

Yes. Yes. Yes. This was what she needed.

She lowered slowly onto his body, hating the clothes and the comforter—more like a frustrater at the moment. She wanted naked skin on naked skin, to press against him cheek to toe, and she wanted it Right Now.

"It's time to move on, Mike," she whispered to him, rocking her pelvis slowly and gently. Push. Release. Push. Release. "For both of us. We both need this."

"You're lying on my omelet." A hint of uncertainty in his stern voice—she was getting to him.

"But Mike, omelets are soft." She whispered again, lowered her lips to his chest and inhaled the warm scent of his skin, curled her hands over his muscular shoulders. Push. Release. Push. Release. Her patience thinned; her desire thickened. She wanted to lose herself in passion, in his strength, to forget all the shit for a few blissful hours as often as he could give it to her. "I don't seem to be lying on anything soft."

His arms moved; he gripped her hips and pushed up against her. Once. Twice. She gave a gasping moan, oh God, it was going to be so good . . .

He strained up, flipped her off him over chez Rosemary, and she found herself on her back—one of her very favorite places to be, thankyouverymuch.

Except instead of starting the lovely trip to happy town, he grabbed her wrists, pinned them over her head, and stared forcefully into her eyes.

"Listen to me, Vivian. Carefully."

"Ye-e-es?"

"When I'm inside you . . . it's going to be about you and me, understand?"

She nodded automatically. Him and her, what the hell else would it be about?

"Not about Ed, not about your anger, not about your grief, and not about mine. Okay?"

She forced herself not to roll her eyes, nodded again, legs open, hips straining upward. "Yes. Fine. Good."

Just do it, Boy Scout.

"Until then . . ."

She blinked. Until *when?*

". . . nothing is going to happen. You understand?"

"*What?*"

He sighed, humor coming back into his eyes. "I didn't think so."

She gaped at him, the beautiful orgasm she hadn't had yet grinding its teeth, shaking the bars, and growling to be let out. "*You're not going to screw me?*"

Mike winced. "God, Vivian, you should work for Hallmark, you have such a way with words."

She giggled when she most wanted to sock him or flounce out of the room in humiliated indignation. "You are the most exasperating, pathetic excuse for a man I have ever *met*. What the hell mind-control drugs do they give you Kettle people?"

He laughed. A loud, ringing, openmouthed, masculine laugh that stopped her struggle. She lay back watching him. He didn't let it last long, but in that second or three, she had a feeling she saw how he'd been with Rosemary, and a dark pleasure-pain settled into her chest.

He stopped laughing, smiled down at her, not saying anything, just smiling right into her eyes, and a weird, soft, gooey thing started erasing the pain.

Worse, he bent down and kissed her cheek, then her other cheek, then her forehead, like she was his favorite sister, or like they'd already made love and were getting to the glowy, sweet part after. The part she loved second best, though Ed hadn't done much more than roll over and snore drunkenly for the past several years.

Worst of all, Mike let go of her hands, slid his arms around her, and pulled her into a gentle embrace that managed also to feel powerful and rock-solid supportive. He laid his cheek next to hers and she closed her eyes and struggled again, this time mentally.

"So help me, Mike, if you start singing right now I'll have to kill you, too."

A low male chuckle—damn, she was even starting to love making him laugh.

"You didn't like my singing?"

"It was agony."

He lifted his head, his smile fading, and she wanted to pull him down and kiss him so badly it shocked her. "Do me a favor."

"What . . ." She wasn't going to like this one.

"You didn't kill Ed. Say it."

"Geez, Mike, will you give me the tiniest break here?"

"Say it."

"If you know, then why do I have to?"

"Humor me." He leaned in close to her ear. "I promise I won't tell anyone the horrible truth of your innocence."

"It's the only innocence I have left."

He squeezed her tight for a second. "Say it."

She turned her head away, throat cramping. "I didn't kill him. He pulled the damn CD player into the tub and gave himself a heart attack. Happy?"

"Yes." He stroked back hair that had fallen over her cheek. "Thanks."

"You're welcome." She rolled her eyes. "So *now* can we have sex?"

"No."

She didn't think so. "Okay, then it's your turn."

Also his turn to look wary. "What?"

"How come you still have Rosemary's clothes?"

He rolled away from her, and her body started to chill in his absence. "I don't want to talk about—"

"Ah-ah-ah. I didn't, either. Spill or I'll duck under the covers and blow you."

"That's supposed to be a threat?"

"The way you are, yes."

"Touché." He grinned, and she wanted to run her fingers through his hair and feel its soft, bristly texture against her palms. She should have done it when he was closer.

"Did she blow you often?"

"Jesus, Vivian."

"Was she any good at it?" She rolled over onto her stomach and scooted closer, trying not to laugh, thinking this was almost more fun than sex. Mike was a blast to tease; he took it in stride, didn't glower like Ed. "Was she sweet on the outside, wild woman in? The whole madonna-whore thing?"

"Get away from me." He shoved her playfully.

She giggled and poked him in the side, gratified when he jumped. Oh happy day, he was ticklish. "Best sex of your life? Is that why you can't let her go?"

"Off. Off my bed." He pushed at her with his body, sliding her inexorably to the edge, and as she squealed in laughing protest, gave her a final push so she landed on hardwood butt-first with an ungraceful thud.

She deserved every bit of that, and they both knew it, but still, he peered over the edge. "You okay?"

She nodded, breathless from laughing, and that tender thing happened again over his concern for her. Great. Next she'd be painting *extra* smiley faces in her kitchen. "I'm okay."

"Good." He frowned down at her, and she sensed he was struggling over something he wanted—or maybe didn't want—to say.

"Ye-e-es?"

"Just so you know . . ." His eyes narrowed, he glanced away, then back. "The sex was boring."

He sat up, tossed off the blankets, and walked, stark naked, into the master bathroom, leaving her on her sore butt on the floor, as surprised as she'd ever been in her entire life.

Thirteen

Original e-mail from Erin, mailed to her list

If you're happy and you know it:
1. *Tell someone.*
2. *Dance in your living room.*
3. *Paint a sunny picture.*
4. *Sing just for yourself.*
5. *Wear clothes that don't match.*
6. *Bake something fattening and forget to count calories.*
7. *Kiss people you love.*
8. *Tell someone you admire that you do.*
9. *Smile at a frowning stranger.*
10. *Do something to make someone else's day happy, too.*

Pass this along to all the happy people you know and make their lives richer and better. Friendships are like plants: The better you treat them, the stronger they'll grow.

"Hey." A finger nudged Erin's cheek, then the familiar rasp of her husband's stubble and the soft touch of his lips. "Wake up, sweet pea."

Erin opened her eyes to find Joe's bedside lamp turned on. It felt like the middle of the night; she knew what that meant.

She yawned and squinted at the clock. "What time's it?"

"Three-thirty." His hand slid under her nightgown, over her breast, his huge palm making slow, warm circles. "I want some nookie from the most beautiful girl in the world."

"Hmmm." She pretended to consider, though they both knew she wouldn't refuse. Times like this, when he was sweet and gentle, she could almost remember why she married him, remember those early years when they'd been kids really, and how awestruck they'd been by the power of what their bodies could do together.

When he was sweet and gentle like this she could still get herself to respond, though it took more work than before Joy was born. "I guess that sounds pretty good."

His hand went lower, teased between her legs, then trailed back up to her breasts. He smelled good tonight—true, like Joe, not booze fumes or cigarette smoke or meat or rage.

She thought he was an okay lover, when he was normal like this, not that she had anything to compare him to. He knew her body inside out, could measure her responses minutely, whether he was doling out pleasure, pain, or that odd middle ground between them. When he wanted to please her, he was expert. When he wanted to hurt her, he was genius.

His mouth settled over hers, and she stifled her recoil. She hated kissing with sleep-filled nighttime mouths, but it had never bothered Joe. His hand fluttered between her legs, and she concentrated on that, on the hot feeling spreading through her, and not on the stale, thick taste on their tongues.

She reached for him, found him hard as he often was when he woke up in the middle of the night. Especially if he'd been dreaming, though she was pretty sure never about her. "Is this for me?"

"Only you, Erin. There's only you." He whispered the words into her hair, breath coming faster, pumping his hips. "You own me, baby girl. You rule me, I'd die without you."

She increased the rhythm of her hand as he increased the rhythm of his fingers on her sweet spot. She used to thrill to words like that, used to think no woman had ever been better or more deeply loved. Until she understood what the words really meant.

She tried to tamp down her anger, tried to refocus on that sleepy, calm place she'd been earlier, when she could almost bring back Joe of long ago and remember how much and how passionately she loved that he adored her. That was a first. Back then that was enough. Back then that was worth anything.

Now in their marital bed, he climbed onto her, slid inside and started to move, keeping most of his weight on his elbows, moving, moving, sweat already forming on his body. Within a few minutes she'd feel the drips from his forehead, his chest, and from under his arms.

Erin rocked up against him, freeing her mind from their bed, from his big, sweaty body, from everything but the hard penis rubbing inside her. She concentrated all her sensations there, and let her subconscious mind go where it wanted.

She was running down a wide, straight, smooth road, at high speed, faster than she'd ever run before. No fatigue in her legs, no strain in her lungs. On either side lay cornfields, stalks waist-high, farmed in straight rows. Each row as she passed flashed on into infinity, the next, then the next. A burst of energy caught her; her speed increased impossibly. The rows and stalks began to blur green, the energy roared inside her, in her pumping legs, in her pumping arms.

Then her feet barely needed to touch the ground anymore; she spread her arms wide, jumped, and soared into space, watching Kettle fall away, her clothes fall away, soaring up and up, feeling the wind blowing over her naked body, up and up into the vastness of space.

The orgasm came, hot and satisfying, and she made herself yell through it, the way Joe liked her to, though left on her own, she'd never dilute such a great feeling with noise.

Joe pulled out immediately and turned her over with eager hands. Erin obediently got on her knees and stuffed a pillow under her belly.

He grabbed her hips, impatient to be back inside her. Her orgasms turned him on, he said, but since she'd had Joy he needed her ass facing him, he said. She was tighter that way.

Erin never mentioned that if he was bigger than a Chicago-style wiener, she would probably be plenty tight.

He pushed in and started thrusting hard, the way he needed

to in order to come. He spread her cheeks while he pumped her in this position, and she knew he was imagining himself in her other hole where he liked to be way too often for her taste. But at least he was only imagining it today.

Now that she'd had her own orgasm, she was tired and wanted to be back asleep. She moaned and panted and made encouraging noises, let her body swing forward and back as if he were slamming her so hard she couldn't help it. He'd brought home porn movies a few times and it seemed he got off most on the women who looked like they were getting pounded the hardest.

Big surprise.

She wanted him to be as turned on as possible. He'd rub her raw if he took a long time, so she did what she could to help him along. Plus she didn't want to be smacked, not in the quiet of the night, not that she was ever wild about it, and he would start doing that if he couldn't come quickly the other way.

Luckily, he was getting close; she could tell by the way he sucked air in and out through clenched teeth, over and over again so that flecks of spit landed on her back.

His right hand left her hip, and she only just had time to register dread before it smacked down on her ass, a slap that would leave a red mark he sometimes spread his semen over when he was done. To soothe the skin, he said. To use his body to heal the pain his body caused her. And besides, what was the point of wasting sperm up her barren cunt? He said that, too, once, when he was drunk, though most of the time he came in her anyway.

The sting from the slap faded. He was in a good mood, he

wouldn't really hurt her, wouldn't hit her in the same place again too soon.

"Oh Erin, oh baby." Another slap. On her other cheek, harder that time. "Ohhhh, ohhhh, ohhhh."

She wished he'd shut up. His moaning embarrassed her; he never used to do it. She dreamed about men with whom sex would be loving and sweet and transcendent, not fresh out of a zoo cage.

At least it was nearly over. He shoved and shoved, shuddered, shouted, shoved again so she felt the sharp stab of him slamming against her cervix.

"Ohhhh, aahhhhh, Erin, ohhhh baby, yes, yes, yes."

She closed her eyes. *Shut up, shut up, shut up.* It mortified her, this loud grunting enjoyment, and it always ruined what started out so tenderly and well.

But now it was done. He'd turn out the light, slump down, moan and sigh a few more times, tell her he loved her more than his own life, and fall asleep, snoring to wake the dead.

"I love you. More than my own life, baby." He hugged her to him and kissed her, his harsh breathing gradually slowing. This was when Joe went softest and most malleable, when she could get things she couldn't any other time.

"Joe? Can I ask you something?"

"Sure, baby." He yawned; then his lips made a pasty smacking sound.

"Vivian's aerobics classes. Can I go?"

Silence that started her adrenaline running.

"You really want to, huh?"

"Well . . ." She held her breath in the darkness. If she sounded too eager, he'd say no. "It sounds fun."

"That woman is trouble. I'm telling you." He squeezed her so hard, she nearly had to gasp for air. "You should stay away from trash like that."

Disappointment stabbed, and angry panic. "But Joe . . ."

"No." His voice sharpened, her sign to drop it. She'd get nowhere tonight. And probably not ever.

"Okay. Good night."

"Good night, sweet baby girl. Sleep well."

Erin pressed her lips together, knowing she wouldn't sleep at all, let alone well. When was the last time she asked for anything just for herself? She couldn't even remember.

She waited until he was asleep. Until the first faint color of dawn started to relieve the blackness of night. Then she eased out of bed, careful, slow. She often woke early and left him, to paint. He wouldn't notice anything different. It was Sunday. He'd sleep until nine. She had hours to herself.

She grabbed a pair of panties from her dresser and a panty liner from the bathroom to catch the postsex stuff, which would drip dismally out of her all morning, and went into her studio, mood lightening as it always did in Joy's old nursery. Joe had been sweet giving the room to her as a studio. Joan had wasted no time pointing out how much nicer the space would be as a family room. But for once, Joe chose Erin over his mother, and the room stayed hers. She was grateful, she guessed. Or ought to be.

In the corner closet, once painted blue with ducks swimming along the bottom of the door, she rummaged until she found the box of personal things she didn't care to share with Joe. He never came in here anymore. Said he thought the room was creepy. She figured he was eaten up with guilt or grief or both.

At the bottom of the box, under the few outfits of Joy's she'd managed to save, under a rattle Joe had only cracked on his ax rampage, a still-new stuffed chick missing a foot, and one fuzzy white infant sock, she found her shorts, and her favorite soft shirt, thick terry socks, her headband and her shoes, broken in and smudged and worn, familiar like old friends.

She wanted to run.

The white nylon nightgown slid easily over her head—she preferred pajamas but Joe didn't like them, too masculine on a woman, he said, and he wanted her in white—and she pulled on the panties with the liner, shorts, the shirt, socks, shoes, the headband, feeling her muscles already strengthening and straining with anticipation. It had been too many years.

Two steps out into the hall, she stopped, put her hands to the hem of her shirt to take it off. What was she doing? What did she think would happen if she got caught? Even if Joe didn't see her, if anyone in Kettle did, all it would take was one comment to Joe . . .

Dampness leaked down between her legs, and she grimaced. Let go of the hem of her shirt. Walked to the front door and unlocked it. Let herself out into the chilly morning that smelled of fall and freedom. She wanted to run.

No one was around. She stretched carefully in the driveway, laughter bubbling up now and then, nervous or happy, she couldn't tell which. Probably both.

She struck out up Maple Avenue at an easy lope, feeling her lungs, legs, and arms groping for their long-ago accustomed rhythms, not finding them yet.

On Main Street she turned away from town, feeling the stiffness in her hips gradually loosening, her feet finding their way, her lungs settling.

She ran faster, farther, leaving Kettle behind. A few cars passed. No one honked. No one made a comment.

Her courage grew along with her elation. She ran until she knew she'd gone farther than a good halfway point, a mistake no runner with her experience should make. But to hell with it. This felt too good to waste, and who knew when or if she'd get out again.

Finally she gave in to the inevitable, jogged in a tight semicircle, and headed back toward Main Street. The town approached and she felt her feet clumping heavier for reasons that had nothing to do with the fatigue clawing at her body.

On impulse, she turned onto a gravel and dirt track that ran into the forest. If she remembered right, it looped around through a few properties and came back to the main road. A small, useless delay, but it felt necessary.

The track was rough going, plenty of opportunities to twist an ankle if she wasn't careful. The surface had been better kept up when she was in high school. Leaves fluttered down here and there; a squirrel scolded from a maple tree; the chill of the air made a beautiful contrast to the heat that had built in her body.

It had been too long since she'd done this. She'd feel it tomorrow, her muscles would be sore and she'd have to force them to move normally so Joe wouldn't suspect. But she couldn't stop, couldn't make herself break down into a walk, couldn't face giving in to the end of this fabulous flight.

The first house appeared, a beige-shingled ranch, who lived there? An older couple used to, would they still be alive?

She turned to peer at the front window, catching a glimpse of movement, remembering the white-haired woman working on her knees in the front garden in the summertime, her husband bringing her a glass of what looked like iced tea.

Erin's foot hit something, a stick or rut, and she tripped and went down, momentum dragging her skin across sharp pebbles sticking out of the dirt.

Ouch.

She lay for a second, letting her brain adjust to the fact that she was on the ground instead of running. Then she sat up cautiously, checking in with her body for any injury. Stupid not to be watching her feet on terrain like this.

"Are you all right?" A male voice, young-sounding. She looked up and saw him stepping through the gate in front of what must be his house now. He must be new to Kettle; she'd never seen him. He was dark, some Mediterranean blood in him, she'd guess. "I saw you fall, are you okay?"

And handsome like the sun had burst over her on a foggy, dreadful day.

"I'm fine." She stood awkwardly, wanting to cross her arms over her chest, wanting to disappear inside herself because there was no way she could appear as beautiful to him as he did to her, and it wasn't fair.

"You're bleeding." He pointed, and she glanced down and registered blood from a surface scratch, dusty around the edges, a child's skinned knee.

"It's nothing." She took a step back, knowing she was staring at him like a weirdo, but unable to stop. His eyes were dark and round, like a baby's. The surrounding lashes were long and full enough to be female, but the thick wiry hair, high cheekbones, strong nose, and angular chin took any chance of being feminine far, far away.

So let him think she was weird. He'd be right.

"Do you want a Band-Aid or something?" He glanced again at her knee, then back up into her eyes, and she felt the jolt of attraction again, even stronger. Thank goodness her cheeks were flushed from running so he wouldn't be able to see them color.

No Band-Aid. She needed to get back to the house. Creep back inside and shower, pull out some paints and let her body cool, so she wouldn't show any signs that she'd been doing anything but sitting inside painting.

"No, I shouldn't—I can't—I . . . don't need one." Her arms crept around her in spite of her telling them not to.

"Okay." He was frowning now, staring at her, and she knew he was coming up with theories to explain her strange behavior, none of them flattering. "I'm Jordan, by the way."

"I have to go." She turned and started off, leaving him standing there expecting her to reply with her own name. She couldn't give him even that much. In another life maybe they'd get to be friends, then lovers, then marry and have children. But she wasn't living another life. No one got to do that. All you got was your own, and if it sucked, that was tough shit.

She got to the sharpest part of the loop, where it started curving back to the road, and she slowed and stopped. Turned, hoping he'd still be standing there, wondering about her, so she could call out, "Good-bye," and at least give him that.

But he'd already gone inside, probably shaking his head over the crazy woman who hadn't even had the sense to accept a Band-Aid for her scraped knee. So she jogged home, let herself silently into the silent house, stretched carefully, took a shower, and put on her own Band-Aid, set out her paints and her half-finished canvas, then sat by an open window to erase the pink from her cheeks and cool off completely, while her running clothes washed and dried.

Then she put the clean shirt and shorts and socks and headband and shoes back in the box under the few baby things of Joy's she couldn't bear to get rid of, tucked the box back into the closet, and told herself to forget any of the morning had really happened.

Fourteen

Entry in Sarah's diary
April
Freshman year at Cornell

Dear Diary,

Well I did it last night. With Ben of course. It wasn't quite like I expected. Not that I thought it would be fireworks and the earth moving the first time. Well, maybe I did. It was just . . . personal and naked and sort of . . . unnatural. I know that sounds stupid, but that's how it felt. And I wanted to scream with how much it hurt, but I didn't want him to think he'd messed up or to feel bad about it.

I love this guy so much it aches in my heart all day long. He acts like everything I say or think is the

*most amazing thing he's ever heard. He says he can
lie there and listen to me all day and never get tired
of hearing what's going on in his Sare-bear's brain. I
know we're going to be madly in love forever.*

*Thank God I didn't have sex with Tom when he
wanted to back in high school. It's so much more special having waited for Ben.*

Gotta go study.

"*Dinner.*" Sarah carried the hollowed pumpkin—one of
her Harvest Moons—to the grand table in her dining room
that used to belong to her maternal grandparents, an elegant
lawyer couple from upstate New York who thought Sarah's
mother married beneath her.

Sarah set the pumpkin, three-quarters full of fresh, homemade pumpkin soup, on the silver trivet she and Ben had
gotten from the Clarks for their wedding. The trivet sparkled
like new; she needed to use it more often so it could develop
a proper patina.

"*Dinner.*" She called out again and waited, poised and proud.
The table was decorated with a tray of greens on which she'd
arranged Red Delicious apples, carefully carved into candle
holders. So pretty.

No one from her family materialized or answered. Sarah
sighed. She'd made dinner early tonight, since it was so nice
for the family to be together, before all its members disappeared into their evenings, Ben at his computer, Amber into
homework or three-hour phone conversations with her
friends or that boyfriend of hers. Sarah thought it would be
nice to have a relaxed meal. Especially one as enticing as

pumpkin soup, roast pork loin with figs, couscous, and salad. For dessert she'd made a deep-dish apple and dried cranberry pie with walnuts.

Extra effort for dinner on Sunday was always special. Sarah's mother had faithfully made a roast every week. People knew now that so much fatty meat wasn't good for them, but that wasn't reason enough to stop the tradition entirely. Besides, pork was so much leaner than it used to be.

"*Dinner.*" She called louder, trying not to sound exasperated, but really, she shouldn't need a megaphone to summon her family to the table.

"I'm going out, Mom." Amber's voice came hurtling down the stairs along with her body. "I thought I told you."

Sarah frowned. Amber most certainly had *not* told her. Sarah would have remembered something like that and wouldn't have put so much effort into making an elegant family meal. "Amber, you didn't tell me, and I'm sorry, but I want us to have a nice dinner together. You're always rushing off. Besides, it's Sunday, school tomorrow, and you shouldn't be out."

"But it's a special night."

Sarah folded her arms across her chest, picturing her own mother doing the same thing, and wasn't it funny how you suddenly found yourself a parent on the other side of the child-parent divide. Sarah even remembered how exasperating her mother had seemed to her, as doubtless Sarah seemed to Amber. Now she just wondered how common sense could desert teenagers so thoroughly, as doubtless her mother had wondered about her.

"Special, how?" She tried to picture Amber middle-aged,

facing a rebellious teenage daughter, crossing her arms and pulling down her mouth and brows.

"We're going to Tanya's house to work on costumes for the party."

Sarah's pulled-down brows lifted. Tanya was probably the least likely person in all of Kettle to plan ahead and put serious work into a Halloween costume. "Really."

Amber started to play with a strand of hair. Liar, liar . . . But such a beautiful girl. Her skin was still so smooth and young and perfect. It hadn't started to turn saggy traitor under her chin, hadn't started to puff out under her eyes. "Will Larry be there?"

"I dunno." Amber scowled at the hardwood under her feet.

Sarah sighed. He was going to be there. He was going to take Amber out in the bushes and try to get his dick in her if he hadn't already. Sarah detested him, his stringy hair, dirty nails, strange body odor, and appallingly sloppy clothing. And that attitude. A living, breathing, extended middle finger.

Where was her husband?

She called out his name. No answer. Ben was nursing a cold; had the congestion affected his hearing? "*Ben?*"

"Just a minute." His voice carried out from his study with more than a hint of annoyance, and Sarah had to force her face to stay pleasant in front of Amber. No one was going to be gladder than she when that book of his was finished. Then she hoped he'd get this whole writer thing out of his system.

"So can I go?"

"Not on a school night."

"Geez, Mom, I'm not in elementary school anymore."

"That's exactly why you need to stay in. Now come to dinner."

"Mom." A tear spilled from each pretty eye and rolled over the fine-pored slopes of her cheeks. "I'm begging you. Please, can I go out? I'll be home by nine, I swear."

"Will Larry be there?" Sarah insisted on honesty. She'd told Amber since she was two years old that nothing she could do could possibly be worse than lying about it.

"Yes." Amber barely got the word out, wiping away a tear.

Sarah was proud of her. "I just don't want you getting in trouble with that boy, Amber."

"He's not trouble, Mom. I wish you'd try to—"

"Is he pressuring you to have sex?"

"*Mom*." She practically shrieked in outrage and embarrassment.

Sarah put her hands to her temples. She hated this type of discussion. Her mother had never had to have it with Sarah. She gave her a book and trusted Sarah would do the right thing, which she had. Sarah didn't have that kind of trust in Amber. Amber seemed ripe for sex in a way Sarah never had been. Amber would probably have an orgasm her first time.

"Just remember this." Sarah took a deep breath. Her soup would be cooling, maybe getting an unattractive skin across the top. "If he really cares for you, he won't pressure you to do something you don't want to."

"I know, Mom." Her voice was softer, conciliatory. "He won't. He's really a sweet guy."

Sarah supremely doubted that. And she wasn't at all sure Amber didn't want to have sex with that animal-boy in the first place. But she'd said her piece as all mothers had said theirs since time began, and there wasn't a lot more she could do. "Homework done?"

"Yes." Amber brightened, sensing Sarah about to relent.

"All of it?"

"All of it. I swear." She fixed shining, hopeful eyes on her mother.

Sarah sighed. She supposed having a nice romantic dinner alone with Ben would be pretty wonderful. They'd had so few chances to talk recently. Like in the past sixteen years. "All right. You can go."

"Thanks, Mom." Amber rushed forward to hug Sarah, and Sarah felt like a gold-medal winner. A gold-medal winner concerned about her daughter's virginity.

"Back by nine, young lady."

"I promise." Amber gave another squeeze and rushed out the front door, probably afraid Mom would change her mind.

Mom went to close the door behind her daughter, who bounded down the street, skirt flouncing behind her, reminding Sarah of a fleeing white-tailed deer. Except the danger wasn't here at home. The danger was out there in the direction she was heading.

Sarah closed the door, letting herself be sad for a moment that the darkness settled so early this time of year, and that her sweet child had grown up so quickly.

"Ben?" She headed into his office, hoping the roast would keep warm enough tented with foil in the kitchen until they finished their soup. Maybe she should bring out some really good wine and put on some Vivaldi. Maybe she and Ben could talk and make love, and maybe she owed it to him tonight to tell him about the orgasms she hadn't been having for two decades.

"Ready for dinner, sweetheart? It's on the table." She took two steps into his office, and her heart sank clear to the bottom of her brass-bit loafers from Talbots.

Ben was wearing his Packers sweatshirt, green sweat pants, and white socks and green and gold athletic shoes. Packers night. Of course. He always watched the game with his buddies, George and Bob, rather coarse men to her way of thinking, but Ben was devoted to them. Which meant he'd be leaving right after dinner.

He finished blowing his nose, checked his watch, and started the process of shutting down his computer. "Sorry, honey, I have the game tonight."

"The game is at seven-thirty. You have time for dinner. I made a special one. Pumpkin soup and roast pork loin with—"

"George made his six-alarm chili so I'm going over early." Her words must have registered all of a sudden because he had the grace to look stricken. "Didn't I tell you?"

"No." She drew herself up straight, wishing she'd told Amber she couldn't go to the party so someone would be home to enjoy her food. "You didn't tell me. Or maybe I forgot."

She added the last so she wouldn't sound accusing, though if he'd said something about skipping dinner, she would have remembered.

"I'm sorry, Sarah."

Yes, he was sorry, she could see it in the way his eyebrows met up high in the middle, and the way his voice cracked. But not yet sorry enough to say he'd cancel. Not sorry enough to stay home and enjoy her cooking and spending time with her. She waited, still hoping. Stupidly hoping, as she'd stupidly hoped in situations like this for years and years and years.

"I'm already late." He glanced at his watch again.

"Sure." Her voice might as well have blown across six glaciers, one right after the other, for all the warmth in it. "You wouldn't want to miss the pre-pre-pre-game show."

"Oh now, Sare-bear." He kissed her, and it was a miracle his warm, moist lips didn't stick to the deep freeze of her cheek.

She was pissed. Royally. Unattractively. Ragingly. What part of her cycle was she in? She heard that women's PMS brains scanned the same as brains of crazy people. Given how she was feeling right now, that did not surprise her.

"Have a great time, honey." She wanted to add that she'd enjoy a quiet evening alone, but knew she would sound insincere and possibly furious.

She'd always felt it important to keep perspective in times like these. Amber and Ben both had occasions that were important to them. Just an unfortunate coincidence that she had put so much effort into the meal and so much anticipation into the thought of her family enjoying it together.

Ben kissed her again, gathered up his keys, and after asking if Sarah had seen his Packers parka, and after she found it at the bottom of the coat closet where it had fallen, he left through the front door, blowing his stuffy nose, and she was alone.

Well.

She went back into the dining room and sat at her own

place, and poured herself a rather large glass of the Alsatian Gewürztraminer her cooking magazine recommended with the soup.

The soup was delicious, the sweetness of the pumpkin balanced by onion and a good kick of fresh ginger, a touch of curry and another of cream.

After the soup, she lingered until her wine was gone, enjoying the candlelight and the Vivaldi, then she brought out the roast, tepid now, but it couldn't be helped. She served herself a nice portion, and into her red wineglass from Williams-Sonoma, she poured a healthy amount of Syrah from the Northern Rhône, which had been recommended online as a good choice to balance the sweetness of the figs.

Next, the excellent salad with romaine and butter lettuces, radicchio, and arugula, and a dressing of extra virgin olive oil and aged balsamic vinegar, sea salt, and fresh garlic.

Drinking wine with salad was a faux pas, but she didn't really care at that point, and the Syrah was excellent and getting better all the time. It must be breathing nicely in the bottle. Or in her glass. Or who knew.

With the apple cranberry pie, she thought a snifter of brandy would do nicely, and she was right.

After dinner, she took her dishes to the sink and left them there. Blew out the candles and took the Vivaldi off the CD player. After a while all that deedle-deedling got irritating, frankly. She was more in the mood for music with balls.

So. A whole evening to herself. What appealed? She was too restless for TV or reading. If she hadn't had that much to drink she might like to dig out her ballet shoes and dance.

Or if she lived in New York still, she could have called any of a dozen friends and gone dancing at a club. She did that often in New York. Ben was never much of a dancer, but he didn't mind that she went. She went out quite often, in fact.

For some reason—probably that she was thinking about New York—she wondered what Vivian was doing tonight. How she liked the quiet nights in Kettle, compared to the wild orgies of her life in the Big Apple. It must be quite a come-down, not that she deserved anything but.

Though of course Vivian had been through plenty of quiet nights in prison recently. Six months of them. Probably making out with the other women, wasn't that what prisoners did?

Sarah would prefer not thinking about that.

She went upstairs, lurching at one point and catching her shoulder hard against the wall, which brought tears to her eyes, but made her laugh. A little too much to drink, Sarah?

She giggled. Harmless fun. At least she got to have fun too, since no one had invited *her* to a party tonight. She probably should be working on the Kettle Halloween bash. Worrying about the decorations, since Joan was chairing that committee, and the food and the entertainment. Or sending another encouraging note to little Katie, in the hospital for heart surgery, who would benefit from whatever money Sarah's pumpkins made. Sarah hoped it would be enough to make a difference; lately she'd been worried about that.

She hoped the party was a success. Sometimes she thought about Vivian's idea of Come As You're Not, and wondered if that theme would appeal to more people. She'd have to give that some thought. But not right now.

In her and Ben's bedroom, she dragged out her laptop. Maybe she'd have e-mail from a friend. Maybe she could write to her college roommate and find out how Karen was doing. Or one of her other friends from New York. She needed to be in touch with them more frequently. Find out what their evenings consisted of now they'd all had kids. Less wild, probably, but with New York at their feet, anything was possible.

She waited impatiently for the machine to boot up, singing a little bit of the hymn from church that morning. *Oh Love that will not let me go.*

The computer warmed and she loaded her e-mail program and scanned the incoming list.

Adrenaline buzzed through her; she felt her cheeks grow hot.

An e-mail from Tom.

Oh my. Oh my, oh no. Without really realizing what she was doing, she'd practically invited him to e-mail her. And now he had. Maybe it was just about the pen? Maybe it was just business? She certainly hoped so.

Sarah,

I hope you won't think me forward. But I wondered if you'd like to get together sometime. For a drink. Or a meal. Or whatever sounds good to you. It seems like we don't get enough of a chance to say what's on our minds.

Tom

Sarah inhaled sharply, taking in oxygen and carbon dioxide as if she'd never stop. At the very puffed-up peak of her breath, her lungs clamped tight shut and wouldn't let the air out.

Or whatever sounds good to you . . . we don't get enough of a chance to say what's on our minds.

Dark, crazy excitement started burning through her, especially down *there*. She put a hand to her chest, to see if she could feel her heart pounding. He wanted her. It was right there in black and white, hers to do with what she would.

He wanted her.

Sarah clasped her burning cheeks, struck out with both legs so her chair rolled away from the computer to give her safe distance.

What was she thinking? She wasn't that kind of woman. Tom had to know that. What was *he* thinking? That she'd start some . . . *affair* with him?

Her throat clutched on a swallow and she had to try again before the mechanism functioned properly. Between her legs the excitement hadn't abated at all. She must be ovulating, that was it. Her libido was up so she was spending way too much time imagining something that wasn't ever going to happen. That couldn't ever happen. She wouldn't let it.

She stood, repeatedly smoothing her hands down her Casual Corner white ribbed cotton top over her still-tight abdomen, looking around wildly for something to do, something to get her away from the crazy hot rush of excitement and the urge to answer him and build that excitement higher, something to ground her in the reality of her life.

Ben had filled the wastebasket to overflowing with tissues from his cold. And he'd not bothered to empty it, just left it there, overflowing, with other tissues scattered around as if being close to the trash was good enough.

She was tempted to leave it all there. Leave it for weeks and weeks, until the pile of tissues grew so huge she and Ben could no longer see out of their window. Would he even notice? Would he ever *get* it?

She stomped over to the closet where she kept plastic grocery shopping bags to empty the second-floor trash. Stomped back and yanked up the wastebasket, heavier than she expected. She turned it upside down into the bag, wincing at the thought of seeing more big clumps of tissues, telling herself he had a cold and that's why there were so many.

There was a clunk, and a split second later, the plastic bag jerked in her hands. She frowned. Tissues didn't clunk.

And then she remembered. The vibrator.

Her body wouldn't move for a long, long time. Then her arm reached in among Ben's bounty of tissues, and pulled the horrible thing out. She stared at it, not even sure what or whether she was deciding to do. Her thumb flicked the switch and the loud buzzing started.

Immediately she turned it off. How stupid. She was embarrassed and disgusted just hearing the noise.

Sarah tossed it back into the bag and gathered up the discarded tissues on the floor. Then she straightened and fished it out again; she couldn't help it. Took it to the bathroom, washed and dried it, came back into the bedroom, tossed it onto the bed, and stared at it, most of it sleek and smooth and white where the battery must be housed, then a thin turquoise rod on one end capped with a gray, soft-looking rubber tip. Which must be where one touched it to oneself.

She tied a knot in the plastic bag over the tissues and let it fall to the floor. Stood for a moment, hands on her hips. Then she climbed onto the bed and knelt over the little plastic toy, gazing down at it, pushing her hair behind her ears.

What did it feel like?

Her loafers clunked to the floor. She picked up the little machine and turned it on again, ready this time for the brash, horrible sound.

No. She couldn't stand it. It was humiliating even thinking about it. How often had she been told by her parents that touching yourself was wrong? Sinful. Even being adult now and knowing she'd been misled, she couldn't.

The silence in the room made her feel guilty. For what, thoughts? She turned on the little radio, CD, and tape player Ben bought Amber for Christmas years ago. Amber wanted a new one last year, so this one came into their room. Sarah turned the classical station up loud, then glanced back at the white plastic instrument of promise still on her bed.

What did it feel like?

Stravinsky's *Rite of Spring* tore through the room, savage, rhythmic, primal music. Impulsively, she danced steps from the choreography she'd learned in college. Her body came alive to the music, even if her synapses and balance were shot from alcohol. Wonderful, wonderful, alive and graceful and female.

She danced away from the bed, and without even having consciously made up her mind to, she turned out the lights in the room so the white-blue glow from her laptop became a nightlight, danced back, climbed into the center of the bed over the hollow Ben's body had made over the years, and turned the vibrator on again. This time she could barely hear the buzz.

What did it feel like?

Eyes closed, cheeks flaming, she leaned back on her elbows and opened her legs. Oh Lord. Was she going to do this?

She giggled, giggled again. Yes. Yes, she was.

She lay back farther. Put the thing at the crotch seam of her Liz Claiborne stretch pants.

Her eyes shot open; she gasped. Oh my God.

The arousal was immediate, intense, like nothing she'd felt before. Her breath came faster, she fumbled to pull down her pants, kicked them to the floor, followed them with her panties. Closed her eyes. And slowly drew the buzzing miracle over her again, where it was supposed to go.

Oh my God.

Almost immediately she felt her body gathering forces for something so deep and strong, she hardly knew how to react, how to slow it, how to get it to stay so she could understand the experience, hang on to the feeling.

Then a burning wave of pleasure so intense, she heard herself crying out in a voice like a movie actress, a voice she assumed exaggerated for male entertainment.

Her sex started pulsing, contracting, and the strong stimulation wasn't so good anymore, though the feeling was still delicious. She moved the vibrator slightly to one side, wishing she could keep it in place so the feeling could go on forever.

Except it subsided too soon and the vibration hurt when she tried to move the rubber tip back front and center. So she switched the machine off.

Stravinsky swelled through the room, suddenly overblown

and intolerable. Sarah moved from the bed and turned him off, too. Then she let herself fall back onto the burgundy and gold duvet from Bed, Bath & Beyond and found herself smiling like a beauty pageant contestant. Oh, how *amazing*. She felt drugged, languid, sexy, delicious. She wanted to feel that feeling again. And again. And again. How had she lived this long without it?

Come as you're not.

The pun made her giggle stupidly, and right then and there, she decided it wasn't too late to change the party's theme. Even if the idea had come from Vivian.

Irony smacked her between the eyes and narrowed her smile to nothing. The vibrator had come from Vivian, too. Vivian Harcourt had handed Sarah the key to her own body. A key Ben should have given her way back in college.

Her breath became irregular again; a sob wanted to climb out of her tight throat, but there didn't seem to be enough room.

All this time while she'd been doing his laundry, cooking his meals, serving him, loving him, making his own self-absorbed carefree life possible, he'd been holding this back from her, this basic gift of love.

Worse, she'd spent most of her life denying anything was wrong, ignoring other women's descriptions of their rapture, tamping down the uneasy feeling that there was something missing from her body, that she was somehow not quite right.

She was perfect.

Rage flooded her like a wall of water, like a tidal wave, moving steadily in to destroy beaches and homes and towns.

He'd kept this from her. While he sat in his damn office, typing his damn books, jerking himself off and leaving the tissues for her to empty and put out for trash day on Fridays. Over twenty years of orgasms he'd had without her, including all the years they dated. Over twenty years.

Well, now she knew how to have them, too, and she was going to make damn sure she made up for lost time. With him or without him, she was going to make the rest of her life one big freaking climax after another.

One sob managed to make it from her lips before she heard the chime of another incoming e-mail.

What was she going to do about Tom?

Sarah scrambled to the computer. The latest e-mail was from her mother, somewhere in rural USA. But Tom's still sat there.

Usually, she opened her parents' e-mails eagerly, wanting to hear the news from whatever state they were touring, to hear of their adventures, to know Mom and Dad were okay.

This time she wanted only Tom's. To read it again. To enjoy the danger and the temptation before she sensibly deleted it. Or answered in no uncertain terms that she was married and nothing could happen between them. Except in her private fantasies. Those belonged only to her and did no one any harm.

After all, who knew what Ben thought of when he was pulling at himself without her. She'd put down her life savings he wasn't thinking of his wife.

She swiveled her chair back and forth, keeping her eyes on the screen while her body turned. *Or whatever sounds good to you.*

What did Tom think about? Did he think about Sarah?

Her breath went in and rushed out, and the heat started building again between her legs. Ben's was the only penis she knew. What was Tom's like? Long and thick? Clean and strong and proud?

She crept to the bed, only mildly guilty. Her hand searched, then closed over the smooth, cool plastic. The buzzing didn't bother her this time, even in the silent room.

She lay back, opened her legs, imagined Tom coming into the room. Undressing her slowly, reverently, kissing her everywhere, especially *there*, where Ben hardly did anymore. She used the vibrator like a tongue this time, long strokes where she imagined Tom's tongue would go.

Her moans came out without her having to plan them. Her head thrashed on its own. A second orgasm built, this one stronger, wilder, deeper.

She called Tom's name, and the excitement of another man's name on her lips fueled her higher. This time she knew to move the vibration out of the way when it became too much. This time she knew to expect the change from the initial ecstatic rush to the pulsing.

Next time she'd know even more.

The orgasm faded to the same delicious weariness as the last one, but Tom's image stayed with her, holding her now, telling her she was beautiful, sexy, the best he'd ever been with. How he'd loved her all his life, how there were no other women who could take her place in his heart.

The vibrator stayed on the bed; she moved swiftly to the computer. Opened his e-mail and hit reply.

Anytime is good, Tom. Whatever you had in mind.

Sarah

She stared at what she'd typed for ten agonizing seconds, knowing she needed to delete it now, before she started something she had no intention of finishing. Before she started something that could hurt innocent people she loved.

The adrenaline buzzed higher, crazier, more seductive, and she gave a sudden wild laugh, like a woman crazy with grief and rage, and hit send with a vicious click of her mouse.

She watched the program search-connect-send, too quickly for her even to register what she'd done, and she suddenly thought of Vivian at Harris's, leered at and jeered at by a bar full of Kettle men, baring her breasts and laughing at them all.

And for one crazy second before she crumpled onto the bed to wonder exactly what she'd just set in motion and how she could both desire and dread the consequences, Sarah could understand exactly why Vivian had done it.

Fifteen

AD IN THE CHICAGO TRIBUNE
OCTOBER 1985

DANCERS WANTED, **NO HOUSE FEES.**
We are currently hiring dancers at our lounge/club located on Kingsbury Street. With experience or without. Great money, accommodations available, flexible hours. Phone: 312–555–8763. Auditions held any day of the week.

Vivian paced back and forth in her newly bare living room, occasionally circling her shoulders or stretching her neck. Last night Mike had helped her move the ugly furniture into the dining room so the space could be free for her first class.
If anyone showed.
Amber said she'd come, maybe try to bring a friend. Vivian

had put notices up around town, but big whooping surprise if no one responded. After a few weeks people might accept her more, trust her more, *if* she managed not to do anything too outrageous.

God, how depressing. Outrageous was what she did. But outrageous fit her in New York. Here, it ended up biting her in the ass and spitting out regret.

Maybe Erin would come, though Vivian had a feeling the Beastman wouldn't let her. Bad situation. Vivian got the vibe about three seconds after seeing Erin in her own territory, and his appearance clinched it. El creepo in the extreme. At least Ed could be charming and sweet when he was sober and in the mood. They'd had plenty of really good times.

She'd bet life was a lot of really bad times with Joe. Damn shame, but Erin had to wipe the boot marks off her backside and fight. No one was going to rescue her from her life. She needed to take the power into her own hands.

A movement caught Vivian's eye out her front window, and she squinted at the street, surprised to be so nervous. She was certified, fair and square, as a fitness instructor through the American Council on Exercise, but this was her first real gig. Ed had thought she was nuts. He teased her through the entire course and the long weeks of studying anatomy, exercise physiology, kinesiology, designing routines . . .

In the end, okay, just as he predicted, nothing came of it. But she'd pulled out determination and discipline she hadn't used since she earned her GED in her early twenties in Chicago, studying days and dancing or working as a female escort nights. She'd been proud as hell passing that exam. No, it wasn't Abby's graduate degree in art history from Wesleyan. But it was hers.

So who was lurking on her lawn? A shy customer? She started for the front door, when her brain registered a man. With a camera.

Her nervous excitement turned sick; she ducked away from the window. Paparazzi. They found her. *Shit*.

Served her right. For all its surreal Mayberry qualities and the closed-minded hostility of its residents, Kettle had been a haven, one she'd managed to fool herself into thinking was safe. Given how much of her private life had come out in the trial, it would take only minor digging to find out this house was still in the Harcourt name. If she'd had her head out of her ass, she'd be surprised they'd taken this long to track her down.

Well, she was happy to give them a piece of her new life if not her mind. Perhaps she should open the door butt-naked? Perhaps when Amber and her friend arrived, Vivian could shout, "Oh goody, the members of my lesbian three-way have arrived." Perhaps she could tell them she was setting up Kettle's first brothel and recruiting teenagers to hook for her.

Except the more scraps she threw them, the longer they'd keep coming around and the longer she'd have to stay here. She needed to keep back the temper, smile graciously, and act like Sarah Gilchrist.

Pause for intense nausea.

Okay, so it wouldn't be fun, but it was probably her first good idea in a very long time.

She crept to the front window and peeked out again, hoping the sheer curtains would hide her long enough to see what was up.

Two of them now, and a third by the driveway, possibly more around the side of the house. The two in front—one short and round, one taller and thin, like Laurel and Hardy—had Amber and her friend in their greasy clutches. Amber would be okay. She'd focus on the aerobics classes and Vivian's dubious membership in the Kettle Social Club and leave out things like, oh, say, Vivian wanting to know if she was screwing her boyfriend.

But she couldn't control what the rest of the town said. These guys were pros at getting what they wanted. Even those good citizens of Kettle who weren't out to persecute Lorelei Taylor would fall, like kids playing in a minefield.

More headlines, more invasion of privacy. More humiliation. More nationwide opportunities for people who didn't know her from a pillbug to despise her, pontificate, lay more blame for the disintegration of modern society at her feet.

Vivian slumped against the wall next to the window. She was tired. Just tired. Six months of fighting, of attitude, of making sure people knew they could kiss her ass for all she cared . . . she wanted to be done with that.

She heard a motor and peeked again. Mike's truck, coming home from work. Already two men were heading for his driveway.

She ran to the back door, feeling like a hostage in an FBI movie. Mike was getting out of the truck, shaking his head, looking so tall and handsome and save-the-day noble next to the evil reporters that she actually got hero-worship gooey.

Get a grip.

A third reporter, the in-between one, neither Laurel nor Hardy, shoved the mike forward, doubtless shouting some gross, intrusive question. What was it like living next to Lorelei Taylor? Did she sunbathe nude? Did she lure small boys into her house with drugged candy? Had she tried to seduce him?

Mike wouldn't betray her. She knew that as certainly as she knew cheap shoes weren't worth the money you saved. And so help her, that certainty made hero worship run even gooier.

Vivian moved away from the window and let her head bonk to the wall. She did not need to go soft on Big Wholesome Mike. For one, nothing she felt in this horrible rebound period could be trusted. For another, anything she started would end badly for one or both of them. She'd already made the mistake of getting involved with someone too different. Fool me once, shame on you, fool me twice, shame on me. The sooner she could get out of Kettle, the better.

Her front doorbell rang and she moved cautiously back into the living room, peered through the fishbowl hole in the door and saw Amber, Amber's friend, and men with cameras in their hands and prying on their minds.

Deep breath. Stay lovely. Be Sarah. She opened the door. "Hi, Amber, come on in."

"Ms. Taylor, would you answer a few—"

"It's Ms. Harcourt." She pulled Amber and her friend inside. "I have no comment at this time."

Door closed. Fine. She'd done what she could. The townspeople would do the rest . . . or she could hope not. But any damage resulting from the first round, she'd have to mitigate by being a model Kettle citizen from now on.

Yippee. If she wasn't acting one way, she was having to act another.

She turned and smiled broadly at Amber and her friend,

who looked like a short-haired Avril Lavigne, the kind of pouty brat Vivian used to love to torture. "Hey, guys, ready to work out?"

"Sure." Amber shrugged out of her red parka and gestured to her friend. "This is Tanya. I'll get more girls next week."

"Sure. Hi, Tanya."

"Hey." Tanya nodded, looking as if she wasn't sure she should be in the same room with Vivian, but whether because Vivian was exalted or villainous, who knew.

Exalted or Villainous Vivian collected their three dollars, led the girls into the living room, and turned on the music while they shed their street clothes.

"Ready?" She sounded too chirpy. Nothing she'd done for the past . . . ever had felt quite this naked. She felt practically more on trial here than in New York. Earning the certificate was one of the very few constructive things she'd done for herself, and she needed to prove she'd earned it fairly.

But no pressure.

"Let's do it." She led them through simple warm-up steps, then stretches. This part she could do without thinking.

Then the hard part. Her routine. Keeping the flow logical, repeating to let them learn each segment, cueing in advance so they wouldn't be surprised by the next steps and stumble.

She didn't start well. Got lost. Called steps by the wrong name. Cued after the switch happened. The girls did their best, but their smiles faded. They exchanged a glance.

Vivian started to panic, which pissed her off. She was *not* going to fail at this. Her fault for assuming her Vivian pluck would see her through, the way it saw her through everything.

Well, this time it wasn't fucking working.

"Okay, change-up here." She got them doing a simple step-touch. What the hell now? They'd been at it for twenty minutes, she'd promised them twice that, plus toning. What routine could she pull out of her ass in the next ten seconds?

Inspiration hit. "Try this."

She started doing a PG-17 aerobicized version of her "exotic dancer" routine, which she could still, unfortunately, do in her sleep. She taught the steps by sections, adding bounce, jumps, arms overhead to increase the cardio benefit.

The smiles came back. Giggles. Laughter. Vivian started to have fun. Let the bump and grind back into the routine. Amber and Tanya went nuts.

"And one and two, work those hips, baby, give it to them."

The girls whooped and worked their young bodies in a pretty convincing imitation of sexual nirvana—all in the name of good health of course.

The shadow of a paparazzi flitted across her window, and Vivian groaned. If this got out . . .

She looked at the two young faces, flushed and glistening with perspiration, shining eyes watching her every move. Screw the risk. Next time she'd have a proper routine worked out and rehearsed, a performance worthy of Sarah and her committee.

She led them in a gyrating cool-down, then twenty minutes of leg work, push-ups, abdominal crunches, then the final stretches, impressed with their stamina. At their age she got most of her physical activity flat on her back.

"Deep breath in." She lifted both arms over her head, inhaling. There. She'd done it. Earned six whole dollars fair and square doing something healthy and satisfying that didn't involve men. "And exhale. Good job."

The girls joined her applause and gathered up their things.

"You hot babes wanna stay for a *pop?*" She winked at Amber.

"Um. I gotta go." Tanya threw Amber a significant look and headed for the front door. "Thanks, though."

"Tanya?" Vivian took a few steps after her. Amber she trusted. This girl was an unknown. "Those guys would give teeth to hear about the routines I just taught. And what they'd—"

"*Those* routines?" Tanya blinked, her voice artificially high. "Like our gym teacher does? March, march, grapevine to the right, jumping jacks, stuff like that?"

"Yeah." Vivian grinned. "Like that. Thanks."

"Sure." Tanya threw Amber another meaningful look and left.

"So, girlfriend." Vivian put her arm around Amber's shoulders and walked her to the kitchen. "What's this about?"

"Um . . . what do you mean?"

Um . . . you know darn well. Vivian opened the refrigerator and grabbed two Diet Sierra Mists. "Why was Tanya giving you the eye when she left?"

"Oh. *That.*" Amber popped the top off her soda. "I wanted to ask you something."

"Ye-e-e-es?" Vivian grabbed a bag of Cheetos Twists and offered them, watching a blush creep up the girl's already rosy cheeks.

Uh-oh.

"Well, Kettle's a really small town, right?"

"I noticed that, yeah."

"So if I wanted to buy . . . something at the drugstore, the Stottlers might see me and tell my mom."

Uh-oh, uh-oh. "I see."

"And I don't have a car, so I can't go to Ladysmith to get anything."

"Hmm." Vivian downed half her soda and suppressed a belch. "What type of 'anything' and 'something' are we talking about?"

"Um . . ." Amber swallowed a mouthful of Cheetos. "Condoms?"

"Condoms." Oh crap.

The teenage face went from red to fiery. "Yes."

"Come upstairs with me."

"Yeah?" Her face turned hopeful.

Vivian came around the counter and put a hand on Amber's shoulder. "Not for that. I want to show you something."

"Oh." She didn't try to mask her disappointment. "Okay."

Vivian led her upstairs into the horrifically wallpapered bedroom, winked at Jesus, imprisoned, doe-eyed, on His clock, and gestured to the dollhouse. "Check this out."

"Oh my gosh, look at that." Amber rushed forward and eagerly peered into each of the six elegantly furnished rooms.

"I thought you'd like it."

"This was your grandmother's?"

"Her father built it for her. They got a lot of the furniture from England."

"It's like a real house. It's beautiful." She picked up the

girl-doll, Emily, from her seat at the wooden table in the kitchen and smoothed the yellow hair, straightened her cloth-and-wire legs. "Did you play with this when you were a kid?"

"Yeah." Vivian picked up the boy from his chair in the elegant chandeliered dining room. "Paradise for a little girl."

Amber narrowed her eyes. "Wait, is this some stupid you're-still-young lecture waiting to happen? Because if it is, thanks, I get enough of those from Mom."

Busted. "No, I just thought you'd like it."

"Right."

"*I* think it's cool and I'm adult and sexually active, okay?"

"Okay, okay." Amber turned back to the dollhouse, touching and exclaiming. The old-fashioned laundry room with tub washer and wringer. The kitchen with the black iron stove and miniature pots of herbs glued to the tiny windowsills.

"Amber."

"Yeah." She didn't look around.

"Why are *you* having to buy the condoms?"

"Oh. Well . . . Larry doesn't really like them. So he said if I wanted to use them I'd have to buy them myself."

Vivian grimaced. Why did women everywhere of all ages put up with so much goddamn shit in so many goddamn forms? "Isn't that touchingly supportive."

"No, I mean, I understand how he feels." She tucked Emily into the dream-come-true white canopy bed. "It's me that wants to use them."

And him that wants to use you. "So the plan is that I buy them for you."

"Yes." She practically deflated with relief not having to spell it out.

"And who will the cashier think *I'm* having sex with?"

"Uh . . ." Amber stared as if Vivian had sprouted an extra head. "You don't care what anyone thinks of you."

"Oh. Right." Of course not. As anyone who'd watched her life on TV could tell you. "So you think you're ready."

"Uh-huh." Amber ducked her head when Vivian tried to hold her gaze.

Damn it. How was she going to deal with this? She wasn't a parent, she had zero dealings with kids, she had no idea what to say to this young person. And yet, she could understand the pressures on Amber, remember her own teenage experiences like they happened yesterday. Only her first time hadn't been her idea, and it hadn't been with a boyfriend.

"How many times has he made you come?"

Amber started, then tried to act nonchalant by leaning forward and taking inventory of the objects in Emily's lacy bedroom. "Oh. Well. He says that's part of real sex."

Oh brother. "Are you taking care of yourself in that department? When you're alone?"

Amber dropped a tiny silver hairbrush and had to pinch it up carefully off the Oriental design rug. "Uh . . . Sometimes."

Vivian had to be screwing this up to the maximum possible. "So why haven't you explained to him how it works?"

Amber raised horrified eyes. "I can't just *tell* him."

"Why not?"

"Because it's private. And personal."

"And sex isn't?"

Amber frowned. "I thought you'd be cool about this."

"Believe it or not I am being cool about this. How many times have you made *him* come?"

Amber glowered at the living room.

"Oh, I'll bet a whole bunch of times." She stuck the male doll back with his head in the toilet and lifted Amber's face. "Repeat after me. I am woman."

Amber rolled her eyes. "I am woman."

"I am powerful alone."

Big sigh of disgust. "I am powerful alone."

"My boyfriend is a selfish, manipulative bastard and will be lousy in bed."

"*Vivian.*"

Vivian rubbed her forehead. If she was tired before, she was even more tired now. "Honey, I've screwed them all. I know the type. Trust me. You want your first experience to be good, with a guy who will care as much about what he can do for your body as what yours can do for his."

"Was your first time like that?"

"Hell no, it was horrible. I don't want you to go through that."

Amber pulled her chin out of Vivian's fingers. "So you won't buy them for me?"

Jesus. This was about as bad as it could get. If Vivan didn't buy them, Amber could have unprotected sex and catch God knew what. If Vivian did buy them, she was, in effect, condoning something all her instincts told her was a bad idea. At sixteen Vivian could handle whatever life threw at her, because by that time life had already thrown plenty. But this girl had been raised in fucking Kettle, Wisconsin. By *Sarah*.

If Amber didn't have a nice pair, Larry wouldn't even

have looked her way. Tits were power. Sometimes too much. Sometimes you were given that power before you were ready to use it.

"If I don't buy them for you, will you sleep with him without them?"

"I don't *want* to . . ."

Her sentence trailed off with the implicit *but I might have to*, and Vivian suppressed a dry chuckle. Sarah must have her hands full.

"Wait here." She went into the bathroom and grabbed a couple of condoms from her just-in-case supply, which at this rate she probably wouldn't need until the next millennium.

Back in the bedroom, she grabbed Amer's chin again. "Listen. If I help you, you have to do something for me, too."

"What." Said with rebellious apprehension.

Vivian sighed. Please God, let her get through to this kid. If this worked, she'd even keep Jesus up on her wall. "I don't need to meet Larry to know how it will be. First, it will hurt. He'll shove it in because he thinks he needs force to break through, because he's heard and made 'bust her cherry' jokes all his life. Second, it will bleed. Third, it will feel great to him, because he hasn't just had his privates ripped open. So he'll hump away as hard as he can which is what he's seen in porn movies, while you're lying there with a giant this-is-*it?* exclamation point over your head. Then he'll be done and unable to understand why you're not writhing in ecstasy. Trust me. If he can't make you come now, he can't that way, either."

She let go of Amber's chin. Immediately Amber crossed her arms over her chest and took a step back, but Vivian knew she was listening. Whether she was hearing was another question.

"I'm giving these to you." She held up the condoms. "If you get in a situation where you need them, for God's sake use them rather than don't. But if you can say no to this guy, I guarantee you will be doing a favor for every woman on this planet, most of all yourself. Plus I'll give you a certificate for a makeover at the Halloween party. All you have to pay me with is these. Unused."

She put the condoms in Amber's hand and closed her fingers over them. "Deal?"

"Deal." Amber took back her hand, not meeting Vivian's eyes, and opened her fingers to peek inside. "I better go."

"Right." She stepped back, wanting to pin Amber down until she promised to stay away from this Larry creep, feeling helpless to convince her, remembering how little she listened to anyone at that age—hell, at any age. Was this what Sarah went through?

They went downstairs; Amber retrieved her coat from the living room and shoved the condoms into the pocket. "Thanks, Vivian."

"Just think about what I said."

"I will."

She was solemn enough that Vivian hoped she would. Except all rational feeling would go out the window when she was alone in the dark with the guy and her inherited need to please. "See you Wednesday."

A smile returned to Amber's pretty face. "You know it. I'll get more girls to come, too. It was awesome."

"Good." She escorted Amber back to the front door. "Watch

out for the creeps with the cameras and mikes. You don't have to say anything."

"I'll tell them you're handing out free condoms."

"Out. Out of here." Vivian opened her door and shooed the giggling girl out. Watched while she walked past the reporters, paused for a few sentences, and kept walking.

God bless her. And keep her hymen safe. Amen.

The reporters turned back to the house, and Vivian slammed the door shut. Okay. So she'd be under siege for a few days. Eventually they'd get bored and leave.

She went upstairs to shower in the pink-and-green-tiled master bathroom, pausing to reinspect the dollhouse. Looking pretty dusty. Maybe she'd dust all the little furniture tonight after dinner. Ironic since she didn't give a rat's ass about dusting big furniture. Then at some point she'd like to go through the attic, see if there was anything her grandmother had left that Vivian might want to take when she sold the house.

Selling the house. Moving again. Having to re-re-reinvent her life. Ouch. A weird, sad pang in her middle.

Oh for God's sake. She couldn't be turning into that much of a sap. The house represented peace and security and some good memories. That was all. She'd suffocate living here longer than it would take for the trial to fade from public view.

Male voices outside made her roll her eyes. Damn it. The jerks would hang out there forever. Or at least until they got what they wanted—an interview with Lorelei Taylor.

Until then, what was she going to do, stay in her house the rest of her life?

Screw that. She'd face them right now. Go out and buy

chamomile tea or crumpets or something. Show them how she'd changed, make sure the stories they heard were dull enough that they wouldn't bother staying. Then she could move on and be deep-down glad about it.

After her shower, she dressed in the outfit she'd bought for her fitness instructor exam. A black, below-the-knee, pleated skirt; a red sleeveless sweater; and a black, red, and white plaid bouclé waist-length jacket.

Hot damn, she looked like somebody's cutie-pie secretary.

Forgo the matching red Manolo Blahnik spike-heeled sandals and the red Kate Spade purse, and go with a black, low-heeled, Stuart Weitzman mule and a small, black, Ferragamo shoulder bag she'd bought when Ed took her to Italy. She even resisted the red fishnet stockings.

Makeup went on with a lighter hand, less mascara, thinner liner, bare smudges of shadow, natural blush. There. She looked mahvelously proper. Vivian reborn. Vivian calmed and simplified. Vivian enriched by her love of small-town living.

Vivian choking on her own bullshit.

She sighed and tucked the white quilt more firmly around Emily in the canopy bed. Smoothed her already-smooth thread hair and smiled into the painted-on face. Vivian and Erin had played here when they were both girls. She did remember something of it. More an impression, a feeling, than concrete memories.

Back then she'd been preteen, not yet aware of her father's growing interest, though she'd felt his temper. A model student. A loving daughter in a generally peaceful suburban Chicago home. Was life really simpler back then, or did it just feel that way because she'd forgotten all the shit that really went on? Maybe someday her life now would seem simple.

God, she hoped not.

She marched downstairs, mules making double-clacks hitting the stairs and then her heels. At the door, for an uneasy second, her courage failed. She'd gotten lazy about keeping up defenses. In retrospect, that had felt pretty good. Going back into this three-ring circus decidedly didn't.

Hand firmly on the knob, she flung open the back door and stepped out into her leaf-strewn driveway, into the crisp, bare beginnings of mid-October twilight that even the intruders hadn't been able to turn cheap and stale.

See? Some things they had no power over. Today that would include her.

Laurel and Hardy already approached with microphones, the photographer and the other reporter sprinted around from the front. Her stomach churned. Maybe they'd ask a few easy questions and she'd be done?

Yeah, or maybe they'd respect her privacy and apologize for bothering her and she could get back into her spaceship and return to whatever planet she thought she was from.

"Ms. Harcourt, how do you like living in Kettle?"

"Very peaceful." She kept walking. "Nice to be out of the public eye."

They didn't blink at the dig, not that she expected them to. "You've changed your name to Vivian Harcourt. Is it safe to say Lorelei Taylor is dead?"

Vivian's throat thickened. "She's behind me, yes."

"How do you like small-town life?"

"It's refreshing." Like an arctic breeze.

"What's it like having to earn your own way with Ed gone?"

It sucks. "I'm adjusting."

"How do you think the residents of Kettle feel having an acquitted murderer in their midst?"

Miserable. "I'm trying to fit in."

"Like when you bared your breasts at the local bar?"

She stopped walking and turned, unable to believe what she'd heard, even realizing she should have expected it. Someone couldn't wait to share that tidbit. Someone couldn't fucking wait. What did anyone know about what had driven her that night?

The reporters waited, practically quivering in excitement. They knew they had her, vulturish, tiny-dicked creeps.

"Nothing to say, Ms. Harcourt?"

"Plenty." The bile rose in her throat. Damn it. Damn it. She was going to say something stupid. Do something stupid, and it would all start over again.

Deep breath. "Wardrobe malfunction."

"Not how we heard it."

"You heard it wrong." She turned back and kept walking to her car, kicking viciously through a clump of leaves.

"Mike Curtis took you home that night; anything happen between you?"

God, leave Mike out of it at least. "He followed me home in his car, that was it."

"Apparently you suggested a hand-job booth for the town Halloween party. You planning to follow through with that?"

She reached her car, barely able to focus on what she was

doing. They knew it all. Was this Sarah's revenge? Would the vibrator be next? Then the condoms she gave Amber? God, what headlines those would make. The bitch. She must have had the time of her life, describing the horror that had visited Kettle.

"That was a joke." Her voice came out low and tight, every instinct desperately needing to tell them to fuck off.

"Are you sure?"

"Yeah, I'm sure."

"Is Mike your new lover?"

"No." Her breath came faster. Damn it, damn it. She'd like to rip every perfectly coiffed strand of hair off Sarah's scalp and burn it in front of her.

"Must be pretty tempting having a single man next door."

"I'm past that."

"You brought him breakfast the other day, stayed quite a while. That sounds pretty romantic."

She clenched her teeth. Did the woman have a goddamn telescope trained on Vivian's door? No matter how Vivian answered that one, it would come out damning.

What was the point? What was the fucking point? She couldn't win. Nothing would sway them from the twisted crap they'd print about her, whether she fed it to them or not.

"You want something to print in your papers?"

They leaned forward eagerly. Her brain scrambled; she had to squeeze the car door handle tight to keep from shaking. "Then print this . . ."

Her eyes caught movement in Mike's living room window. He was standing there, watching her.

Crap.

She could read the tense message in his face as if he were right here shouting at her.

He was right. She knew it. The satisfaction would be short-lived. The consequences long and wearying.

A leaf from the elm between their houses drifted onto her car, yellow and vivid and perfect. She bent and scooped up a handful, threw them into the air, and smiled in conscious imitation of Sarah as they rained gently down.

"Vivian Harcourt is turning over a new leaf as a model citizen of Kettle, Wisconsin." She beamed, mentally giving each man the finger. "And for once, you're welcome to quote her on that."

Sixteen

Anyone wondering where Ms. Lorelei Taylor, hot off
her not-guilty verdict, has holed up? Wonder no more.
The Sublime Ms. L has hightailed it back to live in
her grandmother's house in, believe it or not, a small,
tightly knit community in northwestern Wisconsin,
under her real name, Vivian Harcourt. Kettle residents
had plenty to report regarding their new neighbor.

It seems shortly after her move, Lorelei was seen
at the local watering hole, Harris's Tavern, consum-
ing whiskey as if there were soon to be a shortage.
But that's only the beginning. On her way out, Lorelei proved you can take a girl out of the strip joint,
but you can't take the strip joint out of the girl. Male
patrons of the bar got a boobs-eye view of exactly
what she'd been hiding under her sweater.

That not enough? An anonymous source indicated

>Vivian intends to set up a booth at the town's annual Halloween party to perform manual sex acts on local men.
>Did anyone really think she'd try to fit in?

Vivian opened the middle drawer of her old-lady antique dresser and stared at the contents in disgust. Social Club meeting this morning, day three of Media Hell. What horrendously ordinary article of clothing should she put on to blend in with the other horrendously ordinary residents? After her lofty announcement that she was turning over a new leaf, she'd jumped into the car and taken off for a demonic shopping spree at the closest generic mall, buying the least Vivian-like clothing she could find.

Paisley button shirts; long-sleeved, nontight tees; loose sweaters with high necklines. Even a pair of pleated pants. And—shudder—sensible shoes at reasonable prices.

Help.

But if she was going to convince the idiot media and the idiot American public that she had changed into a subject unworthy of coverage, she had to start with the package.

At least she could still wear exciting underwear. Leopard print today, with matching bra and panties. Her little secret. Over that, the beige pleated pants. The loose, multicolor, horizontal striped shirt. The cream-colored cotton cardigan. And, God forgive her for the sin she was about to commit, the brown, low-heeled, nondesigner pumps.

Gag.

She added light makeup and studied herself in horror. She could pass as Sarah's stepsister. Maybe she should cut her hair in a bob and buy an assortment of pastel headbands.

She rolled her eyes at her reflection. Going to another Social Club meeting was fairly low on her list of things she wanted to do, like . . . oh, say . . . last, but she was going for two reasons. One, so the reporters Velcroing themselves to her life would see her engaged in a healthy and community-minded activity here in her new prison—er, home. And two, so she could find out which bitch leaked the crack about the hand-job booth.

She'd bet her ugly clothes it was Sarah, little Miss Self-Righteous, who couldn't wait to spread tales of the dreadful intruder into her perfect world.

Vivian should fire a warning shot across her bows, ask within earshot of the media if she was picking up any good vibrations lately and watch her fall apart. Except the tabloids would find a way to make the comment reflect badly on Vivian. They couldn't disappoint millions of readers with stories that didn't support her harpy-of-the-year image.

Something more compelling than a prude with a vibrator would be necessary to deflect interest from Lorelei Taylor. When you didn't want a kid playing with the old toy, give him a new one. A shame no other scandals had cropped up recently to engage the nation's short attention span.

Her back doorbell rang and she jumped like a teenager in a horror movie. Damn reporters. She crossed to her bedroom window and raised it. "Who's there?"

"Mike. I have your paper tiger."

Oh great. She had to open the door as Helen Housewife and it was Mike. "Coming."

She ran downstairs and opened the door slowly, already annoyed at how he'd tease.

"Hi." She stuck out her hand, staring at his chest. "Thanks. I couldn't stand this wallpaper another—"

"I'm sorry, do I have the right house?"

She sent a warning look up to his smug grin. "Hand over the tool or risk damage to your other one."

"I'm looking for a Miss Vivian Harcourt? Is she not at home today?"

"*Mike*."

He chuckled and backed her into the kitchen. She tried to stand her ground, but that would put them in full frontal contact, which was not a good idea. Well it *was* a good idea in the abstract, but not with her dressed like a PTA mother.

"You look incredible," he whispered. "Sooo sexy."

"Oh pleez."

"I'm *serious*." He did some pretty convincing heavy breathing. "Like a centerfold . . ."

"You're *not* serious."

". . . from a Sears catalog." He barely finished the last word before he started laughing again.

She put both hands to his chest and shoved. "Cut it out."

"Okay, okay." He stopped laughing. "You look fine, Vivian. Thought about what I said?"

"What you said?"

"About hiding behind the clothes and attitude."

"Oh, bite me. Typical male, taking credit for everything." She glared at him, grabbed the sides of her cardigan, and stretched them open. "This is not change, this is 'let's show the paparazzi Lorelei is no longer worth reporting on.' Okay?"

"Um, yeah, okay." He stepped back. "Guess I hit a nerve."

"I don't like looking this way. It's not me."

"So you keep saying."

She could cheerfully slug him, but the tabloids would probably hear about that, too. "Okay, it *is* me. I've discovered my inner dullness and I can't get enough."

"Hmm." He looked her up and down. "Any chance you bought gray sweats and plain white T-shirts?"

"No. Way." She emphasized each word by poking him in the chest.

He grabbed her finger. "Do."

"Why?"

"Because . . ." He rubbed her finger over his lip, then gave the tip a brief, sucking kiss that shouldn't have shot thrills through her, but since when did her body react the way her head wanted it to? "Seeing you dressed that way is my secret fantasy."

"Right." Vivian snorted and yanked her finger out of his grasp. "What's got *you* all whupped up today?"

"You looking real."

"Give me a break."

"Okay, okay." He grinned, blue eyes shooting sexy amusement. He was going to drive her insane. "Where is this wallpaper?"

"Up where I've wanted you for weeks, sailor."

He gazed at her, brow lifted, until her insides started to cha cha. Damn it, these yearnings were bullshit. She wanted to stay in control and have fun.

"In your bedroom. I might have known." He sighed as if he were resigning himself to the slaughterhouse. "Lead on."

"My pleasure. And if you're lucky, yours." She headed up to the blue-and-brown bedroom, where she turned and leaned provocatively against the wall. "Okay, Mike. Show me how to use your tool."

He held his hands up in surrender and let them slap down against his jeans. "Okay, you haven't changed."

"Did you think I would?"

"I was hoping."

She frowned. "Seriously?"

"Of course not." He moved to the wall next to her and started whistling Billy Joel's "I Love You Just the Way You Are."

She fought giddy laughter. "What is up with you today?"

"Just being Mr. Sunshine. Thought you might need some today." He held up the roller. "Ready to learn?"

"Sure." Sunshine? Had he read the article? She wanted it to go away. Everything about the world felt more manageable and more hopeful when she was around Mike. She wanted to roll in that like a dog in a favorite scent, so the feeling would cling to her after he left. "Show me how."

"You roll the paper tiger over the very ugly wallpaper to perforate it. The more holes, the easier to get it off."

"Can I make a more-holes-easier-to-get-off joke?"

"Not unless you're dressed for it."

She sighed loudly and watched him roll the funky little tool over the brown-and-blue paper.

"When that's done, you soak the paper with hot water. Use a spray bottle, hot as you can stand it." He handed her the paper tiger. "You try."

"Mmm, hot and wet." She winked and pushed the spiky roller over the paper, glorying in the rows of tiny holes starting its ruination. Even her clock Jesus couldn't forgive this print.

"When it's good and wet, use the scraper to peel off the paper. It should come pretty easily. The worst part is scrubbing the glue residue off the wall after. There are all kinds of solvents on the market, but nothing beats hot water, a little detergent, and elbow grease."

"Got it." She stopped rolling. "Thanks for this, Mike. I'm sure you had other things to do this morning."

"You're welcome." He faced her, hands on his hips, features troubled.

She felt suddenly nervous and didn't know why, and that made her more nervous. "Now get out of here, I have a Social Club meeting to go to."

"A what?" He looked incredulous, not that she could blame him. "Why?"

The bile started rising again. "Because a certain prissy Kettle missy is leaking everything I do to the press, and I want to teach her about accountability."

"You think it's Sarah."

"Who else?"

He frowned. "Actually, it would surprise me if it was her. Underneath the Sarah-thing she's got a strong sense of decency."

"Decency?" She blinked faux sweetly. "You mean you couldn't get any?"

"Vivian."

"Ye-e-es?"

"Cut the shit."

She took a deep breath and let go. He was right. She'd been a brat. Again. "Did you see the article?"

"Yeah." His voice dropped. "I wanted to punch something."

Ohhh no. Nothing got to her like a man willing to rush to

her defense. It was so . . . female of her. "I don't deserve this after the crap I've been through."

He shrugged. "To them you're a product."

"I know." She brandished the paper tiger, imagining reporters riddled with holes. "And the way I was, I played right into their hands."

"Was?"

"*Am.*"

He grinned. "Couldn't resist."

"Maybe I should borrow Rosemary's clothes, save me having to shop a whole new wardrobe, what do you think?"

"I think that was low."

She exhaled, suddenly out of steam, tossed the paper tiger onto the bed, and sank down on the eyelet spread. "You're right. It was. But you deserved it at least a little."

"I guess." He sat next to her, put his arm around her shoulders. "You'll make it, Vivian."

"Yeah, I'm a goddamn survivor." But tired of just surviving. She wanted to live.

"With a mouth like a sailor." He squeezed her in a brief hug. "At least you're on the right track with the mother-of-the-year outfits."

"Yeah, um, thanks."

"You're welcome." He leaned close, pressed a brief, warm kiss to her temple.

Oh God. The kiss was so innocent, so restrained, so tender, it was twice as sexy as the usual male assault.

She wanted to turn and start what they should have started the night he followed her home from Harris's. Back then it would have been simple. But nothing about it felt simple now. She wasn't herself. She felt confused and vulnerable, and as if her only strength was anger.

"What was up with you and Rosemary?" She asked because she wanted to know, and she asked because bringing up Rosemary would push him away, and she asked because she wasn't sure she had the resolve to push him herself.

His body tensed. "Why does Rosemary come up every time we're together?"

"Because it doesn't make sense."

"What doesn't?"

She couldn't explain. Because she couldn't picture Mike with some goody-two-shoes chick he had boring sex with? She couldn't picture herself with Ed, but there you had it, fourteen years of nonmarital occasional bliss. What did she really know about Mike?

She was probably trying to turn him into as much of a fantasy of what she wanted as he was of her, going all sweet on her dressed like this. "The two of you. What people talk about. Like you were Mr. and Mrs. Perfect Love."

"That's what people saw."

"There was more?" She made the stupid, horrible mistake of turning to look at him, and he was so close to her, she could imagine how his lips would feel on her mouth and skin, and how his unshaved cheek would feel on hers, and how about on her inner thighs while she was at it.

"Why do you care, Vivian?"

Busted. She shouldn't. She didn't want to. But she had a visceral bitchy need to see Rosemary de-haloed, and she really didn't want to know why. Because she had a feeling it was starting to run deeper than cattiness. "I don't care."

"Right." He whispered the word and bent forward.

Shit, and hot damn and hot flashes that had nothing to do with perimenopause. He was going to kiss her. His lips touched hers, and before she could decide if she was going to back away or give in, sound and movement at the window intruded.

"*Jesus.*" She reacted on instinct, jumped to her feet, and threw herself downstairs. Taking pictures through her bedroom window! She was going to catch the bastard before he got back to the ground, yank his camera away, and stuff it so far up his ass, he'd never be able to crap on people's lives again.

Two feet from the front door, she reached out, caught the knob, and stood there, panting with fury.

And stood there. Still panting, but not as hard anymore.

Something was wrong with this picture. Something was very wrong.

She let go of the door and turned to find Mike halfway down the stairs, watching her, arms folded across his broad chest.

He didn't stop her.

He wasn't going to race down the rest of the stairs and grab her while she struggled and swore at him. Wasn't going to stop her from going out there and making a huge ridiculous mistake she knew damn well she shouldn't be making.

She'd actually been waiting for him to rescue her from herself.

Christ.

She moved stiffly to the yellow-and-blue furniture shoved into the dining room and sank on an unforgiving wing-back, feeling like she'd just swallowed lead.

How often had she depended on Ed like this, to keep her

from self-destruction? Now it was Mike's turn? One man to the next to save her from taking responsibility for her actions and herself? And what had she been thinking about Rosemary depending on Big Mike for every breath?

Mike came down the stairs, stood in the middle of the living room, and watched her until she felt like an art exhibit. "What are you staring at?"

"Smart not to go out there."

"What are you, my father? I made a good choice today? Wanna check my homework?"

His jaw tightened and she could practically hear him telling her to shut the fuck up.

She mumbled an apology. God knew why he put up with her. Unless he loved damsels in distress.

"Did Rosemary need you to—"

"Are we back to Rosemary?" He tipped his head to the side, eyeing the wall as if he'd like to put his fist through it. "Okay. Go. Get her out of your system."

"*My* system? Like you've gotten her out of—"

"The clothes are gone. Pictures. All that stuff. You were right, it was time I got over it."

Holy shit. Vivian traced a small stain on the chair; her fingers looked short and plain and weak without their talon-nails. "Did she need rescuing a lot?"

"Constantly."

"And you loved that about her?"

"No. I didn't."

Vivian slid out of her chair. She wanted to see his eyes up close when he spoke. "You're not into the knight-in-shining-armor thing?"

"No." He answered in the usual wooden syllables he used when talking about Rosemary, his face frozen and robotic. Only this time it occurred to Vivian his paralysis might not stem from the pain of missing her, but maybe from something less noble. Which made wild hope rise in Vivian's chest even though she didn't want it there.

"But she wanted you to be Sir Galahad?"

"Yes."

She should back off this topic. She should back away from this man. She should pack up her house, sell it, and go somewhere the reporters couldn't find her. Like Antarctica.

But when the hell did she do anything she should? "So why am I starting to think the perfect love thing was bullshit?"

Mike shifted his weight, and she had a sudden strong intuition that he wanted to run away as much as she did, and probably as far.

His jaw tightened further; he looked away. "Because, Vivian, it was."

Seventeen

E-mail from Tom Martin to Sarah Gilchrist

Sarah, I read your note at least seven times. You've
really had feelings for me for that long? After all
these years wanting you and getting only occasional
smiles to feed me, my hunger is enormous.

I remember every dance recital you gave in grade
school, every speech, every part you had in the school
shows. You're the brightest, most talented woman
Kettle has ever seen. You have so much to offer. I
wish I was the man taking it from you.

Write soon. Time seems to stop between your
e-mails.

E-mail from Sarah Gilchrist to Tom Martin

*Tom. I remember everything about you, too. How
talented you were on the trombone. How smart you were
at everything, and how ambitious. Do you think our
lives would have been different if I'd said yes the
night of the dance?*

*The road not taken. How it will always haunt us.
Must go, though I'd rather write to you than anything
in the world.*

Sarah pushed the vacuum in short, jerky strokes over the
upstairs hall rug her parents bought from a Turkish man in
Chicago. Usually she enjoyed vacuuming, the way rugs and
floors came free of dust and bits of paper and threads, and
enjoyed the fresh, clean look of the house afterward. Today,
vacuuming felt like slave labor. She wanted to be in her bedroom checking e-mail, to see if Tom had written in the last
half hour.

She was obsessed; it was so unlike her. But since she and
Tom had been e-mailing, she felt as if she were coming alive
again, as if for the last four years of her marriage, after moving back to Kettle, she'd been in a mere coma of existence, a
continuous suppression of her sexuality, her vitality, her talent, *herself*.

How had she allowed this to happen?

Ben had brought her back to Kettle from their thriving,
thrilling existence in New York and buried her under a stu-
pefying pile of housewife responsibilities, so he could sit in
his study, every need anticipated and satisfied before he was

even aware he had it, and write a novel that, if he ever finished, she'd bet would repel any editor misfortunate enough to encounter it.

Tom understood her. Tom wouldn't have insisted she move away from her friends and a career in dance. He would have stayed in the city with her and found a job for himself. She could have inspired him to go to law school as he'd one day dreamed of doing. He could have become a prominent New York lawyer, and she would have been his dancer wife. They would have been an exciting and interesting couple people would have admired and wanted to get to know.

Not to mention if she'd married Tom she undoubtedly would have been having orgasms from day one. Maybe if she hadn't been so stupidly infatuated with the idea of giving her virginity to the so-called love of her life, she would have slept with Tom in high school and had her first orgasm right there in his car. Maybe then she would have known not to marry Ben. Maybe she would have discovered, as could easily turn out to be the case, that Tom was the love of her life, and that she'd saved her virginity for the wrong man.

Which made a horribly poignancy out of the night in Tom's parents' Volvo, with his hands and mouth all over her, his erection thrusting against her graduation dress through his khakis. She'd said no and felt like virtue personified. It could have been the biggest mistake of her life.

Maybe if she'd tasted even part of the deep passion that still, after all these years, simmered between them, she'd have had the sense to foresee the barren existence ahead of her with Ben, where her only use was finding misplaced clothes and cooking his food and providing her body for him to masturbate on. Because she might as well face it, that's what sex between them boiled down to.

Life with Tom would have been full of ardent and interesting discussions, he would have respected and encouraged her point of view, instead of finding a way to bash it down as her husband did every time she ventured an opinion. Why hadn't she seen all this when she was so smitten with Ben at Cornell?

Hindsight was twenty-twenty. Love was blind. The expressions existed for a reason. She'd been so sure the calm feelings she had for Ben were proof of their depth. That other people might be swayed by wild agonies of longing and lust, but those people would be in divorce court within the decade. Not Sarah. Hindsight would be her validating ally. What she had with Ben would last and last.

Why hadn't she noticed the passion was missing? The true soul connection she had with Tom?

She shouldn't be so hard on herself; she *had* noticed. But everyone said passion wasn't important, everyone said passion faded, everyone said what lasted was a strong, healthy friendship and respect. And so she'd climbed onto the soapbox and trumpeted The Truth along with everyone else, *Oh, what I feel for Ben is so much deeper and quieter than anything I've ever felt.* And therefore it was True Love.

Not boredom and suffocation waiting to happen.

What were you left with when you found out everyone had lied? When you found out friendship and respect *could* fade? And what were you left with when you didn't even have memories of passion to rekindle?

Not even hope.

So Sarah had buried herself in a sensory deprivation chamber. See no problem, hear no problem, speak no problem. She'd martyred herself to her child and husband, denied everything she wanted and needed for so long, she could barely remember how to want and how to need. Until Tom.

Want and need didn't begin to describe the dam-bursting flood of emotion, starting with the Night of the Vibrator, when she'd written to him inviting anything he had in mind, and he'd written back three minutes later with everything he had in mind, as if his dam had burst, too, as if he'd been sitting at his computer all day, all week, for nearly a generation, waiting for her. For her, for his Sarah.

"Honey?"

She barely heard Ben over the hum of the vacuum cleaner, the red Samsung they'd bought online for much less than they would have spent at Channing Vacuum on Highway J. Barely, but she did hear him. And decided she had dropped whatever she was doing and run to him probably a thousand times. This afternoon he could jolly well come upstairs himself to get her attention.

"Honey?"

She kicked the machine to more power and therefore more noise, vacuumed the same spot furiously, over and over. He would stand there at the bottom of the stairs for three hours if that's what it took. *Honey? Honey? Honey?* It would never enter his mind that she'd be anything but at his beck and call.

And look at her, trembling over how hard it was to deny him. How deeply she'd conditioned herself to serve.

"Sarah?"

If she managed to hold out against the need to turn off the vacuum and run downstairs calling out, *Yes, Ben?* he'd be irritated, as if it was her fault she hadn't heard him.

"Honey? Sarah?"

Damn it, Ben. Sarah stomped the power switch off. *"What?"*

She never yelled. Ever. Occasionally if she raised her voice the teeniest bit, Ben would get an aggrieved look on his face and answer with exaggerated calm, as if he needed every bit of patience he was born with to deal with his child of a wife.

"Well, Sarah . . ." Gentle, gentle voice, like Fred Rogers about to fall asleep. "I'm going out, and I wondered if you needed me to pick anything up for you."

It was a ridiculous ritual they'd perfected. He'd ask. She'd refuse and thank him for his thoughtfulness. Today she was not going to refuse.

"Yes. Would you pick me up a gallon of skim milk from Stenkel's?"

No response. Her heart rocketed into an erratic beat; her face grew hot. He was undoubtedly letting the shock settle. She wanted him to *what?*

She thought of Tom, scouring the Internet for cards and poems she might like, for pictures of just the right jewelry to suit her, and pictures of the perfect color flowers whose beauty reminded him of hers, since of course he couldn't risk sending the real thing.

"I wasn't planning to go past Stenkel's."

One. Two. Three. Four. Five—she couldn't make it to ten. Was she *planning* to spend all Monday morning last week trying to get the chili stains out of his Packers sweat pants?

"Well plan to now." Adrenaline burned, the fear-excitement of a child deliberately displeasing its parent.

"Sarah?" His footsteps coming upstairs, the shuffle-shuffle of the slippers she bought him. "Are you okay? You seem . . . angry recently."

She gripped the vacuum. Yes, Ben, she was angry recently. She was angry recently and retroactively for all the lost and wasted years of her life.

"Oh." She gentled her tone into regret. "It's probably hormonal. I'm sorry. I'll get the milk later."

She flinched at her words. *Why* couldn't she point out, even diplomatically, that she went out of her way for Ben every day of their marriage, and buying milk wouldn't be more than a ten-minute bite out of his twenty-four hours? And ten minutes of his day spent making her life easier would make her feel happy and cared for. The way she felt with Tom, even just on e-mail.

Ben frowned; she looked him full in the eye with a hopeful, loving look, and it hit her right then that everything hung in the balance. Everything.

If he said no, no, it was fine, *he*'d get the milk. If he'd do that one thing for her, she'd tell Tom she was sorry, very sorry, but she was married and nothing good could come of this. She'd call Dr. Dodson and make an appointment for marital counseling and who cared if Joan found out, working as she did next door at Dr. Marlowe's.

No, sweetheart, you work so hard. I'd be happy to get the milk, it's only a small detour. And why don't we go out tonight, you and me, so you don't have to cook, maybe catch a movie after dinner, it's been so long since we went out on our own . . .

If only he'd get it. The milk and the bigger picture.

"Maybe you should ask Dr. Swanson for some female pills or something. I worry about you, sweetheart. You're not usually like this." He leaned in and kissed her forehead, walked past her into their bedroom.

"I can't remember where I left my shoes. Have you seen them?" A deep chuckle. "Oh here they are, in front of my face."

Sarah started the red Samsung Quiet Storm 9069G, tears trying so hard to rise up in her eyes and sobs in her throat that her body shook with the effort of keeping them down. She vacuumed over to Amber's room, took one look inside at the mess strewn everywhere, on the bed, on the desk, on the floor, her coat, her books, shoes, pens, clothing.

How was Sarah supposed to vacuum with all this crap on the floor? Had anyone given one second's thought to *her*? Anyone, anywhere except Tom?

She heard her husband thud past behind her, finally able to part with the slippers she bought him that he hated, calling out a hearty "Bye, Sarah" that made her want to scream.

One step forward, one powerful kick from her dancer's right leg, and Amber's bright red down Christmas parka from L. L. Bean, warm and stylish, which Amber nearly always refused to wear, sailed into the air and onto the bed.

And a two-pack of condoms fell on the floor, between an ugly orange blouse Amber had worn the day before and a copy of *A Wrinkle in Time* from Sarah's childhood that she and Amber had both read so many times, the pages were falling out.

Sarah turned off the red Samsung Quiet Storm vacuum cleaner.

Amber was having sex. Or planning to.

She couldn't be having it yet, could she? Wouldn't Sarah have noticed? Wouldn't something have changed in her baby girl and wouldn't Sarah be able to tell?

Just two condoms, not a pack. Nothing she'd bought herself . . . unless the rest of the box was here somewhere?

Half an hour later, the last inch of the room examined and carefully put back, she could conclude they weren't part of a box Amber was hiding.

So where *did* they come from? A friend maybe, sharing her stash? Tanya? Beverly? When had Amber last worn the coat?

Early in the week it had been chilly enough that Sarah worried her pumpkins could succumb to frost. That day, Monday she thought, she'd overruled the usual objections and insisted Amber wear her coat. And then what? Had she gone somewhere after school?

Aerobics at Vivian's.

Now that Sarah thought about it, Amber had come home looking defiant and guilty, but Sarah assumed it was because Amber knew Mom wasn't thrilled about her daughter's association with that . . . person.

Who else was there taking the class?

Trampy Tanya, as Sarah called her privately. In two steps she was at the hot-pink and silver phone they bought Amber for her birthday last year, dialing Tanya's number with shaky fingers.

Tanya's mother answered, "Jefferson residence," as she always did, which Sarah thought unbearably pompous.

"Helen? Sarah." She didn't mince words, stayed tough through the horrified gasps of denial from Tanya's mother—if

Helen thought her daughter was saint material, she was the only one who did—and while Helen went to confront Tanya, who must just be home from school, Sarah waited, tapping the phone and pacing on the adorable pink Cinderella rug Amber had thankfully gotten so used to, she didn't notice it was too little-girl for her now.

"Sarah." Said in the snooty tone Helen excelled at, the one that made Sarah want to grit her teeth. "On that day the girls were at Vivian Harcourt's. And you suspected *Tanya*?"

Sarah stopped pacing. She was pretty sure if she took the hot-pink and silver phone away from her ear and inspected the hand holding it, she'd find her knuckles had turned white. "Vivian gave condoms to sixteen-year-old girls?"

"Not to *Tanya*."

Sarah's teeth gritted. As if Tanya would admit something like that to her mother. "I see. Thank you, Helen."

She pushed the off button on the phone and set it back carefully in the hot-pink base.

Well.

Of course Tanya could be lying.

Or she could not be.

Which would mean Vivian Harcourt had given condoms to Sarah's sweet girl. Which would mean Vivian Harcourt had practically pushed Amber into sexual activity way too early for a girl like her. Maybe sex at sixteen had been old news to Vivian, but they did things differently in Kettle. They did them decently and at the proper time.

Sarah opened the hand that held the condoms and stared at them, twin packs of ribbed, lubricated evil. She felt the flush in her face grow hotter. A strange ringing started in her ears, and she couldn't hear as well as usual, as if they'd been stuffed with cotton.

She shoved the condoms in the pocket of her navy washable linen pants, leaped over the red vacuum cleaner, and raced down the stairs, not even stopping to put a coat over her blue and beige cashmere sweater with faux pearls.

She and Vivian were going to have a little talk.

Down the street, crossing it, running past parked cars, the cold air fierce and fortifying in her lungs, her navy-shod feet barely touching the pavement or the sidewalk or the cement of Vivian's driveway.

She hammered on the back door, stabbed the bell three times, mama bear in action, barely breathing hard from her sprint, ready to sink her teeth into Lorelei Taylor's lovely white throat.

Vivian's face appeared in the window, registered surprise, then hostile unwelcome. *Are we feeling a little guilty?* Vivian was many things, but not stupid. She undoubtedly knew why Sarah was there.

Vivian glanced toward the street; Sarah followed her look and noticed men getting out of the cars parked by her house. Men staring with unabashed interest.

The media. Why didn't they leave Kettle alone? Two days ago they'd approached Sarah as she shopped at Stenkel's and asked all kinds of questions about what Kettle's newest resident had been up to. Until the condom incident, Sarah had almost felt sorry for Vivian.

No longer.

One of the men pointed a camera. Sarah pounded on the door again. "Let me in."

She did *not* want to be associated with Lorelei Taylor on the front cover of some sleazy tabloid that uneducated people would pick up in the supermarket and devour as truth.

The door opened and Sarah pushed past Vivian, not caring if she was being rude.

"Well, well, Sarah, what a nice surprise." Vivian shut the door behind her and leaned against it, arms folded, lids half closed, as if Sarah would be lucky to get out alive. "Did you stop to chat with our friends out front before you came in?"

Sarah held up the condoms. "About how you're encouraging teenage sex?"

Vivian's eyes shot wide and Sarah was surprised to see her look hurt for a flash before the rage returned. "You bitch. Is that what you told them this time?"

"Did you give these to my daughter?"

"Did you tell the reporters I did?"

"No, did—"

"You didn't tell them?"

"It's none of their business what goes on here." Sarah took two steps forward and shook the condoms so hard, the bottom one flapped as if it was trying to break free. "Did you give these to Amber?"

Vivian's eyes returned to their natural shape; her shoulders lowered.

"Come sit." She gestured to the stool at her counter.

"I don't care to sit in your house, thank you."

"Oh come on, Sarah. We have to talk about it, you might as well be comfortable."

Sarah inhaled two breaths' worth of air. Vivian had this infuriating way of making her feel uptight and ridiculous.

"Fine." She sat reluctantly on the stool, totally discomfited when Vivian sat next to her. Bits of blue and brown printed paper—*wallpaper?*—clung to her loose striped top and her plain beige pants and her hair. She looked disconcertingly normal, especially now that she no longer seemed about to commit her second murder.

"Have you talked to the reporters at all?"

Sarah made a sound of impatience. "Is this some tactic to sidetrack—"

"No, it's not a goddamn tactic. My life is being fucked with all over again, someone is telling these people everything I do, twisting it so I sound—" Her voice cracked, and she immediately resumed looking furious. "Just tell me. Did you say anything to them? Even innocently?"

Along with the new nonslut outfit, lighter makeup, and short plain nails, Sarah noticed a strain around Vivian's eyes, an erosion of the cocky confidence she always had so firmly in place. "They approached me but I had nothing to say to them. I think their prying is disgusting. And the article they printed about you and about Kettle was . . . unfortunate."

Vivian gave a strained laugh and put her head down so her rich brown hair flecked with wallpaper bits spilled all over the counter, and touches of her natural brown color revealed themselves at her roots, occasionally striped with gray.

Sarah didn't remotely see what was so funny, and she found it insulting that Vivian assumed she'd betray her. "You know, if you were more careful about what you say and do they'd have nothing to report."

Vivian lifted her head, all wide-eyed innocence. "Ya *think?*"

Damn it. The woman was impossible. Sarah slapped the condoms down on the counter. "How did my daughter get these?"

Vivian sat up slowly, and Sarah braced herself for the load of bull that was about to spill out of her, the same brand she used on the witness stand.

"I gave them to her."

The answer was so unexpectedly honest that the furious yes-you-did accusations Sarah was ready to hurl had nowhere to go. More than that, there were no grand, gloriously raging, and articulate accusations rising to take their place. Just choking anger and sadness and fear for her child. "She's not ready."

"That's what I told her."

Sarah held herself still on the stool. How stupid did Vivian think she was? "So you gave her birth control."

"She asked for them."

"That's reason enough? What if she asked for heroin?"

"Sarah." The beautiful brown eyes were troubled, but steady and sincere. Of course they'd been that way on the witness stand, too. "I *told* her she wasn't ready."

"Then *why* would you give her these?" She flicked at the black foil packages; they slid several inches and stopped just shy of the counter's edge.

Vivian got off her stool and rounded the counter to the refrigerator. "Do you want some tea or something? A soda?"

"No. I want to know why you gave my daughter condoms if you know she's not ready for sex."

Vivian sighed as if Sarah were a dunce pupil she'd already had to explain the same thing to over and over. "I know she's not ready, and you know she's not ready, and I think even Amber knows she's not."

"Exactly." Sarah gestured at the black square packages. "Which is why I don't want her to have encouragement from any source apart from that dreadful boyfriend of hers."

"Tell me." Vivian popped the top of a diet soda and took a drink. "In high school, were you ever with a guy in the backseat of a car, or in the bushes at a dance, or in an upstairs bedroom at a party?"

An adrenaline thrill threatened, and Sarah forced herself to resist the memories and to say with pride, "I told him no."

Vivian took another sip, watching Sarah over the top of the can, and Sarah fought not to cringe, hearing her words reflected back in that way Vivian always managed, and knowing what she was thinking. *Yeah, well, not everyone's a frigid bitch like you.*

"Sarah."

"Yes, Vivian." She kept her tone as chilled as the can in Vivian's hands.

Vivian leaned forward, put her elbows on the counter between them. "Haven't you ever lost control?"

Sarah took a quick intake of breath, not quite a gasp, but nearly. The flush on her cheeks deepened, she was sure of it, and Vivian would see, leaning so close. A picture popped up, of herself writhing on the bed, Tom's name on her lips, convulsing in her second-ever orgasm. "Of . . . course."

"Sometimes." Vivian watched her intently, and Sarah hated her for always seeming to know what Sarah was thinking. "It's good to lose control because it frees you. Know what I mean?"

Sarah looked down at the clean counter and at Vivian's fabric-covered elbows. *No comment.*

"And sometimes it's not good to lose control and you want to take the whole thing back." She sighed, sounding genuinely frustrated. "In my case it's usually the second."

Sarah glanced up, completely unsure how to take this lowering of Vivian's guard, one part of her daring to wonder if it was real, the rest of her waiting for the confession to turn into another joke featuring Sarah as the inevitable punch line.

"You want to go into the living room?"

"I . . ." Sarah looked around her. What was wrong with this room? Nothing, especially now that Vivian—or Mike—had painted some of the over-the-top cuteness out of it.

But Vivian was already leading the way, heading for Stellie's old yellow-and-blue couch shoved to one side of the room, and throwing herself down on it, feet extended, hair splayed out over the cushioned back behind her.

Sarah sat next to her, knees together, ankles to one side, wondering why the rest of the furniture had been moved into the dining room. The room without carpet did look much nicer, more sophisticated, cleaner, sharper, more like Vivian herself.

"Relax, Sarah, you're making me nervous."

Sarah leaned back gingerly, hating the view of herself through Vivian's eyes, perched on the edge of the couch like a nervous bird ready to take off at the first sign of trouble.

"Okay." She let her head drop. "I'm relaxed."

Vivian gave her shoulder a playful swat. "Good for you."

Yes, good for her. Except lounging on the couch with Vivian made this seem less like a confrontation and more like a girls' visit. Like the endless ones she'd made to her friend Nora's apartment in New York. The two of them, sprawled on Nora's burgundy striped couch, gabbing the night away, nursing wine and Pepperidge Farm cookies from the Chocolate Collection.

"See, Sarah." Vivian put her soda on the hardwood floor and folded her arms across her flat stomach—for once completely covered by her shirt. "The media must have heard from a member of the Kettle Social Club. I'm sorry I thought it was you, but let's face it, we haven't exactly hit it off. And it seemed the perfect way to get back at me if you wanted to."

Sarah nodded, very wary now. This explained the move to the comfy couch. To soften Sarah up, get her on Vivian's side so she'd spill who was leaking news to the tabloids. Yes, Sarah knew who had talked and why. But to whom did she owe her allegiance?

"I'd like the leak to stop." Vivian turned her head, dark against the yellow cushion.

"I . . . can speak to her." Her voice came out low and nervous. The power in those brown eyes was considerable, even when they weren't threatening.

"Who?"

Sarah swallowed convulsively and started to say, *I'm afraid I don't feel comfortable sharing that information with you*, but caught herself in time to avoid ridicule. "I can't."

Vivian sat up and leaned elbows on thighs, hands dangling between her knees. "I came to Kettle to get away from this. I need it to stop, so I can move on. But I can't do it myself."

Sarah desperately wanted to leave. She did not want to feel either kinship or sympathy for this person. This person could turn on her in a heartbeat, use whatever vulnerability she found in Sarah to her own advantage, anywhere down the road.

"It's like stripping wallpaper." Vivian pried a gluey piece off her shirt. "No matter how hard you try to peel the stuff away cleanly, bits of it are going to stick to you."

Sarah nodded, thinking of Tom, wishing she could go back to viewing morality in black-and-white terms. So much tidier. So much simpler to live that way. "I understand."

"I'd like to know who, so I have some hope of stopping it."

"Knowledge is power." Sarah laughed self-consciously, full of dread. Her father's favored philosophy had popped past her self-censor, and now Vivian was going to have her for lunch.

"Knowledge?" Vivian turned her head, eyes full of engaging mischief. "Actually, Sarah, *tits* are power."

"*What?*"

"Tits." She pointed to her own, for once not on obvious display, and grinned infectiously. "Tits are power."

"Oh, come on." Sarah felt a smile starting in spite of herself. "I hardly think you can equate knowledge to . . . breasts."

"Tits."

"Fine." She lifted her hand and let it drop on the sofa arm, feeling a rogue giggle tickling to come up. "Tits. Happy?"

"Ha!" Vivian held up her hands, framing a shot. "Ladies and gentlemen, Ms. Sarah Gilchrist says 'tits.' "

Sarah choked the giggle back again. "I meant that knowledge, especially knowledge of yourself, is—"

"We'll compromise." Vivian gestured broadly and winked. "Power is knowledge that your self has great tits."

Laughter burst out of Sarah without her permission, a wave that rolled merrily along, capped with a foam of hysteria. This was too unexpectedly like talking to Nora. Where had those friendships gone? How had she survived here so long without them?

"Oh my." She wiped her eyes, let a few more chuckles escape, and took a deep breath. "I haven't laughed that hard since . . ."

She tried to remember, and was horrified when nothing came up. Not even in the past several years. Nora. And now Vivian.

"Since when?"

Sarah looked down at her hands in her lap. Perfect French manicure aside, they'd become loose-skinned, tendons forming vein-draped ridges. Her mother's hands. "It's not important."

Immediately she regretted speaking, especially in a small, anxious voice. Hadn't she just had the good sense to caution herself about revealing vulnerability to this woman?

Vivian touched her shoulder again, more gently this time. "Jail is only one kind of prison, Sarah."

A lump gathered in Sarah's throat, which irritated her immensely. She stood up. "I should go."

Vivian stood up, too. "Yeah, okay."

For an awkward moment the women faced each other, as if something still needed to be said, though Sarah couldn't for the life of her figure out what.

So she turned and went back into the kitchen where the pack of condoms were still a black mark on the old-fashioned tile counter. "I don't know what to do with these."

"Here." Vivian grabbed them and held them out. "Amber's boyfriend sounds like a real jerk. And the only things worse than losing your virginity before you're ready are unwanted pregnancies or incurable STDs."

Sarah shuddered and extended her hand. Vivian had her there. Tom had been honorable. After a few attempts at convincing Sarah to go all the way, he'd given up. But that animal, Larry, there was no telling what he'd do, or whether he'd stop when Amber wanted him to.

If he did that to her baby, Sarah would castrate him with her teeth. "I'll . . . think it over."

"I don't know shit about parenting, but I remember being a teenager." Vivian put the packets on Sarah's palm and closed Sarah's fingers over them, keeping hers on top. "The harder my mom came down, the more determined I was to do the opposite."

"That's Amber." Sarah nodded, desperately wanting to pull her hand away. "I was different."

"*Really?*" A wink took the sting out of the sarcasm, and Sarah could even smile along, albeit stiffly.

"Amber seems like a good, level-headed kid." Vivian squeezed Sarah's hand and, thank goodness, let go. "I wouldn't be surprised if she doesn't need them."

"I hope not." Sarah backed toward the door, intensely uncomfortable without the cushioning hostility between them. She had no idea what to say or how to react to this version of Vivian, who made sense, who seemed to have a better and clearer grasp of her daughter's situation than Sarah did. "Thank you."

"You're welcome." Vivian opened the door and gestured

Sarah out. "So back to the trenches now, huh? You Martha Stewart, me Madonna? The great pumpkin wars?"

Sarah reached the bottom step outside in the chill, condoms clutched tightly in her fist, and turned. Vivian glanced over at the men already getting out of their cars.

The beautiful face aged suddenly into fatigue, eyes losing brightness over dark circles concealer couldn't quite cover. It was suddenly impossible to believe this woman had killed anyone.

"Vivian." She cleared her throat. "I think Come As You're Not is a better theme for the party. And if you want to offer makeovers, that would be fine."

Vivian smiled, and seemed sincere. "Thank you."

"You're welcome." Feeling ridiculous, she took a few steps toward the street. The men immediately went on alert, clearly hoping for more human waste to buzz around. They must be camped there 24/7, watching everything Vivian did.

Jail is only one kind of prison.

Sarah turned back and approached the stoop where Vivian stood watching her. She looked up into the beautiful, tired brown eyes and couldn't help herself.

"Joan. Joan is talking to the press."

Before Vivian could react, she turned again and strode to the end of the driveway, held up her hand to indicate she had nothing to say, walked swiftly to her own house, up the stairs, into her daughter's room, and carefully replaced the condoms in Amber's coat pocket.

Eighteen

Excerpt from Erin's diary
Eleventh grade

I went out with Joe again last night. I told Dad I was going to the Spring Dance, but we went out on our own. He wanted to go all the way, and I let him. He said he'd never felt like this about anyone. That he loved me so much it hurt and if I didn't love him back, he might die, and that he wants to marry me and have kids.

It is so amazing to be loved like this. So different than the way anyone else acts. And when he was touching me and wanted to do it, I couldn't think of any reason not to. It hurt, but it was good pain. He held me so tight after that I almost couldn't breathe. He called me the center of his world and said I'd be protected and loved by him for the rest of my life.

I said I would marry him when I finish high school. I want to do that first, for me. Then I want to go to college and study to be a nurse. Or maybe a social worker.

He didn't use a thingy, but he said if I got pregnant what did it matter because I was going to be his anyway for the rest of my life. I don't know. I think he should use them from now on. Until we're married anyway.

I feel like things will turn around for me now. Joe will take me out of this house away from Dad and into a normal life.

I've done my time.

Erin ran up the steps to the front door of Joan's house. She found herself running almost everywhere these days. Ever since that first day when she'd sneaked out of bed and dug out her running shoes, she'd found time nearly every day to get her body going. At least during the week when Joe was at work.

It felt so wonderful to be out and moving and free of the house. To feel her body building back strength, endurance, challenging herself to go farther and farther. She'd even gone past the dark, handsome man's house, Jordan's house, a few more times, though she tried not to make that the point of running. There were already enough things she couldn't have.

But a few times she'd gone past his house anyway. Twice she'd seen him. The second time he smiled and said hello, which made her blush and run faster to get away. She'd gone home and showered, did laundry, and hid her running shoes and shorts the way she always did, but somehow when Joe came back from work he knew something was different. As if he had a monitoring device set to detect her slightest pleasure spike of unknown origin.

He'd already become uneasy from her wearing the pink sweater as often as she could get away with, without looking like a weirdo who wore the same thing every day. She was even thinking of how to ask for another sweater in a bright color, maybe blue to match her eyes, though that would bring on more interrogation.

She'd shown up in a headband one morning, to keep the hair out of her eyes, and she thought Joe was going to have a fit. Why was she dressing up? Who was she trying to look good for? There was someone else, wasn't there?

No, no, and endlessly no, she was doing this for herself.

The day Jordan had said hello to her, Joe had come down on her even harder. What was it? Who was it? She looked different, had she been meeting someone while he was gone? His hands had gone around her arms, his lip had curled, he'd squeezed until her skin bruised.

She'd stayed quiet this time instead of pleading, instead of insisting she was innocent. Stared at him, silent and calm. And he'd been the one to break. Gone down on his knees and begged and cried. He hadn't meant to hurt her, but how could he be good to her if she gave him no reason to trust her? God knew he couldn't love her any more than he already did. No one could love anyone more than he loved her.

His tirade hadn't made her feel guilty or even that frightened. His tearful apologies after hadn't soothed the bruises or melted her heart. Nor had they brought back to life the love she'd initially felt for him as they usually did. Instead she'd felt only mild disgust and detachment.

This frightened her more than his threats.

She knew she should stop running by Jordan's house and put the headband and the pink sweater away. As rebellions went, her efforts were pretty lame. But since Joy, she hadn't experienced much new or hopeful in her life. She didn't see why she should have to give up something so small as a new sweater and exercise. Running gave her something to look forward to. Something to do besides read *What to Expect When You're Expecting*, which she hadn't in a few days. Something besides painting, besides sending out junk e-mail to see if it would come back.

And speaking of despair, here she was ringing the doorbell at Joan's house. Joan wanted to speak to her. To spend time with her daughter-in-law, she said.

Joan only wanted to speak to Erin when Joe complained. This gave Joan the opportunity for her own tirade, to tell Erin that Joan wasn't allowing her to live in a house Joan owned in order to cheat on her son. And that Erin was lucky not having to work like Joan did. And that Joan had moved into this crappy two-bedroom place so her son and his wife could have her childhood home, so Erin better watch her step or she'd be out on her ass.

Which was sort of ironic because there were times being out on her ass was everything Erin hoped for. At least until reality set in. Where would she go? What would she do? She had no skills, no money, and no family who'd welcome her.

But Joan's version featured lazy Erin freeloading on Joe's

salary. Joan's—make that everyone in Kettle's—version of events had little to do with reality. Like the article Joan engineered for the tabloids about Vivian, which made Erin angry and sick.

Sometimes Erin wanted to interrupt one of Joan's tirades and tell her Erin would love to work. That she'd love to go back to school and get her GED and then an associates degree. She'd get a part-time job to pay for tuition, and when she graduated and got a full-time job, she'd work her fanny off. Imagine feeling useful and productive.

She'd also love to throw out that Joan knew damn well the only reason Erin didn't work was because then Joe couldn't control her as absolutely as he did now.

Joan opened the door and parted her lips in the ghastly smile that was as close as she got to looking pleasant. Her ghastly smile used to be yellow, which suited her, but Dr. Marlowe must have given her a whitening treatment because now her teeth were so white it was startling.

"Come in, Erin."

"Thanks." She trudged into the cigarette-fouled air, fly to the spider, and took her seat in what she had dubbed the whipping post, a squat, overstuffed, priggish chair from Joan's recently reupholstered living room set. Joan had chosen bright white fabric with giant red and yellow and green tropical flowers and birds on it, as if she lived in Kettle, Florida.

"Coffee?"

"No thank you." Erin gritted her teeth. She'd never drunk coffee, had even given up tea when she got pregnant in high school. Who knew what effects caffeine could cause in a fetus? Things scientists might not find out about for years. After all the miscarriages, and then after Joy, Erin never went back to caffeine in case a miracle pregnancy occurred and she'd cause damage to her baby before she knew she was pregnant.

But Joan kept asking if Erin would like coffee. Because then she could mention how Joe liked coffee, and Joan's late husbands liked coffee, and what a nice thing for married couples to share tastes. She loved pointing out all the ways in which Erin was a disappointment to her. And whenever she could find some way to imply *and to Joe*, you could bet she did.

Someday Erin wanted to mention that Joe hadn't really turned out to be her dream husband, either. Maybe she even wanted to today. That's what kind of mood she was in.

"That's right, you don't like coffee." As if this was a character flaw so gross, Joan could hardly stand upright while thinking about it. "Joe drinks his every day alone."

She didn't offer Erin anything else, but went to the kitchen and brought her own cup back to the immaculate living room, lined with gray carpet so clean and perfectly even-piled that without the vacuum cleaner tracks, it would look like plastic. She sat back in one of the tropical chairs, and a parrot appeared perfectly positioned to peck at her dyed hair.

"So, Erin. How was the Social Club meeting this morning?"

"Fine." Erin stared at the parrot, hoping its beak was very sharp. Joan hadn't been at the meeting; she had "important details to attend to" on her day off. Erin guessed the article about Vivian had been worse than anticipated and Joan was lying low, though Vivian hadn't shown, either. "Betty said Sidler's will have the cakes for the Come As You're Not party ready by four on Saturday. Nancy said the band booked a wedding in Ladysmith, but they'd still be on time. Sarah will harvest her pumpkins and move them onto the flatbed. I said we had enough volunteers to set up and run the haunted house."

"Good." Joan rubbed the edge of a nostril between her thumb and forefinger, the way people thought didn't qualify as picking.

Erin crossed her legs and laced her fingers behind her head. She never sat like that, always slouched with her legs together and her hands in her lap. But she looked forward to Joan's reaction to the next part of the meeting report.

"Sarah said Vivian is going to get a makeover booth. She'll sell certificates at the party and do them later, in her home."

"What?" Joan was so agitated, she spilled coffee onto her pink top, which had a puffy white daisy sewn on the front. Erin thought Joan could use about a month's worth of makeovers, but then she wasn't one to throw stones. The coffee stain spread above the daisy, brown on pink, until it looked like a cloud or a map of France. Or a coffee stain making an ugly shirt on an ugly person even uglier.

"*What?*"

"Vivian will sell makeovers." She knew Joan wasn't really asking her to repeat herself, but she couldn't resist.

"That trash making people over? As what, hookers?"

"She's beautiful. I want one myself." Erin couldn't believe she'd said that. She might as well go to the garage, haul out a shovel, and start digging her own grave. It would get back to Joe that she was concerned about looking prettier. Joe would want to know why, and things would all go downhill farther and faster and steeper than they were going already.

Erin thought about how she felt when she was running. How she felt when Jordan smiled at her and said hello. How she felt when she was around Vivian. And she decided that she didn't care. She'd had pain all her life. Now at least she had some pleasure to go along with it.

Let Joan tell him. Just let her.

"I've noticed changes in you lately, Erin. Joe has also."

Erin took her hands back down to her lap. She couldn't help the tremor of fear; in fact she expected it. But this time there was also a little anger, and a little contempt, and a little indifference. And just the beginning of a feeling of power. Not some big, courageous tidal wave of it, like people got in the movies. Not like the Grinch on top of Mount Crumpet when his heart grew three sizes and he got the strength of a dozen Grinches. Nothing that would give her the courage to stand up and dump the rest of Joan's coffee on her ugly clothes and stalk out into the promise of a new life. She was still Erin. But it was nice to feel signs of life after too long feeling barren and weak. Like a recently rain-soaked desert coming into bloom.

"How have I been different?"

"Oh, little things. Anything you want to tell me, just us girls?" The cow eyes lined raccoon-black blinked; the red lips stretched over the oddly white teeth, and Erin wondered how Joan could think Erin was that stupid. Even a developmentally delayed person could see this trap. Even Erin.

"Nothing but me wanting to look better."

"Any reason?" Joan took a sip of coffee. "Hmm?"

"No." The word was curt. For once, Erin didn't feel the need to elaborate.

Joan's lips thinned; her eyes grew cold. "Don't think you're fooling either Joe or me."

"I don't."

The doorbell rang, and Joan put her coffee down on the scuffed end table Joe made for her in high school, which looked ratty next to the bright new chairs. "Who the hell is that?"

Erin shrugged. Probably someone selling candy, or an alarm system, or magazine subscriptions, or someone thinking he could change a person's lifelong beliefs in a two-minute visit. Erin was prey to all of them, being at home all day. Sometimes she wanted to tell them she was sorry, but she was in the middle of Satan worship and the goat was getting restless.

Joan heaved her stomach and breasts out of the chair and teetered on her skinny black-pants-clad legs to the front hall to answer the door.

"What the hell do *you* want?"

Erin got up from her chair. Even Joan wasn't rude enough to talk like that to a fund-raiser or salesperson or missionary. Which meant this must not be a stranger. And there was only one person Erin knew of who rated Joan's open hatred, though doubtless many more, including herself, endured it silently.

Erin's heart started beating a little faster as she turned the corner. Joan stood like a guard dog in the middle of her door, but Vivian was tall enough that half her face was visible over the monochrome teased black hair.

Erin wanted to laugh and pump her fist. Joan might think she was tough, but by the end of the conversation, Joan would find out what tough meant. Erin looked forward to it.

She crept closer, anxious not to make noise in case Joan remembered she was there and told her to go away.

"Hi, Joan, how are you doing?"

"Fine." Joan crossed her arms, angry, defensive, and no doubt guilty. Erin loved it already.

"My, you are looking lovely today."

Erin barely missed snorting. Lovely like a coffee-stained pink-and-black buffalo.

She wanted to get closer, miss none of the action, and it suddenly hit her that she was being ridiculous cowering back here in the hall. If Joan told her to go away, she could say sorry, no. Sometimes her timidity disgusted even her.

She moved forward so she could see Vivian's face.

"Oh, hi Erin."

"Hi." She beamed. Vivian looked a little tired today, but stunning even dressed with less than her usual fashion sense. Erin was pretty sure Vivian couldn't look ugly if she tried.

From Joan, Erin got a glare of disapproval, but Erin was used to those, so she stood her ground. Yes, she felt different today. And nothing could touch her when Vivian was around.

Joan turned back to her visitor. "What are you doing here?"

"Well, Joan." Vivian's smile conveyed zero warmth. "I wonder if I could talk to you."

"About what?"

Vivian held up the flyers. "About advertising my aerobics class at the Halloween party. I know you're in charge of the decorating committee. And a very important job that is, too. I'm sure the school gym will never have looked lovelier."

Joan grunted. "Flattery will get you nowhere."

"No? That's a shame, Joan. Because I think this is a great chance for some of Kettle's residents to get in shape." A deliberate glance at Joan's stomach. "Don't you?"

"We're in a lot better shape than you are." She pointed an accusing finger. "Morally speaking."

"Oh now, Joan, it's funny you should say that." Vivian's smile became broader and more fixed and more threatening, and Erin wanted to rub her hands together with glee. Here it came.

"Because actually, Joan, if you'll notice, I have no more skeletons left in my closet. They're all out, dancing in public, bones clattering away. You know what I mean?"

Joan recoiled a bit, enough to signal that yes, she knew what Vivian meant. "You reap what you sow."

"Oh absolutely." Vivian nodded and looked away, her profile lovely and proud, then she turned back and skewered Joan with those gorgeous lively eyes. "Except that some people, Joan, still have those skeletons tightly locked away."

"What do you mean by that?" Nervousness crept into Joan's voice even though she tried to keep it tough.

Erin wanted to start dancing right there in the hall. Vivian was getting ready for the kill. What form that would take, Erin didn't know, but she had absolute faith it would be crushing and fatal, and she couldn't wait.

"You believe in honesty, don't you, Joan." Vivian's voice was low, sweet honey. "In protecting innocents from moral decay."

"Yes, I do." Joan pulled herself up self-righteously, but her voice was wary. She knew something was coming and that it wasn't going to be good.

Erin bit the inside of her cheek to keep from laughing.

"And that's why you think it's important that the truth be told, no matter how ugly it might be."

"Absolutely."

"I agree with you, Joan. I really do." She tucked the flyers behind Joan's folded arms, smiling the smile of a predator who has finally trapped its prey. "And that's why I think next time those reporters ask me questions, I'm going to feel it's important to tell them what Joe's doing to Erin."

Erin gasped. She shrank back, step after step, until the wooden banister of the stairs to the second floor stopped her. No one had ever said it. Not one single word. Not about Joe. Not about her father. Not in all the years she'd lived it.

Suddenly it was out there, lit neon, flashing, blaring like a car alarm, *what Joe's doing to Erin.*

This was not at all what she expected.

For a blissful, unprecedented second she allowed herself to taste what could happen, what Vivian clearly thought would happen. That Joan would crumple. That Vivian could have her media cake and free Erin, too.

Then reality closed back in. In any other town, among any other people, it might work. But not here. Not in Kettle.

Vivian had about five seconds of triumph. Erin had fewer.

Joan threw back her head to cackle like a ridiculously overdrawn movie villain. Erin folded her arms around herself, wishing she was out running. Wishing she was home painting, or on e-mail, or reading.

"Who the hell is going to care about Erin? It's the dirt on you they want. Shit happens all over the country to all kinds of people. But it takes someone special to make it news." She cackled again. "You are that kind of special, Vivian."

"You haven't experienced the power of the media the way I have." Vivian took a step closer, still thinking she had a chance. "Or the wave of sympathy that follows a good victim story. A few sentences is all it takes to start people wanting blood. In this case, Joe's. And yours."

"Go ahead and try." Joan shook her head pityingly, and Erin wanted to plant her fist in the soft, pink, daisy-covered belly. "All I have to do is talk about how you were here and threatened me, and bang, your stories are as made up as we want them to be."

"The people here know what's going on." Vivian gestured around her. "They'd—"

"We're all very proud of our town's legacy." Joan jutted her head forward until it was only a few inches from Vivian's face. "There's never been a crime in Kettle. Didn't you know that?"

The triumph started to slide off Vivian's face, and Erin closed her eyes. She wanted to stick her fingers in her ears, run off and hide somewhere like she did when she was a kid and her dad got angry. But she wasn't a kid now.

She opened her eyes and took in Vivian's beautiful face, gone frozen and defiant and half disbelieving and trapped.

Erin knew that feeling.

"You know, I've changed my mind. You don't need exercise classes, you're already extremely flexible." Vivian grabbed back her flyers. "I don't know when I've seen someone who could walk around with her head so far up her own ass."

Erin cringed. She wanted Vivian to stop. Preserve her dignity and walk away. Joan would just be warming up. She had the advantage, and now Vivian knew it.

"You don't belong here, Lorelei Taylor. And whatever I can do to make your stay less pleasant, I intend to do it until you give up and get the hell out. Find some other town to pollute with your prostitution and pornography and murder."

Vivian took a step back that nearly broke Erin's heart. The bad guys had always won in Erin's life. She was used to that. Vivian wasn't.

"Joan, I'd stay and chat, but I just remembered I've got pins heating at home and I'd rather go stick them in my eyes."

She turned and strode back to the car, while Joan let loose more of her *bwahaha* laughter, loud enough that the entire town was probably wondering if the Joker had come to Kettle.

Outside, Vivian's car started angrily; Joan closed the door and turned on Erin, as if she'd love to become Kettle's next murderess right that minute. "What did you tell her about Joe?"

For once Erin held her gaze, hating her as openly as she'd ever dared to. "Nothing."

"Liar."

"I said nothing. She's been where I am; she knows. I didn't need to say a word."

"Bullshit. Joe will hear about this."

Erin's breath started coming high and shallow. She was always afraid, but now she was really, really angry, too. Someone as beautiful and powerful as Vivian should not be brought down. Especially not by someone like Joan.

"She's been there, just like me. But you know what?" She

took a step forward, still breathing funny and still angry, and Joan actually retreated. "She's free of him now. She did what she had to do, the only thing she could do. We both know what that feels like."

Joan blanched. Put a hand to her heart. Erin suddenly realized what she'd said, and how Joan had taken it.

Power started rising in her, like sap rising through a tree in the spring, bringing life and strength and beautiful new color. And for the first time in as long as Erin could remember, she didn't feel afraid at all.

Nineteen

Happy fourteen, pumpkin. Your present is an all-expenses-paid trip to Disneyland with Dad. Can't wait to spend time with my Sleeping Beauty.

Your Prince

Vivian pulled the last strip of masking tape off the cream trim in her bedroom, stood back, and admired. Ohhh, was that better. Instead of blue-and-brown misery, the room had come alive in pale blue-green that reminded her of the sea. Not New York harbor, parts of the Caribbean. All the warmer and more beautiful with the gray sky and wind whipping outside in Kettle.

Even Jesus's clock would look lovely against the color. She'd wanted to get rid of the thing, but how could you dump Jesus in the trash? He'd peer up at her with those soulful Holy Bambi eyes and she'd be haunted for the rest of her life. Plus, she'd gotten kind of fond of Him.

She wrapped the foam brushes in a plastic bread bag, dumped the bag on top of the plastic paint tray liner, and hauled up the old sheets she'd used as drop cloths to protect the hardwood.

So. She'd painted and redecorated the cuteness out of the kitchen. Painted her bedroom. Gotten rid of way too many square feet of shag carpet. All she could afford to do for now. More than that, all she really cared to do. No point pretending this place would ever feel like home.

But then she hadn't felt at home anywhere. Maybe in the early years in Chicago with her parents, before puberty hit and things got gross. After that, no matter how long she stayed anywhere, there was always the feeling of running away or to, until Ed. Except as much as she reveled in the luxury, his condo had been entirely too sophisticated to feel like home.

If he hadn't gotten himself killed, by now he'd probably be sharing the place with Abby, who'd fit there as perfectly as goat cheese on an endive leaf, standing auburn-haired among the copper pots and Château Margaux wines, whirlpool tubs, and goose down pillows, all the things she was born to. And Vivian would be running off somewhere new.

Just not here.

She folded the old sheets, sealed the paint can, and hauled them all to the chilly, gloomy basement. Tossed the brushes and paint tray liner and sticky balls of blue-green splotched masking tape in the trash.

Last thing on her house to-do list was to investigate the attic, see what was still up there before she put the place on the market—after the vultures got tired of her good behavior and went home, which she hoped would be any day now. She'd already noticed them missing for hours at a time. They'd no doubt cover the Halloween party the next night, but when she didn't flash any boob or fondle any penises, she bet they'd lose interest.

And then she'd be free to go. Somewhere.

Her heart gave a painful jab and she went back up to the hall outside her bedroom and pulled down the attic stairs from the trap door in the ceiling. She didn't want Mike to pop into her head first thing when she thought about leaving. He was a friend, one she'd made at one of the most complicated parts of what had been a pretty damn complicated life. She'd had a few good girlfriends and plenty of lovers, but never a relationship like this. A man who supported her and helped her but wasn't trying to get into her pants ASAP? What the hell was that?

Something with Rosemary. He still hadn't let out anything juicier than the bare sense that he and Rosemary weren't as happy as the collective Kettle idiocy thought they were.

Whatever. The intimacy of that confession, if he ever got around to it, would only make leaving harder.

The attic stairs creaked on their way down, and creaked again on her way up into darkness and familiar smells. At the top, she fumbled for the frayed string attached to the room's one naked bulb, and was startled when light flooded the room. As if she expected the bulb to have crossed into death with Gran.

The place looked so familiar, she got silly sentimental sniffles. To a nine-year-old, an old woman's past equaled vast tracts of treasure, waiting to be explored. Ancient ice skates, discarded pictures, antique dolls, boxes of papers, trunks of clothes. One trunk in particular held fabulous flapper creations of satin and silk and beaded velvet from the twenties. Vivian had hauled her favorites down to try on endlessly in the mirror in Gran's bedroom, imagining herself on the arm of a dapper beau.

Yeah, well, she never got the dapper beau part down quite the way she dreamed it then. But the dresses would still be here. One of them would probably be a good costume for the party the next day. Come As You're Not. No one could argue that she was a flapper. She'd die to see what Sarah would show up as. A Playboy model? A garage mechanic? Roseanne?

She moved toward the place she remembered, behind a massive carved wood headboard that stuck out into the room.

Bingo. The old green metal trunk. And a new one, next to it, smaller and black, with labels slapped on by ocean liner personnel and worn by time. The New Amsterdam. The Rafaello. Italy. France. England. What was in there?

She crouched and lifted the brass clasps, undid the catch in the middle, and raised the lid. A waft of grandma-scent rose, lavender and a hint of that god-awful apple pie potpourri that smelled like apple pie only if you made yours entirely of chemicals.

This trunk was full of clothes, too. Not flapper costumes,

but clothes Vivian remembered Gran wearing when she visited them in Chicago. Powder-blue and green traveling suits, knit pants, bathrobes, piles of dresses. In particular, one dress Vivian remembered vividly. A scoop-necked tight bodice with a full skirt in cream-colored cotton, with tiny climbing roses in neat alternating rows, some growing up, some growing down.

She carefully pulled the dress out, and shook it unfolded. A Stepford Wife dress, a dress worn in the summer when you'd made homemade lemonade and cookies for the kids and were on the back porch calling them in for a snack.

This she could wear to a Come As You're Not party.

Dress laid aside, she rummaged further and hit something cold and hard. Gran's recipe file, the wooden one Grandpa Lester made for her, still full of cards. Swedish meatballs, salmon loaf, party punch . . . and cardamom butter cookies.

Vivian used to love those cookies more than her own life.

She extracted the card, slung the dress over her shoulder, and climbed down into the warmth of the house, strangely excited. Making cookies wasn't something she did much, to put it mildly. In New York if you had money, you didn't cook. Baking was twice as foreign, unless you did it to brag about at your next cocktail party. Everyone ate out or ordered in. The best of everything waited right outside the building, why put out any effort?

But in Kettle, Wisconsin, with the house done for now—what else was she going to do? She had butter in the freezer, she could let that sit on the counter for a while, or nuke it gently in the microwave until it softened.

Downstairs, she got out two sticks of butter—she could give some cookies to Mike and bring the rest to the Halloween party—and left them on the counter to thaw and soften. Then back up to her paint-smelling beautiful room, where she gingerly moved furniture back into place, taking extra care with the dollhouse so as not to disturb its occupants, hating having to think about getting rid of it when she moved.

God, she was a mess today. She needed activity, she needed people. Tomorrow she'd go help set up for the party. Yesterday's Social Club meeting had been the usual ridiculous affair, but Sarah was planning a pretty good time.

Beyond the party, the weeks stretched entirely too long ahead with no concrete plan to fill them. She hated that feeling more than anything else. It made her restless and jittery and irritable, like she'd ordered a double espresso at Dean & Deluca, they'd given her two, and she drank them both.

Okay. Despairing sigh. She'd bake cookies.

Back downstairs, she set the recipe card in Gran's holder— a tiny clothespin glued to a felt flower glued to a tiny dowel sticking out of a miniature flowerpot. Honestly. The things people found to do with their time.

Two minutes later, she'd found a bowl and a mixer, nuked the butter fifteen seconds to get it soft enough, and plopped the sticks into the bowl along with the sugar. Funny how it was coming back to her. Gran in this kitchen, wearing . . .

Vivian grinned and went upstairs. Two minutes later, she was back in Gran's dress, which fit her frighteningly well. No question where she inherited her shape.

On with the radio to the nearest local station, playing easy listening hits. Perfect. She started the mixer, singing along to "Islands in the Stream."

She added two eggs to the butter and sugar—the curdled

yellow mess was so dearly familiar from so many recipes, she wondered how she could have gone this long without it. Vanilla, dark and fragrant; dry ingredients measured, sifted: flour, baking powder, salt, cardamom, cinnamon, allspice. The scent of heaven. She spilled the cinnamon and had to brush it off her dress, pushed back her hair and probably got flour and cinnamon on that, too, and who cared?

"To all the girls I've loved before . . ."

God, what a putrid song.

She shaped the dough into a log and put it in the freezer, too impatient to let it chill slowly. What else? On a sudden inspiration, she searched her grandmother's larder and came out triumphantly with a tin of Hershey's Cocoa.

Sugar, salt, and the precious dark brown powder, rich and bitter, eschew the microwave from now on. This was her old-fashioned afternoon, layers of clouds whizzing along in the sky, leaves doing elaborate gymnastics all over her lawn.

She mixed the dry ingredients in the saucepan, cutting the sugar to make it dark the way she liked it, then added hot water and let it boil for a couple of minutes to keep brown powder lumps from forming on the surface when milk was added.

While that boiled, she turned on the oven, impatient for the scent of baking cookies.

"Yooooou light up my liiiiife . . ." Flashback to her high school friend Deena's wedding, Deena six months' pregnant, both sets of parents glowering, bride and groom equally horrified. What had happened to her? Vivian didn't have a soul from her old life in Chicago she kept in touch with. Not a soul from her life in New York, either.

Nearly forty years old, and Kettle was all she had.

Dough out of the freezer, she sliced the cookies, a little soft still but who cared, and put them on the ungreased million-year-old cookie sheets—flat pieces of metal, not the double-layer, nonstick, carbon steel ones she lined with silicone mats at Ed's. And used maybe once.

These sheets had seen cookies by the thousands, decade after decade.

She set the timer, poured milk into the cooling chocolate syrup, and lit the flame under it. Eight minutes later, a buttery, cardamom-dominated smell permeated the kitchen. She inhaled greedily, setting out her grandmother's old round cooling racks in preparation for the bounty they were about to receive.

The timer's ding sent her into action, the cookies slid obediently onto the rack. Doubtless her impatient tongue would be burned by the first bite, same as it was when she was a child.

Hot cocoa in one hand, scalding cookie in the other, she glanced out the window and dropped her jaw.

Snow. *In October*.

She took one bite, burned her tongue, and followed it with a bittersweet sip of cocoa. An Olivia Newton-John song her mom had adored came on the radio. She listened, watching snow dancing with fallen leaves, pointlessly nostalgic for the warm, wonderful memories she didn't have, to the point where tears began slip-sliding down her face.

And God, there he was on cue, Mike, striding across her driveway, breath streaming white, cheeks wholesome pink. Superman, answering a cry for help he hadn't even heard.

What was she going to do about him?

He knocked on her back door and she didn't move, not wanting to answer and desperately wanting to see him at the same time. Maybe she needed to move to a place with a name like Shady Elms Home for the Utterly Wacked.

He knocked again; she wiped her eyes, probably even the light makeup gone now, and answered the door to the sneaking rush of cold.

"Hi, Mike."

"Mmm, what smells so—"

A double take. Like in the cartoons. Glance at her, then to the kitchen to locate the scent, then back to her.

Oh no. Here it came. Cried-off makeup. Flour and cinnamon smudges on her face. Donna Reed dress. *She had finally found the real her.* He probably had a stiffie the size of the Eiffel Tower.

"God . . . Vivian . . ."

"Well, which is it, God or Vivian?" She hated the way he stared.

"You look—"

"I know, I know. Amazing, beautiful, and most importantly, virginal. Right?"

"Like shit." He closed the door behind him. "What happened?"

Vivian let out startled laughter. "I was baking cookies."

"Since when does baking cookies run your mascara and turn your nose red?" He reached to smooth her hair, and she ducked under his arm.

"These cookies are a bitch to make."

He caught her shoulder, made her face him. "You want to tell me?"

"No."

"Why does that not surprise me?"

"Because I'm a hard, jaded, fucked-up woman you shouldn't be talking to in the first place."

"Where did you get that dress?"

"Attic."

He took a step closer, still gripping her shoulder. "I was kidding before, you do look beautiful."

"Glad you think so." She took a step back so his arm went straight. "It's my costume for the party tomorrow."

He stepped forward again. "This is where I say you've been wearing costumes all along, right?"

"Whatever floats your boat." She stepped back.

Step forward. "Vivian."

"Yes?" Step back.

Forward. "Hold still."

"Why?" Next attempt to step back thwarted by strong muscular pressure from strong muscular arms belonging to Mike.

"Because I'm going to kiss you."

Sharp intake of breath on Vivian's part cut short by one of the most amazing kisses she'd ever been privileged to receive.

And another one. And . . . oh God. More. And she was kissing him back like the affection- and sex-starved fool she was, only as the kisses progressed, it started being less about her needs and more about Mike, which scared the shit out of her. "Stop."

His hands traveled from her shoulders to the sides of her breasts and made the sweet, virginal, cotton feel extremely sexy. Not to mention the woman wearing it.

"Why?"

"I don't know." What reason would make sense?

His thumbs found her nipples, which practically barged through the nylon of her bra, like the Incredible Hulk, whose inflating muscles shredded his human clothes.

"Mike."

"What?" He backed her against the wall, wedged his thigh between hers, and proceeded to work magic that made her brain beg to be released from the burden of common sense. Hell, of conscious thought.

"I forget."

"Good." He painted a tiny circle on her neck with his tongue, and she pushed her pelvis instinctively against the erection promising heaven through too much fabric.

Then he stopped, and her moan of disappointment came out much too loudly.

"Cookies."

"They're—" She wrinkled her nose and sniffed. "Burning."

Classic interruption. Had to be either that or a knock at the door, which, at the rate the cookies were burning, would probably be the fire department.

One pan of charred cardamom butter cookies out of the oven, and of course, as in any good farce, the smoke detector went off. While she dealt with the cookies, Mike climbed a chair, yanked out the battery, and went around opening windows.

"Whew." He waved smoke toward the fresh air and winked. "Surprised *we* didn't set it off."

"Yeah." She put the pan on the tile counter, where it sizzled against some water left there.

"So?"

She turned and found him standing in the center of the kitchen, hands on hips, giving her the where-were-we? look, which made his blue eyes hot and sweet, and which made her chest fluttery, and which made every warning signal go off at a decibel level that made the smoke detector a lullaby. "So-o-o?"

He took a few steps toward her and she took the last step to him, though she hadn't intended to.

"It's lucky the cookies burned," he said.

"Why? They were good cookies."

"Because I want you to make the decision about us with your brain, not your . . . not the rest of you."

She laughed. "You mean not with my c—"

His hand made sure the rest of the word couldn't come out of hers. "You are such a foul mouth."

She blinked up at him, moved back from his hand. "Is that exciting to you?"

"Possibly."

"Come see my bedroom."

He frowned. "Vivian . . ."

"No, no, I want you to see it. It's painted."

"Listen to me." He took her shoulders and planted her solidly on the floor. "If we go up there, we're not coming back down for several hours."

"Gee, Mike, you take a long time to look at paint."

"And if we go up there and spend several hours, that's not going to be the only time we spend several hours."

"Fine by me. Paint is endlessly fascinating."

"Vivian." His jaw tensed; his hands on her shoulders clamped harder. "We are going to do this like normal people."

"You know any?"

"We're going to be together exclusively, and see this through until we either decide it won't work or get married."

"*Married?*" She put her hand to her thumping heart. "What are you, nuts?"

"Relax. I was making a point."

"Christmas, you scared the crap outta me."

"Yeah." He grimaced comically. "I think I wet myself."

She laughed and didn't resist when he took her hands and put them around his neck, though she felt as if she should.

"Let's go upstairs, Vivian."

"To see the paint?"

His hands gripped her waist; she felt the quiet strength in them, and her heart did that weird squeezy thing again. "And more, if we have a deal."

"Mike, I'm leaving as soon as—"

"That's immaterial. Do we have a deal?"

"How is that immaterial?"

"Because I'm talking about you and me, not where we live."

"I've just been through hell. When I leave here, I want to leave. I want to put this whole miserable chapter of my life behind me. I want to start completely over."

"With some other sugar daddy who beats you up?"

She took in a deep breath, half begging for patience, half in horror at the thought. "No. Maybe on my own. Or with a man who is good to me."

"And?" He spread his arms what-about-me? wide.

She laughed. "Not in Kettle. I don't belong here."

He looked down at her dress and over at the cookies. "You're underestimating—"

"I put on a costume and baked some cookies, Mike. You

might think you don't want another Rosemary, but you're asking me to be her every time you talk to me."

"I'm not asking you to be Rosemary. Trust me." He took in a breath that hunched his shoulders up by his ears, then blew it out and let them drop. "I want to tell you."

Oh God, here it came. The outpouring. She wanted it desperately, to know she could hold a place in his heart Rosemary couldn't. At the same time, she was going to leave soon, and if she was the first person he'd told, it was like shooting a wild dog you'd taken a month to make trust you. "Why do you want to tell me now?"

"I've been doing a lot of thinking."

"This is new for you?"

"Shut up, Vivian." Only he said it as if he meant he adored her.

"Go on." How could she refuse? "I'm listening."

"I . . . knew Rosemary from childhood. We dated through high school and got married because Kettle expected us to. I was young and infatuated and I didn't have the strength to say no even though it felt wrong." His face shut down. "She was a sweet woman. But she didn't challenge me, not in any way, not ever. My needs always came first. My opinions and decisions ruled. It drove me nuts."

"I can imagine."

"I'd pick fights to try and get her to stick up for herself. I was cruel sometimes. I'd make her do things in bed she didn't want to, to see if she'd say no. And she'd just lie there looking martyred." He closed his eyes briefly, and it hit Vivian that what she'd always read as pain was mostly anger. "After a while I realized she *was* fighting back. Bitterly."

"Damn right." Vivian snorted. She wanted to dig Rosemary up and sock her in the nose. "Bitches come in all flavors."

"So I stopped trying to have a marriage. I smiled. I let her cater to me. I gave up on sex. I felt trapped. On more than one occasion I hoped she'd die."

"And you got your wish."

"Yeah." He looked down at his feet. "Aneurysm. Bang, she was gone. And you know where I was?"

Vivian cringed. "Not on top of someone else?"

"Close. In a bar, drunk off my ass, with some woman I'd just met doing some serious lap dancing." He ran his hand across his forehead, looking so miserable, she wanted to do whatever it took to make him smile again.

"Oh God."

"That was the first time I let another woman touch me."

"Oh God, Mike." Vivian put her hands over her mouth and laughed in total dismay. "So you came home from this other woman messed up and guilty, and Rosemary was dead?"

"Yeah."

"Don't tell me. In your bed. Waiting for you."

"Yeah."

"Oh no. Oh no." She reached and touched his chest, feeling as if a truck was parked on her own. "The ultimate passive-aggressive victory."

He grabbed her hand and pulled her close; she forced herself to relax against his solid, hard warmth. If God screwed up and sent her to heaven, it would be full of guys like Mike. "So . . . what then?"

"I made it through everyone's shock, and left. Went far and

wide, holed up with a friend in Portland, Maine, worked too hard, drank too much, fucked too many."

"No such thing." She squeezed him to show she was kidding. "Just don't tell me you blame yourself for her death."

"No, I don't blame myself for her death. Her body did that to her. The doctor said even if I'd been there, nothing would have saved her. But I feel guilty as hell that I—"

"Get over it, Mike." She lifted her head and forced him into eye contact. "She got you in the end, didn't she? Probably died with a smile on her lips."

"I was with another woman and she was dying alone."

"You were starving, Mike. She was starving you. I'm amazed you didn't have your dick in half the county. You deserved to."

"Not that many people around here would agree with you."

She took in his grim expression, and it bonked her over the head what it must have been like for Mike to live in Kettle. Way worse than for Vivian. "Why the hell did you come back here?"

"I wanted to make peace with it, with her. I couldn't do it while I was away. I thought if I came back, maybe . . ."

"But it didn't work."

Meaningful look. "It's starting to."

"Oh no. Oh no." She unwrapped her arms and pushed him away, totally nonplussed when he started chuckling. "I am not your personal savior, Mike. I'm an unstable mess of a person and I will take no responsibility for—"

He lunged toward her and, oh crap. Kisses again. Hard ones. Hungry ones. Kisses with serious intentions that overwhelmed her, scared her, and turned her on madly.

Now on her feet, then suddenly lifted off them and plunked down on the kitchen table. Her skirts up, panties pushed aside, and his tongue . . .

Ohhh, let's just say she was currently a very happy woman. Getting happier all the time. In fact she was going to leave him in the dust. "Mike, you're going to make me come."

"That's the plan."

"What about you?"

"No condoms."

"Oh." She gasped and leaned back on her elbows, let her head tip back, gave herself over to the heat and warmth until she felt the orgasm building, faster than she'd expected it to, a big, long, pulsing explosion. Damn he was good. Rosemary was a fool.

Then he lifted her—oh my God, he really did—and carried her, while she giggled like a teenager, up into her room.

"Okay, nice paint. Where are the condoms?"

"Glad to see you have priorities."

He set her down and she giggled harder, lit up with anticipation. This was all going to be fine. Carnal sex was her expertise. She'd expected emotion, warmer and stickier than anything that would come out of their bodies. That she couldn't handle. But a guy who'd yank up her dress and stick his tongue between her legs, yeah, he was speaking her language.

Quick trip to pull the shades in the room, then into the bathroom, and she tossed him the condoms. "Lie on the bed."

He shed his pants and his shirt and lay on the bed and, oh my goodness. They shouldn't allow men that beautiful to be naked in front of anyone who wanted her heart to keep beating.

She desperately wanted to touch him, but first she wanted to get this girl-next-door stuff out of the way and be sure he knew what he was getting.

So, dress first—a long, slow pull of the zipper, while he watched and his briefs rose to a lovely pyramid shape.

She started humming, "*What Lola wants . . .*" and let the material fall off her shoulders. Then turned partly away, gave him a come-hither look over her shoulder, and gyrated her—

"Don't do that."

She froze. "Don't do what?"

"I want you to take your clothes off for me."

"Gee, I thought that's what I was doing."

"No. You're doing it for men everywhere." He lifted on his elbow, unselfconsciously GQ. "I want you to do it for me. Not the stripper routine. Just take them off."

She didn't move. "You want me to stand here and take my dress off? What's sexy about that?"

He rolled his eyes. "For someone who's done it all, you are clueless. Just let the dress go."

"Fine." She let go. The dress swished to the ground, skirt billowed out, then slowly sank flat.

And there she stood in zebra-striped bikini underwear and a matching zebra-striped push-up bra. Not dancing. Not pouting. Not undulating. Not seducing.

"Now take those off." He was whispering. His cock jumped under his briefs.

She shifted her weight. She felt naked and stupid. And vulnerable. "But I'm . . . just a woman in underwear."

"Geez, Vivian, you're *you* in underwear. You're incredible." His voice was low, husky; his own underwear began to look painful. "Take them off for me."

She unhooked the bra and slid it off. Pulled down the panties and stepped out of them. Not a shimmy. Not an exaggerated self-caress. Not a peekaboo tease. She felt squashed. Suppressed. Unnatural.

He groaned, dragged his briefs off, pulled a condom on so fast his fingers were practically a blur.

"Come here," he whispered again, as if his voice didn't work around her when she wasn't fully dressed.

She stared at him, beautiful and naked on her bed, and didn't want to go. He'd taken all the fun out of it, all the playfulness, and all the . . .

Safety. Shit.

She was in over her head. He wasn't going to tumble her, or screw her, or fuck or force or humiliate or worship. He was going to make love to her.

What had he said? *It's going to be about you and me.*

Crap.

She knelt on the bed and waddled toward him, let him draw her down and fit her to his body. Instead of jumping on board, he lay there, stroking her gently, her arm, her hip, her belly.

"When I was in Portland, I bought a house."

"Oh?" She was out of her element. Bizarrely afraid. Since when was Vivian out of her element in bed with a man?

"A small two-story. A fixer-upper close to downtown. The neighborhood is coming up."

"Nice." Why was he telling her this now? His hands explored everywhere, warm and sure. She lay still, feeling she should be touching him, too, but not able to do it and not understanding why.

"You'd like Portland, I think."

Instant freakout. "What, so you're asking me to move there?"

"Vivian. I just said you'd like it."

"Oh." Why was she panicking? Why was she so sure he had her already in his Portland kitchen, wearing her grandmother's dress, baking him cookies?

"Relax." He turned and kissed her, long, slow, dreamy kisses.

She responded automatically, barely able to contain the urge to push him away.

He pulled back and held her chin so she couldn't look away as she desperately wanted to. He knew. Of course he knew. Damn him. "Okay, what's up?"

"I'm . . . scared." Harsh laughter burst out. "You're scaring me. This is so fucked, Mike. It's too soon, I don't know. This has never happened to me. Ever."

A grin spread over his face, which had gotten so dear to her that it hurt. "You're fal-ling in lo-ove with me-e."

He said it in the singsong way kids tease each other, and she adored him for that. Because it broke the weird intensity and she could playfully smack his chest. "In your dreams."

"You are." He rolled her onto her back, grinning triumphantly. "Admit it. Say it. 'I lo-o-ove you, Mike.' "

His words came out in a killer imitation of her voice, and she laughed so hard, her stomach started aching.

"C'mon. It's true." He moved over her, supported on his rock-solid arms. "I lo-o-o-o-ove you, Mike."

"Stop." She gasped the word out, tears rolling down her temples, perilously close to falling into her ears.

"Oh, Mi-i-i-ike." He spread her with his fingers and pushed himself inside. "Say it."

The sexual adrenaline hit. She gasped and lifted her hips to meet him. "Oh, Mike."

She meant to continue the joke, but his name didn't come out that way. At all.

He dug his arms under her, pulled her close, and moved in a slow, gentle rhythm, cheek pressed to her cheek.

She hesitated only a second—who was she kidding?—then wrapped her arms around his strong, wide back and gave in.

Twenty

E-mail originally written by Erin,
forwarded back to her from
her freshman year tutor, Fran Sterling
October 29

*Erin—A friend sent me this and it made me smile. I
thought you might enjoy it.*

Fran

Everyone knows David rose up to slay Goliath with a
perfectly aimed blow from his sling. What the story
doesn't tell you is that his mother made the sling
when his father was too busy or too tired and the boy
grew impatient.

It doesn't tell you that she had to nag him every

day to practice, that she took the time to help gather the smoothest and best stones for her son. Nor that she set up the targets, and gave him encouragement and praise as his skill grew.

Undoubtedly as he faced the giant, David called not only upon God, but upon his mother's faith in him, that he heard her voice along with the Lord's, telling him not to doubt his strength or his aim or his heart.

Nor should you, as you face your daily Goliaths, hesitate to call on the women you know for the same kind of guidance.

Send this e-mail to all the underappreciated, powerful women you know.

Erin secured the last white plastic skull from the pile she'd lugged into the Kettle High School gym, to the last piece of black rope she'd measured and cut that morning. At the Halloween party that night, when visitors to the haunted house rounded the bales-of-hay wall, the skulls, glowing with black light, would seem to swoop down to attack the intruders.

Why anyone would pay money to be afraid . . . well, let's just say Erin got plenty for free. She'd agreed to help Joan set up the haunted house, but refused the job of dressing in black, lying on the floor, and grabbing the ankles of unsuspecting patrons with hands that had been clutching an ice pack. Scaring people that badly would probably make her sick.

So Erin would serve punch on the other side of the gym, where the band played. She always served punch. Stood behind the table with the big plastic bowl, holding the big plastic ladle and made sure high school kids didn't pour in grain alcohol, though the party would probably be more fun if she let them. Someone always tried. Yet another tradition, among too many in Kettle.

Though one untraditional element had been added this year. Vivian had shown up to help decorate, and to set up her makeover booth. Erin was surprised to see Sarah talking to her, and even laughing at one point. Something weird was going on with Sarah. She was manic or something. Erin had never seen her snap at anyone, and she'd nearly bitten Audrey Bender's head off for suggesting they bring her pumpkins indoors a day early. Sarah wanted to make a big entrance the day of the party.

Nancy, not surprisingly, followed Sarah's lead and helped set up Vivian's booth, helped her paint it shocking pink with a big red kiss mark on the front, and a sexy black winking eye. Beyond that, she even offered to staff the booth so Vivian could enjoy the party, though Erin was pretty sure Nancy was just trying to get out of having to mingle.

Even Betty, waddling along toward her due date, praising the Lord for this and that, put her considerable lettering skills to work on a *Make Yourself Over* sign to go on the table.

So the decree had come down. Vivian had been if not accepted, then tolerated. Reporters and photographers hovered in the gym and outside, easily recognizable from their big-city clothes and attitudes. They'd find nothing to report today. Now that Vivian was keeping the lid on, Kettle was, as usual, about as devoid of tantalizing news as you could get. At least on the surface.

Erin stepped out of the haunted house and peered around

bales of hay set at the entrance. The sliding wall that would block off the haunted house and keep that side of the gym in darkness hadn't been closed yet, and she could see across the room. Vivian sat at her booth, arranging certificates and sample cosmetics. Even from this distance, even dressed down from her initial splendor, she glowed with beauty and poise. Erin was going to go talk to her.

That morning Erin had nearly jumped out of her skin when an e-mail she'd written came back to her. The one about David and Goliath. She made that one up five months ago, snorting to herself over how corny it was. But people ate that stuff up.

Where had it gone? Who'd read it? She'd love to know what they thought, how many people were moved or delighted or slyly amused and passed it along, and how many skimmed it, rolled their eyes in disgust, and hit delete.

She loved thinking she'd had an effect on so many people. People she'd never meet who lived in places she'd never go. Maybe some of them even wondered about the woman who wrote the note. It was as if in all these towns and cities outside Kettle, Erin had started to exist.

She didn't usually believe in signs. Too many times she'd thought her luck was about to change, like when she finally told Mrs. Flatley about her father in grade school and thought she believed her. Like when she married, and when she carried Joy into the third trimester. Too many times she'd been wrong.

But this wasn't a bad decision she'd made, this was the collective force of the world, the passing from in-box to in-box of an e-mail that had started with her, and that had made its way back like a large and powerful ocean salmon coming home to the stream where it began as a tiny wiggling thing inside an egg.

So this sign she'd take. This sign told her she could walk up to Vivian and ask for a makeover. Joe would freak if he found out, but Erin didn't seem to care. She was in the grip of something that had started the day the jury found Lorelei Taylor not guilty, and she couldn't break free even if she wanted to. Maybe it was fate, maybe it was her own will—yeah, maybe she had one after all. She didn't know. She didn't care. She wanted to look pretty, even if it was for one afternoon of her life.

Her feet must have moved her because she found herself standing in front of Vivian.

"Erin, hi."

"Hi." She glanced up and looked back down at the table. Damn it, why was this so hard? She knew what she wanted, she just needed to say it. But with Vivian there, looking so calm and beautiful and untouchable, the words froze in her throat.

"Are you interested in a makeover?"

"Yes." She was able to look up then. "I am."

"Excellent." Vivian clapped her hands together. "You are stunning under that shyness; I've been dying to do you. Beautiful eyes. Very sexy cheekbones."

"Thanks." She felt herself blushing. Beautiful? Sexy? Vivian was just being nice. Never mind that Erin suddenly wanted to be that way with the desperation of a preadolescent.

"What's your costume tonight, Erin?"

"I'll be a hobo." She was a hobo every year. Dressing as a

man was Joe's answer to the risk of letting her out among them.

"A hobo? Are you serious? Do they even have those anymore?"

"Probably not." She laughed, awkwardly, stupidly.

"Screw hobo. I'm done here for now. Come home with me, and I'll do your costume." She stood and walked around to where Erin stood. "Come as you're not. I'll make you into a glamour girl, how's that?"

"No." Erin took a step away from the pink booth.

Vivian's perfect dark brows drew down in the middle. "You can change back when we're done if you decide you want to."

"I don't think . . ." Erin swallowed. The denial had been automatic. She reminded herself that she'd had a sign that morning. That this was something she wanted. She didn't have to go to the party made up. Or let anyone see her but Vivian. "Yes. Okay. Thank you."

"Good." Vivian smiled and picked up a lock of Erin's hair, testing it between her fingers and thumb the way Erin's mom used to test material in fabric stores. "You're going to look fabulous. Let's go."

In a daze, Erin walked beside her toward the double doors with the red exit sign above them. People were noticing the two of them together, throwing them looks. Already Erin had started doubting her decision.

"Erin." The familiar bark made her skin contract and the hair stand up on her arms.

Joan. Shit.

She turned back, stiff and stretched tall, imagining Joan as a giant cyclops, wishing for a sling and a smooth round stone. "What."

"Where do you think you're going?"

"The haunted house is finished. You said I could go when it was finished."

"Home. To Joe."

"Joe is at Rick's."

Joan's black-lined eyes narrowed, which made them about the size of a normal person's. "You're asking for trouble."

"I'm sorry, are you Erin's keeper?"

Joan didn't turn her head. Didn't even acknowledge that Vivian had spoken.

Erin put her hand on Vivian's arm, surprised at how tense the muscle was. But she shouldn't be surprised. Vivian had lived this, too; her reactions would be deeper than most people's. "I'll be home in time. He'll be at Rick's until dinner."

"What's he going to think of you tramping off with this woman?"

"How is he going to find out?" This from Vivian, a direct challenge. Both Joan and Erin ignored her. The battle was between them, over patterns established too long ago.

Erin lifted her chin defiantly. Which for her meant she barely met Joan's eyes. More like she met Joan's nose. "I'm sure Joe would *love* me to do something that makes me happy."

Vivian snorted next to her, and Erin tightened her grip on Vivian's arm, not sure if she was restraining Vivian or if Vivian was propping her up.

Joan's arms crossed over the Mickey Mouse head smiling on the front of her pink sweatshirt. A blob of black paint had fallen on its cheek, like a mole gone bad. "I hope you know what you're doing."

"I hope maybe I finally do." She turned and walked away, thinking she had just dropped the most perfect movie exit line ever, and wishing she could be wildly proud of herself. The truth was, her legs were shaking, and she suddenly understood what people meant when they said you could feel someone's gaze burning into your back. Joan would tell Joe. Joe would come down on her when he got home. Worse, he'd be drinking at Rick's all afternoon. Was lipstick and mascara she'd never get to wear again worth all that fear and pain?

The gym doors swung shut behind them, the damp air felt like a release. Vivian burst out laughing and held up her hand for a high-five Erin felt dumb giving her. "You go, girl."

"I'm not sure this is a good idea."

"Why?"

"You know why."

"Look." Vivian turned so she was standing right in front of Erin, and Erin could see her perfect skin and smell her fresh scent. "You always have a choice. You can bend over and take it or you can fight. Sometimes it's a new choice every day, sometimes twice a day, sometimes more. Sometimes the old choice will stick for a while, until it's too much and you need to switch. But every new second and every new day you have the power to make a choice again."

Her eyes were deep and intense, and a thrill scurried through Erin's chest. She'd never thought of her situation that way. She'd always felt locked into a black-and-white life sentence. Either she stayed or she left. She liked Vivian's version better. She liked to think that she was choosing to stay.

Or choosing to fight. And that the choice was always open to her and would always be open to her.

That feeling made the world around her brighter and more hopeful, even though the clouds obstinately covered the sky and the dampness made the air colder than it was.

"Okay. I'll do it."

"Good for you!" Vivian hooted, and Erin felt as if she'd won a coveted and special prize she'd been wanting for years.

The feeling lasted all the way up to Vivian's house and into the kitchen, touched up so it looked more like a place Vivian would live, ditto the living room, and up to the faintly paint-smelling bedroom where Stellie had slept, now pale blue-green instead of the too-busy dull wallpaper that had been there.

The dollhouse still stood in its corner by the closet. Erin caught her breath, treating herself to the precious memories of the day she and Vivian first met, of Vivian's deliberate casualness sharing the treasure, of Erin's awe. She approached the house now, three floors, six rooms, as tall as she was, and picked up one of the little figures who'd been stuck with his head in the toilet. She didn't ask why. "Nathan, wasn't it?"

Vivian came back into the room with a makeup case the size of a suitcase and laughed. "Probably. I haven't a clue. Did Gran have you back here to play after I went home to Chicago?"

"Until Dad made me stop."

"Why?"

"He was perverse that way."

Vivian scowled and heaved the case onto the bed. "Mine was perverse, too, in ways that involved me."

She said it offhandedly, as if she was talking about her grocery list. Erin nearly dropped Nathan. How could she talk so easily? Erin couldn't. Not even to Vivian. Not always even to herself. "I'm . . . sorry."

"Me, too. But that's life." She put a sturdy wooden chair in the middle of the room, and patted the cane seat. "Sit."

"Okay." Erin tried not to show how nervous and excited she was. She carefully put Nathan back in a tiny wing-back chair in the living room and adjusted him so he looked comfortable. Then she turned to find Vivian watching her thoughtfully.

"I'm leaving here soon."

Erin's brain shut down, the way it always did when instinct told her bad news was coming. "What do you mean?"

"Leaving Kettle."

Panic started. "Leaving?"

"As soon as the media goes away and the fuss dies down. I'm just here to ride it out."

"But . . ." Erin threaded her fingers together and squeezed at the knuckles until it hurt. Vivian. Gone. She thought Vivian had moved here to stay for at least a year or so. That she'd be here long enough to be Erin's inspiration and maybe her friend, the one person who could understand her. That she'd help, that she'd somehow make things change, if not for Erin, maybe for Kettle, in some of the ways it badly needed to change. That Vivian herself was a sign, the way the e-mail this morning had been. Like an angel helping David's stone fly straight. "You just got here."

"This isn't really my kind of town."

"No." She shook her head, trying not to sound as miserable as she felt. "No, of course not."

"I was wondering, though, since I'll have to sell the house and get rid of stuff, would you like the dollhouse?"

"Would I like it?" She forced herself to concentrate.

"Yes. I'll give it to you."

"I'm . . ." She stared stupidly. Vivian would give away a happy piece of her childhood? To Erin? "It's too much."

"I'd like you to have it. It means something to you. I don't want some spoiled princess getting it from Daddy and playing for ten minutes before she's begging for the next thing."

"I couldn't." Erin's voice went whispery. "Joe would—"

"Fuck Joe." Vivian gestured violently. "Do *you* want it?"

Erin plunked herself in the chair, frightened, desperate, miserable. Why had she allowed herself to hope? Vivian was leaving, and once again there would be no one here for Erin. No friend. No hope. Nothing.

Except, maybe, a dollhouse, that would remind Erin of the one time she had someone to escape with, to hide in the woods and put her arms around and laugh with from fear.

That was something.

She cleared her throat so her voice would come out stronger. "Yes. Thank you. I'd love it."

E-mail from Tom Martin to Sarah Gilchrist
Afternoon, October 29

Sarah, leave the party and meet me at my place at nine tonight. I want you so badly I can't sleep. I'm hard all day long thinking about you, about touching you, about kissing you everywhere, about making you scream with pleasure. Please don't say no. Please say you'll

*meet me. I'm a desperate man. Desperate for you and
only you.*

Tom

Sarah read Tom's e-mail for the fourth time, delicious sensations bouncing around her body, trying to memorize it before she'd have to hit delete so no one poking through her
computer would find it, not that anyone in this house would,
but just to be certain. God forbid she die in a freak accident
and leave this.

She hated deleting notes from Tom. She wished she had
every e-mail he'd ever sent and all of hers back to him so she
could assemble them in a big book and reread them, reliving
the excitement—the timid exploration turned into this glorious, beautiful exchange of passion.

Making you scream with pleasure. Oh my. She was crazy
with desire. Crazy. She put her hands to her hot cheeks, certain a sexual demon had taken possession of her. She deleted
the e-mail and crept to her dresser drawer, fished under her
slips, and came up with the vibrator. Again. She was insane.
She'd never lusted so deeply or purely for any man.

She listened for a second to make sure Ben hadn't done
something radical, like change positions in front of his monitor, then lay back on the bed, turned the magical little blue and
white machine on, and put it to work, fear she'd be discovered heightening her arousal. Ten seconds, twenty, imagining
herself on his doorstep, dressed in her Come As You're Not
costume of black fishnets, torso barely covered in black satin,
black elbow-length fingerless gloves, a headband with fuzzy

ears, and a long black tail. Tom opening the door, the rush of unstoppable lust, the desperate hurry, the driving need to be together, clothes torn off right there in his hall, passionate kisses, then Tom's beautiful face between her legs . . .

Thirty seconds, forty . . .

Oh. She muted the cry, let her body sail through the by-now familiar sensations—rising ecstasy, spilling over, wild contracting . . . and then down.

Tonight. If she dared. For the first time, a body other than hers would make her feel all those things. And so much more in her heart.

Leave the party and meet me at my place at nine tonight. She deserved it, yes, dear God, she deserved it. But—

"Mom?"

Amber. On her way up. Sarah yanked up her black linen pants and lunged for the dresser, reburied the vibrator under several inches of soft, high-quality ivory, black, and peach-colored nylon, rayon, and silk.

"Yes? What." She tried to sound short and pressured. She'd left the Kettle High gym on the pretext of checking her pump-kins, but the pumpkins were undoubtedly fine, cozily loaded on the flatbed next door, ready to make their entrance later.

All she'd really wanted to check was her e-mail.

"Can I come in?"

"Sure honey." She dragged off her apricot sweater so she could pretend she'd been up here changing.

"Hi." Amber came in, hesitant, awkward. "Um . . ."

"What is it, sweetheart?" Sarah's tension rose. If such a thing were possible.

"Can I ask you something?"

"Of course." *Oh no.* Sarah had enough on her plate without another Amber crisis.

"Um. Well . . ." She stared down at the rug Sarah and Ben had bought in Portugal together, twisting her fingers. "Larry wants me to go to a Halloween party in Ladysmith tonight."

Sarah was so upset, she stopped with her sweater still on both arms but not yet over her head. "What?"

"I *said*, Larry wants—"

"I heard what you said."

"Then why did you say, *What?*"

Sarah took a deep breath, because she'd been about to open her mouth and say, *You know perfectly well why, you little shit*. "Don't be sassy with me, young lady."

An adolescent expression was the only response. That damn subversive eye roll that said, *Mom, you are so out of it*.

Well, not quite as out of it as everyone seemed to think. Just wait until they saw her at the party in her costume. Kettle would never be the same.

"Absolutely not, Amber. You are going to be at Kettle's celebration as you have been for the last—"

"Kettle's celebration is for *kids*."

"No. It's for our town. And you're going, like it or not."

From somewhere in the back of Sarah's head, Vivian's voice reminded her that coming down too hard on a teenager . . .

She made an effort to rein in her temper. Damn it, she had a million things to do. It was getting dark, and she still had to get dressed—with a demure cloak that allowed only tantalizing glimpses of what she had on underneath. Then she might as well check her pumpkins before she went back to the gym to make sure everything was—

"You can't keep me from going."

"No." She forced herself to stay calm, wanting to shake Amber until her disrespectful head flew clean off and Sarah could replace it with a new one. "You're right. I can't."

Amber's eyes widened. Obviously she had not expected to win that battle. Though it struck Sarah that after the surprise wore off, her daughter looked more stricken than triumphant.

"But I can depend on you to do the right thing, Amber. The mature thing. Because . . ." She almost said, *Because you're my daughter*, but she couldn't handle Amber rejecting that bond with more sarcasm. "Because I trust you."

Amber's face screwed up as if she were trying not to cry, except she hadn't seemed sad. What on earth was the matter *now*?

Then it hit. Amber had actually been coming to Sarah for permission *not* to go.

"Is that Larry pressuring you to attend this party?"

Amber's head jerked up; she met Sarah's eyes as if she'd just found out her mother was an alien mind-reader. "Sort of. We fought about it."

"What kind of party is this?"

"It's Larry's friend. His parents are away this weekend. I guess there's going to be a lot of beer, and worse stuff, and . . . other things I don't think I want to do."

Sarah's heart nearly broke. She wanted to clasp the sweet child-after-all body of her daughter close, but she was too afraid Amber would roll her eyes again. "Sweetheart, why didn't you just tell me that?"

"Because I promised him I'd ask. He wants me to go."

Oh dear God. New anger added heat to all the anger Sarah glowed with already. Not just at Amber. Not just at Larry. But at herself, now. For spending Amber's life catering to Ben. What had she taught her daughter about the ability to think for herself and speak for herself and make decisions for herself while essentially acting as Ben's slave?

Larry wanted Amber to do something for him. Where did Sarah think her beautiful, smart girl would find the courage or strength to resist or object when all she saw in her own female role model was Cinderella pre-prince? And post-prince, for all the world knew, the fairy tale stopped there.

No wonder Amber had been drawn to Vivian. No wonder.

Well, no longer, because Sarah was becoming a new woman. Or rather reverting to who she'd been before Ben. Life for Sarah and for her daughter was going to be different, starting right now and lasting for as long as they both lived.

"Go out and tell Larry you can't go because I won't let you." She gestured Amber outside. "Blame it on me."

"Really?" The hope in her voice nearly made Sarah cry.

"Yes, of course. I'll take the fall gladly. I'm so proud of you I could hug you."

Amber rolled her eyes, and Sarah had to swallow hard to stay strong.

"Well, duh, Mom, you don't need permission for *that*."

Her little girl came into her arms, and Sarah enveloped her, held her tight, letting her senses register every sensation, every sweet curve and sweep of her daughter's body, her warmth, her smell, her ebbing little-girl softness, in case Sarah never got to experience a moment this good again until teenage hell had passed.

"Go." She made herself turn Amber loose. "Tell him. Is he waiting outside?"

Amber ducked her head, kicked at the rug. "Yeah."

"Good. When you're finished, come back in here, because I have something to show you."

Amber danced to the door and pirouetted, a study in opposites to the way she'd come in. "What?"

Sarah smiled. She shouldn't be doing this, she didn't have time, she had decisions to make, responsibilities to attend to. But this mother-daughter moment was so precious, and who knew when they'd get one like it again.

"I want to show you my Halloween costume."

Twenty-one

Erin Hall

"Okay. Done."

Erin held still while Vivian snapped an elastic around the French braid she'd just made in Erin's hair. She'd put makeup on her, too. Eyeliner, mascara, blush, lipstick, nothing that had ever touched Erin's face before. Her eyelashes felt heavier, and her eyes felt as if they were open wider. A lot of girls wore makeup in high school now, but back when Erin went, only some girls did, and she wasn't one of them.

So she was a late bloomer. Better than never blooming at all. "Can I look?"

"Not yet. I want to give you something to wear."

"Why?"

Vivian looked down at Erin's baggy jeans and the long-sleeved cotton tee fraying around her neck, and her gray cardigan sweater, and lifted an eyebrow.

"Yeah, okay." Erin laughed. Stupid question. But it made her kind of nervous to think of wearing something else. Especially something of Vivian's. Erin's clothes might be baggy and horrible, but they'd been who she was for so long, shedding them felt threatening.

"I'm taller than you but not by much. I think you can fit into my stuff." Vivian was already at Stellie's massive bureau, opening drawers, pawing through piles, checking her closet, turning around now and then to look thoughtfully at Erin.

Erin reached to touch her hair. Her face felt cool and exposed, the braid tugged pleasantly on her scalp when she moved.

"Here. Look. This is perfect."

Erin turned to look and immediately started to blush. A black miniskirt, shorter than anything she'd ever worn except her running shorts, but those didn't count. And until recently, she hadn't worn those, either. Besides jogging, she doubted anyone in Kettle had seen more of her legs than a sock-covered ankle.

The top Vivian chose was hot pink, searing pink, pink enough that people miles away would know it was pink, and wonder about the person wearing it. The shirt also looked about three sizes smaller than anything Erin was used to.

"You'll need hose, too." Vivian darted back to her dresser, rooted through another drawer. "Sheer black, with tiny black dots. Thigh-high so the lace tops flash when you cross your legs. Very sexy but more comfortable than stockings and a garter. Men go wild for black stockings."

But men didn't go wild for Erin. If a man even looked at her, it was at most with a flash of curious pity. Even those looks got her the third degree from Joe. Jordan didn't look at her like that. But he'd only seen her running with her hair in a careless ponytail, looking strong and free. He didn't know her the way she usually was.

"And heels of course." Vivian was back at her closet, poking among enough shoes to stock a store. "Aha! These."

Erin gasped. She doubted she could even stand in those. The heels had to be four inches, ending in a tiny spike. Little would cover her foot, just thin straps cascading down the steep incline of the sole. They'd be incredibly sexy. On Vivian.

"Jimmy Choo criss-cross sandals. The man is a genius. What size do you wear?"

"Eight."

"Ha! We're twins. Here." She brought the clothes over, a black and pink armful.

"Vivian. I can't . . . I can't wear this stuff. Joe—"

"Joe's not going to see you. This is just fun for us. Unless you want it to be more, that's up to you."

Erin laughed nervously, about the only way she laughed. She might as well admit she desperately wanted to wear the clothes, just here in Vivian's room. Even knowing she'd carry back excitement that Joe would sense no matter how hard she tried to conceal it. "Okay. For here."

"Good for you. I'll help you dress."

Erin stopped smiling and crossed her arms over her waist.

Her parents, her husband, and medical personnel were the only people who'd ever seen her naked. "I don't need help."

"Why? It's fun girl stuff." At her dresser again, Vivian held up a bright pink matching bra and panties that still had the tags on. "Never worn. They'll be great under the outfit."

"You can't."

Vivian tossed the underwear on the bed. "Can't what?"

"Be here. See my body."

Vivian came over and stood close. Gave Erin a long, searching look that made Erin want to cry. "Why not?"

Erin's breaths started coming too fast, too short, a ball lodged in her belly. She was horribly afraid she was going to build up to one of her fits. She couldn't stand to do that to Vivian. She'd die of embarrassment first.

"Modesty?"

Erin shook her head, looking past Vivian, lips pressed together to keep the truth back.

"Scars?" Vivian said the word strangely, as if something was lodged in her throat.

Erin swallowed. Swallowed again, though there was nothing in her mouth to swallow. She'd told one person. One. About Dad, too. Her teacher, who seemed so nice, so worried. Then a few days later, Mrs. Flatley told Erin to be a good girl and to stop making up stories about her father, because that kind of thing didn't happen in Kettle.

"He cuts you?" Vivian whispered in a choked way, standing so close her breath hit Erin's cheek. "Burns?"

Erin shook her head, unable to speak. The ball inside her moved up into her chest . . . only it didn't feel like one of her fits now.

It wasn't a fit. It was the urge to spill, filling her until she thought she'd explode. She hadn't felt that for so long, she didn't even recognize it.

"You can tell me." Vivian was still whispering.

"I cut myself. Used to. When I . . . was a kid." Her breath heaved up and down so the words bounced out of her, nearly unintelligible. "Joe . . . he just . . ."

"Okay." Vivian put her arms around her. Erin was shaking so badly she didn't know how Vivian could hold on to her, but she did. She was strong. Erin laid her head on Vivian's shoulder and screwed her eyes shut. She was tired of being a basket case. She wanted to suck vitality and courage out of Vivian. To be strong like that all the time, every day.

"Shhhh. It's okay. It really is." Vivian rocked her like a child, then started humming the Irish lullaby with the "*too-ra-loo-ral*" part, which was kind of nutty, but which made Erin feel a little more stable. "Erin."

"Yes."

"I'm going to take off your clothes and put the new ones on. I want you to relax and let me."

Erin lifted her head, keeping her eyes shut. Vivian took off her sweater, gently pulling it over her shoulders. Erin didn't let her protest out. Nor did she open her eyes. Vivian took the T-shirt and pulled it up, stretching the neck to get it over Erin's head, careful not to touch her made-up face or muss her perfect hair.

Erin stood stiffly in her old cotton bra and jeans, feeling vulnerable and shaky. She could do this. It would be fine. When it was over, she'd open her eyes and see a new woman.

Vivian's hands tugged at her waistband, unsnapped, unzipped, pulled down the jeans. If she was shocked at the scarred mess at the tops of Erin's thighs, she didn't let on.

Then Vivian's warm hands again, unhooking her bra, slipping it off, easing her panties over her hips, the air in the room cool on her naked skin.

Erin lifted her feet one by one to let the panties go. Her eyes were still screwed shut, her breath still coming too high and too fast. What next? The shocking pink underwear would go on. She felt herself bracing, as if it would burn her.

Instead of underwear, she felt touches. Small ones with one finger, tiny gentle strokes. Vivian was tracing her scars. Every one. Circling the bruises still on her arms. And two on the insides of her thighs where Joe had been rough.

Then a hand under her chin, a brief warm kiss on her mouth, and a whisper in her ear. "You can get free of him. There's help out there. You just need the courage to do it."

Erin didn't move. She felt Vivian's absence, sensed her walking away. She wanted to open her eyes, but her breathing had slowed, her heart had slowed, the ball in her chest nearly dissolved. If she opened her eyes she might have to go back.

She felt Vivian near again, a tap on her foot. "Lift."

She lifted that foot, then the other, and felt the smooth glide of underpants back up, soft and slidy with lace, the cupping of her breasts by another bra, not hers. Then the swish of a lined skirt, cool against her skin, the unfamiliar embracing tightness of a top over her torso.

"Lift again." Another feeling, stretchy cobwebby material sliding up, then the firm soft grip of elastic around her thigh. Repeated on the other side.

Erin opened her eyes.

"And now, prepare for a shoe-gasm." Vivian brought the sandals over, smiling wickedly, and it was as if the previous scene had been a crazy dream out of Erin's crazy head and all along they'd been two normal girls dressing for a party.

She stepped up into the shoes, giggling at the way her feet felt so scrunched and unnatural, and realizing the giggle wasn't stupid and nervous-sounding. But happy, like they were young again, playing dress-up, with no idea how their lives would turn out, with their faith that things would get better still intact. "How do you walk in these?"

"Practice and attitude." Vivian looked Erin up and down and shook her head. "You're going to drop dead when you see."

"Okay." Erin giggled again. That sounded promising. She teetered over to the mirror facing the street, thankful for her strong legs and ankles to keep her upright.

Her image stared back at her, as shocked as she was.

"Wow." She started laughing and tented her hands over her mouth. "Wow."

"See?" Vivian appeared in the reflection next to her, beaming. "You are a total hot babe."

"It's not even me."

"Oh yes, it is. Trust me, you carry it naturally. You want to go as you're not to the party, wear the ratty stuff you've been hiding in your whole life."

Erin brought her hands down. She did look hot. Her eyes had become large and glamorous, framed with dramatic dark brown. Her face glowed with color, her lips looked sensuous and sexy, even with the muted shade Vivian chose. The hairstyle was chic without being too chic for her and framed her features perfectly.

Isabel Sharpe

And the outfit . . .

Her body had never looked like that. It had never occurred to her she had a body that could carry off sexy clothes. She didn't spend a lot of time examining it. Her body had betrayed her by not carrying Joy to term; her body was a vehicle for pain more often than pleasure.

But this . . .

"Thank you." In heels she was Vivian's height, and their eyes were on the same level. "Thank you."

She couldn't say anything more, but Vivian nodded, looking straight back at her, and Erin knew she understood that Erin wasn't just thanking her for the makeover, but for the whole afternoon. The healing touches, the encouragement to get herself free from—

Joe. Erin looked around wildly for a clock and saw the old one with Jesus's face on it, which she thought Vivian would have gotten rid of. But maybe even Vivian couldn't bring herself to throw Jesus away.

Five-thirty. "I'd better go."

"Okay." Vivian said it regretfully, as if she'd really enjoyed being with Erin this afternoon, and Erin's heart swelled. How different would her life have been if Vivian had moved to Kettle to stay all those years ago? Maybe both their lives would have been different.

She started gathering up her old clothes. "I can pay you—"

"You don't need to pay me."

"Yes. I do. I—"

"Erin." Vivian laid a warm hand on her arm. "Count this one as fun between friends, okay?"

Erin choked up. She knew Vivian must have had tons of friends in her life. She was already friends with Mike, if not more than friends, and might even end up friends with Sarah. Calling someone a friend wasn't that big a deal. If Erin cried, she'd look like a bigger dope than she already was.

"Thank you." She started pulling off the clothes, gratified when Vivian didn't ask why or urge her to keep them on.

"Is he home now?"

"No. Not for a while, probably an hour or so." And he'd be drunk from partying at Rick's all day, and things would get even nastier later after the bourbon he snuck in to the party every year. "I need to make him dinner."

"Keep the hair and makeup. Enjoy them a while longer. You can comb out and wash off quickly before he gets home."

She desperately wanted to. She wanted to go home and park herself in front of a mirror and stare. Memorize exactly how she looked in case she never saw herself this way again. "Okay. I will."

She went reluctantly downstairs, trying to hang on to the glow of the afternoon, knowing it wasn't going to last nearly long enough.

She said good-bye to Vivian quickly, so the moment wouldn't seem symbolic or stupid. Just casual friends saying good-bye after a pleasant afternoon they assumed they'd have to do over and over again.

At the end of the driveway she turned in the descending darkness, saw Vivian standing illuminated by her back porch light, looking after Erin, and they both waved. When Erin glanced again, she saw Vivian had gone inside and shut the door.

The next time she glanced up, she saw Joe had gotten home early and was storming up the street to meet her.

Sarah Gilchrist

Sarah pulled her cloak more tightly around her in the chilly darkness. She was late. Sharing time with Amber, wonderful as it had been, had put her behind schedule. She'd sent Amber and Ben off to the party while she stayed to check her pumpkins one more time before she'd get Ben or one of the other men to drive them over. Or maybe she'd drive them over herself.

But even more than checking on her pumpkins, Sarah wanted to take a few deep breaths of chilly, breezy Kettle air and come to some decision about Tom. The scene with Amber had been an eye-opening experience. Sarah was proud of her daughter for having the guts to tell that Larry animal that she wasn't going to be his lay for the evening.

Of course he'd been furious, told Amber she was tied to the apron strings of a bitch, and plenty of other ludicrous and insulting things. Happily, his testosterone tantrum hadn't endeared him any further to Amber. Amber had gone happily to the Kettle party with Ben, who had dressed as Stephen King, a joke no one would get, and he'd have to explain it a hundred times.

The decision about Tom was turning out to be a bigger decision than just infidelity. This decision was about choosing the kind of person she was going to be, the kind of woman she wanted Amber to have for a mother. One who stayed home in servitude, not living up to the promise of her education and ambition? One who was forced to sneak out to meet the man she hoped to love soon? Or one who got what she wanted honestly and openly when she was free to do it?

And yet, the idea of meeting Tom, of the passion and tenderness he'd bring her . . . Maybe this once she could allow herself that on the sly. Maybe once would be enough to make clear whether her marriage and her life here were worth fighting for. Maybe just this once. To feel like a real woman, indomitable and powerfully feminine and free. Like Vivian probably felt every single day of her life, no matter what she'd been through.

And yet Sarah was not Vivian. She'd built a life here, confining as it seemed in her clearing vision of the last few weeks. She was unofficial chairperson of the Kettle Social Club, a responsible citizen with an unblemished reputation. Everyone liked her. Everyone respected her. In Sarah people knew they had a friend, someone they could depend on, someone they could trust to do the right thing.

Was she willing to risk that? Would little Katie and her parents rejoice quite as purely over the money from the pumpkins if they knew it had been raised by a philanderer?

Up in the field ahead, she saw the flatbed truck, the tarp covering the pumpkins . . . Something was wrong. The tarp wasn't up high enough. Had someone stolen some? Stolen her hard work, and Katie's hope for recovery from her accident?

Sarah ran for the truck, reached for the tarp, peeled it off with a few heaves from her strong arms.

And brought both hands up to cover her mouth.

Her pumpkins had been smashed. Methodically. One by

one. Where there had been a glorious pyramid of flawless specimens, now there was only pumpkin flesh and pumpkin seeds and stringy pumpkin guts.

Who could have done something so cruel and so heartless and so . . . personal.

With utter certainty it came to her. Larry. Because Sarah had come between him and his humping, panting, revolting teenage orgasm in her sweet, pure daughter.

Damn him all the way to hell.

She backed up, needing to put distance between herself and the horrible sight. Her foot hit something, and she fell on her butt and stayed there, staring at the chaos, smelling the sweet, overpowering pumpkin smell. Gone. All that work. All that nurturing. All that perfection.

The tears that slid down her cheeks were expected. As were the pair of warm-up sobs. Sarah covered her face with her hands and prepared for the torrent that would follow.

Instead, inexplicably, Sarah started to laugh. She laughed and laughed and laughed, doubled over onto the long damp grass, straining and writhing, nearly vomiting from how desperately the laughter wanted out of her.

Screw it. Just screw it all. She'd go see Tom. *Now.*

Ten minutes later, she turned onto Maybelle Street, thankful for cover of darkness, thankful for most people already gathered at the high school gym. Tom would be home, hoping for her, half out of his mind with anticipation. He'd explode into relief when she showed so much earlier than he suggested.

She strode up his driveway, glorying in her resolve to do something really good for herself. Her marriage to Ben was over. It had been over for years; she'd just been too stubbornly convinced that someone like Sarah Gilchrist would never make such a stupid mistake as to marry the wrong person. Not Sarah. Sarah did everything right.

Well, this time Sarah was doing something really right. Something wonderful and beautiful and passionate and right.

She rang his back bell, breathing slightly fast from her speed walk over here, parting her cloak to give him an enticing glimpse of what lay underneath. She'd waited so long for this—they both had. All their adult lives. She could hardly wait to be in his arms, feel his lips on hers. It would—

His door swooped open. "Sarah."

He sounded surprised rather than carried away by his burning desire for her.

"Tom." She started toward him, expecting him to grab her, and was startled when he moved back to let her pass into a dingy back hallway adjoining a kitchen that looked as if frat boys had camped there for weeks. "I'm . . . early."

"Yeah, um . . . yeah." He turned to look at her, one hand still holding the door as if he was afraid of closing it. Or had forgotten to. "Chilly out there, huh."

Maybe he was just nervous. Maybe he was embarrassed because he hadn't cleaned yet this century. Maybe her beauty in the uncharacteristic getup stunned him.

A girl could always hope.

"Yes, but it's warm in here." She unfastened her cloak and let it drop to the floor. Stood there in her teeny black satin outfit with the push-up bra, the black fishnet stockings, and the furry ears and tail.

"Wow." He laughed and closed the door, put his hands on his hips, shaking his head. "Wow. Look at you."

"Do you like it?" She posed provocatively, one leg slightly bent, a dancer's pose, only instead of holding still, she rocked gently, which made him laugh again.

What was the matter with him? He couldn't possibly think she was here for a neighborly visit.

"Yeah. I like it all right." He laughed again, kind of a hyuck-hyuck, gosh-'n-by-golly laugh, and Sarah started to have trouble holding her irritation at bay.

Where was her passionate man? Where was the fiery excitement he promised? Where was the chemistry that sizzled every time they met?

She didn't come all the way over here to be laughed at.

Three steps and she was pressed against him, arms around his middle, which was softer than she expected, but okay, none of them was eighteen anymore.

"Tom." She lifted her face for his kiss . . .

His arms came around her fiercely, he breathed her name with just the right amount of reverence, and she started to heat up. Yes. This was it. This was right. This was what she—

"Oh baby, you feel good." Then he kissed her, a huge, passionate, fiery kiss, which left enough of his spit on her face to fill a medicine dropper.

Funny how time erased certain memories.

His breathing became short, shallow, as if he was about to have some kind of seizure. He grabbed her hand, covered it with more wet kisses, and pressed it urgently to his crotch, which appeared so far to have nothing going on whatsoever.

Nausea replaced the sexy tingles of anticipation, reluctance nearly overcame the willingness of her heart to melt into his. She rubbed him halfheartedly through his pants, and though he moaned embarrassingly loudly, and thrust his hips and moaned some more, what God intended penises to do when undergoing focused manual stimulation did not happen.

Apparently that part of him wasn't eighteen anymore, either.

He pushed down on the tops of her shoulders, as if he wanted her to kneel. "Sarah. Suck on my cock and I'll get hard as a rock for you."

Sarah sank down obediently. *Oh my God.* What had she done? Betrayed her marriage and morals for the chance to kneel and service another man? A man who used the detested C word?

Be patient, Sarah. What was she going to do, leave because he hadn't greeted her the way she fantasized? She'd come here for Tom, for what they'd meant to each other, what they still meant to each other. They were both nervous. This was normal.

She opened his fly and took him into her mouth. He was soft, small; sucking him was like mouthing a little balloon partially filled with water. But that wasn't his fault. Most men encountered this situation in their lives at one point or another. Or so she'd heard.

A few minutes later, the balloon was still in the same flaccid state as when her efforts started, and Sarah's jaw was getting tired.

"Sarah. Baby. Let's go upstairs. To my bedroom." He laughed nervously. "I want to get you naked, I want my hands all over you. I want to see your tits, and your pussy. I want my tongue all over you, sucking your clit."

Sarah froze. Her what? And her who? And her *what*?

Under her now-motionless lips, his penis finally started to swell. She jerked back and let it flop out of her mouth. She wasn't turning him on. He was. With his own nasty words.

If she went upstairs . . . oh God, she couldn't. He'd probably have her on the bed on her hands and knees so he could do her like a dog. She'd probably have to talk dirty to get him off. Or worse, he'd talk dirty and get himself off, and how was that any different from sex with Ben?

This was ridiculous. Worse—she was ridiculous. She didn't want Tom. She wanted the fantasy of Tom. She wanted to feel loved and worshipped and desired. And that had nothing to do with who he was, just what she wanted him to make her feel. "I can't go upstairs."

"What?" He looked crestfallen, like a kid told Santa wasn't bringing him toys this year.

Sarah got to her feet, not bothering to wipe her mouth surreptitiously. "I thought this was what I wanted. But it's not. It isn't right. Not for Ben, not for Amber, not for Kettle, and not for me."

"Because I couldn't get it up right away? Well, I'm sorry, I was nervous." His voice became nasal and petulant. "Just give me a few minutes and I'll be fine."

"It's not that." She looked into his eyes, and instead of the blazing fruition of a spark from long ago, there was nothing but an old friend she'd built up into something more.

Saved from herself by a small, limp penis.

"I should go. I'm . . . truly sorry about this, Tom."

"You're a tease, Sarah. A cockteaser. First in high school,

now again. Is that what you get off on? How many other men have you done this to?"

"None." She was beyond weary. Beyond humiliated. Beyond empty. She picked up her cloak and headed for his door.

He followed her. "Well, I've done quite a few lonely wives favors, and they were *all* satisfied."

"In *Kettle*?" Couldn't be. People here didn't—

Tom gave her a look as if she hadn't passed first grade yet. *Oh God.* Lonely wives. In Kettle. Sarah was one of many. In spite of her beyond-everything exhaustion, that managed to hurt.

"Well, Tom, congratulations. Keep up the good work."

She left him sputtering, calling her names that would probably have more of an effect on his penis than she had. And how she longed for antiseptic wash for having had something in her mouth that had invaded women she probably knew.

The chilly night air in Kettle was no longer invigorating and freeing, but cold and lifeless, oppressive and damp.

She walked to the end of his driveway, tears welling up in spite of her valiant efforts to stop them and save her face from telltale black channels of mascara.

What was she going to do now? Where could she go? Where could she possibly feel safe after tonight?

The party was out of the question. Even she wasn't brave or strong enough to act normal. Smiling, chatting, wondering which of her friends Tom already had his dick in. Impossible.

Nor could she go home and sit thinking about what she'd done, waiting for her betrayed husband and daughter to come home, which they would when Sarah and pumpkins didn't show.

She needed a friend. Not on the phone. A live body with a warm shoulder to cry on. Someone who'd understand what she'd done and why; someone who wouldn't judge her or be shocked or condemning when she found out Sarah wasn't what she'd pretended to be for so long.

She stopped walking. Her head lifted. She caught her breath.

There was only one person like that in the whole damn town.

Twenty-two

Erin

Erin stopped walking and waited. Joe would get to her soon enough.

Why was he home so early? He always stayed forever at Rick's . . .

Joan had called him from the gym. Joan had told him he better get his ass over here because his bitch wife was at that slut Vivian's house, working together to find Erin a boyfriend, or plotting to kill Joe, or sinning in some unimaginable way together. Erin wondered if despite two husbands, that was something Joan would like to watch.

It was a miracle Joe hadn't come home even earlier. Maybe Joan waited until she thought the evidence would be most damning. Or maybe the football game hadn't been over yet, or he wanted to ponder her rebellion to work himself into more of a rage.

He hesitated in his approach, a slow, bizarre suspension of movement that knocked his stride off, and she realized he was staggering drunk.

At first she wanted to turn and run. He wouldn't be able to catch her. He was strong, but hopelessly out of shape. She'd leave him in the dust.

But where could she run to? Vivian might protect her, but for how long? Vivian was leaving. This battle was Erin's to fight or not fight, exactly as Vivian said.

"Er'n." He was using his calm, quiet voice, which meant he was at his worst. When he yelled, it usually wasn't so bad. Passion and anger got in the way, and he was sloppy and more threat than punishment.

"Yes, Joe."

He'd see the hair, even in this dim light. But if she ducked her face, maybe she could get home and wash off the makeup before he noticed. It wasn't much, but it was all she had besides her usual plan of taking whatever he dished out.

"What the hell're you doing out here?"

"Coming home to make dinner for you." She stared at the ditch beside the road, a black stripe in the near-darkness. She couldn't believe it but she wasn't afraid. Maybe she was too cold and hard and dead inside to feel fear anymore.

"What's this?" He grabbed her hair, yanked the braid so her neck snapped back and her face was exposed to the faint light from the streetlight across the street.

"What's *this?*" He took hold of her jaw, squeezing, forcing her face up to him. "You whore. You painted whore."

Of Babylon? Erin muffled a gasp of laughter. His mother would have written those lines for him.

"Who did this?"

Still no fear. But something else. Maybe she was angry. Maybe she was just plain sick of it. "Vivian."

"Vivian." He spat the name out. "I'll deal with you first. Her later."

Erin muffled more laughter, not as carefully this time. As if anyone like Joe could come close to conquering the fire and passion and power that was Vivian. Vivian had already rid herself of one man. Joe would simply be next.

He yanked on her braid again, squeezed her jaw harder. "What. Is. So. Funny."

She couldn't answer the question with her jaw clamped in his harsh fingers, apart from weird mumbling sounds, but she tried anyway. "Nff-ing."

He held her there, and she heard a rumble of gas through his belly, a beast-growl of hunger. He was shaking, sweating. She prayed he'd drop dead of a heart attack and roll into the black stripe of the ditch, so she'd be free, cleanly and faultlessly.

She used to think she was like the bird she'd tried to let go in the woods. That after an initial taste of life in the wild, she'd try to get back into the cage, too. Not tonight. Tonight she felt she'd eventually learn to fly on her own.

"We're going home, Er'n. You're going to wash that shit off, then I'm gon' take my bath before I touch you. You unnerstand?"

She instinctively waited for the fear, off-balance when it still didn't come, like a meticulous friend forgetting a regular lunch date. Maybe after the mirror glimpse of what she could have been—what she still could be if she dared—and after the sweet touch of Vivian's fingers, Joe seemed more pathetic than threatening. If he finally killed her tonight, he'd feel only her contempt.

"You unnerstand me?" He shook her, pinching her jaw harder, breathing heavily, and she knew he already had a hard-on from thinking about what he was going to do to her.

"Ysh."

He let go of her face and grabbed her arm. "Let's go home."

Sure thing, Joe. She followed him, outwardly meek, into the house and the master bathroom as she'd followed him truly meekly so many times.

But now it was her turn to breathe heavily, perspire, feel the churning in her belly. Contempt, a slow, rising anger, and for the first time, resolve.

This was the last time he was going to do this. The last time. The only way she'd submit was to keep repeating that to herself, over and over, and then find some way to make it true.

Joe ran water into the tub, grabbed the elastic off her hair, and raked the braid out, using his fingers like a claw-comb. He tested the water, grabbed the back of her neck, and forced her to her knees, bending her over the tub.

The last time.

The water was hot. Scalding. She didn't scream. Not from the heat and not when he used Comet powder on a wash-cloth to clean her face.

Something was building in her. She recognized the force immediately and wondered how she could have mistaken it at Vivian's. The only kind of power Erin had ever had was building, the ball in her gut, swelling and squeezing. It hadn't happened for a long time, not since a year after Joy died, when Joe had taunted her for losing their child and being barren since.

She didn't fight the pressure. She let it build, nurtured it along. Screwed her eyes shut against the sting of the chemicals, forced herself to bear the scraping of the abrasive on her skin, choking on the bleach that powdered her nose and lungs.

The last time.

"There." He hauled her to her feet, examined her dripping, raw face, exhaling foul alcohol fumes. "You're clean. Dry yourself. I'll make you mine again after my bath."

She winced even at the cautious dab of the towel on her skin, fighting not to gasp for air, the hot, angry ball up in her chest now, wider and wilder. Behind her, the metallic thunk of the drain stop falling into place, water still running.

He undressed, body bloated and hairy, penis sticking out from its tangled nest of hair, a foolish pink bad design, and he slipped into his ridiculous ritual purifying bath.

Erin stood sentry at the side of the tub, stiff, unmoving, waiting for the blazing ball in her chest to rise further, expand further until it took over her brain and her vision started fading to snowy static.

"Dry your hair. Then take off your clothes." He pawed at his silly stiffening sausage, looking her over greedily. "I need to make you mine ev'rywhere a man can take you."

Not this time, Joe.

She pulled the ancient hair dryer from the cabinet under the sink and plugged it in, surprised she could do that much with the ringing already in her ears, and the false brightness affecting her vision.

"I changed my mind." His voice was higher, strained with arousal. "Take 'em off now."

"No." She spoke calmly, aimed the dryer at her hair, temperature on low since her skin couldn't handle any heat.

"What'd you say?"

"I won't take off my clothes."

"*What. Did. You. Say?*"

She turned, tried to meet his eyes, but only got to his chin, panting not with fear, but with rage. "No."

"You bitch." His penis was harder now, fueled by her defiance into hotter lust for control and discipline. "You think you're something now Vivian put crap on your face?"

"Yes."

He laughed. "You're wrong, sweet pea. You're nothing."

"So far."

"What the hell makes you think you're something? Lipstick? You can't work, you can't have children, you sit home all day painting ugly pictures, what're you exactly?"

The ball rose into her head, pressure on her brain, burning and bright. "I had Joy."

"Joy wasn't even a kid. She was a deformed thing they pulled out of you dead and threw in the incinerator with the garbage."

"How . . . could they do that?" she whispered, panting, barely able to get the words out.

"I told them to."

The ball exploded. Erin opened her mouth to scream. Scream and scream and scream the way she'd screamed and screamed and screamed her whole life when the ball built and caught fire and rose into her head and exploded like that.

But this time the scream didn't come. This time she looked her husband right in the eye and tossed the still-running hair dryer into his bath.

Vivian

Vivian pulled her grandmother's dress over her head, still not sure why she was going to this stupid party. A few weeks ago she'd have wanted to go for the sole purpose of pissing everyone off. A few days ago she'd have wanted to go to prove to the media she fit in here. Now she just wanted to leave Kettle. Start over somewhere entirely new, fresh, exciting, somewhere she belonged, somewhere she'd be accepted, or at very least somewhere she'd be anonymous.'

Like . . . nowhere on this planet.

She caught back her hair and wrapped it into a severe French twist, then wrinkled her nose at her schoolmarm reflection. Why bother partying if she wasn't in the mood? No articles about Lorelei Taylor had come out in the last week or so. Nothing newsworthy was going to happen tonight, whether she went to the pumpkin bash or not. Nancy had slavishly volunteered to staff the makeover booth; Nancy could handle it. God knew Vivian wasn't anxious to spend the evening listening to her. And she'd sell more certificates without Vivian's foul presence anyway.

Early next week, she'd put the house on the market. It was time. Mike was getting intense, mentioning Portland again this morning before he left. She wasn't biting. All her life, from one man to another, leaning on this one, depending on that one, betrayed by all of them.

Yeah, Mike seemed different. Yeah, she'd fallen pretty hard. But hello, she was massively on the rebound from a disastrous dysfunctional relationship. Any man who didn't beat her up and involuntarily frame her for murder would look good.

She stepped into a dreadful pair of plain beige flats she'd bought to complement the dress, annoyed at herself for being flip. Her feelings for Mike ran deeper than that. But if she moved to Portland, it would be Mike's house, Mike's friends, Mike's choice.

It was time for Vivian, on her own. Cue swelling background music and shots of widowed pioneer women chopping down trees. Time for Vivian to make it in some capacity not involving men, for the first time in her life.

She was evolving.

Stellie's house would bring enough money to buy somewhere. Nothing fancy. No more East Side luxury for a while. If she found she needed big city living, she could get a roommate, teach aerobics, maybe hair dressing.

She didn't know. It sounded lonely and dull and ungrounded. But she couldn't stay here. Couldn't face Mike's loving eyes anymore, the eyes that increasingly said "mine" and "wife" and "forever."

Forever was too damn long to be talking about at this point in her life, no matter how she felt about him.

A knock at her door, the bell. Mike. Again. Her heart rose in anticipation of seeing him, and she told it to calm the hell down, scowled at the mirror and pulled the pins out of her hair. Ran downstairs and flung open the door—to the most unexpected apparition she could imagine: Sarah. Looking as if she'd just been struck by lightning.

"Whoa. Come in." She waited to close the door until Miss Zombie America managed to walk past. "What the hell hap-pened to you?"

"I think . . ." Sarah swallowed as if she had zero moisture left in her body. "I made a mistake."

"Okay. You want some tea? Coffee? Whiskey?"

Sarah stared with eyes that reflected a complete lack of comprehension. Or possibly a complete lack of brain func-tion. "I . . . don't—"

"Whiskey." She pulled Sarah into the living room, since otherwise Sarah would have stayed standing in the kitchen for the rest of the night. "I'll get you a drink."

In the dining room, she opened the cabinet of what had originally been a writing desk, pulled out Irish whiskey, and filled a glass with a healthy dose. She'd guess Sarah was in no mood for partying Kettle style with sugary virgin punch.

"You've done nice things for this place."

"Thanks." She crossed through the living room she'd spent the morning putting back in shape and held out the glass. "Here. Take off your . . . cape thing and have a seat."

"Yes. Okay." Sarah yanked at the ties and let the cape fall from her shoulders, swung it around, and dropped it across the arm of the couch.

Vivan's eyebrows shot up. "Holy shit, look at you."

Sarah took a long swallow of whiskey and smiled wryly, her eyes coming back to life. "I'm a sex kitten."

Vivian guffawed. "Come as you're not. You're perfect."

"Yeah." She looked down at the glass resting on her knee, sniffed, and drank again. "I'm just perfect."

Okay. No laughing. Vivian sank down beside her, wondering what could be bad enough to keep Sarah from her pumpkins and reduce her to this state. Had she ordered the wrong color frosting for the cake?

Or please, not Amber . . .

"So what was this big mistake?"

"I'm leaving Ben."

Whoa.

"Hold that thought." She scrambled off the couch and headed for the dining room. "If we're getting that heavy I need a drink, too."

She poured herself a double, took a healthy gulp, then returned to the couch to face As Sarah's World Turns. Being this particular woman's confessor was about the last thing she'd ever expected. "Okay, run that by me again."

"I'm leaving my husband. Ben. For the last decade of our marriage, he's been . . ." She grimaced and looked over at Vivian. "You don't really care, do you."

"No, not really." Vivian patted Sarah's fishnet-covered knee. "But that makes me a good person to tell."

Sarah laughed dryly. "That's one way of looking at it."

"So you were on your way to the party, you decided to leave your husband, and you came to me why?"

"Oh." She gestured aimlessly with her drink and nearly

sloshed whiskey over the rim. "You were the only person I could think of who wouldn't judge me."

"For leaving your husband?"

"Uh-uh." Sarah swallowed her latest sip. "For cheating on him."

Ha! Vivian smiled her most delighted smile. "Well now, Sarah darling, that's one thing I never did."

"No?" Sarah turned to stare in horror. "You never did?"

"Nope." She leaned back on the couch to enjoy the moment.

"I . . ." Her face flushed crimson. "I thought you'd understand. I thought for sure—"

"It's okay. I can't throw stones at anyone for fucked-up behavior."

"Well this was . . ." She gulped more whiskey, staring off into space. "This was quite fucked-up."

Vivian snorted behind her hand, hoping it sounded like a cough. Sarah was the only person who could make "fucked-up" sound like polite conversation at teatime. "What was? The marriage or the cheating?"

"Both." Another big swallow of whiskey. Sarah was looking to get derailed as fast as possible. "The marriage was slow, painful, endless fucked-up. The cheating was fast, painful, immediate fucked-up."

"Which happened when? Just now?" She wanted to laugh again. Of all people . . .

"I wouldn't actually say it happened." She shook her head too many times, with the careless emphasis of someone on her way to getting plastered, then shot Vivian a glance. "You see . . . he couldn't get his thingy up."

"His *thingy*?" That was too much. Vivian giggled helplessly, relieved when Sarah joined in.

"He couldn't." Her brows drew together and quivered while she tried not to laugh any more. "I probably could have worked on that little wiener for the rest of my life."

"Oh *God*." Vivian shrieked with laughter. Nothing in the world could be funnier than Sarah talking about sex. Nothing. "So what happened?"

"I walked out." Her smile faded.

"Because he couldn't—"

"No." She gripped the glass on her lap. "Because I realized I was full of shit. Deeply and thoroughly full of it."

Vivian's giggles committed abrupt suicide. "Oh."

"You knew that. Probably everyone did. It just took me a while." She drank again; her glass was almost empty. "Not a pleasant discovery."

"But self-knowledge is power."

"Not tits?"

Vivian shrugged. "Sometimes I wonder."

"So you're finding out you're full of shit, too?" Sarah's eyes were hopeful, let's be best girlfriends and find out we're not who we seem together okay?

Vivian rolled her eyes. She got enough of this from Mike. "Hell, I don't know. Can we talk about something else?"

"Oh sure, sure, sure." She made a fluttery motion with her fingers. "So . . . Do you really drink beer with carrot cake?"

"No."

"Did you flash your boobs at Harris's because you were miserable and angry?"

"Yeah."

"Did you kill Ed?"

Vivian twirled her whiskey, watching the legs gather inside the glass and run themselves dry. She wasn't sure she liked this unmasking. "No. I didn't."

Sarah nodded and drained her glass. "Mike tried to tell me when you first moved here, but I wasn't ready to hear."

"He did?"

"Uh-huh." Sarah smiled a sweet, tipsy smile. "You look beautiful in that dress. Has he seen you in it?"

"Yes."

"It's the kind of dress Rosemary would wear."

"Oh, ducky."

"Funny me being dressed like this and you like that." She frowned and tipped her head. "Did you ever stop to think that maybe we're closer to our real selves like this than—"

"God, I don't know, ask Dr. Phil." Vivian snatched Sarah's glass out of her hand, took it with hers to the dining room, refilled both and came back in, not sure Sarah should have any more, but she needed all of her second one. "Cheers."

Sarah clinked her glass and raised it. "Here's to being full of shit."

Vivian kept her glass in her lap. She did not care to drink to that, thankyouverymuch, though she noticed Sarah had no trouble at all.

"You're not going to hurt him, are you?" Sarah indulged a puppy-eyed, fuzzy-focus plea. "He's been through enough."

"I'm not planning to." *Liar.* It was exactly what she was planning. And guess what, now she could drink to being full of shit openly and honestly, and thank God for that.

"It's so good at the beginning, isn't it." Sarah put her glass on the coffee table, sighed, and laid her head back.

"Yep." Vivian didn't want to think about how good, nor did she want inevitably to hear how good it used to be for Sarah and Ben. "When are you leaving?"

"Soon. I'm suffocating here."

"Tell me about it. Where will you go?"

"I want to take Amber and move back to New York." She slid off the couch and started walking around the room, as tall and graceful and slender a sex kitten as there ever was. Vivian could actually picture her enjoying New York. "I was happy there. I had a good life, friends. I danced professionally."

"You have enough money to live there?"

"Yes." She picked up a tiny cross-stitch sampler Stellie had done for a miniature frame, *Home Is Where the Heart Is*, which Vivian had cleared out in her original sweep and replaced the day before in a sentimental moment she now regretted. "My grandparents were wealthy. I've been supporting Ben here. And serving him. I can't do that anymore."

"Have you talked to him?"

Sarah shook her head and replaced the miniature. "I'm done. I just want out. Of the marriage and of Kettle."

Vivian put her glass down. Not that she began to be an expert, but for Amber's sake, Sarah should at least try to see if there was anything worth staying for.

Kind of like Vivian wasn't planning to do with Mike. Shit.

The back doorbell rang; Sarah recoiled, pressing herself against the wall. "Oh God, if it's Ben looking for me, or—"

"Relax." Vivian moved past her toward the kitchen. "Who'd think to look for you here?"

She rounded the corner and saw Erin dimly through the back window, looking strangely mottled and wide-eyed.

Apparently Vivian was hosting the other Kettle Halloween party tonight.

She opened the door; Erin ducked her head.

"Hi, Erin."

"Can I come in?"

"Sure." She started to move back; Erin burst into the room as if she were afraid of the dark. Vivian glanced out to make sure there were no signs of Joe in pursuit, then locked the door, turned, and got a good look in the light of the kitchen.

"*Your face.*" She grabbed Erin's thin arm and held on, wanting to throw up. The bastard. Bruises all along her jaw. Cheeks and forehead that looked as if they'd seen the business side of a cheese grater. "He saw the makeup."

"Joan called him from the gym."

"The bitch."

"He came home before I could wash it off. So he did."

"With sandpaper."

"Comet."

"Oh my God."

"It's okay." She laughed a weird, manic laugh. "It's all okay now."

Vivian nodded cautiously. "Joe . . . let you come over?"

Again the laugh. Vivian frowned. Had she been drinking? Had she snapped? She was acting really strange, even for Erin.

"He doesn't know."

The light bulb went on. "You left him? You snuck out?"

"I walked out. Right out the front door." She laughed, a big

gasping rush of air, laughed again, and Vivian realized what
was up. She was terrified.

"Come on in, honey." She led Erin toward the living room.
Erin followed, docile and trusting, hand like ice in Vivian's.
"You want a drink? Or hell, you probably need one."

"Yes. I need one."

"Come in." She turned the corner and wasn't sure whose
face registered more surprise, Sarah's or Erin's.

"Hi, Sarah."

"Erin, what . . . your face."

Erin took a deep breath and stared at the ceiling, as if trying to recall a speech. "Joe did this to me. For years. And my
father before that."

She pulled up her shirt and showed bruises, scars.

Vivian smiled. Good for her. Good for her.

Sarah gasped, put her hand to her mouth. Tears gathered,
and spilled down her cheeks and over her fingers. Predictably,
Sarah could even cry tastefully.

"I didn't know. I'm so sorry. I didn't know."

"It's okay. It's over now." Erin accepted the glass from Vivian, downed the entire thing, then coughed and gasped, her
raw face reddening further. "People drink that on purpose?"

"Sit." Vivian led her to the couch. "We should—"

The back doorbell again. The women tensed.

"I'll check." Vivian got up quietly and peeked down the
hall, bracing herself for the sight of Joe about to put his fist
through her window.

Mike.

She ran to him and opened the door, storm no longer
squeaking after he fixed it, as he'd fixed so many things.

"Hi." She smiled, hating the way she wanted to lie on her back and wag her tail in ecstasy. Hating more that she wanted to invite him in for protection. "I've got company."

He frowned and cocked his head in that quirky way she adored. "Who?"

"Sarah and Erin. I don't think we're going to the party."

"*Sarah's* not going? What about—"

"No. She's not. I'm not. Erin's not. We're all staying here. Okay?"

"Can I help?"

"No. This is girl stuff."

His eyes narrowed. "Vivian, what—"

"Look, Mike. I just can't be with you."

His face froze. "That sounds ominous."

"We can talk tomorrow."

"About?"

"Us. The future. Whatever you want. Not now."

"Oh, I see. So I have a nice, peaceful night ahead waiting to see if my heart gets trampled?"

"I didn't plan this."

"Right." He sighed, scrubbed his hand across his forehead, and gave her a look. "I hate being Mr. Nice Guy."

She grinned and knew leaving him would probably take twenty years off her life. But staying with him might take thirty. "You can't help it, you were born that way. Now go."

He leaned in and kissed her, long and hard and thrilling, and she felt guilt and confusion wrapping themselves around her heart and trying to squeeze all the happy, good stuff out.

"Okay. I'll go." He walked down her steps and crossed her driveway. Her entire being screamed at her to call him back.

But that's what she'd always done. Asked for protection, used them for safety. She'd start the whole destructive dependency cycle again. Self-knowledge was power. Right?

Though tits weren't bad on a cold, dark night.

She closed the door and strolled, deliberately casual, back into the living room, where the two women stared apprehensively.

"No more interruptions." Especially if one of them turned out to be Joe. He'd need a night to cool off at least, and Erin would need a good lawyer. Too bad Vivian had put so much effort into pissing off Mr. Combover, Esq., at every turn. Going forward, she might want to see about keeping more bridges unburned.

"Girls' night only." She started turning out lights. "Party's moving upstairs. We're not home."

Sarah and Erin giggled and helped her darken the downstairs. Clutching their drinks, they climbed the stairs, into Vivian's room.

"Okay." Vivian pulled the blinds and put one lamp near her bed on the floor. They sat down around it, faces lit strangely by the low light.

Her buddies. A desperate housewife and a wacko. Nice.

"What a sweet dollhouse." Sarah crawled over to it, her tail dragging behind her, picked Emily up, and cupped her gently in her hand. "Was this around when Stellie was here?"

"Yes." Erin nodded several times. "Vivian and I played with it when we were little."

"Really?" Sarah looked back and forth between the two women as if this association was impossible to digest. She touched a miniature couch, drew her hand over a little lamp.

"Way back then. I was going to be a dancer and a famous scientist."

"I wanted to be a nurse," Erin said. "Or a social worker."

Vivian snorted. "I wanted to give the best head this side of the Mississippi."

Sarah laughed so hard she dropped Emily. "Well, you probably got closest. But I doubt any of us thought we'd end up here tonight, together, in this situation."

"Oh for God's sake." Vivian drained her glass and filled it again. "End up? Life begins at forty, right? I think we have some time left. Here's to first steps."

Erin held up her empty glass. "To no more Joe."

"To no more Ben."

Vivian bit her lip. *To leaving Mike.* She couldn't say it.

"Mike's wonderful, Vivian." Sarah spoke dreamily, misunderstanding her silence, and Vivian found herself glad Mike wasn't here to see Sarah drunk and loose, dressed as a sex kitten.

"He is." Erin held out her empty glass to Vivian, who shook her head, then relented and poured her another half-finger. "And he's much happier since she died."

"What?" Sarah gaped. "Rosemary?"

Erin nodded and downed her second drink with barely a shudder. "I think he was relieved. I was. She drove me nuts."

Sarah stared at Vivian, who shook her head, frowning. Better let Sarah think Erin was off her rocker. Though Vivian was starting to think Erin was probably the only person in Kettle who saw through all the bullshit.

And Mike.

"You know what?" Sarah replaced Emily in her perfect

house, sat, and arranged her long legs to one side. "We're like those women in 1920 who holed themselves up in this house Halloween night, away from their men."

Vivian's drink began to taste like gasoline, and she put it on the floor.

"One of the women went home and her husband beat her to death."

"Oh, but Erin, that was an acci . . . dent." Sarah retreated under Erin's scowl. "I'm an idiot, aren't I."

Short silence, while they apparently agreed with her.

"Well that's not going to happen tonight." Vivian leaned over and kissed Erin's ragged cheek. "You can stay here."

"No. It won't happen." She giggled, her eyes shiny and glazed in the light.

Sarah flicked Vivian a glance. "We should call the police and report him in case he comes after you."

"Good idea." Vivian got up and headed for the phone, dragged the white pages onto her bed.

"No police."

Vivian ignored her. Police, non-emergency . . . there. She stabbed her finger on the number, surprised to find she no longer mourned her long nails. "It's a good idea, Erin. At this point he'll come after me, too. I'd like to think Sarah can do 911 fast, but I'd rather it didn't come to that."

"It won't."

"What makes you so sure?" Vivian started to dial. Five . . . five . . . five . . . six—

"Because." Erin shrugged and drew her knees up, rested her chin on them, and stared at the lamp, two bright reflected spots in her eyes. "I killed him."

Sarah gasped so long and so loud, Vivian had time to be surprised she didn't inflate and go sailing around the room.

"Relax, Sarah. She's not serious."

"Yes. I am."

"Not funny, Erin." She heard the fear in her own voice, and punched off the phone.

"I'm not kidding. I did it like you did. A hair dryer in his bath. Now I'm free." She lifted her head and gazed triumphantly at Vivian, student to master.

"Oh God." Vivian had to breathe to make sure she didn't puke Irish whiskey all over her grandmother's hardwood. Erin's odd behavior explained: She was in shock. "You're sure he's dead?"

"I'm sure."

"Erin." Vivian walked over and crouched next to her, wondering how life could keep going so horribly wrong. "I didn't kill Ed."

Erin turned those strange, fixed eyes on her.

"Yes you did." She spoke calmly, with absolute certainty. "You freed yourself. You told me to do the same thing."

"No." *Oh God, oh God.* Vivian put her hand on Erin's arm and shook gently. "The CD player fell into Ed's bath. It was an accident. I wanted you to *leave* Joe, not kill him."

Erin's smile started to droop. "An accident? You didn't kill him? To free yourself?"

"No, I didn't." Vivian's voice cracked. She had a sudden urge to live her entire life again. Different parents, different state, peaceful suburbs, college education, a white-fenced house, husband who adored her, two-point-five kids and a dog. Was she evolving leaving Kettle and Mike? Or running away? "I loved Ed. Or . . . I thought I did."

Not the way she loved Mike.

Erin stood. Turned and staggered out of the bedroom, catching her side on the doorjamb, stumbling down the stairs.

"Jesus." Vivian scrambled after her, Sarah close behind. "Erin, don't go anywhere, we can talk about this, we can figure out what to do, get you a lawyer. It's going to be okay."

"I have to go running." Erin reached the front door, opened it, made a tiny, helpless, animal sound, and froze.

Vivian came up behind her, moved her aside, and found herself staring into the stony, pale-as-paper face of Joan.

Twenty-three

Vivian quickly stepped in front of Erin.

"You killed my son." Joan stared past Vivian with the same shocked, too-wide eyes Erin was undoubtedly using to stare back. All made more sickeningly bizarre by Joan having dressed for the Kettle party in black and painted her face ghostly white.

"Come in, Joan." She pulled the woman in, glanced past her into the street, and any urge to giggle evaporated.

Cars pulling up. Men getting out. The media, the reporters, paparazzi. Hadn't she said only a few hours earlier with naive confidence that there would be nothing to report tonight? She'd barely had time to react to Erin's announcement, but she saw it clearly now. The copycat crime of the century. The feeding frenzy was only beginning.

They'd extract from Erin that Vivian urged her to get free of Joe, that she'd offered to help. They'd catch on to Erin's admiration, paint a picture of a disturbed woman idolizing Vivian, of her transformation culminating in a makeover using Vivian's makeup and Vivian's clothes. This was going to be beyond nasty. Because this time it was really about murder, and the facts would be used to paint a picture that flattered no one in it.

And if Vivian thought she never understood the value of a white-picket-fence existence before, she understood it double now. Only the house with the fence had Mike in it, and was located in Portland, Maine. The kids were theirs, and the dog was named Lorelei or Taylor, so Vivian would never forget to appreciate what she had.

As soon as the dream snapped into focus, it fuzzed and faded into impossibility. What had she thought she could accomplish shaking Kettle up, besides drawing attention to herself? Well, congratulations, she had. Now a husband and son was dead, and a troubled woman who'd finally freed herself the only way she knew how would pay by starting a new life in yet another prison.

Unless Vivian could stop it here. For Erin's sake and Mike's sake and hers, and if Vivian could just make her see it . . . Joan's, too.

Joan pointed a shaking finger at Vivian. "You gave her the idea with what you did. Joe is dead because of you."

Erin made a choking sound. "I was—"

Vivian grabbed Erin's arm, relieved when Erin got the message and shut up.

"I'm going to see you get life without parole for this, you bitch." The huge eyes were unblinking in the startlingly white face, teeth eerily white to match. Erin shrank back. "You were never good enough for my son. I'm going to see you and Lorelei both locked up. You're both guilty, you're both—"

"Joan?" Vivian spoke as gently as she could, trying to keep her breathing smooth and regular. "We need to sit down and talk this out."

"I've got nothing to say to you. The police are at the scene, I told them to come here when they were done. I knew you'd be here, both of you, twin murderess bitches celebrating."

"Not celebrating." Erin sank into a chair. "We're not."

"Think about what will happen, Joan."

"She'll get put away, that's what will happen."

"It's not that simple. Someone told Joe that Erin was at my house this afternoon. That person knew he'd be furious." She touched Erin's raw cheek. "Would this have happened if he'd come home at his usual time?"

"You can't pin this on me. She was trying to be something she's not."

"She deserved this for trying on makeup?" Vivian kept calm, but it was close to the hardest thing she'd ever done.

"Joe didn't deserve to die." Joan's voice cracked; she wilted to one side as if one leg stopped being interested in holding her up. Sarah caught her, led her to the faded couch, and sat next to her.

"No. He didn't deserve to die." *Though he came close.* "But the two of you left Erin feeling she had no other way out."

"This has nothing to do with me."

And that was where Vivian's only hope lay. In proving her wrong. "Did you see who's outside?"

"Reporters. They were all over the party."

Sarah exchanged glances with Vivian and nodded nearly

imperceptibly. "They'll make a huge deal of this, Joan. It will be very unpleasant."

"Murder is unpleasant."

Vivian sat on her other side. "Because I'm here, it will make national news."

Joan leaned away from Vivian to glare at her better. "I'm glad. They'll drag you through the mud all over again, maybe this time get some of it to stick where it belongs."

"And Joe." Sarah's voice was pure honey. "They'll drag him, too. It will be awful."

Joan leaned the other way, and Sarah got the glare. "What?"

"It will all come out, Joan." Vivian adopted Sarah's soothing tones, though she'd rather shriek and throw punches. "What he's done to Erin for so many years. Stories. Details."

Sarah shook her head mournfully. "The whole country will think he's a monster."

"Much worse than me. And you know, Joan, most abusers were abused themselves as children." She tried to keep her tone sympathetic, praying this risk would be worth it. "The press will ask a lot of questions; there will be a lot of speculation. Is that what happened to Joe as a boy? What kind of mother could stay silent while something like that went on?"

Joan started to breathe too quickly; her body shook.

No joy leading up to this hoped-for triumph. Vivian wished she could take back the whiskey; her stomach was sick at what she was doing. But she'd gotten Erin into this. She owed it to her to try and get her out. And to herself. And even to bloody fucking Kettle, which would be torn apart if this went public.

"I'll tell people. Finally. I will." Erin popped out of her chair and started pacing. "He had the hospital throw my baby away like she was garbage before I even saw her. He smashed up her nursery with an ax. He wouldn't let me get a job or see anyone or wear what I wanted. He hit me. He put things up me that hurt during sex. He liked to go in the wrong hole when I was on my hands and knees and pretend I was a boy. He wanted me to dress like a little girl and call him Daddy and suck his—"

"*Stop.*" Joan made a ghastly sound that was probably supposed to be a laugh. "You say that, and here's my response. Joe came to me one day and said you liked the kinky stuff, and it upset him. I was there when we told them to take the baby. Trust me, you didn't want to see that thing. Joe did it to protect you from that nightmare for the rest of your life."

She laughed too loudly, trembling, demonic. "See how it will go? Her word against mine. None of you scares me. I told you how things work here. No one will back her up. They just don't want to know."

"You are absolutely right, Joan." Any sympathy Vivian might have felt for the grieving mother died quicker than her son had. "And that works both ways."

"What the hell does that mean?"

A pounding on the door. "This is the sheriff. Open this door."

"Erin killed Joe?" Vivian took Joan's arm, desperate to get the message across. "That kind of thing doesn't happen here. Who is going to believe it?"

"*Certainly* not me." Sarah took up her cue so beautifully, Vivian could have kissed her. "I can't imagine such a thing happening here. I don't *want* to imagine such a thing happening here."

"It was an accident, Joan."

"No." Her voice quavered.

"If it was an accident, Joe will die a hero, mourned by the town. You'll be the noble, grieving mother. If this goes to trial, you'll be the enabler, Joe will be a monster, Erin the victim. No jury would convict her. Is that what you want?"

Pounding again, more urgent. "Sheriff. Open this door."

Joan's torso shook; she moaned and wiped her forehead. "She can't get away with this. She won't get away with this."

Damn it. *Damn it.* "We're not trying to get away with it. We're trying to keep it from getting worse than it already is. Would Joe want his personal life exposed like that? Would he want *you* exposed like that?"

"Open the door *now* or I start counting."

Shit. She'd done what she could in the time they had. Vivian jumped up, opened the door, and let the sheriff in with his assistant, feeling as if she were letting in a carrier of the black plague.

"What's going on?" In keeping with the sick irony theme for the evening, the sheriff was dressed as a convict, features ashen under his bravado. He'd probably never had to investigate anything more than a parking ticket.

"Bill." Joan rose off the couch and stumbled, Sarah shot to her feet and supported her, whispered something in her ear, gazing anxiously at Vivian, who shrugged. They'd done what they could. Everything was up to a top-heavy, cow-eyed bitch. Erin's fate. Vivian's fate. And poor, dopey Kettle's.

"What the heck happened, Joan?"

All eyes turned to Joan, who lifted a trembling hand to her black hair, face pasty and horrifying in the ghostly makeup.

"Joe was . . ." She let out a sob. "Joe had an accident in his bath."

Vivian exhaled. Erin gasped. The relief on the sheriff's face was nearly comical. "But when you called, I thought you said something about murder."

"No." Joan gave a short, weak laugh, tears streaming. "You know as well as I do. There's never been a crime in Kettle."

Erin opened her eyes and turned to the Jesus clock on her sea-green wall. Six A.M. She didn't have to leave for work at Dr. Dodson's for another hour at least. He started seeing clients at eight, but she liked to get there early. On Wednesdays he was nice enough to give her a therapy session for free at seven. But this morning she didn't have to get up yet, though she wanted to run.

In another few months, maybe by summer, she'd have her GED and enough saved to enroll in some college-level courses. After that, she figured there'd be no stopping her. Plus, she'd turned one of the upstairs bedrooms here into a studio and had started painting in earnest. Dr. Dodson had hung one of her paintings in his waiting room, and a few clients had even asked about it. Maybe that could become another source of income. People said her paintings made them feel cheerful.

She rolled out of bed and walked to the dollhouse to say good morning to her doll family, got them out of bed and started on their day. Even she thought this was pretty weird, but she'd begun doing it one day and just kept at it.

After she saw Emily to the table and Nathan making her

breakfast, Erin opened Stellie's bureau and chose some of Vivian's old clothes to wear. Vivian hadn't taken much when she moved to Portland with Mike. Said she wasn't going to need a lot of the outfits, that Erin could have them.

Considering she was also letting Erin stay in her house rent-free until Erin got on her feet financially, Erin felt more comfortable thinking of the clothes as a loan. Vivian had actually borrowed some clothes from Erin before she left, which had mystified Erin. But Vivian insisted on two pairs of gray sweat pants and a bunch of plain white T-shirts. As if that made the trade even, when her clothes must have cost thousands.

Today Erin chose a bright red pair of capris and an electric blue top and laid them on the bed so she'd be able to dress quickly when she came back from her run. Dr. Dodson thought casual dress made clients feel more at ease, and Erin was fine with that. She didn't think she could stand any more beige or gray or navy, even if the colors belonged to a fancy suit.

Things had changed in Kettle since the fall. Sarah had moved with her daughter to a suburb west of Chicago. She and Amber were planning to spend a good part of the summer touring Europe together. Ben had gone to Chicago, too, but Erin had the feeling he was more part of the furniture than the family. She didn't think he and Sarah would be together much longer, but at least they were trying. And Sarah would be happier near Chicago, Erin was sure of that. Amber, too.

Joan had sold both her houses and had gone to live with a sister in Peoria. Erin had helped her move. Kind of an odd dynamic, with Erin helping out of guilt, and Joan letting her help out of guilt. Both women had grieved Joe in different ways, and while they were glad as hell to see the backs of each other, the balance of power had shifted, and they'd managed to work together okay. And maybe helped each other heal.

Erin had buried the hair dryer she'd used to kill Joe along with her *What to Expect* book at the little grave marker in the woods she used to pretend marked Joy's grave. She felt bad burying something nonbiodegradable, but Dr. Dodson said it was probably good closure. Whatever that meant. You couldn't ever really close the door on that kind of grief, for either Joy or Joe. Like trying to put an elephant in the refrigerator; no matter how you tried to stuff it away, something still stuck out.

She put on her shorts and tied her hair back in a ponytail— maybe she'd French braid it later for work since Vivian had shown her how before she left. Erin hadn't run much in the winter, but now there were a few days warm enough here and there, where she could take it up again. April was full springtime in a lot of places, but it took its finicky time in Wisconsin.

Downstairs, she chugged a glass of orange juice and grabbed a granola bar she'd made herself from oats and peanut butter and honey, with chocolate chips just for the fun of it. She went outside, stretched, and started off. Over on Maple, up Spring to Main, and today she chose the direction she'd avoided for a while.

Running, running, feeling the high, the power and ease of her stride, the chill of the air becoming more of a friend as her body warmed. On the way back at the last second—though she probably knew all along she'd go this way—she veered down the track into the woods. She hadn't seen Jordan's house for a while. Maybe he'd be there himself. Or maybe not.

His house came into view, and she saw him standing next to a car in the driveway; he must be leaving for work. He wore a suit and an overcoat and was loading a briefcase into the car, though the engine wasn't running yet.

She passed by and turned her head to smile at him, not tripping this time.

"Hi . . . *Hi*." He looked as glad to see her as she was to see him, which was silly, since they didn't know each other at all.

"Hi." She sped up, feeling herself blush, and ran down the road, five yards, ten, fifteen, twenty . . . Then she jogged in place, breathing the chilly air scented with the coming of spring.

And turned around and jogged back, dropping to a walk several feet from his driveway. He wasn't there, but she knew he'd be back out soon, so she waited, pacing at the edge of the road, letting her breathing quiet from the running, though the nerves wouldn't let it quiet far.

His front door opened and he came out again, this time carrying a bundle that made Erin's heart crash into her stomach like an elevator with a snapped cable.

A baby. He was married and she was a complete fool.

"Hey." He walked toward her, cradling the child, and Erin dropped her eyes to her shoes, new ones she'd bought with her own money.

"I'm Jordan."

"I remember. I'm . . . Erin."

"Nice to meet you officially, Erin. And good to see you." He grinned, and she wanted to die from his warm and gorgeous smile belonging to someone else. "This is my daughter, Letitia."

"She's beautiful." Erin's heart jumped back up into place and beat painfully. Dark eyes, dark hair, regarding Erin with a somber stare. "How old is she?"

"Nearly eighteen months." He cleared his throat. "Her mother . . . passed on shortly after she was born."

"Oh. I'm sorry." She was sorry. Terribly sorry. And also . . . not.

"It was tough." He was looking at her again, dark eyes full of something she couldn't read. "But then life goes on."

"Oh. Yes." She swallowed, touched the tiny red coat, trying not to give away her excitement. "Hi, Letitia. You look very nice in your red coat."

"Wed coat."

Erin laughed. How perfect, how perfect she was. She wanted to touch her own nose to the pudgy sweet cheek and inhale the little-girl smell. "And you have a beautiful name."

Letitia ducked her head against her father's chest and peeked up coyly.

"Thank you." Jordan laughed and kissed the top of her dark soft hair. "I chose it for her."

"Is it a family name?"

"No." He smiled at Erin in a way that made her think something here was meant to be. "In Latin, Letitia means 'joy.' "

A+

AUTHOR INSIGHTS, EXTRAS, & MORE...

FROM

ISABEL SHARPE

AND

AVON A

SQUEAL MAGAZINE, JUNE EDITION, THE M REPORT

Hello and all hail, darlings, your intrepid interviewer salutes you from our cozy and luxurious hacienda in Beverly Hills, or maybe from our fabulous loft in the Village, or perhaps we're on our private Caribbean island? Who knows, who can tell? Just be sure we're somewhere supremely much more fabulous than you.

One thing we know, we were recently somewhere not nearly as sensational as what we are used to, or—we cough delicately—what we deserve. And yet a plum assignment by anyone's standards, even those as astronomically high as ours. An interview with Lorelei Taylor, née Vivian Harcourt, a Where Is She Now piece, two years after the trial that got America's knickers in an unattractive twist.

First, we had to find her, and find her we did, my duckies. Not in Vegas, not in New Orleans, not New York or L.A., but Portland, Maine, the home of . . . well, who the hell knows? Positively not *nous*.

We are to meet her one god-awful, gray, foggy day at a place of her choosing. Please, darlings, by all means go humble if you must, but don't stoop to clam shacks. Not when meeting us. This quite fetching reporter couldn't help wondering how much of the war zone dining was for effect. A dash of sticking-it-to-us by not reserving *un table* at the city's best.

Oh, but tell us we haven't become cynical in our young age.

She's late of course, only ten minutes, but late enough that ours truly went ahead and ordered hot tea, since our internal temperature had been lowered by then to fifty-three damp, penetrating degrees. Have Mainiacs not heard of the concept of spring?

So in she walks, and we can tell you without fear of contradiction, which sadly isn't true of much we say, that she is
gorgeous. We'd seen her on TV, of course. Who didn't follow
America's favorite criminaless's happy trip through the justice
system? But in person—well, let's just say that though our
own beauty is of course legendary, she took our breath away.
We didn't even entertain thoughts of having her offed because
of it, since then we'd no longer be able to gawk. And we are
neither male nor lesbian.

The bigger surprise? Total absence of tarty outfit. Jeans
and a white sweater, not low-cut and not even particularly
tight. She looks—God forgive us for the word we are about to
utter—wholesome.

We, dear readers, are as unflappable as a rock—a beautiful,
gemlike, and valuable rock, you understand—but for a few
seconds after she sits down, not offering her hand to shake, we
notice, our composure is—we blush becomingly to admit—
rattled. In her presence we can see how men fall like bowling
pins around her, and it makes even this jaded—though still
young, of course—heart wonder what she ever saw in Ed, who
we once thought the epitome of gentlemanhood, but of late
have used the term *cockroach*.

Wait, was that a smattering of sympathy for Lorelei Taylor
we heard coming from our collagen-plumped lips? How can
this be? She killed him, right?

We start the interview.

"So tell me, Lorelei, how—"

"Vivian." She says this with a smile lovely enough to be
one of ours, but we get the message that it would be best not
to keep up with the Lorelei stuff if we value our good looks,
which we don't need to tell you we do, immensely.

"Vivian, of course. How are you liking life in this charming . . ." We gesture around the grease-spattered walls of
the clam shack, making sure we drip disdain over the rough
tables and dirty floor. ". . . city? Not quite what you're used to,
hmm?"

"Portland has a lot going on," she opines, like a good chamber of commerce employee, which she isn't unless she's hid-

ing something from us, which of course, us being the ferreting devil we are, she can't possibly be.

"What does it have to offer you?"

"A life." Her lips, painted the subtlest shade of rose, which we are afraid suffers in comparison to our riotous red—or is it vice versa?—tighten, and we suspect she is thinking poignant things about not having had much of a life before, which is not nearly shallow enough for us, so we move on.

"And Mike, your handyman."

"He's part of that life, yes."

Oh God, then she gets that gloopy, superior look on her face that we simply can't abide. We congratulate ourselves for not inviting Mike, since this would be the moment for coupley gazing, and our clams would be hurled across the table before we even ate them.

"So you've been married six months. I'm sure my wedding invite got lost in the mail . . ."

She acknowledges our fairly lame joke with the slightest lift of one dark brow and tells the waiter to bring her fried clams. Before we can open our mouth to insist on salad if there is such a thing on the premises without iceberg, she orders clams for us, too, then stares in open challenge.

"Where was your wedding?" We never back down from a challenge, so we hand the waiter our menu with a charming smile.

"City hall."

"Dress?"

"Suit. Ivory. Small bouquet of white roses."

She scores more points in our personal book for not gushing on, Bridezilla-like, about every detail. "Were your families there or did you elope?"

"My mom came out from Chicago. I hadn't seen her in a while so that was nice. And Mike's parents were there."

"Mike was married before, though, wasn't he?" Oh, and good for us, we got a slight—very slight, since she is a pro—stiffening of her body in response to our shamelessly manipulative question, which we hurled at her after being kind so she'd relax. For you see we are pros, too.

"Yes, he was."

"To a woman he adored who died tragically. Rosemary, wasn't it?"

We are not prepared for the trace of smug amusement on her comely face, which makes us wonder frantically if and how we miscalculated. All our sources had Mike and Rosemary joined at the hip—which by the way there is surgery for now, in case anyone hasn't heard.

"That was a long time ago."

There is more to this story. Our ferret nose is positively twitching. But her stare is uncompromising, her delicate chin held firm, and we sense we won't get much more there. We graciously accede and find ourselves grudgingly respecting her strength. In any case, we have ahead of us plenty of time and resources to snoop further. We make a note.

"You haven't been back to Kettle since you moved here with Mike."

"No. I'll be going back soon, though. For a friend's wedding."

We knew this of course, and are slightly disappointed that she came out with it herself, so we couldn't drop the big bomb.

"How lovely." In compensation, we make sure our voice shows how little we care.

"It is. She deserves a lot of happiness."

"Erin, you mean. Yes." The waiter has brought the clams by now and we spear one, making sure our apprehension and disgust are on our face, though frankly, they smell delicious. "How remarkable that her husband died the way Ed did, so soon after you showed up in Kettle. I hadn't realized bathtub accidents happened so frequently."

Oh we are so *so* good. She is clearly disconcerted.

"People need to be aware of how dangerous it is to mix water and electricity." She slides a clam into her mouth, manages to chew it calmly, and swallows. We give her credit.

"To be sure. Especially when you mix water and electricity and abusive men who need to disappear."

She comes on fierce, as we hoped she would, but to our

immense disappointment, pulls back. "You weren't there. You don't know."

"True." We put the clam in our mouth, expecting to have to deposit it immediately back into a napkin, but our defeat is crushing. It is sweet and rich and absolutely delicious, and we anticipate finishing the entire basket, even if it means extra antacids tonight. "But I want to know, and all my readers do as well."

"They watched me on TV every day for six months. They know as much as I do."

"Do you think you've inspired other women to bump off their husbands?"

"Oh, for—" She half rises, and for a second—please understand how rare this is—we wonder if we've gone too far. Then she leans forward, and we make a note that if we survive this interview, we must ask her about her divine perfume.

"I didn't kill Ed." The words come out so mangled, we almost don't catch what she's said. Then she relaxes, sits back down, and looks us straight in our deeply seductive eyes. "I didn't kill him."

She says it louder that time, and clearly, and we have the odd feeling she believes she's telling the truth. Then she tosses that thick, dark, luscious hair and smiles as if she won the lottery, and we get another feeling—that she's been wanting to say that in public for a long, long time. Immediately we are beside ourselves with confusion. What fun would it be if she really didn't kill Ed as everyone with half a brain knew she did?

Nothing bores us more than purity of conscience, so we move on.

"Back to Erin, kind of a mousy little thing. A strange friend for someone like you."

She laughs, and the sound is beautiful and relaxed, and we realize for all we know about this woman—more than we know about people we've lived next door to for over a decade—we've never heard her laugh.

"Erin has strength I don't. She left her husband. I didn't have the guts to leave Ed."

We lean in to try our favorite trick, rapid-fire grilling, but can't help stuffing another clam in along the way, even at risk of dulling our edge with lip-smacking. "She left him dead, you mean?"

"A suicide, an accident, we don't know."

"Killing yourself by electrocution? How often does that happen?"

"He was a disturbed person, not a statistic."

"How many people dry their hair while they're still in the bath?"

The brow comes up again. The almond eyes turn hard. We brace ourselves. "How many people refer to themselves in the plural and wear heavy black boots with pink capris?"

Ouch. Oh ouch. We are so flattened we actually respect her. A jab worthy of ours truly. Truth be told, we had no idea June could still feel like winter. The boots were a necessity.

"What about the house in Kettle, will you sell?"

"Yes. Erin and her fiancé, Jordan, are going to buy it from me."

Our fabulously accurate instinct perks up. "Or they're going to get it as a wedding present."

Bingo. She looks startled. We smile our victorious smile and move on, because sometimes that's what we do.

"Back to you. Any little Mikes and Vivians on the horizon?"

"Would I tell you?"

"No." We smile and inhale another few clams, terribly disappointed that they're nearly gone, and we find that we are actually enjoying ourselves, and what a surprise that is.

"Are you working? Tell me about a day in the life of Vivian."

"I keep the books for Mike's business and help him sometimes on site. I also teach aerobics three days a week through the recreation department. They had an opening a month or so after we moved here."

"What kind of adjustments did you need to make? To Portland and to being a Mrs." *Mrs.* being a title we have sworn to avoid for all eternity, we can't help uttering the word kissed with scorn.

"I like being in a smaller town." She flashes that breath-stealing smile. "Smaller than New York or Chicago. Bigger than Kettle."

"And to being Mrs. Curtis?" Oh dear. We asked, didn't we. Let the goo flow, like a mighty river.

"That's been a pleasure."

"Care to elaborate?"

"No." Said with soft tone and glowing eyes and, oh God, bring us a bucket, except we can't bear the thought of parting with any bit of these clams.

For the rest of the lunch we are lazy and sinful enough to avoid difficult topics and chat. We are reduced to hysterics a few times by episodes from her life, and yet notice we have not included them even though they could cause her all sorts of delicious complications and embarrassment. In short, we bond. And the lovely M bonds only with those most worthy of us.

We come back to our hardly sumptuous-enough hotel room and type up the interview and are startled to find that even during the earlier part of the meal, we weren't as hard on Vivian as we were so sure we were going to be. More than that, we are in serious danger of reversing our utter certainty that she killed Ed Branson.

Even worse, we have lost ourselves—temporarily, you understand—enough to think that were circumstances vastly different—like for one that she did not live anywhere as nonexistent as Portland—we might want to hang with our girl Vivian once in a while.

Lorelei Taylor is dead. Long live Mrs. Michael Curtis.

This is the always fabulous M signing off for another day.

Home Page of Sarah's Website

Hello, and welcome to *www.SarahCooks.com,* the companion website to my cable cooking show. This week I'll be sharing recipes I'm making for a friend's upcoming wedding.

The first is a truly lovely appetizer that has many possible variations, always practical if you entertain frequently, as my husband and I do in our beautiful Chicago home. I'm presenting it here as a crostini, for passing to guests during the cocktail hour.

Some people believe crostini make a suitable appetizer for a seated dinner, and I have seen it on many restaurant menus, but really, if you want toast with a topping, have it for breakfast.

I'm leaving the amounts up to you since you know how many guests you have and how hungry you'll be. The boursin and arugula are also excellent spread on slices of grilled eggplant and rolled up, or on prosciutto. You can substitute herbed goat cheese, or gussy up plain goat cheese with herbs snipped from your own garden. For the recipe below, please don't use deli roast beef! Roast your own tenderloin medium rare and slice it thin.

Sarah Says: Life is too short to eat indifferent food.

Sarah's Crostini

> *One baguette*
> *Boursin cheese*
> *Arugula*
> *Thinly sliced rare beef*

Slice the baguette and brush the slices with olive oil. Bake or broil until golden brown. Spread thinly with boursin and arrange beef and arugula attractively on top. Drizzle with oil if you'd like—olive, walnut, or grapeseed. Don't waste your truffle oil here. The arugula and cheese are too strongly flavored.

My next recipe this week is for cookies. These are what I'd call once-in-a-while cookies since they're involved and very rich. I'm making them since my friend doesn't want a cake. She's been married before, and wants absolutely everything to be different about this wedding. So I'll be making these cookies, triple chocolate brownies with Valrhona chocolate baked in the bottom of muffin tins so they'll have neat edges, and adorable mini fruit tartlets.

My daughter, Amber, will be making a guest appearance on the cookie show. When she was little, she'd insist I make the brownies at least twice a month. She's grown into such a lovely young lady, though of course she'd be mortified to hear me say that.

Back to the cookies—I don't need to tell you *again* not to use shortening, do I? Not only is it loaded with trans fats, I swear it actually subtracts flavor from your baking.

Sarah Says: Use butter or don't bother making it at all.

Sablé

> 2½ cups sifted flour
> ¼ teaspoon baking powder
> 1 dash salt
> 1 cup butter, softened
> 2 teaspoons vanilla
> ½ cup sifted confectioner's sugar
> 2 tablespoons milk
> Seedless raspberry jam

Sift flour, baking powder, and salt. In the bowl of a standing mixer, beat butter, sugar, and vanilla until light and fluffy. Add flour and milk and stir gently until mixed. Refrigerate dough until easy to handle.

Preheat oven to 350 degrees. Roll dough to one-eighth of an inch or slightly less. Cut out the same number of 2½-inch circles and 2½-inch donut shapes. Bake on an ungreased cookie sheet 12–15 minutes, until just beginning to brown. Let cool.

Stir jam to loosen. Spread onto circles and top with donut shapes.

This week's new ingredient: pomegranate molasses. The pomegranate has become the darling of chefs, have you noticed? They are showing up in the supermarkets looking fresher and happier than in many years, and the juice is being touted for its excellent health benefits as it's simply loaded with powerful antioxidants. Our friends in the Middle East have long known about this wonderful fruit, and of course the seeds nearly brought about the doom of Persephone, daughter of Mother Earth. But you should look that up if you've forgotten all your Greek mythology.

At any rate, pomegranate molasses, look for it in specialty stores or online. It's wonderful stuff, thick and fruity and sour-sweet. Use it to glaze poultry or lamb (Google for a fabulous Persian recipe using it with lamb and ground almonds), or stir a bit into your chicken broth when making rice.

Sarah Says: *Please* make your rice with chicken broth. Plain water makes it taste like library paste.

Another suggestion: Stir a few tablespoons into your pecan or walnut pie batter, then scatter fresh pomegranate seeds on top after it cools from the oven. Superb.

Finally this week, if you haven't bought yourself several silicone baking mats, for heaven's sake run right out and do it now. I use mine for everything from cookies to bread to pizza to anything that would make a baked-on or sticky mess of my pans.

As always, *e-mail me* with food-related items that catch your fancy, new ingredients or restaurants using them in creative ways, kitchen gadgets or shortcuts, or let me know how you liked any particular program! I'm always happy to hear how well I'm doing.

Love and kisses,
Sarah

Erin's Journal, June 29

Tomorrow is my wedding day. The last time I could say that, I was going to marry Joe. I was so excited then to be getting out of my father's clutches. Yeah, well, we all know how that turned out. I'm excited now, and nervous about being a good wife to Jordan, but I'm not at all worried he'll be a bad husband to me. I tease him that he could lie in bed all day belching, and still be wonderful compared to Joe.

I think about Joe sometimes still, though less than I used to. Definitely on his birthday, on our anniversary, and on the day he died. But there's distance now, and strange as it sounds, it doesn't seem as if he ever really was my husband.

Overall, I'm happy. It actually is possible for me to be happy, though I have to fight off the panic a lot of times that I don't deserve this. Or that something horrible will happen and I'll be back to being miserable. Dr. Dodson says that's normal. It helps me to think that at least something about me is normal. I'm kidding, really. I'm normal in a lot of ways now; a lot of things don't scare me as much as they used to. But it's nice to know this fear is an irrational fear and not a premonition. I guess you get used to being crapped on by the world to the point where you keep expecting more crap. And I still keep expecting to be punished for what I did to Joe. I guess I'll have to make friends with that guilt. I can't see it going away completely.

Vivian is coming to my wedding. She warned me there might be media there, too, like that awful M person from *Sleaze* magazine—ha ha, I mean *Squeal*. No one in America really cares that I'm getting married. They'll just want to dig up the story of Joe again.

Sarah is coming to the wedding, too. She's bringing some guy she's been dating for a while, though mostly she'll fuss around making sure the food is perfect. She insisted on donating everything, which is so amazingly sweet, but means I couldn't stop her making all this fancy stuff that isn't really Jordan and me at all. Anyway, it cracks me up that in her public persona she acts like she and Ben are still married. Maybe divorced women aren't supposed to make good crostini.

I wasn't sure whether to invite Joan to the wedding or not. I decided not. Weddings should be a new, clean beginning, not a reminder of past messes. She probably wouldn't come, anyway. We send Christmas cards every year; that's plenty. I have a harder time forgiving her than Joe.

Letitia will be our ring bearer. She will look adorable. How she acts will be up to the fates. Her tantrums are spectacular, but I even love those. Jordan laughed at me when I videotaped one, but I said someday she'll be having them again, at age fourteen, and we'll need to watch this one to remind ourselves we've been through it already and lived. Being her mom is the most amazing gift I've ever gotten except maybe meeting her father. He and I have already decided to adopt a baby boy when the dust settles from getting married.

For our honeymoon, Jordan is taking Letitia and me to Disney World. Obviously when you have kids, an erotic adventure in Tuscany isn't an option. Happily Letitia sleeps soundly. *And* naps. He promised me a second honeymoon sometime when she and whoever her brother turns out to be are old enough to leave alone.

I told him having him in my life was plenty of honeymoon for me. Pretty corny, but I really meant it.

I better go to sleep now. Tomorrow can't come soon enough.

Erin

ISABEL SHARPE was not born pen-in-hand like so many of her fellow authors. After she quit work in 1994 to stay home with her first-born son and nearly went out of her mind, she started writing. Yes, she was the clichéd bored housewife writing romance, but it was either that cliché or seduce the mailman, and her mailman was unattractive. After more than twenty novels for Harlequin and the exciting new direction of women-focused stories for Avon Books, Isabel admits her new mailman is gorgeous, but she's still happy with her choice.

Isabel Sharpe